# BIO RESCUE

## S. L. VIEHL

A ROC BOOK

ROC

Published by New American Library, a division of
Penguin Group (USA) Inc., 375 Hudson Street,
New York, New York 10014, U.S.A.
Penguin Books Ltd, 80 Strand,
London WC2R 0RL, England
Penguin Books Australia Ltd, 250 Camberwell Road,
Camberwell, Victoria 3124, Australia
Penguin Books Canada Ltd, 10 Alcorn Avenue,
Toronto, Ontario, Canada M4V 3B2
Penguin Books (NZ), cnr Airborne and Rosedale Roads,
Albany, Auckland 1310, New Zealand

Penguin Books Ltd, Registered Offices:
80 Strand, London WC2R 0RL, England

First published by Roc, an imprint of New American Library,
a division of Penguin Group (USA) Inc.

First Printing, July 2004
10  9  8  7  6  5  4  3  2  1

Copyright © S. L. Viehl, 2004
All rights reserved
RoC REGISTERED TRADEMARK—MARCA REGISTRADA

LIBRARY OF CONGRESS CATALOGING-IN-PUBLICATION DATA:

VIEHL, S. L.
BIO RESCUE / S.L. VIEHL.
P. CM.
ISBN 0-451-45978-4
1. EMERGENCY MEDICAL PERSONNEL—FICTION. 2. LIFE ON OTHER PLANETS—FICTION. 3. GENETIC
ENGINEERING—FICTION. 4. MARINE ANIMALS—FICTION. I. TITLE.
PS3622.I45B56 2004
813'.54—DC22

Set in AGaramond
Designed by Erin Benach

Printed in the United States of America

PUBLISHER'S NOTE
This is a work of fiction. Names, characters, places, and incidents either are the product of the author's imagination or are used fictitiously, and any resemblance to actual persons, living or dead, business establishments, events, or locales is entirely coincidental.

For my stepdad, Anthony J. Sabella,
with love and gratitude.
You'll always be
the father of my heart.

# ACKNOWLEDGMENT

My thanks to James Milton for many brainstorming sessions that contributed much to this novel, and to the members of the ProWrite group for allowing me to share the experience. You guys are the best.

# CHAPTER
## ONE

Most Allied League pilots didn't like flying around Hsktskt displacer blockades. It was about as intelligent as 'Zangians swimming bloody near a starving mogshrike—they only did it if they weren't particularly attached to their tails.

But Jadaira hadn't become a pilot to preserve her ass.

"I've got a ship on screen," Burn said over her headgear. "Vector ninety-three degrees, one-forty east, seven solar, midfield."

Dair didn't think anyone from her squadron had been foolish enough to blunder off course into an orbital minefield, but she switched to flight band and checked anyway. "Somebody going sand-belly on me?"

All of her pilots answered, by the numbers and in position.

"Acknowledged." Relief made her ease back in her harness. So far the pilots' pod kept their losses at zero, but with all the war junk floating around, that could change. Rapidly. "Burn's found himself a stray. Saree, drop down and have a look, if you would."

Through the viewer Jadaira watched as her wing lead pilot rolled out of patrol formation and flew a short parallel to the field. Saree's strafer made a silver flash against the star-strewn blackness as she came about.

"Target acquired, Commander," her wing leader transmitted. "Freighter class. Could be a League transport."

The League had pulled out of the Pmoc Quadrant months ago, and the war had kept them so busy they hadn't come back to visit. Still, the ship could be carrying reinforcements to the front. "LTF or passenger?"

"Too small to be troop. Debris trail's half a kim wide."

No military pilot would have left that kind of scatter, no matter how smashed-up his ship was. It would be like begging for a rogue or a merc to attack.

"Refugees." Dair shifted her grip on the controls as she considered the situation.

Her patrol could provide safe escort through the system for anyone fleeing the war, if necessary, but this was different. She couldn't send more than one ship in to guide the blunderer out without risking triggering the whole minefield. Also, the patrol's primary mission was search and destroy, not search and rescue.

There were really only two options. She could try to get them out, or she could watch them blow up. "Feeling toothy today, Ensign?"

Her gunner's voice acquired a mocking edge. "You have to ask, Commander?"

Dair recalled Saree before she broke formation herself. "Maintain safe distance until we're clear. Keep an eye out for more strays; sometimes these lost pups travel in pairs." She hesitated. "Onkar, if we blow this, you've got the pod."

Her second-in-command didn't like her giving him orders, mainly for dominance reasons. When there was a threat to the pod in the water, males became aggressive, and very protective of females. Flight training had cured her male pilots of most of that, but Dair knew Onkar still resented her outranking him. Telling him he could take over only if she was dead was just another subtle volley in the silent war between them.

He tossed back one of his own, not so subtle: "I'll note the regs violation on my incident report."

Of course he would. Onkar noted *everything*.

*He's probably rehearsing how he'll give orders already,* she thought as she entered the field. Duo, *keep my tail in one piece.*

The Hsktskt were rather unimaginative when it came to setting up displacer mines, and the best way to enter a field of them was from an angle. Each of the proximity-sensitive mines had been programmed to randomly rotate positions, and carried enough charge to blast a nice-size hole through any slow-moving, unprotected hull. A snap to get around, if one was an experienced fighter pilot.

Unfortunately, the League transport pilot wasn't. Dair saw that as soon as she made visual contact, and watched his inexpert maneuvering set off three more mines. "Oh, not good."

"Mouth-breather," Burn muttered.

"Have a little sympathy for the handicapped, cousin." She disengaged all auto controls and powered up the boosters. "Be slick now; here we go."

Flying fast and straight was the only way to keep from triggering more mines. Fast Dair could do; straight was the challenge. While she avoided colliding with the mines in their immediate flight path, Burn began targeting the rows ahead of them and shooting out a corridor in front of them. Impact shock waves from the explosions battered the hull, but the strafer was uniquely designed to acquire, absorb, and then shed displacer fire. Constellations rippled as the blasts rolled off them in steady, light-bending sheets.

"Transport on center screen, Dair. Vector fourteen degrees, thirty-eight east, point-two-five solar." Burn made a rude sound with his gill vents. "Lurching through on a single thruster, the finless pup."

She still had to make sure she was trying to kill herself for a friendly. "Initiate structure scan."

"Acknowledged." The gunner performed the sensor sweep and patched the data directly to her screen. "It's League standard. Debris trail's fouling the readings, but weapons and stardrive appear inactive."

The civilian pilot must have shut them down to reduce his energy emissions; so he apparently had *some* brains. "Signal and advise him to cut his engines and hold position."

Burn relayed her orders as he cleared the last of the mines between them and the transport. As it came fully into her visual field, Dair swore. The ship was a passenger freighter, designed to haul lots of beings through space but do little else. And it was a flying wreck, riddled with impact craters, hull panels scorched, and engine cowlings close to collapse. What she could see of the fuselage appeared intact, but in some places, probably not for long.

"I've received a response," her gunner said. "Ship's the *Hemat,* private passenger transport out of Sol Quadrant." A sharp clik of disbelief came over Dair's headset. "Cousin, you're not going to believe this."

"Try me."

"He's warning us off."

She changed her mind—the pilot was an idiot—and switched on her transcom. "Transport vessel *Hemat,* this is the *Wavelight,* PQPM Commander Jadaira mu T'resa. We're here to provide assistance. Power down your engines and stand by." *And quit acting like a jerk.*

The voice that replied sounded clipped and unpleasant. "We do not require assistance, *Wavelight.*"

*Of course they require assistance; any half-wit can see that.* But quadrant regulations as well as her own colonial charter required her to respect the wishes of any species that refused aid. If they said no, she would have to leave them alone. Her 'Zangian instincts had no problem with that. In the water, the unhealthy or crippled were abandoned, driven off, or went on their own to an isolated, sacred place to die.

Only Dair wasn't completely 'Zangian.

Perhaps she'd heard him wrong or had inadvertently offended him. "Say again, *Hemat,* and please provide your status."

"We do not require assistance, *Wavelight.*" The pilot's voice came through the transcom, harsher than before, almost like a growl. "Most of the systems on board, including our navcomm, have been destroyed."

*He can't find his way out of the field, that's all?* "Copy, *Hemat,* we'll guide you out. What's your destination?"

"We were in route to Kevarzangia Two, but—"

"Not a problem," she cut in on his relay before he could hand her more nonsense. "That's our home base. We'll escort you."

The voice grew nastier as the pilot snapped out his response. "*Wavelight,* I repeat, the Skartesh are *not* in need of your assistance. This is not your concern."

"Skartesh." Burn produced a weary sigh. "As if we needed more of them."

*"Hemat."* She fiddled with her panel, creating artificial interference. *"Hemat,* do you copy? Your signal is breaking up again."

"Dair," her gunner cut in over her ruse. "The bloody mines are grouping."

That meant the disturbance they'd created within the blockade field had been large enough to trigger a mass detonation sequence. AKA the worst thing that could possibly happen.

*Enough chitchat.* *"Hemat* pilot. Hold your position until we pull ahead fifteen kim, and then follow our track. Push your throttle through the gate as soon as we're clear."

"Unacceptable." He was actually snarling at her now. "I repeat—"

Dair never found it difficult to be genial toward other starjocs, but even her good nature had limits. "Look, pilot, all these floating blasters have just gone communal. Whether we stay or not, they're going to converge on our present positions and blow. You and I have about a minute and thirty seconds to clear the field, or make our peace with our respective deities."

There was a moment of static, then, "Negative. Abandon the field; I repeat, abandon the field."

Dair could have fiddled more with the relay, but whatever coy game the Skartesh pilot was playing aggravated her. "Okay, friend, here's the situation: If you stay, we stay. Should you change your mind, maintain visual contact and prep to get the hell out of here. *Wavelight* out." She terminated the signal.

"Do we really have to die for a bunch of Skittish?" Burn wanted to know.

Part of Dair didn't want to. The Skartesh—commonly referred to as the Skittish—had been forcibly evacuated from their homeworld by the Allied League. Skart's solar system had been one of the first engulfed by the war between the colonizing League worlds and the reptilian raider-slavers of the Hsktskt faction. As a result, the displaced lupine aliens were rapidly becoming the most numerous species on K-2. Because of the strange and often disruptive nature of their behavior, few of the land dwellers on K-2 wanted any more of them to transfer in. The native 'Zangians weren't as judgmental, but the tensions the cult created among the other colonists had everyone worried.

Certainly no one would have called the Skartesh a species to die for.

But Dair felt sure she could get them out intact. "Lock a range and bearing scanner on him. Tell me the minute he twitches."

"Are we staying if he doesn't?"

She routed power to the stabilizers. "What do you think?"

"I think you're stubborn, demented, and you bluff like a Tryti-norn dances." Burn made the strumming sound of 'Zangian mirth. "But then those have always been your best qualities."

"That and I picked you as my gunner." She checked the posi-tion of the nearest clustering probes.

Dair flew over the *Hemat* and took up position in front. She eased her hold on the control grips and watched the screen as Burn targeted the rows ahead and started blowing out a new conduit. Once he'd opened a linear avenue wide enough to accommodate the freighter, she throttled forward and shot into the open conduit. Five kim. Ten kim.

*Come on, come on,* she thought as she watched the scanner. *Quit being such a nail-head and shake your tail.*

Fifteen kim. Slowly the freighter began to follow their track.

"Appears he's not quite as sand-belly as we are," Burn said.

"So much for my dream male." The knot in her chest eased, but only momentarily. Turbulence rocked the strafer as she navigated the channel of clear space Burn had made. Rolling the ship helped them endure the buffeting, but the sluggish freighter couldn't do the same.

"Commander, he won't withstand much more." Her voice of reason patched another sweep of the *Hemat* to her console. "They're barely maintaining environment as it is."

They'd have breathers on board. They had to. "Patience and per-sistence, cousin."

"What about the mines?"

She ran the sharp edges of her top teeth over her bottom lip. She had to divert the clustering mines away from the *Hemat,* which they'd locked on as the bigger target. *Only one way to do that in a blockade field.*

Dair knew there were plenty of ways to die in space. It was a vast, unfriendly void that supported life only if it brought along with it its own heat and atmosphere. She took small comfort in the fact that being blown up by displacer mines was one of the more merciful ends.

At least they'd die fast.

Dair made her decision. "Burn, punch me another hole, wide spread, forty-four degrees port. Make it sloppy." She changed the rate of their emissions, making it appear as if the strafer were a very large, very damaged troop freighter.

The gunner clicked his teeth once and then released a long breath through his vents. "*Duo,* that's pissing blood."

"Exactly." She signaled the freighter. "*Hemat* pilot. Stay on course and don't follow us. As soon as you're clear, signal my squadron. They'll guide you home."

"Commander—"

"Don't debate this with me, pilot." She hated being curt with a stranger, but they had no time for diplomatic niceties. "Follow orders or bid us, your passengers, and your posterior farewell."

Her gunner opened a second, larger swath through the port side of the field, and she abruptly veered off. The concentration of fire and destruction, along with their engine output, acted like a magnetic field on the blockade units, and drew them away from the transport to crowd in around the strafer.

Like any killing machine, the mines went for the biggest chunk of bait.

"Deep with you, Jadaira mu T'resa," Burn said.

Hearing the 'Zangian united-upon-death farewell made her shoulders shake, but Dair didn't laugh out loud. Gunners were so fatalistic—and sensitive—and her cousin was no exception. "At your side, Byorn mu Znora."

As the grouping mines began exploding in chains, the shock waves turned into direct contact displacer hits—something the hull couldn't shrug off. Although the cabin environment remained secure for the moment, Dair automatically pulled on her breather and locked her arms into the control grips, to prevent her hands from being jarred from the console.

What was it her academy instructor had said? *Learn to fly through hell and you'll always find home on the other side.*

The explosions were so close and dense that her viewer became occluded, and Dair had to rely on console readings to follow the narrowing channel. A few kilometers more and they'd be clear, but the communing blasters were already closing off the end and forming a wide, deadly wall. Sealers around the overhead canopy began to whine. She knew her ship better than anyone; the strafer would never hold together long enough to punch through this mess.

*Sorry, Dad, Teresa. I had a good run.*

Sonic fire registered on her screen, making her jerk. She leaned forward; almost convinced it was a ripple. But it wasn't. "Someone wants a court-martial."

Burn's response was lost to the blasts as the squadron moved in on the blockade wall, and vaporized enough mine chains to punch out an exit for them.

As the last impact wave hit them, Dair's console screen shattered, and plas shards floated lazily over to bounce off her faceplate. She lost all data display. "Ensign, where is our lost pup?"

"Sixty-one degrees starboard, Commander. Now clear of the blockade."

Dair needed to make sure their interior atmosphere was intact, and she wasn't going to take the pilot's word for anything. "*Hemat* pilot, hold your position; we're coming around to dock with you."

She turned in a tight circle to fly a pass beside the transport when something glittered in the corner of her right eye. A half second later, something slammed into the side of the ship and sent them into a whirl.

"What the *suns* was *that?*" she yelled, turning to gain control over the spin and the ship.

"The *Hemat* just took a shot at us. Single-chamber repulse fire." Burn's articulated fin ends hammered his console. "Can I return the favor? Please?"

She'd just saved his ship, and he was *attacking* them? "Hold your fire." She leveled out and heard something under the ship tear and groan. "Can't he just say thank-you?"

She tried to signal the transport, but the pilot was either jamming the frequency or didn't care to respond. Another blast hit them. This time she knew what the ripping and rumbling was; he'd disabled both her primary engines.

One shot might have been an accident, but two . . . "All right, that does it. Take away his toys, Ensign."

"With pleasure." Burn directed a short volley of pulse fire at the underside of the transport, and there was a small but gratifying flare of light. "Transport weaponry power cells destroyed."

"Good job." Dair switched to flight band. "Onkar, form up behind the freighter and herd him back to base." If the Skartesh had lost their environment, they could damn well suffocate now.

Her second instantly transmitted back: "Why was that fool mouth-breather shooting at you?"

Burn cut in before she could respond. "They're Skittish, Lieutenant."

Onkar muttered something short and vile.

"Burn, shut up. Onkar, let it go and make sure he lands safely. I'll have a word with the pilot later." Actually, Dair wanted to bite him. Someplace soft and full of nerve endings. Skartesh had lots of them. "My thanks for saving our tails."

"That was prime flying, Jadaira." Onkar made it sound like she'd done it merely to aggravate him. "What's your status?"

"Everything but the main thrusters are shot, but we'll limp along after you. Get these civilians on-planet."

"More transfers?" Saree said, momentarily forgetting protocol. "*Duo,* don't we have enough already?"

"Who knows, perhaps the Ninrana will take some of them off our hands. See you back at base." She switched off wideband and tried to reboot her screen. "Burn, I'm blind here."

"Yeah, but you've got a nice personality," her cousin joked. "Twenty degrees, eleven north, solar four hundred plus."

They both laughed as they headed for home.


Rushan Amariah left one of his relief pilots at the helm of the *Hemat* with orders to fly back to Kevarzangia Two as slowly as possible. Since the pilot, like the entire crew, was also a follower of the faith, he did not question Shan's orders.

Which was just as well, because any opposition might have resulted in the backup pilot having his throat torn out.

A few of the faithful were still crouched on the floors of the corridor that led back to his quarters, and as Shan passed them they timidly reached out to brush their fingers against the hem of his robe. Their deference was automatic; he was the Salvager, the Great Messiah, the Ennobled One who would return the Skartesh to paradise. To touch his garment was to affirm their convictions in the Promise and the Delivery.

All of that, and yet Shan had still been unable to carry out his mission, and had nearly destroyed them all in that blockade field.

*If only that idiot pilot and her patrol hadn't interfered.*

He'd had little experience with female soldiers. His people never permitted their women to work outside the home environment; maintaining the faith, bearing children, and caring for their mates were their primary duties. Certainly no female had ever served in a command position; that was unthinkable. Now he would be forced to dwell among other species who allowed their women all sorts of unimaginable liberties.

And the way she had spoken to him—as if they were equals, then refusing to obey his orders—still made his blood run hot. *If she belonged to me, I would bite her tongue until she learned how to curb it.*

Shan punched the code to access his quarters, then stepped inside and secured the door panel. The transponder he had concealed in his storage unit was small but he hadn't been able to risk bringing anything more sophisticated on board the *Hemat*. Communicating with anyone outside the cult unless under life-threatening circumstances was forbidden by Skartesh laws; laws Shan was obligated to enforce. He could not insist on one thing and do another. His followers were devoted, not blind, deaf, and mentally incompetent.

The relay he had left open was still displayed; the recipient of his signal still patiently waited for his report.

"I located the device," he said over the encrypted channel. "It was planted in the stardrive."

"By whom?"

"Unknown." Someone had been following the *Hemat,* however, and Shan had flown into the minefield hoping to lure the pursuing ship in after them. The patrol's commander and her heroics had ruined that.

"Could it have been one of the faithful?"

"No. They were not permitted access to the vessel until we launched, and I scanned each of them myself prior to boarding. It must have been someone at the quadrant processing station, perhaps on the docks." Shan wanted to return there and take the place apart, platform by platform, until he found the culprit. "How did you know it had been planted on the ship?"

"Our information came from the Ylydii ambassador's envoy. He was found deceased several hours after his last transmission to us." The elderly male's ancient eyes narrowed. "The physicians here say it was natural causes."

Too many friends of the Skartesh had done the same over the last cycle. "I doubt that."

"Indeed. We will need to examine the device." He scratched idly for a moment at his silver cheek fur. "Send it to us through the usual channels."

"I cannot comply." Shan barely kept the frustration out of his voice. "We were discovered by a League planetary patrol. Their rescue efforts made it necessary to eject the drive, along with the device."

The elder considered that for a moment. "Can you recover it?"

"Negative. My ship is too damaged, and we have a military patrol escorting us to the planet." Also thanks to that foolhardy 'Zangian commander and her do-gooder impulses. At least the two shots Shan had taken at her ship had kept her from docking with his. "Colonial security will likely retrieve the drive before I can requisition another ship."

"Indeed." Some of the dark-streaked fur across the older male's low brow bristled, and then smoothed out. "We will attempt to recover it through other channels." A faint smile wrinkled the grizzled muzzle. "We must allow for the occasional error, Rushan. Even a savior such as yourself has been known to make them."

It was not his habit to make any mistakes, but he refrained from snapping that out and dug his claws into his thighs. "As you say."

"You will proceed to K-2 as planned, and reunite with the faithful. Report back to me as soon as you have arrived. And Rushan." The smile disappeared. "There can be no more mistakes."

# CHAPTER
## TWO

Normally it would have taken only a few minutes to return to K-2, but without her primary engines Dair had to fly the way a seastar oozed. She also wouldn't trust the stardrive until she had the flight crew check out the damage from the field and their ungrateful friend, the suicidal Skartesh.

When Dair finally landed, the emergency response vehicles were waiting with chemfoam pumps, a ramp tube, and two mobile immersion tanks.

"Go on ahead," she told Burn as she set the envirocontrols to drain the cockpit. "I'll talk to this guy."

"So will I," Onkar said over the flight band.

The words sounded subdued, but the tone behind them said *furious 'Zangian male, ready to use some teeth.* "You can't thrash him, Lieutenant."

"Why not?"

"You'd win, and they'd make me clean up the mess." She hoped that would placate him, and switched her interior controls to evacuate the cockpit. "Transport, we don't require tank transfer, thanks."

"Copy, Commander."

Because they were amphibious aquatics, 'Zangians were able to breathe above and below the surface, but preferred to breathe liquid. Even Dair and her pilots, who could tolerate gravity and longer periods above the surface, operated more efficiently breathing fluid. As a result the League had modified their strafers to maintain a liquid interior environment chemically identical to K-2's seawater. 'Zangians injured out of water also swiftly went into systemic shock, and were always transferred directly to mobile tanks via sealed ramp tubes before being transported to the FreeClinic for treatment.

Making the transition from breathing liquid to oxygen wasn't difficult, but the sensations weren't pleasant. It took Dair and Burn a few minutes to expel the last of the almost-seawater from their gill vents, and inflate their seldom-used lungs.

"I hate breathing air," Burn said, between coughs.

"*Duo,* who *likes* it?" Dair cleared the last drops from her gills and took her first deep breath. And smothered a groan. Unlike her cousin, she had many major surgical alterations to deal with, including an artificial diaphragm. Which felt like it was bruised; she'd been wearing her harness a little loose and had probably hit her chest into her panel when the *Hemat* had fired on them.

They put in the tympanic inserts that allowed them to communicate with land dwellers, then climbed over the side of the strafer and jumped to the ground. Burn swayed and then staggered a little. So did Dair, despite her greater experience with gravity. The adrenaline rush of the rescue was recoiling on her, and combined with her bruises and need for the water, it was quickly sapping her energy.

Unlike her, Burn also had to coil up his flukes and separate his SEAL-modified lower appendages in order to walk. 'Zangian bodies weren't designed to do any of that for long periods of time.

Dair often envied Burn his flukes. Of course, being small and extremely agile she could swim faster than anyone in her home pod, and her specially designed legs and webbed feet made it easier for her to walk on land. Yet she'd always secretly wished she could look more like the other pilots: more 'Zangian, less Terran.

She couldn't tell Teresa that. Her stepmother's favorite admonition was, *That's pod mentality, Jadaira.*

Burn limped along the side of the *Wavelight,* eyeing the damage to their ship. "Verrig isn't going to like this."

The exterior of the strafer had taken a beating; some of the hull panels had craters in them large enough for Dair to put her fist through. Heat stress had caused seams in the alloy to shrink, and wiring spilled from them like nests of barb-eels. Hydraulic fluid mixed with cabin water rained in steady streams from the strafer to the landing pad. Dair saw her reflection in one of the oily, dark puddles, and made a face at the less-than-'Zangian image.

Her ship was battered, torn, and bleeding, but Dair knew they'd patch it back together. Just like they had her.

"Security wants to see you two." Flight Crew Chief Verrig paced the length of the *Wavelight*. His species were quad-legged but armless, so he wore a prosthetic rig with a number of interesting attachments. Between his huge eyes and tiny mouth was a long, vertical flap he used for speech. His colorless derma generated a continuous layer of gelatinous slime that kept his body temperature regulated. Most land dwellers thought Verrig was a little repulsive, but Dair and her people considered him quite handsome. "A miracle you didn't lose cabin environment."

Burn rolled his recessed eyes. "Going flat-lung was the least of our problems, crew chief."

"Jadaira." Onkar appeared, looking none the worse for transitioning from liquid to atmosphere.

Unlike Dair and Verrig, the two 'Zangian males both had dark hides, the color of sky before moonsrise. Burn was too young to have many battle scars, but Onkar had old clash markings slashed all over him. One deep scar bisected the left side of his face, and three gillets under his right ear were missing—none of which he had gotten in the breeding caverns, as most of the pod's other males had while chasing a female in season. Onkar had been adopted by Dair's pod as an adult. Before that he had lived in the outer currents as a rogue.

Onkar's reticence wasn't from lack of opportunity. Among 'Zangian females, Dair's second was revered more for his scars than his SEAL modifications. His tough appearance could have snared him any mate he desired, too. Except that he didn't chase anyone.

Dair knew he was waiting for her to go into season. In the water he watched her constantly, and every time they were topside he made sure to be somewhere nearby.

She met his gaze, and felt the tension that always hovered between them, unspoken, unmovable. "Lieutenant."

He looked past her at the *Hemat*. "I will deal with this refugee pilot."

"No, you won't." She tapped her chest insignia.

"This is not about rank." He glanced at Verrig and lowered his voice. "He *attacked* you."

She understood his feelings of aggression, but she couldn't allow him to act on them. "*Duo,* Onkar, he made a mistake." She thought of how she had taunted him during the mission, and her voice gentled. "We all do."

"Yours was saving him." He stalked off.

Verrig used a grav-hoist to pull back the huge primary engine cowling, peered inside, and hooted his disgust. "What the blessed *Knti* happened up there?"

Pilots kept their quarrels private, so Dair shook her head at Burn before replying with, "Just caught some friendly fire. Why haven't they released the passengers on the *Hemat*?"

Her gunner nodded toward a FreeClinic transport parked near the passenger vessel. "Looks like Medical's still on board."

She recalled what the pilot had transmitted. He'd said nothing about injured passengers. "Were there wounded?"

"None, far as I know," the flight crew chief told her. "They're checking for bugs."

That was definitely strange. Transport subjected every landing vessel to intense scans to assure they were not carrying any potentially harmful life-forms or diseases. "Biodecon not working?"

"They're Skittish. The council has ordered special inspections for their transfer vessels; you know what sorry shape they usually arrive in." Verrig, who thought any abuse of a starship was grounds for immediate execution, snorted. "Knowing how they love to generate filth, it will take us a solid month or more to sterilize the ship. *Knti* only knows what they've done to the propulsion and navigational systems."

"How many on board?" she asked.

"Couple hundred, plus the one I heard that they've been waiting for. A salvage man or something." The crew chief extended one of his artificial limbs and handed her a datapad. "Sign off on the strafe for me, Commander. I'll req you a temp replacement; you won't be getting her back for a few weeks."

She noted her consent and nudged Burn. "Come on. Let's see what's going on."

"What about Norash?" Verrig asked.

The thought of going on the carpet in front of the chief of Colonial Security didn't thrill Dair. "I'll report in later."

The gunner spotted a couple of pilots walking off the landing pad, and waved a fin. "I want a minute alone with the Skartesh who fired on us, Jadaira."

Like Onkar, Burn was feeling aggressive, but high stress had that effect on 'Zangian males. Dair felt pretty punchy herself. "He's Skartesh, so watch his teeth and paws. Remember they're pretty free with their body fluids, too. Don't bite him, don't swipe at him, and don't try to mark him."

"They don't like acquiring scars?" Burn, who intended to collect as many as he could to impress the pod's females, was utterly mystified by that.

"No. They think it's . . . unattractive," she said, for want of a better word.

"Land's end, have they ever looked at themselves?"

As they walked to the Skartesh transport, Dair took a few moments to enjoy what there was to appreciate while being topside. Kevarzangia Two was a beautiful world, above and below the water. The land dwellers had to cope with far more varieties of chokeweed, which grew all around their dwellings, but it came in pretty colors and smelled, for the most part, nice.

Dair never understood the colonists' need to remain boxed up in the structures they called buildings, but even they were interesting. The cramped conditions sometimes gave her a touch of unease, which her stepmother called claustrophobia, but when that happened all she had to do was look up.

K-2's sky was almost endless, like a huge, clear inlet of good water. A few clouds drifted about, but there was nothing hanging above her but green sky. Another of the reasons she'd chosen to join the military and learn to fly; being a pilot was just as thrilling as being in the water, but she could move faster and go farther than she'd ever imagined.

Space and speed were wonderful addictions.

"Look at this," Burn said.

Dair turned her attention to the *Hemat,* which was in far worse shape than the strafer. Fuel and environment were leaking from a couple of panels, and huge carbon sweeps mottled the outer hull. Part of the fuselage had crumpled in, and the stardrive array was nothing more than a big, empty hole. Technicians were already crawling all over the outside of the vessel, but the docking ramp was guarded by a pair of armed militia.

She walked up and held out her tags. "Commander mu T'resa, Ensign mu Znora. Permission to board the ship."

The guard scanned and verified her ID, then Burn's. "You'll have to go through decon again when you're through."

"Acknowledged, thanks."

Dair and Burn walked up the ramp and signaled for entry, but had to wait a few minutes before the hull doors parted. More militia stood inside, and she had to repeat her request and show ID again before gaining access.

"All this for some Skittish?" Burn looked around as he scratched his hide. He was already starting to flake. "Seems a bit overmuch."

"The council has been strident about enforcing their charter lately. Must be why they've insisted on extra inspections." She spotted a gaunt-looking female in a long white robe standing silently in front of a door panel, and walked up to her.

To an aquatic eye, the Skartesh were not a particularly attractive species, and this female was no exception. A little taller than Dair, she had long, slanted dark eyes rimmed with black lids. A black nose jutted out with a narrow jaw to form a distinct muzzle. Blunt-tipped triangular ear flaps stood straight up from her skull, exposing the pink inner works. Like all her kind, she was covered with fur, but hers was spotty in color and density, and the dullness and odor rising from it indicated that cleanliness was not a priority. A longer, matted brown mane sprouted from between her ears and ran down under the collar of her robe. Her paws had four wide, thick digits tipped with short black claws, and a fifth crooked, longer digit that served as a thumb.

*They look like malnourished werewolves,* Teresa had said once when she and Dair had passed the large compound the Skartesh had set up for their cult at the edge of the colony.

*Is there a great diversity of wolves on your homeworld?* Dair had asked. At her stepmother's blank look, she added, *You said once that 'Zangians look like Terran seawolves.*

*Oh, that's human slang for orca, honey.* Teresa had given the Skartesh inside the compound the same dubious look that the other land dwellers did. *Trust me, if you're going to be described as a wolf, go with sea, not were.*

"We'd like to speak with your pilot, please." Dair didn't expect an answer—the Skittish rarely chose to communicate with anyone, verbally or otherwise—and wasn't surprised when the lupine female turned, punched something in on the wall console, and abruptly walked away.

Burn stared after her. "Does that mean we follow?"

"I guess." She looked down at the small tufts of hair on the deck where the female had been standing, and wrinkled her nose. "Let's go and see what happens."

Burn didn't appear happy at the prospect. "You're sure I can't scar them?"

The silent Skartesh female led them down the corridor to the end, and signaled at a wide door panel. When it slid open, she turned and stood waiting. Since the panel didn't close, and the female didn't try to stop them as they approached, Dair and Burn walked in.

Inside were thirty more Skartesh wearing white woven robes and sitting on the deck around a central helm console. The male manning the console was also wearing a robe, but his was the color of deep water. He had his back toward them, but the black-rimmed eyes of those gathered around his feet moved to stare at the two 'Zangians. No one rose, or spoke, or blinked an eyelash.

*If this is the reception segment of the crew, they needed to brush up on their protocol.* Dair politely cleared her throat. "Pardon the intrusion, but we're looking for your pilot."

The Skartesh male in the turquoise robe turned around. "You have found him."

The pilot wore a thin metallic band around his brow, but unlike the female and most of the Skartesh gathered around him, he had a beautiful silken pelt of dark brown body fur and a long, thick black mane. Pretty as it was, Dair never could get used to seeing another being covered with hair—especially hair the color of dead choke-weed, like his.

*Maybe his will fall out in patches after he's been here awhile, like the other Skittish*, Dair thought. *Would make him seem a lot less . . . menacing.*

His slanted eyes were dark with no whites, like the other Skartesh, and didn't look friendly. "What do you want?"

For a moment, Dair stared. So did Burn. The Skartesh rarely spoke where they could be overheard, but everyone had caught their high-pitched yips in their native tongue. The pilot's wristcom was a model that projected translations while mimicking his natural voice, which was much different, deeper, harsher, and so resonant that Dair imagined she could feel it in her bones.

*He looks like a big canine but he sounds like an aquatic.* Finally she put her own vocal cords to use. "I'm Commander mu T'resa, commander of the planetary patrol squadron." She gestured to her cousin. "This is Ensign mu Znora."

"Rushan Amariah." The Skartesh bared his teeth.

Burn's folded dorsal fin stiffened, straining under the back of his flight suit, until Dair reminded him in clik why humanoids usually showed teeth. *Greeting-not-threat.*

*Shows-too-many*, her cousin clikked back.

*Be-calm-quiet.* Since Skartesh seemed to prefer face-to-face conversing, she pulled off her helmet and shook out her gillets. "Pilot, would you mind telling me why you fired on us after we led you from the blockade field?"

Dair had been told her alterformed voice was rather striking. Underwater she sounded like everyone else, but on the surface oxygen enabled her replacement larynx to work. The blend of Terran organs and SEAL technology had given her a clear, faintly melodic tone that Teresa claimed became quite piercing whenever Dair lost her temper. Certainly it was the exact opposite of Rushan's.

The Skartesh took his turn staring, but mostly at her face. "You have Terran blood?"

*He isn't much of a genius.* "No. I'm a SEAL."

The fine short fur beneath his eyes bunched.

She interpreted that to mean that he didn't understand her. "A
SEAL is a surgically enhanced/altered life-form."

"You were made to look like a human female?" He made an up-
and-down gesture. "Deliberately?"

"Yes. My stepmother is a Terran biologist. She invented SEAL
technology." The silent, blank faces watching them made her uneasy
to elaborate further. "I'd still like an explanation for what you did
up there."

"Would you."

"There was no reason to fire at us; we were only providing assistance." She waited a little longer to see if he would respond with
some sort of explanation. When he didn't, she said, "I was under the
impression that your people don't communicate verbally with other
species."

"Our followers are forbidden to. I am not bound to the same
rule for secular reasons." He stepped forward, and the people sitting
on the deck quickly scuttled out of his way. "Your medical personnel refuse to allow us to join our brothers and sisters. Why?"

Dair didn't answer him. *See how you like it.*

Rushan's gaze shifted to her gunner. "Do you know why?"

"Maybe it's your attitude," Burn said, stepping in front of Dair.
"Cousin, I'd like my moment alone with the pilot now."

Someone entered and came up to stand on Dair's other side. "I
will have mine first, Byorn," Onkar said.

She scanned the faces of the three males. The dark fur around
Rushan Amariah's eyes and muzzle was scrunched up; Onkar had
every muscle tensed to spring. Burn trembled with youthful, scar-
hunting eagerness.

As she would in the water, Dair dealt with the most dangerous
male first. "Are you disobeying a direct order, Lieutenant?"

Onkar didn't blink. "Yes."

"She said I could go first," Burn added helpfully.

So she had, but Amariah's followers were now starting to ex-
change little sharp sounds, and tensing as if to spring. *What would
Teresa say to put everyone at ease?* "I think you're outnumbered here,
boys."

Onkar bared more teeth. "I am not a boy."

"Leave my ship," Rushan Amariah said, and pointed to the door. "And take your intrusive female with you."

The former rogue pilot surged forward.

"No, Onkar." She put her hand on his fin and blocked him with her body. He was displaying mating and protective behavior, so military protocol didn't apply. She had to calm him down. "He's phobic; to him we look like 'shrike. Enjoy the day; forget him."

Onkar didn't stop watching Amariah, but his gillet fringe slowly subsided. He brushed the flexible end of his articulated fin over the backs of Dair's fingers for a moment as he settled his fierce gaze on her. "For you, Jadaira. This time." He gave the Skartesh one more glare before he left the compartment.

"*Duo,* I hope I never have to battle Onkar for a mate." Her cousin stepped toward the Skartesh, and then caught her expression. "I can't have a go at him either?" When she clikked a no, he sulked. "You never let me have any fun anymore."

That left Rushan, who was still regarding her the way he would an overlarge parasite.

Dair exhaled slowly. "Well, pilot, I can't say it was a delight to rescue you, and I think in the future that you should avoid male 'Zangians as much as possible, but good luck with gaining permanent resident status."

"Wait." Amariah turned to her. "Where is this Terran biologist—your stepmother?" He nearly spit out the last word.

*Why does he care?* "Her name is Teresa Selmar. She runs the research station at Burantee Point."

"And you?" He moved closer, invading her strike space. "Where do you live?"

It was no big secret. "I'm either in the water or"—she pointed to the upper deck—"on patrol duty up there."

"I see." He examined her for a moment. She knew how she looked to other species, most of whom had very little love for Terrans. Teresa never seemed to understand that, but she sometimes forgot the widespread prejudice against her native species. Or maybe she chose not to see it.

In any case, Dair certainly didn't expect the Skartesh to reach out and touch her.

Rushan reached out carefully, trailed his fingers down the long, straight strands of hollow white sprouting from her scalp. "She made this your hair?"

All of Burn's teeth reappeared, and she took a quick step back. "No," she told him. "They're my gillets. I breathe water in through them and out through my gill vents."

The Skartesh didn't drop his hand; in fact, he tried to touch her again. "Why are they white?"

"Get off her." Her gunner swiped at him with the curved hook protruding from his fin, but Amariah sidestepped the blow.

Dair clikked a sharp reproval at Burn: *No-knowledge-no-harm.*

To the Skartesh, she said, "It's white because I'm an albino, pilot. Also, among my kind, this sort of touching is reserved for one's mate." And *Duo,* was she glad Onkar had left. He'd have taken off Rushan's limb if he'd seen the Skartesh handling her like a lover.

Rushan didn't look sorry, but this time he said, "My apologies."

The door panel opened behind them, and Dair turned to see a pair of nurses from the FreeClinic pushing in a cart filled with equipment.

One of them, a flowery, fragrant Psyoran, ruffled her frills. "Excuse me, pilots, but you'll have to leave now."

Dair nodded to her, and then turned to Rushan Amariah to make her farewell. "I hope we meet again under happier circumstances." She didn't mean a word of it, of course, but she had been raised to show courtesy and dignity toward strangers.

The Skartesh seemed surprised at that, and even bowed a little. "Perhaps we will."

"Come on, Dair." Burn tugged at her sleeve. "I'm starting to peel."

It took a few minutes for them to get clearance to leave the ship. They underwent a thorough decon before being released from Main Transport. By then it appeared as if all the Skittish on K-2 had assembled in a series of circles around the *Hemat.* One of them, a small female with her head mane braided in long, thin cables, stood up and began yipping and slapping her paws against her chest. The rest of the Skittish did the same, slapping harder and harder until the entire landing area echoed with yelps and thumps.

"Here they go again," Burn said as the rest of the squadron came across the docking pad to meet them.

The pod greeted each other absently as they watched the lupine cult perform their ritual. Dair had seen it before—the Skittish openly performed their circle rituals constantly, wherever they were—but never had she seen so many do it at the same time, or gathered in one place.

It was striking to see. White robes shook and swayed and manes fanned out as the Skartesh began to dance, hopping up and down as they moved in and out of their circles, forming pretty patterns with their bodies. Some took polished alloy bars from their robes and began striking them together, adding a higher metallic top note to the slapping paws, yipping calls, and pounding footpads.

"Strange," Loknoth, the youngest male in the pod, said. "You'd think they want to feed."

"They're not hungry." She hoped.

"The other mouth-breathers don't act like this," Saree said. "One of the others passing by called them fanatics. What does that mean, Dair?"

"Teresa says it means the zeal of their beliefs frighten others not of their faith." They weren't making her feel too safe, either. There were so many of them now, and the pod was too far from the water. "Come on; let's go home."

# CHAPTER
## THREE

The 'Zangians took to the coast a glidebus specially dedicated and adapted for their people and other aquatics, where Dair's pod occupied the waters for a ninety-square-kim stretch. As the native settlement closest in proximity to the land dwellers, the pod had formed many ties with the myriad species who occupied the colony. The coastal pod was also considered the most progressive settlement on the planet, and was held in high regard by most of the other 'Zangian communities.

When they arrived, the pilots' pod climbed out and ran like children for the cliffs. Along the way, some of the younger 'Zangians became so impatient they began shedding their gear.

"You'll have to come back and pick it up," Onkar warned a couple of the younger eager females.

"The water awaits. Who cares?" Madura, considered one of the most appealing females in the pod, gave him a flirtatious look. "Race you to the platform."

Onkar did not run after her, but glanced at Dair. "You should instill more discipline in your females, Commander."

"You should lighten up, Lieutenant." The enthusiasm was infectious, and Dair found herself unfastening the front of her flight suit as she strode across the plateau rock to the uppermost ridge above the ocean. Several hundred feet below them, turquoise waves churned with mild ferocity in a small, deep diving bay, hemmed on either side by a wide ribbon of dark sand.

Seventy percent of K-2's surface was covered by water, and most of it was a shimmering, serene blue. As Dair watched the life of her world rush to embrace the shore, the sense of coming home became complete.

*This is where I was born, where I live, and where I will die.*

Stripping out of her flight suit and the skin shield beneath it that kept a thin layer of water circulating over her limbs made Dair sigh with relief, until she saw that Onkar was still watching her as he stripped and stowed his flight suit in the locker built into the rock. Water gushed out from the open lines as she deliberately dropped her suit onto the ground.

Onkar was the largest and fastest male in the pod, with a heavily muscled frame that he had developed from many years of swimming rogue. No one knew why he had left his natal pod and crossed the eastern sea—asking would have been highly impolite, and everyone was too afraid of him to pry—but the only reason males were usually driven out of a pod was for bad behavior. Dair's pod had adopted him after he had found two lost, terrified pups that had strayed into the outer currents and had guided them home.

In contrast, Dair was the smallest female in the pod, but thanks to her SEAL modifications, she was faster than Onkar in the water. She was faster than any 'Zangian who had ever lived, according to Teresa, who had tested Dair's speed against every adult in the pod and every test record on the colonial database. Naturally her step-mother had custom-designed Dair's augmentations to make her stronger, swifter, and more efficient in the water.

Dair's body gleamed bone-white in the sunshine. She knew it was her color, not her form, that made Onkar look at her. She was the only full-white who had been born to her kind in the last six generations, and her rarity was the only reason he wanted her. Or, possibly, because she was the only female who had never been in season, or lured a male to the breeding caverns.

*And that still gnaws at you, doesn't it?* Dair thought as she expelled the last of the air from her lungs. Sometimes she wished Onkar would value her for other reasons, but he was a male, and gave no sign of ever changing his competitive attitude toward her. That made it impossible not to resent his attention. *Look as much as you wish, Onkar, because this is one female you'll never catch.*

He circled around her, the way he would in the water, and flexed his back muscles before he turned his attention toward the horizon. Sometimes he would do that for hours—stare far away at nothing in particular—but he never said why.

It disturbed her when he did that, too. Dair would rather have Onkar stare at her than at the endless stretch of the outer currents. Out there was nothing but emptiness and waiting death.

"*Duo,* life and pups and full bellies," Hanumatha, an older male, called out to the twin suns. The rest of the 'Zangians echoed the blessing as they lined up to dive.

"All ours, thanks to the commander's skill," Saree teased Dair as she went over.

"More the commander's luck," Onkar snapped before he dove.

Dair and Burn went together, out of habit; her fingers curled around one of his fins. They barely made a splash as they traded air for water, and streaked down deep into the liquid, enveloping blue.

'Zangian water was cool and dense, and the intertidal strip near the sands was busy with all the creatures of the shallows. Fish of countless colors, shapes, and sizes swam beneath free-floating clusters of surface chokeweed, ready to dart up into the protective vegetation should a larger, hungrier group come looking for food. The concerted, side-to-side movements of their flat, scaled bodies churned the light filtering down from the surface.

Beneath the 'Zangians, the less obvious bottom-feeders and sand dwellers kept the seabed tidy. Golden seastars inched along the silt, hunting half-buried bivalves, while scarlet-shelled *sterbol* defended the burrows they built for themselves by stacking and cementing together abandoned shells. Closer to the reef, the more venomous inhabitants of the shallows patrolled the bottom: waspnetters moving slowly, dragging their strainer-shaped lower jaws through the mud before gulping whatever they picked up into their spiked throats to be stung to death before digestion, and the less methodical tube snakes, popping without warning from their hiding places to sink their long, thin fangs into small fish before swallowing them whole to be squeezed into digestible matter inside their long, column-shaped bodies.

Just beyond the seamount ridge, other 'Zangians waited for them. Today there were perhaps thirty adults and a dozen pups, swimming in a roughly oval-shaped formation, with the eldest on the flanks and the little podlings in the center.

They represented only a small portion of the coastal pod, as most spent their days out hunting or swimming up and down the coast, but Dair liked how every 'Zangian within the immediate area always came to greet whomever entered their waters.

*Jadaira.* Her father circled around her, giving her the usual parental inspection before he nuzzled her, snout to nose. *You look sleek.*

'Zangians didn't speak in the same manner as land-dwelling humanoids, and until Dair's stepmother had put her prototype cerebral monitors on them, it was largely thought that the natives couldn't communicate beyond using echolocation. None of the 'Zangians had bothered to correct or try to explain this to the mouth-breathers, Dair's father had told her in confidence once, because they really hadn't thought the mouth-breathers were intelligent enough to comprehend their methods of communication.

*The first time we saw them, we thought they might be some kind of new food,* Dairatha had said. *Noisy food at that. Thank* Duo *they stayed on the surface until they worked out how to communicate with us, or we might have tried to catch and eat them.*

Like all other 'Zangians, Dair spoke three forms of language— clik, fin, and balaenea. Clik was the wordless, tonal sounds and pulses they made to communicate short bursts of vital information to the pod, while fin was purely body language, shared by many other species, which conveyed both words and concepts. Balaenea— named and translated by Dair's stepmother—was something of both, and neither, and only the most evolved aquatics, like the 'Zangians, used it.

*Are you hungry?* Dairatha asked.

*Starving.* Dair paced her father as they swam toward the feeding grounds, which stretched along a wide reef beyond the shallow trenches. *Mom working down here today?*

*She came down as soon as she heard about your run through the blockade. She said something about someone firing on you.* He furrowed his brow and glanced at her sideways, a wordless fin expression of uneasiness and concern. *She also shouted some things about your skill.*

Dair knew better. *My skull, Dad.*

*Skill, skull.* Unconcerned with the specifics of Terran language, he flipped his tail flukes. *She will be happy to see you.*

*I bet.* And equally delighted to lecture her again on the dangers of stressing her augmentations.

As they swam for home, Dair thought about Rushan Amariah and his Skartesh prejudices. She guessed her people would seem frightening to the water-phobic, cultist species; the 'Zangians wore no clothing, owned no possessions, and while the resident pods stayed in one region, they didn't build dwellings or claim their territory as property. They certainly couldn't dance, and clapping the chest was fin for *I-challenge-you.*

Maybe that was why the Skittish made the 'Zangians so nervous. Their behavior made it seem like the entire species was constantly trying to pick a fight.

*Don't call them Skittish,* she reminded herself. *You wouldn't want them calling your people unkind names.*

The construction site loomed ahead, built just on the other side of the reef. Teresa had been the driving force behind the effort to build the first Undersea Research Dome on Kevarzangia Two, and she now divided her time evenly between supervising the construction underwater and continuing the research experiments she conducted in her topside laboratory. The URD was not yet habitable, but several smaller habitat units had been set up to provide living space for the saturation divers and scientists building the dome.

Dair's father glided into the seawater access hatch of the largest habitat beside her, but did not join her in the air lock. 'Zangians could breathe oxygen above surface, but as they got older and heavier it became more of an effort to deal with the accompanying gravity. Dairatha surfaced in the interior pool only long enough to greet Teresa with an affectionate nuzzle before diving back down into the sea.

As Dair walked out, Teresa brought over a med kit and took out a scanner. "Getting a little cocky up there, kiddo, aren't you?" she asked as she passed the scanner up and down Dair's legs.

She wiped the water from her eyes. "Normal duty run."

Her stepmother straightened and folded her arms. "Trying to get yourself and your cousin blown to smithereens is not my idea of normal, Jadaira."

"Then it's a good thing you're not in charge of the squadron."

Burn came out of the air lock in time to overhear them. "It was my fault, Teresa."

That earned him a snort. "Don't try to cover for her, Byorn mu Znora. It didn't work when you were pups; it won't work now."

An older 'Zangian female appeared behind Burn, her generous form almost as tall and half again as wide as his. "I should say not."

Burn's mother Znora was the oldest and most aggressive matron in Dair's family pod, and the most devoted of protective mothers. For some reason, she took particular exception to Dair's existence, and generally referred to her as *that leech-hided runt someone should have devoured along with the afterbirth.*

Thank *Duo* Teresa had thought differently, and had saved her life.

"Hello, Znora." Teresa, knowing her adversary well, bared all her teeth. "Slumming?"

"Come, Byorn." She ignored Dair and Teresa, and only flapped a fin at Dairatha, who had returned to circle around the pool. "You will feed with those who do not wish you dead."

Burn gave Dair a faintly apologetic look, then dove down behind his mother.

"I hate to admit it, but she's almost justified in being pissed off at you." Teresa finished scanning her. "You're being reckless, Jadaira. We've talked about what will happen if you push things too far physically when you're in space."

She'd talked about it, and Dair had agreed with every word she said. The same way she did now. "Yes, ma'am."

"Don't hand me any of that 'Zangian banality, either. I get enough of that from your father. You're still a little dehydrated, and there are a couple of bruises on your sternum. Otherwise, you're okay."

"You rebuilt me well," Dair said, pressing her mouth to Teresa's cheek. Her lips weren't as mobile as her stepmother's, but she could do a fair imitation of a Terran kiss. "Forgive me?"

"I have to. After all the work I've done on you, I can't strangle you." She scowled at the scanner display before pocketing it. "Let me slip into my rig and then we'll go for a swim."

Dair thought swimming with Teresa was fun. Her stepmother didn't have webbed feet or pectoral fins, and her skinny arms weren't very effective in the water, but she was happy to latch onto Dairatha's dorsal fin and let him pull her along. Teresa also couldn't stay in the water very long, and Dair's father had to stay shallow because she couldn't collapse her lungs. Still, Dair always felt they were more like a 'Zangian family when her stepmother joined them in the water.

Because Teresa liked to keep an eye on things, they swam out to the URD. When construction on the permanent dome was completed, more land-dwelling species like Teresa's could live virtually full-time alongside the coastal pod. Her stepmother already had an entire team of marine biologists eagerly awaiting their chance to dwell among the 'Zangians.

Dair's father thought the whole arrangement was rather strange. *I still say it's too small, Teresa.* He circled around the environmental units that would convert seawater into fresh oxygen and desalinated drinking water for the biologists. *Are you sure everyone will fit in there?*

Teresa's headgear was specially adapted to translate the 'Zangian language underwater—as it happened, she had invented that device, too—although she was obliged to take her regulator out of her mouth to respond. *Humanoids don't need much space, Dairatha.*

A shadow passed through the murky column of water just on the other side of the site, and Dairatha went motionless and gave his daughter the fin sign for extreme danger.

Dair used her body to shield her stepmother. *Teresa, be very still.*

She obeyed instantly, and they all watched as the long, wide shadow passed.

Mogshrikes had populated K-2's oceans since prehistory, and were the 'Zangians' only natural enemy. Although Teresa had uncovered fossilized evidence that many similar species had existed prior to the volcanic upheaval that had formed K-2's continents, for some unknown reason only the 'shrikes survived the cataclysm.

Dair wished they hadn't. They were huge, mindless killing machines, ten to twenty times larger than the biggest 'Zangian. Their mouths were so large they could swallow a 'Zangian whole without even bothering to use their endless rows of jagged teeth.

Yet the mogshrikes *always* used their teeth.

The shadow emerged from the outer currents and for a moment swam parallel along the border of 'Zangian water. Countless mvrey clung to the mogshrike's belly, keeping it clean of parasites, and staying on hand in case any scraps came their way. Few did; 'shrikes were greedy and efficient. They also had sharp senses, and could smell blood in the water from a hundred kilometers away. They usually cruised at slow speeds, searching for prey, but Dair had seen them swim faster than her stepmother's surface skimmers went with full-open throttles.

For a moment, it appeared as if the 'shrike might intrude further; then the lunate tail swung wide and it glided away. They all remained still and silent until it disappeared from sight.

*I am getting too old for this sort of excitement,* Dairatha said, and blew out a cloud of bubbles through his vents. *This is the second time I've seen that monster this close to our water.*

Dair was troubled, too. The mogshrikes had always stayed out in the far outer currents, where wrill bloomed heavily and fish and less evolved mammalian aquatics passed during their seasonal migration. 'Shrikes typically avoided the warmer waters closer to shore, and swam in only when they were drawn by extreme hunger or an injured aquatic.

Dair couldn't taste any blood in the water, so she assumed the monster was looking for easy kills. It was disturbing to think that it might return. The 'Zangians knew how to evade their greatest predator, but Teresa and the other scientists weren't fast enough to get away. *Mom, your dome needs a defense mechanism.*

Teresa gave her stepdaughter's arm a squeeze. *I have you and your father, and the pod.*

*If more than one 'shrike attacks, we'll be too busy to look after you.*

*Mogshrikes always swim alone, and so far none of them have intruded on the site.* She stayed on her regulator for a moment to get more oxygen. *Jadaira, you know how important this project is to me. Don't fuss.*

Dair knew there were other reasons her stepmother wanted the dome built. Teresa had never been able to live full-time with her father, and the periods of separation they experienced were growing longer as Dairatha grew older. This was the closest her stepmother would ever get to dwelling in his underwater world.

*The 'shrikes don't care about your project,* Dair reminded her stepmother. *All they want is to kill. If enough blood spills in the water, they'll come from miles around. You know that.*

*Then we will be careful. Come, let's return to the dome. I want to show you the photoscans from our last voyage.*

Dair stared in the direction the mogshrike had taken, then flipped around and trailed after her parents.

This was home for him now. Onkar would never get used to that.

Once they were underwater and among the coastal pod, Madura restrained her excitement long enough to make a few more gliding passes around him. Onkar could tell from the subtle changes in her body that the young female's first estrus was imminent. She was nubile and lively; when she came into season every male in the pod would probably follow her into the breeding caverns.

Every male but him.

Onkar looked past her to where Dair had joined her parents, and felt the ever-present knot in his lower belly constrict a little more. Since coming to the coastal pod, he had been careful not to develop any expectations or intrude where he was not wanted. He would not risk losing another family. Yet no matter how he tried, he could not stay away from Jadaira.

Even when they were apart, he could not rid himself of his irrational longing. It was as if she were a sickness that had seized hold of him, slowly spreading to the center of his bones.

When they were on duty, it was easier to control himself.

Military training overrode his 'Zangian instincts, and Jadaira was, for the most part, an excellent commander. But here, in the water, all of that went away, and he had nothing to distract him from his obsession.

*Come and swim with me,* Madura said, nudging him with her blunt little snout. *We can feed together.*

Because she was barely more than a pup, he gave her a firm but gentle push back. *Go on; I'm not hungry.*

Her gaze went to Jadaira, then back to him. *Your appetite might improve if you would abandon your desire for her.*

He didn't need advice from one who had no experience, and made a curt clik that was essentially wordless but very straightforward in meaning. Dair would have translated it into one of the Terran terms she enjoyed using: *Back off.*

The young female was not cowed, but she traded some of her exuberance for a show of concern. *Someone needs to say this to you; it might as well be me because I know you won't bite me. Dair is a fine commander but not one to give you pups. You know she has never come into season, and she swims too fast for any male to ever catch her, if she ever does. Also, she doesn't like you.*

*Go and feed,* he told Madura, and then took off for deeper water before the young female could say more.

Swimming away from the pod didn't bother him in the slightest; he had spent years by himself in the outer currents. Years that he wished he could forget. His rogue's existence had been intolerable at first, and several times he had nearly allowed a 'shrike to catch him, thinking to put an end to the unbearable loneliness. Yet something inside him refused to relinquish his life; it was all he had left.

*There is more than this,* he would tell himself. *And I must find it.*

Reuniting the lost pups with their pod had been an instinctive act; Onkar hadn't done it to prove worthy of adoption. He hadn't thought about it at all at the time; he had discovered the distressed podlings and had simply herded them along as he tracked their scent backward through the currents.

When the coastal elders had offered Onkar sanctuary as reward for saving their young, it had been almost as great a shock as being cast out of his natal pod. By then he had been so used to his solitary state that he had been unsure that he could dwell among a civilized pod again, and had nearly refused.

*I am not one for you,* he had started to tell them, when a flash of white had caught his eye, and he had fallen silent.

The 'Zangian female was all wrong: too small, completely devoid of color, and her body was arranged oddly. Yet she moved through the water like a shaft of sudden light, and the happiness in her voice as she called to her larger cousin had made an ache of longing lodge in Onkar's throat.

Seeing young Jadaira, the only full-white 'Zangian he had ever encountered, had seemed at the time like an omen. Every pod had a legend about the place where 'Zangians went to die, and the promise of rebirth.

*We go to die in a nameless place, Onkar,* his dam had told him. *It is small and white and beautiful. And there, if we are worthy, a great power heals us and returns us well and whole to the sea.*

He could only stare and think: *There are second chances, and here is mine.*

Since that first glimpse, Onkar had learned everything that he could about her. She was more than unique; she was a miracle child who had come back from the dead. Her individuality went beyond her altered body and independent manner; while she was as intelligent and inquisitive as other 'Zangian females, she formed arbitrary, uncommonly steadfast bonds that were not based on mating or feeding status.

Onkar wasn't even sure what caused Jadaira to maintain such unwavering loyalties; her relationship with her father's mate completely baffled him. Yet in this and other, subtle ways, Dair was as much an outcast as Onkar was. When she looked at him, he thought he could see the same loneliness and longing hiding behind the bright curiosity in her eyes.

Or he told himself that he could.

*Dair is a fine commander but not one to give you pups.*

Madura was right; Jadaira had never shown the slightest interest in him. In fact, the little white female had gone to great lengths to discourage him. Most males would have abandoned her at once and pursued another, but her indifference seemed only to make the challenge greater for him.

He followed Jadaira and her father from a distance, and watched as Dairatha's odd mate joined them. They were a peculiar trio, but so close that one had only to observe them to feel the warmth of their mutual affection.

Onkar wanted that as much as he wanted to plant his young inside Jadaira's body. Rarely in his lifetime had anyone treated him as anything but a nuisance, an outsider, or a threat. There was much irony in the fact that the only one he had ever wished to think better of him regarded him as all three.

*In time, she will not,* he promised himself as he swam away. *And then I will catch her.*

# CHAPTER FOUR

The next day Dair and Burn were summoned to the colony FreeClinic by Dr. William Mayer, the chief of Medical Services.

"Why would they call us in after a routine patrol shift?" Burn wanted to know as they took the transport to the colony.

"I don't know." Because of the antirejection treatments for some of her more radical SEAL augmentations, Dair had spent more time in the FreeClinic than any of the other 'Zangians. "Maybe the flight surgeon wants to check us out and verify that we're fit for duty."

Just outside the entrance to the medical facility, they encountered a small group of Skittish performing another ritual that evidently involved pulling out tufts of their own fur with their teeth and casting them into a disposal unit designed to resemble an artificial fire. They were surrounded by some bored-looking militia and a few visibly appalled colonists.

"No wonder they look so patchy," Burn muttered. "They're so starved that they're taking bites of themselves."

Dair shook her head. "I'm telling you, they don't do that because they're hungry. Teresa says the high humidity makes them shed. Like we flake when we get dry. So they're like us." She fell silent as the Skartesh circled the fire and collectively urinated on it, putting it out. "Or not."

"I'm sorry, but I don't do that," her gunner said, grimacing at the resulting unpleasant odor. "And that is really disgusting. They should go live on Ninra, then, with the other dirt dwellers."

"Desert dwellers."

"Same thing."

Navigating around all those hopping bodies and undulating white robes wasn't a problem for the two pilots—the Skartesh shrank from them as soon as they saw them—but some of the colonists trying to gain access to the facility had more problems.

"Get out of the way!" an aggravated Esalmalin yelled at the refugees, every spine on his outer hide bristling. "And quit pissing in that fire; you're stinking up the whole place!"

Dair paused and watched as the Skartesh completely ignored the prickly humanoid. *Why are they afraid of us and yet have no fear of someone whose physical form can obviously cause more harm?*

"Can't hear me? Let's see how you like this." The spikey colonist took out a small bottle and began spraying some sort of fluid at the Skartesh, who immediately howled and backed away, tearing at their fur.

"Stop that!" another, furred humanoid colonist shouted. "You're terrifying them!"

"Hey!" One of the militia came up and snatched the bottle away. "What do you think you're doing?"

"It's only water!" the Esalmalin said, his expression more outraged than ever.

"Really nice." The soldier emptied the bottle out onto the ground. "You know that they're hydrophobic."

"How would I know that?" the colonist countered, gesturing toward the cowering Skartesh. "They never talk to the rest of us, now, do they?"

The furred humanoid made a disgusted sound. "Why would they want to, with you dousing them like that?"

"Proximity circuits are heating up around here," Burn said as he scratched a flaking spot behind his ear hole. "We could reschedule, maybe? Sometime when they're not having pissing contests?"

"I don't think so." Given the presence of the Skartesh, Dair now suspected that the *Hemat* was part of the reason they'd been summoned. "Let's just get it over with."

The big red insect nurse who manned the lobby directed them to the teaching unit, where Dair and Burn met up with the rest of the squadron, who were waiting outside the conference room.

"Hey, Dair, what's all this about?" Saree asked her. "I barely got wet before they recalled me."

Onkar looked as if he'd eaten something dead. "You shear off something too big for your gullet, Commander?"

"Not me." Her second-in-command would slash himself in front of a mogshrike if it meant he could take over the pilots' pod, but she had no intention of letting him do so by admitting she'd goofed up. Even if she had. "I think it might be about the Skartesh we saved yesterday."

Onkar went over to the view panel to stare outside, and Loknoth joined him. "Land's end," the younger male said, and looked back at the other pilots. "They've started pissing on each other now."

"Maybe they're . . . hot or something," Saree said.

"You should have seen the mouthful of teeth on that Skartesh starjoc we saw yesterday," Burn told a couple of the younger males. "Nasty. Didn't thank us once for yanking his tail out of that minefield. Plus he had chokeweed growing everywhere on him."

"Hair," Dair corrected. "He wasn't that bad."

Her cousin made a rude sound. "What about when he stroked your gillets?"

Onkar whirled around. "What?"

Madura also turned a curious eye on her. "You let a mouthbreather initiate sex with you? On his ship? Was he any good?"

"Nothing happened. He didn't know what he was doing. I mean, he didn't know what the gesture meant. *We didn't have sex.*" Highly embarrassed now, she tried to change the subject. "Why are we waiting here?"

"They told us to," Loknoth said. "Some healer wants to talk to us."

The healer turned out to be Dr. William Mayer himself, one of the heroes of the Core plague and Dair's personal savior. Dr. Mayer was a tall, older Terran with a scant amount of white hair and a spare, disciplined form. He had a way of regarding people that made even the most virtuous soul want to squirm. In Dair's pod, he easily would have taken leadership and mated with the finest of their mature females. All of the 'Zangians, with the exception of Onkar, greeted him with fins down, a sign of deep respect.

Onkar, Dair noticed, met the older Terran male's gaze directly, and only then inclined his head. Of course, since he was as scary as the Terran doctor, he could get away with it.

"Dr. Mayer." As was proper for the leader of a pod, Dair added a respectful nuance to her fin greeting by blowing a little air through a select number of gillets. "You wished to see us?"

"Yes, Commander." He opened the door panel. "Please come in and sit down."

Inside the conference room, a number of holoprojectors had been set up around a long table. A slim, blond Terran female was placing datapads beside the servers and carafes of water at each seat. She looked up and smiled without teeth at the 'Zangians. "Hello, I'm Administrator Hansen."

"Ana." Dair moved forward and took her hand. The colonial administrator and newly selected council member was one of her stepmother's closest friends, and had done a lot toward helping Dair adapt to humanoid life during her pup years. "It's good to see you."

"You're looking sleek," she said. "Would you and your people take a seat?"

The pilots all shuffled around the table and eased into the chairs. Remaining stationary was difficult for 'Zangians, who were constantly on the move under the water, and could tolerate being strapped into a vessel cockpit only because of the liquid environment through which they could see and feel the movement of the ship.

"Commander mu T'resa, pilots, gunners. Thank you for responding to my request." Dr. Mayer moved to stand at the head of the table. "We've brought you here today to ask for your assistance with a growing problem."

Dair glanced around the table. Only Onkar looked unwilling to hear what the mouth-breather had to say, but she knew he'd stay just to find out what she would agree to do. "How may we help?"

"This is one of the remnants of the League/Hsktskt conflict, with which you are all very familiar." Mayer activated one of the holoprojectors, which replayed the blockade run they had made for the Skittish. "You handled the situation very well, Commander. There were more than two hundred immigrants on that ship. Only your quick thinking preserved their lives."

Dair ducked her head, pleased at the compliment. "We just did what we could."

"You did very well. So well that I wish you had been somewhere else earlier this week." He activated another unit. "This ship was not so fortunate."

The pilots watched the playback as a Psyoran passenger vessel inadvertently wandered into another blockade.

*Edge of the quadrant,* Dair judged from the star positions. *What in* Duo's *light were they doing out there, so far from the transport routes?*

One by one the mines detonated, until the ship was too badly damaged to escape. Seeing the unmistakable glow of a stardrive going critical made Dair close her eyes for a moment. Saree made a mournful sound as the ship exploded.

"Why did no one go after them and provide aid?" Onkar demanded, his voice hoarse.

"There are very few planets in that region, and the quadrant has all remaining forces patrolling more populated areas," Mayer said. "No one could reach them in time. That is why I've asked you here, because I believe you can prevent this from happening again."

Onkar made a curt gesture. "Rescuing civilians is not our mission. It is the responsibility of planetary governments to provide safe passage within their borders. We only defend them."

"I know what your orders are, Lieutenant, but the fact remains that your efforts saved the *Hemat.* There were two other ships caught by war traps this past month." Mayer replayed similar projections. "More than three thousand lives were lost, including some survivors who could have been evacuated."

He cleared the holoimages from the air before pointing to the datapads in front of the 'Zangians. "Those are the statistics on casualties for the past revolution."

Dair activated her pad. Forty thousand, nine hundred and seventy-three life-forms had died over the last year during mishaps with blockades, impact probes, and other battle traps the League and Hsktskt had left behind. Another ten thousand had disappeared, along with their ships, and were presumed dead.

"I regret the loss of life," she said with sincerity. No species trying to avoid war should have had to suffer such deprivations. "What can we do, Dr. Mayer?"

"We have trained medical personnel who can immediately respond to distress situations across the quadrant and provide on-site medical treatment and evacuation." He paused. "What we require are pilots to fly the rescue missions: Locate them, retrieve them, and transport them quickly and safely to where they're needed."

"These pilots would be us?" Dair guessed.

He nodded. "With your flight expertise, knowledge of the quadrant, and experience with the various hazards left behind by the League, you 'Zangians are my only choice."

"*Rescue* pilots." Saree sounded dubious. "Flying what?"

"We will provide standard transport freighters," Dr. Mayer said.

"That won't work. Freighters are too slow; they set off blockade mines and virtually everything else in the traps and clutters," Dair pointed out. "We won't be rescuing anything biological when that happens. The other problem is that our strafers accommodate only two; three at the most. We can't ferry passengers."

"We have nothing else."

Dair thought for a moment. "Maybe we do." She turned to Ana Hansen. "Administrator, may I borrow your panel?"

The Terran woman willingly surrendered her console, where Dair cued up the new holoimages she needed.

"You're probably not familiar with this, but the quadrant has an impound satellite station on Yno, the largest of Ylyd's moons." She brought up a star chart and indicated the neighboring planet. "There are three Hsktskt raider ships there. We captured them during our last strike missions, just before the League left the quadrant." She zoomed in on one of the ships. "The raiders are gstek class, which are some of the fastest star vessels the faction has ever designed."

Everyone watched as the Hsktskt ship appeared. They were beautiful vessels, designed for stealth and speed, and the only way the 'Zangians had caught them was by destroying the propulsion systems. The three Dair and her pilots had brought down had mostly been due to a combination of Hsktskt pilot error and some extremely lucky shots, since the raiders could outfly the League strafers on half an engine.

"We could modify some of them and remove what we don't need." With a bit of fiddling, Dair superimposed another image on top of the raider vessel. "That would make room for your patients and your medical teams in these compartments here, here, and here."

"Why do you want to use raiders, Commander?" Ana asked.

"The gstek is the only ship big enough to accommodate the people you want to retrieve while being fast enough to avoid space traps without initiating the stardrive."

Onkar leaned forward. "No one but the Hsktskt are skillful enough to fly those things."

"The lizards aren't going to come back, and if they do, it won't be to run rescue missions," said Madura, siding with Dair's second. "So you have no one to pilot them."

"That's not true." Saree contemplated the holo. "Dair could pilot it; she trained on enemy ship simulators at the academy. So have Loknoth and I. We could train the rest of you in sims."

"That's the only way this will work." Dair got to her feet so she could take a closer look at the holo projection. "If we're going to rescue and transport people, we'll need to make further modifications. Strip down the nonessentials from the weapons array, reinforce the hull. What's the maximum amount of people you'll need us to move?"

"Up to one hundred injured at a time, based on casualty projections and if you put all three ships into service," Dr. Mayer said as he handed her a datapad.

She glanced at it and then passed it to Burn. "We can fly these ships, and provide transport to and from emergency sites. However, my squadron and I have no medical training, and we won't have time to attend to the casualties." Nor would they have the inclination.

"You'll be flying with a full medevac team on board," Dr. Mayer said. "Each ship will carry a physician, two residents or interns, nurses, paramedics, and orderlies."

The concept of taking healers along with them evidently confused Saree, who asked, "Why can't you wait for the injured to come here? We'll bring them to you."

"The severely injured would not survive the journey." Dr. Mayer, who obviously didn't understand 'Zangian concepts of life and death, looked hard at the wing pilot. "Without on-site treatment, even some of those who do will die."

Ana put a hand on Dr. Mayer's arm. "More will survive if we provide immediate medical assistance, pilot, which serves the mission goal to preserve as many lives as possible. That's the whole point of a rescue initiative."

"To rescue anything alive and save those lives by the process." Dair thought it over. "I've never heard of anything like it."

"It would be the first dedicated biologic rescue effort in the quadrant," Dr. Mayer said.

"Bio Rescue." Ana smiled. "That's a good name for it."

"What you propose violates the natural order." Onkar rose from his seat. "It also falls under individual planetary jurisdiction, so it is your problem, not the quadrant's or the League's."

Dr. Mayer didn't like hearing that, and the strips of hair above his eyes drew together. "We don't have experienced pilots or adequate ships. I have applied to PQPM, but they've refused to offer any help."

"Then as a League officer, I can take no part." He gave Dair a hard look. "Jadaira, do not violate regulations by agreeing to do this." He left the room.

She waited until her grouchy second was gone before she said, "Administrator, with respect, we are still under quadrant command. We will petition them for permission to provide assistance, but I can't abandon my duties if they say no."

"You could resign your commission."

*Now there's a thought.* She met Dr. Mayer's piercing gaze. "I can't speak for the others, but yes, I could do that."

"And leave us to tag after Onkar?" Burn snorted. "No, thanks. If you quit soldiering, I'm going with you."

Other members of her pod voiced similar attitudes, until Dair held up a hand. "Wait. Before we all tender our resignations, how many pilots do you actually need, Doctor?"

"We would like to run four units. Since your people can't be out of the water for longer than twelve hours, we will need four pilots per vessel to rotate duty in regular shifts."

"You'll need gunners and weapons, and guards for the medevac teams as well." She did some calculating. "There are only thirty 'Zangian pilots in my squadron, and not all of them will be able to fly the gsteks."

"We will all resign, if the pod decides to accept the duty," Saree put in. "The pod stays together."

Dair glanced at her wing leader. "Agreed, but even so, we still won't have enough pilots."

"We can recruit candidates from the planetary militia and security," Ana suggested.

"Check into that. In the meantime, the pilots' pod will discuss the matter." Dair rose from the table, and the rest of the squadron followed suit. "When do you need a decision?"

"Every day more people die," Dr. Mayer said. "As soon as possible."

Onkar stood waiting for the other pilots outside the facility, where the Skittish had stopped dancing and pissing on each other and were now sitting in tight, motionless groups on the ground. Dair noticed that they didn't seem to mind getting urine stains on their pristine white robes, which perplexed her. One of her stepmother's main obsessions was keeping her garments free of soil and odor. Teresa wouldn't even release waste in front of her mate.

"You cannot agree to do this, Jadaira," Onkar said as soon as he saw her. "We are soldiers, not scavengers."

"They're not asking us to scavenge, Lieutenant. This is how they care for their injured, and we have to respect that." She looped her arm around the notch that passed as an elbow in Burn's articulated fin. "Besides, it could be fun."

"The quadrant will not allow it." Nor would Onkar, judging by his tone and expression.

"Land's end, what's chewing on your hide?" Saree gave him a nudge. "We'll talk about it later."

"You. 'Zangian."

Dair swung around to see another robed Skartesh striding toward her. She was a female, and beside her walked a male almost as large as Rushan Amariah. Both were wearing Skittish-styled robes, but theirs were green instead of white. Behind them, a dozen white-robed Skartesh followed.

She made a polite gesture of universal greeting. "Yes? May I help you?"

"You are Commander mu T'resa, the pilot who rescued the Skartesh vessel *Hemat?*" the big male asked her. His voice sounded rusty, as if he hadn't used it for some time. He was covered with very dark, silver-streaked fur and wore a strange band of cloth wrapped around the top part of his skull.

"That's me," she said, and gave him a close-lipped smile.

The female stepped up to her. Like her companion, she was dark-furred, but had many patches missing from her skin. Her eyes were small and fierce, and she showed nearly all her pointed teeth.

Dair was a foot taller than her and had at least fifty pounds more bulk. So when the Skartesh female lashed out with a heavy paw and hit Dair in the face, she was more shocked than anything.

Onkar was there, shoving the Skartesh female back so hard she nearly tumbled backward. The white-robed followers moved restlessly, as if not sure what to do.

"Easy, Lieutenant." Burn put himself between them, and turned to the Skartesh. "What's inflated your bladder, woman?"

"You sullied the Salvager." The female ignored him and spoke only to Dair. "Never approach my son again."

"Okay." She rubbed the sore spot on her cheek. "Mind telling me what the Salvager is and who your son is?"

She swiveled around and stalked off. The big male stayed behind, his squinty eyes fixed on the mark Dair could feel forming on her cheek. "You met our son, the Salvager, Rushan Amariah, on the *Hemat.* The faithful saw you touch him." He gestured to the white-robed followers, who ducked their heads and tried to look invisible.

Dair was totally bewildered until Burn tugged on one of her gillets to remind her of what had happened. "Oh, right. But I didn't touch him. He, uh, touched me."

"You lie. Our son would never lay hands on a heretic. Keep your distance in the future." With that, the big male walked off after his female.

The white-robed followers eyed the 'Zangians for a long moment, as if wishing to speak. A sharp sound from the female who had hit Dair made them hurry off after her.

"What was that all about?" Madura wanted to know.

"I'm not sure." Dair scratched a spot under her jaw where it didn't hurt.

"You violated one of their taboos," Onkar said. "Stay away from them, Commander."

"No one knows anything about their taboos," Burn said. "How are we supposed to know when we violate them? And what about him violating ours?"

"Doesn't really matter." Dair thought of Rushan Amariah having to endure such a violent parent, and felt sorry for him again. "Anyone know what a heretic is?"

No one knew. She would have to remember to ask Teresa.

The Skartesh myth of the Promise was an incredibly complicated, convoluted tale that had been handed down from father to son for centuries.

*There shall be great upheaval visited upon the children of the Promise, violence from above and below the world. It shall cause the children to scatter like seed upon the four winds of creation. This is the time of the Hand of the Salvager, who shall gather them up, and bring them to the Place of Decision, until all who are to be judged shall be seen, and measured, and found wanting or deserving. Only then shall the Salvager choose those worthy of Paradise, and bring life to them through the Great Burning.*

Studying it made Shan's head ache, but memorizing every word was not enough. The meaning behind even one of the eight thousand passages might be all that separated triumph from complete disaster.

No one had ever been permitted to study the Promise outside of the Skartesh, and among them only a few high-ranked males had ever been allowed access to all of the scrolls. Unfortunately, every single one of the holy men was now dead. *It is here. All I have to do is find it.*

His door panel chimed once before it opened.

"I have prepared your midday meal, my son." Yersha Amariah set down the plain food she had arranged on a tray and slipped her paws into the sleeve ends of her robe. When he did not look up from the Promise scroll he was reading, she added, "Forgive me for interrupting your study, but does the food displease you?" When he met her gaze, she nodded toward another tray, one she had brought the night before and that he had not touched.

"No." He rolled up the elaborate list of prayers and placed the scroll aside. "It is satisfactory. You may go."

She gestured to an empty chair across from him. "May I sit and speak with you? There are matters that require your attention."

Shan had no desire to listen to her female complaints. "My father can attend to whatever domestic problems you have."

"These matters concern the faithful, and the Promise."

He gave her a sharp look. "They are not your concern."

"Even a woman can be called upon to defend the faith." She defied him and gracefully arranged herself on the chair. "And you."

Shan's parents had nearly drowned him with their faith, and he was heartily sick of it. Yet by his own choice faith had now become his life. He considered throwing the tray of food in Yersha's face, but quelled the urge. He could show her the respect she deserved as a mother. *For now.* "How so?"

"We were told of this aquatic female who assaulted you on the ship. Your father and I tracked her, and confronted her." She adjusted the folds of her robe. "She will not inconvenience you again."

She had confronted Jadaira? "What did you do?"

"I did what was proper. I administered correction."

Skartesh methods of correction ranged from beatings to ritual sacrifice. If Yersha had killed her . . . "What manner of correction did you use, precisely?"

"I marked her, that is all." Her eyes narrowed. "Rushan, she touched you. Such offenses can not be tolerated."

"She is not Skartesh, and I will decide what will or will not be tolerated." He rose from the table and went to the view panel. "You will consult with me before you administer any future correction."

"But to preserve the faith—"

He swiveled around and looked at the doorway she had left open. "Are you questioning me?"

"No." Yersha quickly rose and then prostrated herself. "I sought only to perform my duty. I beg forgiveness for whatever offense I have caused."

"You are forgiven." He made a negligent gesture. "Go."

When she left, Shan went to the console and immediately signaled the FreeClinic. Only when the reception clerk confirmed that Commander mu T'resa had not been treated or admitted for any injuries did the tension leave him. He terminated the signal and accessed the colonial database.

*Inquiry: List any/all available data on mu T'resa, Jadaira.*

Her files were not extensive, and he was surprised to see that she was only seven years old, the same age as a preadolescent Skartesh. A quick cross-reference to the 'Zangian biodatabase revealed that the K-2 natives matured quickly, attaining adulthood as young as three years of age.

Jadaira had enlisted in the League at age four, and had spent a year undergoing intensive in-flight and command training. The League had set up at a special branch of the academy on K-2's eastern continent exclusively for the 'Zangians, who could not survive away from their homeworld long enough to complete training at the main PQM training base on Hlagg.

Training in her home system, Jadaira had excelled in all her flight courses and had gone on to graduate first in her class. From there she had repeatedly distinguished herself in combat during the Hsktskt attempt to occupy the Pmoc Quadrant. According to the dates, she'd attained the rank of commander within her first year of duty. He could not access her military records or performance reports, but Shan had seen her in action, and suspected they were equally impressive.

*All this from a female.*

It went against every one of his personal beliefs, but Shan had trained himself to think outside his faith and culture. He sensed Jadaira was just as skilled and dedicated to her profession as he was to his. In essence, an excellent source of strategic information as well as a strong, ideal ally for the coming crisis.

And Yersha had attacked her for touching him.

Shan summoned one of the faithful who regularly attended the Skartesh leaders, and asked for an account of the incident between Yersha and the 'Zangian pilot.

"Your mother confronted the aquatic female, accused her of laying hands on you, and struck her in the face," the older female attendant told him. "She warned her to stay away from you in the future."

He heard the note of shame in the female's voice. "You told Yersha that she touched me?"

"No, Ennobled One. We told your mother exactly what happened." The female stared at his feet. "I and the others . . . we were disturbed by her twisting of the truth."

Shan dismissed the attendant and considered his options. He had little time or opportunity to make new contacts; few if any of the colonists felt sympathetic to the Skartesh. The only viable contact he had made outside the faithful since arriving on K-2 was with the aquatics, and as reluctant as he was to involve himself with a female, Jadaira had shown the most empathy toward him.

*Perhaps I intrigue her. I can use that.*

He could also use the incident with Yersha as justification for his next contact with the commander. Certainly she had not deserved to be struck for touching him—the attendant was correct, as Jadaira had not, in reality, touched him at all—so his apology for the incident would be completely sincere. Being a female, she would doubtless look favorably upon him for inquiring after her. He could build on that. Once he had her trust, she would give him what he needed.

He took the tiny transponder out from where he had hidden it, and tested it. "And if she does not, I will get what I want anyway."

# CHAPTER
## FIVE

Teresa Selmar finished the latest scan of her alterformed-wrill tank and downloaded the readings into her database.

"If you little guys keep on reproducing like this," she murmured as she inspected the new batch of semitransparent wrill hatchlings, "we're going to have us a whole new listing on the menu."

In the wild, the tiny crustaceans matured to a maximum of three centimeters in length, but her bioengineered strain would grow twice as big and live three times longer. There were a hundred more tests to be performed under controlled conditions, but Teresa hoped the results would allow her to introduce them to the native wrill population. Interbreeding would increase the size and stability of the biomass for the hundreds of native aquatic species who depended on it as their primary food source.

"You've earned your lunch." She released the daily infusion of nutrient-rich algaplankton into the tank. "And as long as you don't prove harmful to the natural food chain, you should be out of here in no time."

"Not every transplant is a bad thing," her N-jui assistant T'Kafanitana said as she carried one hundred half-gallon water samples from the remaining tanks to the analyzer. Tall, multijointed, and bearing a strong resemblance to a maroon-colored preying mantis, T'Kaf provided her skills as an expert chemist as well as handling most of the heavy work around the lab. "You have proven to be a most valuable addition to our colony."

Teresa smiled up at the towering female. "Some would argue that point."

Teresa Selmar had never been popular wherever she went. She had alienated her human family by leaving her native homeworld the day after she'd reached majority age. Her parents hadn't bothered to plead with her to stay on Terra; by that time they'd mostly resigned themselves to their daughter's bizarre and repulsive predilection for studying alien marine life-forms.

*You'll come to a bad end, Teresa,* her mother had predicted. *All those alien oceans are teeming with diseases and filthy creatures.*

Teresa had picked Kevarzangia Two as her destination simply because it was the closest planet whose aquatic inhabitants had never been comprehensively studied. Admittedly she had done so in order was to make a name for herself at first. Being the first to study K-2's marine life was far more appealing than forcing herself to make overtures and garner the favors of more established xenobiologists in a field polluted by inherent cronyism.

So she had come to cover herself in glory, but she had ended up finding so much more. Like Dairatha, and Jadaira.

Teresa had not planned for her relationship with Dairatha at all. For one thing, they lived in environments that were mostly hostile to the other, and they had no way to communicate with each other for the first six months she had spent on-planet. Then there were the more subtle differences. The 'Zangian male was twenty years Teresa's junior—although comparatively speaking, he had twice her life experience—and he was completely devoid of ambition.

Still, there was something about Dairatha that got under Teresa's skin, and every time they met she was instinctively drawn to him. The unexpected sexual attraction was simply an added nuisance. By the time she had found a way to easily communicate with the 'Zangians, she had already fallen half in love with the big male.

Teresa kept her distance, however, for Dairatha had already mated and was awaiting the birth of his first pup. His mate, Kyara, also became one of her best friends; although it wasn't as if she were the jealous type.

*We share ourselves with each other,* Kyara had told her once after catching her watching Dairatha. *If you want him, make him chase you.*

By then Teresa had understood the 'Zangians' polygamous natures, and their total lack of jealousy away from the breeding caverns, yet still she had felt awkward. *I am better off with one of my own kind.*

A short time later the colony had been infected by the Core, microscopic organisms with a collective sentience that had been accidentally removed from their native botanical environment. The Core had acted like a plague, killing carriers and contaminating others in their frantic attempt to escape their hosts. Several 'Zangians who regularly dealt with the land dwellers became infected, and then brought the pathogen back to the coastal pod. Because she had remained isolated at Burantee Point, Teresa had not fallen ill, but Dairatha's physician brother had accidentally brought the infection back from the colony and transmitted it to the rest of the pod. By the time the doctors at the FreeClinic had discovered how to cure them, a third of the 'Zangians had disappeared to a sacred place that Dairatha would identify only as "for the dying."

Kyara had been in her last weeks of pregnancy when she fell ill, and rather than swimming off to die she had begged Teresa to save her pup. Knowing how badly damaged the unborn female was from her mother's Core infection, Teresa had spent long hours alternating between watching over her friend and experimenting with replacement tissues.

Kyara had barely lived long enough to expel Jadaira from her body. As she died, what was left of the pod had drawn back, shocked by the pup's diseased appearance. Then, being true to their nature, the 'Zangians had abandoned Kyara's ruined child.

Teresa had been attending, and knew what to expect, but still the summary rejection of the pup by the coastal pod enraged her. Only Dairatha defied his people's traditions by helping her to transfer the tiny, dying 'Zangian infant to a mobile tank. Teresa took her directly to the FreeClinic, where she had spent the next twenty hours in surgery with William Mayer, repairing the damage done to the little white pup by the Core.

It took another five operations before Jadaira began to show any improvement, and for a full revolution after her birth it was still touch-and-go.

In the seven years since Dair's birth, Teresa had never forgotten those terrifying months sitting up by the immersion tank, night after night, watching the little female move sluggishly through the water. If it had not been for Dairatha staying at her side, nudging his pup through the water when she grew tired, Teresa might have given up a dozen times.

"Hello? Teresa?"

"Back here." She looked up as an older, blond Terran woman entered the lab. "Ana." She checked her wristcom and frowned. "Oh, God, did I forget we were having lunch again?"

"Not this time." The administrator smiled and held up a datapad. "This is an official visit. Of course, if you want to ply me with some of your excellent coffee, I won't refuse."

Teresa chuckled. "You're such a caffeine addict."

"This from the woman who regularly decimates my imported chocolate stores." Ana smiled at the N-jui. "Will you join us, T'Kafanitana?"

"Thank you, Administrator, but I must finish analyzing these samples." The chemist nodded toward the tank. "I'll keep them on monitor for you, Doctor."

"Thanks, T'Kaf."

As they walked from the lab into the living area, Teresa inspected her friend's smartly tailored uniform tunic, which was in the new turquoise and green colors chosen by the postplague administration. "Did I eat all your chocolate the last time we got together? You look like you've lost some weight."

"No, I've still got a stash, just no time to break into it. Lots of double shifts lately, trying to process all the new transfer applications. Then council meetings three days a week." She sighed as her wristcom chirped and she checked the incoming signal. "Make that four this week. I'm also training a new assistant; a Tribirrun named Carsa."

"They're not so bad"—Teresa dialed up a pot of coffee and some pastries from her prep unit—"unless you got a young one."

"Nearly mature, but Carsa still hasn't decided which gender it wants to be." Ana shook her head. "So it's actively transgendering. Mostly at the office."

Teresa winced. "Yikes."

"Last week it tried extruding breasts and a penis at the same time, and had to have emergency hormonal treatment. This week it's trying out menstruation." The administrator sighed and rubbed her forehead. "Yesterday it burst into tears every time I forgot to say 'please' and 'thank you.' "

"Well, if anyone can handle a waffling Tribirrun, it's you, Ana."

Teresa had never expected to become friends with another Terran; until she came to K-2 she could hardly stand being in the same room with one of her own species. But besides sharing her interest and tolerance for alien life-forms, Ana had something other Terrans usually didn't come equipped with: an unusually strong empathic ability to sense other beings' emotions and, at times, even their thoughts.

She put it to use as soon as Teresa sat down with her. "You're worried about someone. Jadaira?"

"No, I . . ." She put down her cup and gave her friend a wry smile. "You know, it would be nice if I could lie to you once in a while and get away with it. Yes, I am a little worried about Dair."

"You're her mother." Ana patted her hand. "You're entitled."

"I sometimes wonder if I am, still." Teresa stared absently into her server. "She's a grown female now, and a highly trained soldier, and totally in control of her life. She's in fine health, and Lord knows, she's achieved everything I've ever hoped she would and more. And yet, no matter how I try to restrain myself, I nag at her every time I see her, and worry all the time when I don't."

"That's a mother's prerogative as well."

"More like a mother's curse." She rolled her eyes. "But enough about me and my kid. What's this official business you brought? Not another request from the Quadrant Census wanting me to count how many tentacled invertebrates we have on-planet, I hope?"

"No head or tentacle counts, I promise. Although the timing

could probably be better"— Ana drew out the datapad and set it on the table between them—"I do think you need to be involved in this."

Teresa took the datapad and studied the proposal outline. "Bio Rescue medevac operation to perform search-and-rescue missions in space." She read down through the proposed services. "Ambitious. Dangerous, too, what with all those battle traps and ordnance floating around out there. You'll need some experienced people to handle the missions." She met Ana's gaze. "Ah, I see. You want the SEALs to fly them."

"They're the logical candidates. William Mayer and I met with the pilots' pod this morning." Ana moved her shoulders. "They're going to consider the matter."

"They're soldiers, Ana, not medics." Teresa set the pad aside. "They're also 'Zangians, and you're going to have a very hard time getting them near any patients."

"I picked up some feelings of distinct revulsion from them when we talked about the injured patients." The administrator frowned. "I know their instincts are logical in the water, this isn't the same?"

"You're asking a lot of them. The 'Zangians' natural aversion to anything wounded is a basic survival instinct."

"Blood draws predators, I know. But is it really instinct, or custom?" At her blank look, Ana nodded, "The big male lieutenant— Onkar?—mentioned that what we proposed to do violated the natural order."

"He was referring to the act of preserving life, and that is custom, not instinct. The aquatic culture here has a very different attitude toward that than we do." Teresa sat back in her chair. "For example, they think that instead of trying to save the injured and diseased, we land dwellers should simply produce more children to replace them."

"Dr. mu Cheft at the FreeClinic doesn't believe that," Ana pointed out. "If he did he wouldn't bother saving any of his patients."

"He's one of the exceptions. You have to remember that mu Cheft left the coastal pod to live among the colonists during the first settlement, which was when he obtained his medical degree." Teresa nodded toward the coast. "The majority of the natives here have actually had very little in the way of cultural exchanges with the colonists, mainly because of the environmental factors. They've upheld traditional 'Zangian beliefs because there is no one underwater to challenge them."

Ana looked disappointed. "They'll probably refuse to help, then."

"It's hard to say. The pilots are an exceptional, unpredictable bunch." She smiled at her friend. "Do you want me to talk to Dair about it?"

"I honestly just wanted to keep you in the loop, as you are closer to the 'Zangians than any of us." Her blue eyes twinkled. "But if Jadaira asks for advice and if you want to put in a good word for us, it would be greatly appreciated. Liam tried, but . . ." She searched for the right phrase.

Teresa arched her brows. "William Mayer is not known for his persuasive charm. In fact, I'd guess that he's one hundred percent charm-free."

"Now, Teresa. He's an extremely busy man."

"He's also an overbearing, tyrannical pain in the ass. I considered drowning him quite a few times, you know, when Dair was a pup." She studied her friend's expression. "Why are you running interference for William?"

"I'm not. He's a brilliant surgeon and innovator, and I only want to do my part to help with this project."

Teresa concentrated, and imagined her friend in William Mayer's arms, being passionately kissed. Despite the fact that the doctor was Terran, they looked very good together. She was almost tempted to play matchmaker.

Ana's cheeks flooded with pretty color. "Stop thinking that, right now."

She heard something in her friend's voice that relayed more than annoyance, and cleared the image from her mind. "Sorry. I didn't know." She tilted her head. "Does *he* know?"

"There's nothing to know. We work together, that's all." The administrator tried to sound stern, but an unwilling smile curved her lips. "All right, I think he's very attractive; I always have. But he sees me only as a professional associate."

"Dairatha felt the same way about me, until I swam naked with him for the first time." Teresa eyed the immersion tank at the back of the house. *If those walls could talk* . . . "Telling him Terran females are selective breeders and basically always in season helped a little, too."

Her friend chuckled. "Somehow I don't think the same approach would work with Liam."

Teresa winked. "Never know until you try."

Dair stayed at the FreeClinic long enough to request that more information on the Skittish from the colonial database be sent to Teresa's dwelling. Normally she would have accessed a public console and punched it up herself, but the pilots' pod was anxious to discuss Mayer's proposition, and her throbbing face made her just as eager to get away from mouth-breathers for a while.

The 'Zangians didn't bother to head back to the coast, but stopped at Teresa's land dwelling and headed for the enormous immersion tank in back of the structure. Teresa intercepted Dair on the way to the wet room, where the aquatics stored their suits before climbing into the tank.

"Jadaira, Ana came to see me and told me about Dr. Mayer's proposal." She looked troubled. "You know this will be more than just ambulance duty."

There was no translation into 'Zangian for the last phrase Teresa had used. "What is ambulance duty?"

"It's . . . Never mind. It's a very worthy mission, and I wanted you to know that I'm on hand if you want to talk about it."

"I have to discuss the matter with the pilots' pod." She nodded toward the tank.

Her stepmother stared at her. "What happened to your face?" She put her hand on Dair's cheek, and her lips went white. "You're bruised. What did you do?"

"It's okay." She eased her fingers away. "A small misunderstanding with one of the Skartesh." Before Teresa could speak, she added, "It was my fault; I inadvertently violated some religious taboo. It won't happen again."

"Damn it. Hold still." Her stepmother wasn't going to be put off, and scanned her augmented mandible. "At least there's no permanent damage. You have to report this, Dair."

"Mom, it's best forgiven and forgotten." She started unfastening her suit. "I've really got to get wet."

"All right. Bring the pilots in to visit later, if you want." Teresa headed back for the house, but paused as someone came around the side of the structure.

By then Dair had stripped to the waist, and when she saw the Skartesh she politely covered her bare chest with her hands. "Hello." She turned to her stepmother. "Mom, this is Rushan Amariah, the pilot of the *Hemat*. Pilot, this is my father's mate, Dr. Teresa Selmar."

"So you're the one." Teresa's face turned pink as she walked into his strike zone. "Did you hit my daughter?"

Rushan made a strange gesture, lifting both of his paws and displaying them palms-out. "My mother caused the injury. I came to apologize for her behavior."

"Apology not accepted." Teresa pointed to the glidecar path beyond her home. "Leave."

Dair gave up trying to cover her chest and strode over to them. "Mom, *he* didn't hit me." She rubbed a digit over an itchy spot on her arm as she said to Rushan, "I'm sorry, I didn't know that I offended your parent. It won't happen again."

"Quiet, Jadaira." Teresa faced the Skartesh. "You think you can come here and smooth things over? Forget it. I'm human; I know what prejudice is. You're not spitting on my child."

"We do not spit on others, and I only wish to explain what happened." Rushan seemed very agitated, and wouldn't look at Dair at all. "My mother and father founded the Promise movement. Their beliefs are very stringent, and their faith strong."

Dair was eager to settle the matter. "Well, then, no harm done."

"That's pathetic," her stepmother said.

"It's more than adequate, Teresa." She sent a longing glance toward the tank where the pod was waiting for her. "Thank you, pilot. Enjoy the day."

She walked away, hoping that would end things. But Rushan followed her, and Teresa followed him.

*If they want to preserve their mouth-breather modesty, they'll just have to go into the house.* Exasperated, Dair stripped down to her skin and dove into the tank.

Burn stared through the transparent wall at Teresa and the Skartesh. *Dair, is your foster dam having problems breathing?*

*No, she's angry.* Arbitrary anger toward another, being on neutral ground, was a difficult emotion for most 'Zangians to grasp. The closest they came to it was mild annoyance, unless it had to do with food or mating, and generally only then on feeding grounds or in the breeding caverns. The aquatics had strict customs about the acceptable ways in which to resolve anger, but serious fights were very uncommon and grudges even more rare. *You know how protective she is of me.*

*She acts as if you'd just slipped from her birth canal,* Saree said as she swam over to them. *What's that male doing here? Does he wish to mate with you?*

That was a possibility, given his behavior: touching her, pursuing her, and coming without prior invitation to a place she considered one of her homes. In 'Zangian society, males never demonstrated such blatant interest unless they meant to warn other males of their intent to fight over a female as soon as she came into season. But Rushan Amariah wasn't an aquatic, and he'd shown just the opposite behavior when she'd met him on the *Hemat*.

*I don't know what he wants, but we need to talk about this land-dweller issue now. Let Teresa handle him.*

The pilots' pod had much to say about Dr. Mayer and Ana Hansen's proposal, and Dair gave everyone the opportunity to speak his mind.

*I think it is too dangerous,* Curonal, Madura's sibling, said. *If they were in the water, it would be one thing. But they are asking us to retrieve beings all over the system. We will be too far from home if anything goes wrong.*

Saree was not as negative. *I'm not afraid of a little dry hide, but the idea does have its perils. We've only flown patrol missions, and have done very little retrieval work. This medevac crew will be handling people with new wounds.*

They were all a little leery of being close to injured life-forms.

Out of sheer self-preservation, 'Zangians avoided anything spilling blood in the water, and it was hard to ignore the instinct.

*You know land dwellers aren't like us,* Dair reminded them. *If they are diseased or injured, nothing attacks them topside, and they don't devour each other. They have nothing that would compete for the victims, or threaten us.*

*It's bizarre, the way they cling to life.* Blunt as always, Burn got right to the heart of what was bothering everyone. *Even after they are too hurt to feed, they still struggle to preserve each other. Why is that?*

*We do the same, in some ways,* Dair said. *How many of you would abandon a newborn calf? Not counting me, of course.*

Everyone suddenly looked somewhere else. Reminding them that she had been cast off as an infant wasn't very courteous, but Dair thought it served as a good example of the possibilities.

Onkar jumped into the tank and came to Dair. *That mouthbreather is out there, watching you, Dair. He stinks of chemicals and lust.*

Competitive 'Zangian males identified each other by the smell of pheremones broadcast by their swollen seminal glands, but the Skartesh gave off no such scent that Dair could detect.

*Ignore him, pilot.* Refusing to use Onkar's name or rank in the water was a deliberate insult, but he deserved it for being late and thinking so poorly of her. *We are obliged to give Dr. Mayer a response on this proposal. I will resign my commission and offer my services to the Bio Rescue team as pilot. If you wish to accompany me, I will be glad of it. If you refuse, I will understand.* She looked at the faces around her, and then swam apart from the group. *Choose what pleases you.*

Burn joined her. *At your side, cousin.*

Saree and Madura also swam over.

*I am not certain this duty will suit me, but I must try it first to see if it will,* Loknoth said.

Curonal somersaulted, and then joined them and echoed his sentiments.

Dair noticed Onkar's mood growing more agitated, and turned her head to see Rushan standing just beyond the tank wall. He was indeed watching her. She couldn't detect any physical signs of arousal—Teresa had indicated most mouth-breathing male lupines displayed some sort of engorged genitalia when drawn to a female—but his expression and the movement of his eyes indicated some interest in her physical form.

*They are fascinated when we shed our garments,* Madura commented as she noticed him. *Is undressing an aphrodisiac to them?*

*Hardly, or they'd be jumping on us a lot more.* Dair's gunner flipped his flukes. *Naked skin must be another of their taboos. That's why they hide under all those clothes.*

*How can they read each other's bodies when they are wrapped up like that?* The young female slipped around Burn, playfully gliding her hide against his. *No wonder they whelp only once or twice in a lifetime.*

Dair glanced at Teresa. Her stepmother's inability to provide Dair's father with a pup had made her something of an object of pity among the 'Zangians, but Teresa had explained it was a matter of choice, not instinct.

"After your dam died, I had my hands full with keeping you alive. I didn't have time to try breeding with your father," Teresa told Dair once. "Other females offered to be surrogates, but we wanted to give you our full attention." She had made a face. "All right, and I didn't want your father breeding with anyone else."

Complications from Core infection had killed Dair's biological mother shortly after birth. Born premature and devoid of proper hide pigmentation, Dair had also suffered massive tissue damage from the plague while in utero. Only Teresa's alterform procedure and Dr. Mayer's skills as a surgeon had saved her.

As an albino, she would have been different even without the SEAL procedure. Full-white pups who survived to adulthood were revered by her people, which gave her status other females could never attain.

Yet Dair didn't want to be valued for her color. She didn't want to spend her mating years being chased because of it, either.

"There's no reason to rush breeding, Dair," her stepmother always said. "You have your career to think of, and you can always have pups later."

Monogamy appealed to her on several levels. It was, to use one of Teresa's human expressions, very romantic. Dair suspected her father didn't always appreciate the restrictions her stepmother's beliefs placed on him, but he respected them and had curtailed his mating habits accordingly. As a result Teresa and Dairatha shared the kind of intimacy and knowledge of each other that Dair envied.

*I want someone like that for me.*

Rushan Amariah walked over to the tank, and placed his hand on the wall, apparently trying to get her attention. Dair swam closer. Odd that he showed no fear of being so close to so much water. The small amount the Esalmalin had sprayed on his followers outside the FreeClinic had absolutely terrorized them.

"I must speak with you," the Skartesh's muffled voice came through the wall of the tank.

Before Dair could respond, Onkar suddenly shot past her and rammed his head into the tank wall, which made Rushan stagger backward in surprise. *Mouth-breather! Go away!*

*What is the matter with you?* Dair collided with Onkar before he could ram the side of the tank again. *He isn't bothering us; he's just curious.*

He nipped her hide with the edge of his teeth, hard enough to leave a mark. *Let him be curious about his own kind. There are enough of them here now for him to have his pick of the females.*

*I don't want him any more than I want you.*

She hadn't meant to be so rude, and wasn't surprised when Onkar drove her back to the opposite side of the tank. *Then stop encouraging him.*

Dair knew arguing over mating practices with an aroused 'Zangian male was useless. *Fine. I will stay over here. He will take that as a refusal.*

Onkar watched her as he rounded up the rest of the pod, who were darting around them in high agitation. Attack behavior outside feeding or mating grounds disturbed the 'Zangians, who considered it a sign of illness. Onkar's continued aggression forced them out of habit to remain silent and docile as he grouped everyone together.

*Who agrees with Dair to resign from the PQPM and join this Bio Rescue program?* Onkar demanded.

Everyone surrounded Dair, and clikked their approval.

*Very well. I will do this thing.* Onkar's fins churned the water for a moment. *But if it fails, Jadaira, you will surrender leadership of the SEALs to me.*

*Agreed, Lieutenant.* She looked at the serious faces around her. *You'll see, this will be good for us.*

# CHAPTER
## SIX

The pilots elected to leave Teresa's tank and catch a passing transport out to the coast, but Dair stayed behind to talk to her stepmother about Bio Rescue and Rushan Amariah. She still had some questions that only a nonaquatic could answer, and she suspected Teresa had a few of her own.

Her stepmother came into the wet room as Dair finished dressing. "Did you all come to a decision?"

"You mean that your tank monitors are all malfunctioning?" She gave her an amused look. Teresa had no qualms about listening in but she would never admit to doing so. "We're going to fly for Bio Rescue." She looked out through the window at Teresa's grounds. "Did that Skartesh leave?"

"After Onkar went ballistic, I made him go." Teresa handed her a towel for her wet face. "He's a bigot and a fanatic, honey, and his people are isolationists. You should really avoid him in the future, if possible."

"I didn't ask him to come here." Dair followed her into the house. "I should feed. May I make you something?"

"Just a cup of tea, dear, if you would. Excuse me for a moment; I promised Ana I would signal." Teresa went to her console.

Her stepmother's prep unit only held a couple of varieties of unprocessed fish, as there were few that didn't spoil quickly, so Dair chose a double serving of raw *peixe* for herself and made Teresa a pot of tea. 'Zangians rarely had the urge or the need to drink fluids the way mouth-breathers did, but Dair's altered digestive system could handle larger amounts of fluid, so she brought two servers to the table. Drinking tea was a sociable thing to do among land dwellers, and sharing the custom always pleased her stepmother.

Teresa returned after a few minutes and sat down with her at the kitchen table. "Thank you, sweetheart." She poured for both of them. "Dair, do you ever regret being a SEAL?"

That startled her. "Why would I?"

Her stepmother made an odd gesture. "You didn't exactly give me permission to experiment on you."

"You and Dr. Mayer saved my life." She sipped some of the heated liquid from her cup. "If I had been able to talk, I'd have said yes."

During her pup years, no one had told Dair how or why she was different. For one thing, the other 'Zangians had shunned her entirely at first. Only very gradually did they learn to tolerate her presence, and eventually accepted her back into the pod. Her father had been too busy teaching her where to swim, how to feed, and which neighbors not to annoy to talk much about why she was the only all-white, and why she was arranged so oddly.

Over time she'd wondered about the physical differences. Her gillets and genitalia were stuck in odd positions, and her shape was wrong. She didn't have the articulated fins and flukes like other pups, and her hide had no coloration. Her eyes appeared to be recessed at first, but as she grew her cranial bioaugmentations expanded and flattened her face. Dr. Mayer had given her a small, cosmetic nose and ear-shaped flaps on her haffets like a humanoid, though hers were nonfunctional. Her limbs and torso were an odd mix of 'Zangian musculature and humanoid form. Her feet didn't attain the graceful tail form like 'Zangian flukes did, but the webbing between her toes served just as well.

She regarded her stepmother, who still seemed troubled. "I am happy with how you made me, Mom."

"That's not entirely true. You've never quite forgiven me for altering your gillets."

Teresa's desire to give her "hair" had created much grief for Dair when she had been a pup, but she didn't hold a grudge. "Don't be silly."

Instead of being in the proper positions on either side of her jaw, gillets sprouted all over Dair's scalp. Her cousin and the other males had thought this particularly hilarious. Since her stepmother was covered with hair in the same place, Dair at first had thought she'd done it to make them look more alike, so that other land dwellers would think Teresa was her biological dam.

Dair's father had later explained why her stepmother had decided to make her look more like land dwellers. How the pod had rejected her and refused to provide donor tissue, and how Teresa had had no choice but to adapt the most compatible humanoid prosthetics available. All Dair could see was that Teresa had to wear a breather rig when she swam with them, and that living topside seemed very inconvenient.

She smiled at her stepmother. "What I haven't forgiven you for was the first time Dad beached me."

Teresa ran a fingertip around the rim of her server. "That wasn't much fun for you, I know."

It had been horrible. The memory of the first time she'd breathed air still made her chest hurt. Her throat had burned, her stomach had heaved, and for a few minutes she'd just shook and shuddered on the sand, letting everything come up and out. Finally the pain dulled enough for her to start crawling back toward the waves.

"No, Jadaira." Her father, who was not so graceful on land, had awkwardly crouched down to pull her up. "You must do this."

She hadn't wanted to do the things he called *standing up* and *walking*. She'd never lived under the burden of gravity before. Standing made her dizzy. Walking made her fall, and landing hurt more than both of them.

"I remember, I thought Dad had gone feeble and was trying to kill us both," Dair said. "Then I saw you standing at the top of the dune."

"First time you'd ever seen me without my rig."

"I didn't know you had a face under all that stuff." She picked at her fish. The image of Teresa laughing and calling her name still made her artificial toes curl with delight. She'd held out her arms that were like Dair's arm-shaped fins. She'd run toward her on legs that were like her legs.

"You knew my sound and my scent," her stepmother reminded her. "You took your first steps into my arms." She watched her feed for a moment before she added, "You're not eating much."

"It always tastes funny out of the machine." Dair took a mouthful of raw fish and restrained herself from jerking her head the way she would have in the water, to kill it before swallowing. "I like it better when it wriggles in my teeth."

"Your stomach will become intolerant if you eat only unprocessed foods, and you do need to practice your land behavior, Dair. It's more important than ever that you fit in now."

She eyed her stepmother across the rim of her server. "Why?"

"You'll be required to act as a land dweller would now. You can't abandon the patients who are mortally wounded, the way your pod would in the sea. You will have to preserve life above all other things."

"Why do your kind feel that's so important?"

"It's partly culture, and partly environmental. Take Terrans, for example. As we developed our civilization, we advanced enough to preserve the lives of our tribes when they became injured, rather than let them die. This perpetuated bloodlines and provided experienced elders for each community."

Dair argued the 'Zangian point of view. "But if you whelped more pups, you wouldn't need to save them all."

"I think it has a lot to do with the human understanding of death. We are aware at all times that we will die. Life is very precious to us. We cling to it."

Her people understood what death was, but never applied the concept to themselves until it happened. 'Zangians lived in the *now,* not *the future* or *what might be.* Dair felt almost the same, although she had a different perspective because she had always been aware of her own uniqueness. *Still, why think about death when you could enjoy the moment?* "If I die, Teresa, will you alterform another pup born like me?"

"No, Dair. You were dying; it was the only way to save you. The pod would never accept it, either." She sighed. "The elders have made their position on radical alterforming very clear."

She finished her fish. "Okay. If anything happens to me, you can always adopt Burn. His dam is driving him sand-belly lately, and he likes your tank."

Her stepmother laughed until her eyes leaked. "Oh, Dair. My life would be so dull without you."

Dair left Teresa and headed for the coast a short time later. Instead of taking transport, she walked, both to exercise her augmented limbs and to enjoy the novel feel of the suns on her face. She wasn't as uncomfortable out of the water for long periods of time as other 'Zangians were; something to do with her SEAL skin reacting to the suns-shine.

"As a natural albino, you would never have been able to tolerate the light," Teresa had told her once. "The synthetic biochrome I used to augment your derma acts as a permanent sunscreen."

She didn't notice the Skartesh following her until Rushan Amariah caught up. "Commander."

*My, he is a persistent male.* "Pilot."

"Call me Shan." He lost a little of his stride. "You don't like me, do you?"

She stopped and eyed the dozen white-robed followers walking in a straight line behind him. They stopped when he did. "I don't like or dislike you. I don't know you."

"My apology was inadequate, and my mother overreacted. I want you to know I'm sincerely sorry for what she did."

"Forget about it." When he lifted his hand, she stepped back. "Please don't touch me." She gestured to the crowd. "They'll see, and I don't want to offend your mother again. She hits hard."

Shan turned and said something in a fast, lilting language that her TI didn't translate. His followers abruptly turned around and marched off, leaving them alone.

Dair wasn't so sure that was an improvement. "What do you want?"

He eyed a pair of colonists approaching from another direction. "Is there someplace we can have some privacy?"

She understood the many needs for privacy. None of them she wanted to share with Shan. "No."

"I see." He held out something. "Open your hand. It's all right; I won't touch you."

Warily she stretched out her open palm, and he dropped a small, golden disk of metal onto it. She turned it over. The disk was inscribed with strange pictographs, and in the center was a glowing purple stone. There was a chain of tiny metal links, cleverly interwoven, attached to the disk.

She'd never seen anything like it. "What is it?"

"A gift."

Dair knew land dwellers often gave each other objects as gifts. 'Zangians weren't too sure what to make of the custom; they didn't own objects, and allowing first-feeding privileges was a much more sensible method of showing gratitude or friendship.

Gift giving was only one of their strange customs. The woven weeds they called garments smothered their skin, and they wrapped and draped themselves with more before sleeping. Dair couldn't sleep without being immersed, so Teresa had kept her in the immersion tank with her father every night that they stayed with her, and reluctantly let them keep a couple of mvrey in the tank as well. Letting the parasite eaters attach themselves to her skin kept Dair very clean. Why Teresa didn't let them do the same for her seemed silly.

Strange, strange behavior. Like Shan offering her this gift. Well, she could be polite. Unsure of the fastener, she looped the chain around her wrist. "It's very pretty. Thank you."

"No, Commander, it's a necklace." He traced the air around her head. "You place the chain around your neck."

She unwrapped it and gingerly draped the necklace over her head. The chain got caught on some of her gillets, then slid down and hung from her neck. It felt heavy. She tucked her jaw in so she could see it resting against the front of her flight suit. "Does this have some special meaning to you?" She hoped it wasn't some sort of mating gift.

"On oKia, it is the symbol of friendship."

"oKia?" She'd never heard of that world. "What quadrant is that in?"

"It is . . . far from here. A planet that once traded with the Skart homeworld." Dark fur bristled across his brow as he reached down and lifted the disk with his fingers. "The stone is a rose star sapphire. When light refracts through it, it becomes the same color as your eyes."

The way he said that bothered her; she felt sure he didn't mean it as a compliment. "I must go now. Thank you again for the neck-gift."

"Neck*lace*. Dair—that is what they call you, is it not?" He didn't wait for an answer, but closed his paw around the disk. "Don't go. I wish to know more about you."

"I don't understand why you would," she said, couching her words carefully. "Yesterday you fired on us. Today your dam hit me. You say kind words, but your body speaks differently. Your gaze is critical."

His voice turned unpleasant. "I want to know more about you and your people. I want to understand you."

"No, you don't." She was pretty sure he wanted to mate with her, and thought it sad that Rushan's family had so badly neglected his sexual education. She wasn't in the water, so she couldn't physically evade him. That left being verbally blunt. "Rushan Amariah, I am not in season, and even if I were, I wouldn't want your pup."

He nodded, seemingly unperturbed by the very rudest remark she had ever made in her life. "We could be friends."

"Perhaps, if your mother and my stepmother and your religion and your people saw no harm in that. However, they all seem to." She had no need of his friendship. "I must go."

"I wish to see you again." He seemed to be forcing the words out now. "How can I persuade you that I mean no harm?"

She thought of Onkar. On rare occasions, pod males sometimes killed each other over females. It was part of the rarest form of extreme 'Zangian behavior—a kind of sexual frenzy—but they had never told the land dwellers about it. Dair's father had explained once that even her stepmother, as enlightened as she was, wouldn't understand. Teresa and the other colonists considered all such acts illegal.

Given the possessiveness Onkar had already displayed around the Skartesh, Dair worried that a direct confrontation between the two males would end up in just such a disaster. "I just don't think this is wise."

"Wise or not, I will see you again, Jadaira. Soon."

She started to walk away, then looked back to see him watching her go. He stood there with his hands curled at his sides, and never turned away.

Dr. Mayer, Dair's stepmother, and Ana Hansen had only begun to set up for the meeting with for the pilots' pod when Dair found them at the FreeClinic. Both Terran females were discussing something in low tones and missed the 'Zangian's entrance, so Dair politely cleared a few of her gillets.

Ana looked up. "Hello, Dair. We weren't expecting you until later."

They were supposed to be beginning medevac orientation that day, but Dair had received a signal earlier that threatened to shut down Bio Rescue before it ever got initiated.

"I bring some bad news. All of our resignations were rejected," she told them. "PQPM has suspended all discharges until the war is finished. We are not excused from our regular duties, and have to stay on planetary patrol."

"Oh, no." Ana looked distressed.

*Now for the good news.* "I think I know of a way we can do both jobs."

Dr. Mayer looked up from the console he was manning. "Administrator, I won't have my people carrying arms or being fired upon by hostiles."

"There aren't any hostiles left," Dair said, before Ana spoke. "We don't engage the enemy like that anyhow."

She explained why 'Zangians had been put on permanent patrol duty. "Quadrant wanted a strong military presence here, to protect the heavily populated worlds, major trade routes, and mining belts. However, all of their fighter and recon pilots, as well as the bulk of their troops, were needed in the combat zone and to protect military installations and supply routes. Since 'Zangians can't survive away from the homeworld, we were the logical choice to stay behind. That situation won't change until the war is over."

"Then how can you do both jobs?" Mayer asked.

"This is how it can be done: The modified raider flies in formation with the patrol. If an emergency comes in while we're on patrol, the Bio Rescue team responds, and the strafers provide backup and protection. Otherwise, we stay on patrol."

The physician frowned. "I still don't like it."

She had the feeling Dr. Mayer was one of those Terrans who didn't like a lot of things. Perhaps she would introduce him to Rushan. "It's the best we can do. Otherwise you'll have to recruit from another, nonmilitary pod. Add to that the time it takes to train them to fly the raiders"—she spread her hands—"you would not have trained pilots for at least another two or three seasons, maybe more."

Ana looked at Dr. Mayer. "Liam, she's right."

The door panel opened, and a security officer stepped in. "Excuse the interruption. Security Chief Norash requires Commander mu T'resa at HQ. Immediately."

She'd forgotten to report in about the Skittish. "I'd better go and see him. I'll return to join the orientation as soon as I can."

The officer transported her over to Colonial Administration headquarters, the lower floor of which was occupied by Security. She'd visited there only once or twice during the occupation, so she let Norash's man lead her to his duty station.

'Zangians had always felt a little intimidated by the Trytinorns, who were as large as yearling mogshrikes, and had thick, unlovely hides with the same yellow-and-brown striping as wasp-netters. Although they didn't have much in the way of teeth beneath the elongated nasal appendage they used like an arm and hand, and displayed irritable but otherwise mild dispositions, all that bulk was troublesome. It certainly made any smaller life-form nervous.

Dair didn't like the head of security much because nothing made him happy, but she always tried to be polite. "Chief, you summoned me?"

"Three rotations ago I summoned you. Where the *suns* have you been, Commander?"

She tried to look innocent. "Oh, you know. Just hydrating."

Norash lifted his prehensile nose, which was as long as Dair's entire body, and pointed to a corridor. "In my office. Now."

She'd taken plenty of verbal assaults in the past, and endured them with little difficulty. Land dwellers liked purging their gullets with a lot of huffing and shouting. Dair was pretty sure it had something to do with their digestive systems. She positioned herself in front of Norash's console, and when he began ranting, she stood silent and accepting until he settled his belly.

"So in the future, Commander, when I send for you, you will report at once, is that clear?"

"Yes, sir." No, she wouldn't, and they'd do this another time. It was becoming something of a meeting ritual between them.

"Good." Before she got to the door panel, he added, "Come back here, Jadaira. I'm not finished."

She couldn't help the "You're not?" as she resumed her position. Usually she had to stay only through to the end of the shouting.

"We retrieved the drivecore from that passenger freighter you fished out of the blockade. It was rigged to blow." He pushed a photoscan across his console toward her. "This is what my people pulled out of the control circuits."

She examined the image of a very small transmitter attached to a very large block of molecular accelerator. A teaspoon of it would have vaporized the entire building. The photoscan showed a hand pistol beside the device, for scale. "There's enough here to wipe out the whole colony."

"And it would have, if the pilot hadn't ejected the core before entering that blockade." Norash retrieved the photoscan. "Someone doesn't like our new residents."

"That would be basically everyone on the planet, sir."

"I received this from one of my patrolmen." He showed her a second image, one of herself speaking with Shan. "The pilot is the son of Yersha and Kabod Amariah, founders of the Promise movement."

"I'm sorry, the Promise?"

"It's a new form of an old Skart religion practiced by this cult. Why was he speaking to you?"

"Rushan? He wished to apologize for some inappropriate behavior." She saw no reason to give Norash the specifics; he had already violated her privacy by photoscanning her with Shan. "He gave me this"—she tugged Shan's neck-gift out of her collar to show him—"and asked for my friendship."

"Refuse him and give him back the bauble. He's nothing but trouble."

Dair felt a twinge of perverse anger. It was one thing not to wish to have anything to do with Rushan Amariah herself, but to be ordered to avoid him? That didn't sit well with her. "Chief, would you mind clarifying how this Skartesh male poses a threat to me or the colony?"

"Firing on you and finding the bomb from his vessel aren't enough?"

"Obviously he discovered it and wished to safeguard his passengers, or he wouldn't have ejected the core. As for firing on me, that was more out of . . . bad temper than anything." She made a casual gesture. "His kind subjugate their females; being saved by one likely bruised his pride."

"He ejected that core shortly before your squadron showed up at the blockade. He could have seen you coming, and decided to rid himself of the evidence."

That made no sense. "He ejected it so that it wouldn't kill his passengers."

"Jadaira, let me give you some advice." He wagged the end of his nasal appendage in her face. "This young male is the religious leader of the Skartesh now. The current census indicated there are more than twenty-seven thousand of his followers on this planet. Another ten thousand are in route to the Pmoc Quadrant. We've been unable to crack their internal security and find out why they've chosen to mass here, but more are coming."

"They filed for official asylum," she said. "The League drove them from their homeworld. They must want a safe place to live."

"We don't know that because they refuse to communicate directly with anyone. They shun any involvement in the community. They constantly create public disturbances." Norash backed up to an odd object sticking out from the wall panel and rubbed one of his brown-and-yellow-striped flanks against it. "If not for the revisions to the charter, I would have already found a way to deport every single one of them."

In order to tempt more life-forms to settle on K-2, some of the stricter passages of the charter had been revised to allow public assembly. As a result, the Skittish had official sanction for any sort of group dances they wanted to hold.

Dair could understand why Norash was upset. No species since the Bartermen, who had left K-2 en masse during the First Exodus, had maintained such consummate secrecy about their religious and cultural practices. Norash liked to know exactly what was happening in the colony at all times.

And, although they never came out and said it, so did the 'Zangians. K-2 was their homeworld, and while its colonists could always move on to another world, the 'Zangians could not survive anywhere else. There were complex mineral components in the indigenous seawater that could not be found on any other world. It was Teresa's theory that being deprived of them was what killed every aquatic who had left or had been removed from K-2.

This gave her an idea. "Why don't I try to find out what the Skartesh are planning to do? Rushan wishes to be my friend, and friends often confide in each other. You say he is one of their leaders; leaders usually know what their people have planned."

Norash's wide ears flared. "You're not trained as a security operative."

"I'm a soldier, not a spy." She gave him an ironic look. "However, I can usually persuade others to trust me. It has something to do with the pink eyes, my stepmother tells me. I look harmless."

Norash considered this. She could see the indecision in his little eyes; wanting the intelligence, not wanting her to be the one to provide it. "You'll have to file regular updates on your progress. The minute you discover anything, and I do mean *anything* that represents a threat to the colony, you report to me at once. Is that clear?"

"Yes, sir."

"Very well. Dismissed."

# CHAPTER
## SEVEN

Dair returned to the FreeClinic and was directed to join the rest of the pod, who had finished the meeting portion of their initial orientation and had begun their first training session. As soon as she turned the corner to enter the assessment unit, Saree rushed past her.

"Sar—" She stared after her as the other 'Zangian female darted into a lavatory.

Loknoth came staggering out after Saree, and paused long enough to choke out, "Dead thing," before he occupied the lavatory beside Saree's.

Dair went up to the assessment desk. The little Psyoran nurse who had been on board the *Hemat* greeted her in a pleasant voice. "Good day, Commander."

"Nurse." Dair glanced toward the lavatory units. "What's wrong with my pilots?"

"Oh, they're just experiencing a bit of nausea. You're Dr. mu Cheft's niece, aren't you?" When Dair nodded, the nurse shifted pigment, showing a beautiful rainbow array of color on her front frills. "I'm Ecla; nice to meet you. How is your stomach?"

Her stepmother claimed she'd made it to outlast biosteel. "Fine."

"Excellent, then you can join the class in pathology." She used one frill edge to indicate a corridor leading off from the lobby. "Three panels down, on the left." She gave her a kindly look. "Just breathe through your mouth and you'll be fine."

Now totally bewildered, Dair followed Ecla's instructions and entered the panel she indicated.

The smell of chemical preservatives hit her first, followed by what they masked: flesh rot.

There wasn't a 'Zangian on-planet who hadn't resorted to eating something that was already dead. Dair knew most of her people would deny it until their gill vents swelled shut, but it was something everyone did, whether out of hunger or curiosity or sheer spite. 'Zangian parents contributed to the problem by forbidding podlings to even go near the dead. It was sensible advice, for a creature's death throes as well as release of body fluids attracted mogshrikes and a whole horde of lesser nuisances.

It never worked, though, because podlings were insatiably curious. Still, after one had a taste of rotting flesh, once was usually enough. The stench was a good reminder.

Dair looked around the pathology lab. A few members of the pilots' pod were standing with their backs to the wall panels, watching Dr. Mayer working on something with another physician, a red-carapaced being with very nasty-looking claws. Their subject was spread-eagled on a stainless-steel table, and had been dead for some time, Dair judged by the body's condition and stink.

"Now, when you transport a patient with an injury to the torso, you must compensate for any turbulence you encounter." Dr. Mayer peeled back the outer layer of the creature's torso. "As you can see, in this species the internal organs have little protection—"

The sight of all those inedible guts and spilling fluids made the rest of the pod with the exception of Dair flee the room.

"Sorry, cousin." Burn gave her a faintly apologetic look as he darted around her.

"Commander." Mayer looked up, his frustration plain. "I need them back in here to see this."

"I don't think they're coming back, Doctor. 'Zangians don't like carcasses," she told him. "Dead things attract scavengers, who fight and spill blood, which brings the bigger predators. The scent of dead flesh is a fear trigger." Despite her altered sense of smell, even she was starting to sweat. "Perhaps you could use photoscans to illustrate your point?"

"That isn't the same." Mayer tossed down his instruments in disgust. "Your battle-hardened warriors become ill at the sight of a cadaver. What are they going to do when we're loading the injured into the holds?"

"Probably stay at the helm, out of the way." She glanced at the dead thing. "You need us to fly your medevac missions. That's all we're going to be able to do, Doctor, and you'd better accept that or find someone else."

"And if there are more wounded than the medevac team can handle on their own?"

She scratched an itchy spot on her brow. "You'd better stock a lot of purge bags on board."

"This isn't going to work."

Ana looked up from the monthly community service allocation reports she was reviewing as William Mayer strode into her office.

Her assistant, Carsa, trailed after him, its luminous eyes looking distinctly watery. "Administrator, I told this male that you were occupied, but he ignored me." It made *male* sound like *killer* and *ignored* like *assaulted*, but Ana knew its hormones were still running unbalanced.

"It's all right, Carsa. Dr. Mayer and I are working together on a project. If you would—please—hold my signals. Thank you." As Carsa retreated, she switched off her datapad and indicated the seat in front of her desk. "Sit down, Doctor. Would you like something to drink?"

He paced back and forth. "I'd like some pilots who don't puke at the sight of a dead body. Do you have forty of those?"

"The 'Zangians didn't do so well with their first training session, did they?" She rose from the console and dialed up some tea. "You should give them a little time to adjust, you know. You're throwing concepts at them that are very new and a little frightening."

"They're soldiers; surely they've had some related battle experience." He stopped pacing when she brought the server of oolong to him and absently accepted it. "Jadaira was the only one who didn't run shrieking out of the room, and even she turned three shades whiter than she already is."

"Come and sit down." Ana took his arm and guided him over to the chair, then sat in the one beside it. "This isn't all that's bothering you."

He eyed her. "Can't you read my thoughts?"

"If I concentrate hard enough, maybe, but it gives me a terrible headache." That was a bald-faced lie, of course. She had never tried to, mainly out of her own fear that she would discover what he genuinely thought of her. "You could save me a considerable amount of pain and an analgesic injection by telling me."

"Someone sabotaged the Skartesh ship that Jadaira rescued from the orbital minefield. The stardrive was rigged to explode, but not until they landed here at the colony."

Ana's smile faded. "How did you find this out?"

"Norash. He informed Jadaira, and he thought I should know." He placed the untouched server on the edge of her desk. "If someone is using refugee vessels as weapons, they may try again."

This could have significant impact on how they handled all incoming transfers. "I'll have to inform the council of this."

He nodded. "Norash is preparing a report for tomorrow's meeting. You'll want to touch base with him."

She released a long breath. "Why would someone want to destroy the colony now?"

"Any number of reasons: the war, revenge, Core paranoia—even the Ninrana may have decided they have tolerated us long enough. They've only been promising to conquer every other world in the system for the last, what, hundred, two hundred years?" He rubbed his eyes. "We need these pilots more than ever, but if they can't handle the job, I might as well shut down the program now."

She thought for a moment. "The first time you attended a dissection, how did you feel?"

"Impatient to do the cutting myself." He glanced sideways at her. "I've never been squeamish, Ana, so you won't get any sympathy from me that way."

She inclined her head. "And the first time you lost a patient? Did you sail through that without any difficulties as well?"

"No. I went to a tavern, drank too much, picked a fight, and spent the next day in detention." The side of his mouth curled. "I broke my right hand and couldn't operate for eight weeks after that. Gave me some time to think."

She tried to imagine the distinguished man beside her drunk and brawling. And couldn't. "Our pilots are some of the best in the League, and no one knows this system better than they do. Perhaps you could give them a little more time."

He regarded her for a moment. "And understanding, I suppose?"

"You're the doctor. I'm just the data pusher." Feeling self-conscious, she tucked a stray tendril of hair back from her face, then winced as it caught on the stone setting of her ring. Since she had a server in her other hand she tried to tug it free. "Ouch."

"Hold still." He caught her wrist in one hand and gently detangled the golden strands, then held on to her hand to study the one ring she never removed. His silver brows drew together. "You're married?"

"I was." He had never asked—or noticed—before this. She didn't know if that should have made her feel angry or depressed. "My mate, Elars"—she nodded toward the photoscan on her desk—"was killed in a transport accident on Trunock. It's been seventeen years, now."

"I didn't know. I'm sorry." His tone was crisp, a doctor expressing sympathy to a patient's family.

It should have comforted her. Instead it made her want to slap him. "So am I, every day."

Ana retrieved his server and went to dump out the tepid tea. She had never felt like this with Elars, but then he had actually cared about her heart. Liam would show an interest only if it stopped working.

"Is there anything else I can do for you?"

"Unless you can lend me some of your inexhaustible patience, probably not. I simply wanted you to be aware of the situation." He watched her busy herself at the cleanser unit. "Perhaps I shouldn't have burdened you with this. I've upset you."

She kept her back to him until she could compose herself.

"Not at all. I would have found out at the council meeting anyway, and I appreciate the heads-up going in." She resumed her place behind her desk. "My advice would be to concentrate the pilots' training on what they can do without physical discomfort or distaste. Once they've had more exposure to patients, I think they'll develop more tolerance for the less appealing aspects of the work."

"I'll try to give them some space." He checked his wristcom. "I'd better head back to the clinic. Will you be attending the Hlagg ambassador's reception next week?"

Ana nodded. She went to all of them, but he knew that.

"We should go together." He rose and went to the door, and then glanced back at her. "I'll pick you up a quarter-hour before the reception starts, if that's acceptable?"

No, it wasn't.

Liam assumed that she had no escort, which instantly infuriated her. He was offering only to be courteous. Or perhaps to use the occasion for his own reasons. He had never before asked her to go with him to any colonial function. In fact, he avoided them.

Ana didn't need him to escort her anywhere, for that matter. She was a council member, a highly respected leader, and had many, many friends around the colony. She was certainly still young and attractive enough to command attention wherever she went. Why, at most events she spent more time discouraging interested males than anything.

That was what she should do: tell him she planned to spend the evening with another man. A much younger, extremely virile male. One who found her utterly mesmerizing and treated her like a goddess. One who couldn't wait to leave receptions so he could make love to her all night long.

Yet the moment she opened her mouth, the only thing that emerged was, "Yes."

He smiled a little. "I'll see you then." Out he went.

She stared at the closed door panel for a moment, and then rested her face against her hands. *Damn the man.*

\*　　\*　　\*

Dr. Mayer grudgingly excused the pilots' pod from further direct exposure to the dead, and concentrated on instructing them as to how to properly lift, carry, and secure the injured. The 'Zangians had a difficult time understanding the necessity for certain procedures, but they were used to being weightless, in space and water. The effect of gravity wasn't a daily concern, unless it meant flying out of the lower atmosphere.

The medevac team went over what would be needed on board the raiders, and the pilots spent a few shifts rearranging the equipment. There, too, they butted heads; the med pros wanted everything easily accessible, while the pilots and gunners wanted everything secure. Dair tried to act as liaison between the two groups, and spent most of her time smoothing frazzled nerves on both sides.

It took three weeks, but at last the day arrived when their training was complete, and they were prepared to launch the first patrol carrying the medevac teams.

As squadron leader and the most experienced pilot, Dair took the helm of Bio Rescue One. The Hsktskt control consoles had been modified by Verrig and his engineers to read out in 'Zangian pictographs and stanTerran, and Burn was already hooting over the multifunction weapons panel. It was odd to be piloting from a flight deck instead of a cabin, but Dair had flown plenty of freighters and other large transport vessels during training. She simply had to get used to the unusual rigging, and to breathing air instead of liquid while she flew.

Dair signaled the medevac crew to strap in before she powered up the engines. Hsktskt tech had an array of dynamic thrusters unlike anything the League built, and she'd spent long hours in the tank, studying the design schematics.

"Ensign, weapons at ready?"

Burn's dark hide flushed, showing his eagerness and satisfaction. "Ready and ample enough to blow up a small moon, Commander."

"Try to restrain yourself, cousin. We like the ones we have." She requested permission to launch.

Flight Control from the main transport tower responded at once. "Rescue One, you are clear to launch."

Rescue One—she liked the sound of that. Every ship should have a proper name. "Acknowledged, Control."

Lifting off with so many thrusters at her disposal was a bit like being a hungry podling in the center of a newly hatched *mackla* cluster. Dair couldn't help pushing the throttle up a little more than was necessary. The next moment they were soaring up into the green, so far and fast that she wondered if there was such a thing as a raider stalling in midatmosphere.

Then the g-forces hit her, and she thought, *Who cares?*

"That old Terran said that you were checked out on raiders," Burn shouted over the engine roar.

"Simulator runs, sure." She released a strum of laughter from sheer exhilaration. "But this is the first time I've ever actually *flown* one of these monsters."

Burn muttered something about *next time* and *Onkar.*

Flying the raider was almost like getting caught in a tide current. Even the cabin equalizers couldn't compensate fast enough to counter the g-forces, which tugged at her body with greedy fingers. Her flight suit, specially designed to keep the blood in her body from pooling in her extremities under such conditions, contracted and kept her from losing consciousness.

Dair rolled into a starburst maneuver, straightening out with another laugh when Burn yelped.

"*Duo,* Dair, quit flipping your tail!"

"Haven't really got one," she reminded him.

"I can see why!"

As Dair leveled out with no small amount of regret, someone staggered into the cabin. She looked over her shoulder and saw it was Dr. Mayer, and he didn't seem happy. Maybe it was the faint green tinge to his coloring.

"What do you think you're doing?" he shouted. "My people are too terrified to remove their harnesses!"

*Oh, dear.* She'd scared the civilians.

"Sorry. Just some altitude adjustments." Dair hoped he didn't know enough about flying to know she'd been goofing off. "We're leveled out now; it's safe."

"Keep it that way!" He stumbled back out.

Burn gave her a look, and she rolled her eyes. "Can't help it they've got delicate bellies."

"Show-off."

Though it flew like a dream and made maneuvers the strafers couldn't hope to mimic, the raider was not without its handling problems. She cut through space like a fin edge, but the ticklish throttle and hand-trigger directional thrusters weren't designed to be handled by humanoids. Even the slightest correction could send them sheering off course. As a result, Dair had to handle the controls like a bottom-basker rising to top feed: slow, slow, slow.

That could be adjusted, once they returned to base. The communications array, on the other hand, turned out to be a real nightmare. The Hsktskt relayed only one signal at a time, and only to other Hsktskt ships. What signals Burn pulled in from the rest of the squadron were distorted and choppy, and from what they could pick up, theirs sounded equally warped. Burn couldn't raise Flight Control at main transport at all.

"Let me try. Flight leader, this is Rescue One." She fine-tuned the relay as best she could. "Advise main transport that we are audio-down for this patrol. They're going to have to patch the calls through you."

"—thought they repaired the shreddy thing—" Saree's voice squawked over the panel.

"Must have been a drone who worked on it, because I'm not picking up a damn thing."

They flew last in formation, mostly because Dair still wasn't sure of the controls. It wouldn't do for Rescue One to cause their first call, either. About an hour into the mission, one of the nurses, the big red one, lumbered on deck.

Dair looked up into her four eyes. "Help you?"

"We've got a signal coming in over the diagnostic transponder. Transport's received a relay from another passenger vessel. They were caught in an orbital energy shunt, and their last transmission stated that they were going down fast."

Aside from Ylyd and K-2, there were only a couple of marginally habitable planets in their solar system. "Which one?"

"Ghalt Major."

That was one of them. Dair pulled up the system chart and punched in the general location. They were a few minutes away. "Did they give you exact coordinates?" The nurse handed her a datapad. "Thanks. Tell your people to rig up. Burn, signal Saree and tell her we're breaking formation."

As Burn sent the relay, she plotted a short run course. There wasn't much fancy flying involved, just a fairly straight shot from their position through three clutters before they hit Ghalt orbit.

Clutters, or remnant battlefields, were another legacy of the war. When the big League and Hsktskt cruisers attacked each other, they sent out swarms of various-type ordnance. The ordnance didn't always detonate, so when they left, a lot of it remained behind, floating in space. Most were too small to be picked up by a sensor sweep until a ship was right on top of them.

"Burn, engage your targeting array."

"Confirmed." Burn watched his board. "Do you know that this beast has more boom than a star carrier?"

"Good, then you won't run out." Dair flew to the brink of the first clutter and switched to thermal scan. Sometimes old ordnance corroded and leaked trace amounts of radiation, which made them easier to spot. "Patching through to your panel. I'll dodge as much as I can."

Negotiating a clutter was like swimming through a chokeweed field and hoping not to get entangled; it was simply not possible. She guided the ship over, under, and around the largest blips on her screen. Impact shudders from the ones Burn fired on and blew rolled over the raider. The ones he missed began pelting them hard. They exited the zone and flew clean space for another thousand kim before entering the next one.

"Here we go again."

She had the feeling Mayer would show again, so by the time they hit the last zone his entry on deck didn't surprise her. "Commander—"

"Not now, Doctor." She set the ship into a controlled spin and bottomed out at the densest part of the zone.

Mayer grabbed on to a support railing and ignored her request. "Can't you avoid these minefields?"

"They're not minefields; they're clutters. Yes, I can avoid them, if you don't mind taking two days to reach our destination." She spared him a glance. "Otherwise we have to fly through them."

"Can the ship sustain the damage?"

"We'll find out," she said. "Now, please leave the deck and don't return unless your section is collapsing, without atmosphere, or on fire."

He stomped back out. In between firing, Burn gave her the eye.

"Oh, don't look at me like that," she said. "If we don't establish some authority with these medical people, they'll be nipping at our flukes every two minutes."

"I'm not arguing with you." Burn vaporized another full spread. "Hull is holding up, but the discharge vents are overheating. Guess the lizards don't sustain full thrusters for very long."

"No one engages them that long." She adjusted the fuel supply, trying to compensate, but most of her attention had to remain on navigating through the zone. "We're going to need an engineer on board to handle this stuff until we work out the bugs."

"Verrig won't do it," her gunner said. "He hates flying with you."

"He'll get over it." She saw the cluster of ordnance ahead and decided a few minutes' lag time wouldn't kill them. "Turning to forty-eight degrees port. See if you can open a window through those derelict ships for me, cousin."

It was sad, flying through the blasted remains of so many vessels. Pmoc Quadrant, like so many other parts of the galaxy, had become a graveyard. She thought she saw something glimmer off the starboard through the viewer, but they were clear of the zone before she could identify the source.

"Entering Ghalt upper atmosphere," Burn said.

"Prepare for emergency landing." She altered their trajectory and eased through the short, bumpy ride to the surface. Below them, the cloud cover parted, and she tried to get a visual on the transport. "See it anywhere?"

"On my screen, ten degrees by two minutes north of our position."

"Adjusting approach," she acknowledged, moving the nose just a fraction as she changed headings.

What was left of the transport lay on a relatively flat portion of a high, flat-topped plateau. Survivor flares burned brightly, but the layout was so erratic and the wreckage so close to the edge that Dair bypassed the site for safety reasons and landed a kim away.

She pressed the internal relay to the cargo hold. "Doctor, we've arrived. Looks like you've got some business out there." She checked the environmental conditions. "Oxygen is negligible, so I'd recommend you mouth-breathers suit up."

"I need you both to accompany us to move the injured," Mayer reminded her.

Burn scowled. "What joy."

"Part of the new job, cousin. Just think, you could have sucked onto Onkar's hide and had it easy."

"Don't remind me."

Since Burn and Dair didn't have to breathe through their mucous membranes, and carried twenty minutes' worth of oxygen in their blood, they collapsed their lungs and put on their emergency packs. Even if they spent hours on the surface, they'd need only a small amount of oxygen occasionally to keep going.

It was something Dair had done only underwater, so the feeling was a bit odd, but as soon as they stepped out of the ship, the cold slap of carbon dioxide and nitrogen made her glad that she didn't have to breathe for a while.

Ghalt was a dead world, filled with the same odd rock formations and meteor craters as any moon above K-2. The temperature hovered just above freezing. The downed survivors weren't going to last long under these conditions, especially if their cabin air lock had been breached.

"You set down too far away," Mayer said, using the envirosuit's helmet comm transmitter to relay his displeasure.

"I didn't want to knock anyone off the cliff or squash them under the landing gear." She pulled out a remote and activated the emergency surface vehicle. "Next time I'll hover and you can jump to the surface, if you like."

The big red N-jui nurse appeared next to her. "Some may be too badly injured to transport over this distance."

"Don't worry. I'll bring the ship closer once we locate the survivors and assess the situation."

The ESV dropped out from beneath the ship and landed on the rock with a huge thump. The Hsktskt had designed it to accommodate raider teams, so they all fit in with plenty of room to spare. The ESV sped over the uneven terrain with gratifying speed, too.

Beside Dair, Burn adjusted his gauges, then scoped the horizon. "Flares sighted, Commander. Crash dead ahead."

They stopped at the first sign of heavy debris, and got out to search the wreckage. The ship had broken up into three sections, one of which was emitting high levels of radiation.

"They went down with their stardrive." She took readings and calculated from the dispersement how much time remained before core meltdown. "You people have fifteen minutes to retrieve whoever is breathing, and then we're gone."

"You and the ensign search." Mayer had already pulled some poor being out of a tangle of alloy. "We'll triage and prep for departure."

Dair saw Burn look away from the bright orange body fluid pooling on the rock. "Acknowledged. With me, cousin."

Their rapid search turned up plenty of bodies, but most were dead. Burn's own skin color chalked over until he looked like he'd bled out himself. Of the two hundred passengers, they found only another ten still alive, and all of them were badly injured.

As time ran out, Dair left the medical work to the pros and took the ESV back to the ship. Landing near the triage area would be tricky, but Burn volunteered to talk her in. Less than five minutes remained when she disembarked and ran to snatch the injured.

"Careful!" the big nurse snapped at her as Dair flung a female over her shoulder.

"We're out of time." She hefted another limp, bleeding body with her free arm. "Everyone, back on board. Now!"

Since Dair and Burn were much stronger than the Terran or his team, they were able to carry four survivors between them. While Mayer and his people got the rest through the hull doors, Dair simply dropped her burdens on the deck and ran for the helm.

"Commander—" Mayer tried to grab her as she raced past him.

"Just strap them down and hold on!"

Burn was already at his console, staring at her with wild eyes. "The drive core from the wreck is collapsing."

# CHAPTER
## EIGHT

"Shoot it." Dair powered up the engines and bypassed all safeties across the board.

"What?"

"You heard me. Use a full pulse charge and skim the shot along the outside. It won't detonate." Not instantly, she hoped.

She was slapped back in her seat as the thrusters engaged and shoved the raider straight up off the surface. At the same time, her gunner followed orders and fired on the critical stardrive. If her theory was right, the angle of the shot and the impact would blow the core off the plateau and down the other side into the valley below, buying them a couple of seconds. If she got high enough, the explosion might even give them a thermal boost.

Dair saw stars appear across the viewer just before a huge white light flared beneath them.

Burn inflated his lungs. "There it goes."

Shock waves and superheated air slammed into the ship from beneath, sending them faster into the upper atmosphere. For a moment, Dair wondered if the hull would withstand the rads, and watched her panel without blinking.

"Shielding," Burn muttered. "We didn't check the shielding."

"We've got something cushioning us." Whatever the Hsktskt had used as hull alloy didn't allow radiation to permeate it. According to her readings, the interior of the ship remained free of contamination.

She looked over at her cousin. He was as filthy and delighted as she was. "Clean and clear. Pretty shooting, gunner."

"Spectacular flying, pilot."

The door panel opened, but Dr. Mayer remained on the threshold. His hands were stained with three different colors of blood. "Commander, about those cluttered zones."

*Not this again.* "What about them?"

He inclined his head back toward the cargo hold. "Some of these people won't be able to hold on much longer. Can you fly through them again?"

Would she ever understand Terrans? *No,* Dair thought as she nodded. "Strap them down tight and hold on."

The Terran's stern face relaxed a few degrees. "Thank you."

Because they had cleared a path through the clutters getting to Ghalt, the return trip was much easier. Burn had to shoot out only a few strays before Dair crossed the last zone and reached K-2 orbit.

She requested emergency reentry assistance and went down as fast as she dared. Response vehicles from main transport and the FreeClinic crowded around the ship as soon as the gear touched the landing pad. By the time she'd shut down the engines, the medevac team and the ten survivors were already scanned, offloaded, and en route to Trauma.

Burn and Dair spotted a harassed Verrig shouting at one of his people as they tried to release a half-melted panel under the gstek. "Check for radiation first, you idiot! You want to sprout another head that glows in the dark?" He saw them and abruptly headed their way. "What did you do to my ship?"

"Your ship?" She folded her arms. "Your ship has no space-to-ground communications. Your ship has helm controls that make hair triggers look tardy. *Your ship,* crew chief, is a big floating chunk of 'shrike feces."

"Fine, next time, bring more of it back and I'll fix it."

"Oh, no." Before he could walk away, Dair grabbed one of his prosthetic arms. "From now on, you're flying with us."

Verrig's mouth flap spread. "What?"

"I don't have time to tinker with this reptilian junker. Get yourself rigged and fitted for flight duty by next shift."

He yelled something as Burn and Dair walked away, but her cousin was too busy snorting air through his blow valve for her to make out what.

She stopped him before he climbed on the glideshuttle. "Let's go by the FreeClinic and see how they are."

"I need to get wet, cousin. Let's not."

She let Burn go. He truly didn't understand the reasoning for half of what they'd just risked their lives to do, and the fact that he had withstood close proximity to the injured was enough. Dair herself got off at the FreeClinic and went in to satisfy her own curiosity.

The charge nurse eyed her as she came through the door. "Are you injured?"

"No, I'm the Rescue One pilot." She nodded toward the treatment rooms. "I thought I'd see how our passengers made it."

"Two were dead on arrival." The nurse ignored her shocked expression and picked up a chart. "Dr. Mayer is in surgery with one, and has another four waiting."

"I understand there were one hundred ninety missing passengers who were not identified before their bodies were destroyed," someone said from behind her.

Dair turned to see a small, bald humanoid in a fancy tunic carrying an official-looking case.

He consulted a datapad and then her face. "You would be Commander mu T'resa?"

"I would be." She looked him over. "Who are you?"

"Pmoc Quadrant Judge Advocate General Operations Supervisor Njal-Geir." He made a small, universal gesture of greeting. "Sloppy work, Commander. How are we to account for those individuals who died on Ghalt, now that you've blown a gigantic hole in it where they once were?"

"I don't know. Make a guess?"

His flat face scrunched up. "That is not acceptable. The judge advocate general wishes precise data."

Dair rubbed an itchy spot on her brow. "Well, you could go by the passenger manifest they had to file before routing through Pmoc space."

"My dear." He unscrunched enough to give her a pitying smile. "No one files proper manifests during wartime."

"I see. Well, you could go sweep up the ashes and run DNA, or go back to my first suggestion. Excuse me." She spotted the big N-jui nurse who had flown the mission and waved to her. "T'Nliqinara, right? Your people make it through okay?"

"Orderly Springfield suffered a sprained wrist, and Nurse K-Cipok received a number of contusions." She glared. "My nether regions are also rather bruised."

"Sorry. I heard two of the people we rescued didn't make it." She looked at the floor. "I guess I could have flown a little more carefully."

"Then the other eight would likely be dead now, too." She swept her arm out toward a corridor. "I am needed in surgery. Excuse me."

Njal-Geir tried to get in Dair's face again before she left the FreeClinic, but she referred him to Mayer. "I'm an aquatic, supervisor. You don't want to see me get dehydrated. It's really disgusting, the way my hide peels when I do."

"You will be required to answer for your actions on Ghalt, Commander," he called after her. "If not today, soon."

Not today was fine with Dair.


After the maiden flight of Rescue One, things began to slowly fall into place. The flight crew finished modifying one of the other two gsteks needed for regular patrol with the fighters, so the entire burden didn't fall on one vessel. Onkar, Saree, and Loknoth were the most experienced pilots in the squadron, so they usually worked prime shift, alternating with Dair and four other pilots. Curonal, Madura, and Hanumatha divided the auxiliary shift work with the other, non-'Zangian pilots recruited from the militia to provide adequate cover.

Because so many members of her family pod were now flying medevac, Dair's uncle often accompanied them instead of Dr. Mayer. Daranthura mu Cheft had never done much jaunting before, but enjoyed the thrill of dodging through the clutters immensely.

"Feels like we're racing rip currents," he told her as they took a team to retrieve a handful of Aksellan miners stuck on a rogue asteroid after their transport had been destroyed by a Hsktskt surface trap. "Too bad space isn't fluidic."

"It is, in some ways." She adjusted their course as they cleared the clutter. "There isn't any water, but there are gravitational fields and other spacial anomalies that act the same way currents do. We have to skirt around the edge of that moon that's breaking up over K-1, for example, or the ship would be pulled down the grav-drain. Kind of like swimming out from an abyssal whirlpool, so you don't get sucked in."

"I've got the Wanderer on-screen," Burn told her. "Want to see it, Uncle?"

"Please."

A holoimage of the huge, tumbling rock appeared above the main console. As her Uncle Daran inspected it, Dair studied the readings. It was a planetoid-class rogue, solid mineral, and was generating its own droplet-shaped magnetic field. The surface temperature was a mean minus seventy-nine degrees Celsius and, if it had contained more carbon, it would have been a comet.

"Why did it come here, I wonder?" her uncle asked.

"Probably roamed by a little too close and got pulled in by the Twins." The binary suns dragged all sorts of space junk in, rather like *sterbol* acquired burrow shells. "Burn, it's tracking erratically on my sweep." She didn't quite trust the instruments yet. "Yours?"

"Confirmed."

Dair suspected that there might be some gravity on the surface of the asteroid, given the rapid tumbling way it traveled, but the clash of its field with that of the Twins was causing some course fluctuations. Course fluctuations meant stress tremors and, if the center of the asteroid was molten, surface eruptions.

"I think this might have to be a hover-and-scoop job." She checked inventory. "Verrig activated some of the onboard retrieval drones; might as well ruin a few of them."

"You can't use the drones," Daran said at once.

She peered at him. "That's not a bad imitation of Dr. Mayer. Now cut it out."

"I'm serious, Dair. Those junkers were programmed to retrieve slaves from raided colonies, and you know the Hsktskt don't take sick or injured beings."

Just her luck, he was right. "Then we'd better come up with an alternative, because I can't set this ship down under these conditions."

"Don't look at me; I'm just here to shoot things," Burn said. "Any suggestions, Uncle?"

She continued studying the inventory. "Wait a minute. We could drop the ESV, and then pick it up with the cargo extensors."

"Would that work?"

"It might," her gunner said, his voice a little testy. "It also might kill the miners, wreck the ESV, and crash the ship. All at the same time."

"If I maintain reverse thrusters, I know I can hold a controlled hover while you get the miners out." She wasn't going to speculate on what would happen if there were ongoing magma eruptions, or whether the cold would affect the gear, or if the extensors wouldn't tolerate the weight of all those bodies on the ESV, et cetera. "Burn, you can man the laser on the ESV, and shoot any rubble that flies your way."

"As long as it's under a quarter-kiloton, sure. What about the big stuff?"

"Uncle Daran can drive around it."

"Excellent idea." Her uncle seemed satisfied. "Let's get prepared."

"Tell me something," Burn said as he cleared his screen and unfastened his harness. "Are there ever going to be any *unexciting* jaunts on this route?"

"Why do you think they call my place of business Trauma, podling?" her uncle asked.

Dair set up as even an approach as possible, and went into orbit above the Wanderer. Bits and pieces of the asteroid smashed continuously against the hull. The fragments ranged in size from grains of sand to huge boulders that would have filled her stepmother's land dwelling. She signaled the cargo hold and told the medevac team to board the ESV, then relayed their plans to the clutch of miners below.

"There iz no way to zafely retrieve uz," one of the miners buzzed over the audio. "There'z magma zpewing all over thiz faze. We appreziate the effort but we can't rizk any more livez."

"Tell my uncle that when you see him, huh? He'll be the tall, flaky guy behind the driver's console." She terminated the next squawk of protest and checked her comline to the ESV. "Burn, did you heat that rig up?"

"Laser's powered and ready." He cleared his throat. "If we die, you have to tell my dam."

She imagined Znora's reaction to such news. "If you die, I'm crashing the ship on purpose so I don't have to." She got as close to the surface as she could without risking a hull-to-surface collision, then opened the cargo hold doors. "Prepare for drop."

"Keep your hover steady," Burn transmitted. "Watch your boards, too."

The ESV eased down the ramp and fell a short distance before slamming upright on the asteroid. There was enough atmosphere in the envelope to transmit the whomp it made all the way up to the helm.

"ESV operational," her gunner said. "You made me bite my lip with that drop, Commander."

"Next time, Ensign, quit running it on the way down."

Dair monitored the team as they drove to the edge of the mine shaft, where a tight cluster of eight-legged beings were waiting for them. Along the way, Burn had to use the laser several times as the surface continued to shatter and float up around them. She could see everything that happened clearly on the viewer, but it didn't make her feel any less helpless.

*Don't think about failure. Think about maneuvering those extensors to clamp onto the ESV's chassis. Think about making Burn stay on the ship next time so he has to watch.*

Dair had already extended the cargo-loading arms to their full length, to see how far they would go. Not far enough; she'd practically have to land on top of the ESV to use them, which added another element of fun to the task. If she lost control of the ship while retrieving the surface team, they'd all end up permanent residents of the Wanderer.

Dair caught her breath as magma exploded out of a vent shaft, too close to the medevac team's position. Surface faces shifted, a conical fountain of orange-purple molten rock solidified into chunky black hail, and the thermal disruption effectively erased the forms of the rescue team from her screen.

"Uncle Daran?" She punched the console pad with frantic fingers. "Burn? Someone answer me!"

"Dair," her uncle replied, his voice hoarse. "We got out of the ESV, but the eruption destroyed it. We're cut off on all sides. We can't move."

"Stay where you are." Dair ignored the fifteen warning lights flashing under her nose and slowly guided the ship over to the mine shaft. Magma was still rising in a terrifying column only a few hundred meters from the team and the surviving miners. None of them should have survived exposure to that much heat, but for once the icy temperature of the asteroid did everyone a favor and cooled everything down.

"Burn? Burn, respond."

"I'm here, cousin." He sounded strong and unconcerned, which meant he was scared out of his wits.

Dair couldn't risk picking them up one at a time. She put the ship into a controlled hover, left the relay channel open, and grabbed an envirosuit from the desk's storage bay. "Is there something everyone can get in, like a surface transport or a piece of their ship?" She began pulling the protective gear over her flight suit.

After a long pause, her gunner said, "There's something they were using to haul minerals up from the shafts. It's like a cargo container but with an open end. I think we can fit everyone in it."

"Do it. Make sure you're secured inside. I'll lower the extensors." She punched his coordinates into her console, and activated the automated retrieval program. "When they reach you, clamp them on either side; then signal me."

As soon as Burn verified that he had the clamps locked on the container, Dair began reeling in the loader arms. Something began pummeling the port side of the ship, and a claxon went off as the helm began rapidly losing cabin environment.

"Commander?" Burn called.

"Blast, not now." She should have insisted on Verrig accompanying them; she had no time to fiddle with this engineering nonsense. "Stand by, Ensign." She sealed her helmet, put the extensors and the controls on auto, and went to see how bad the leak was.

It was bad. The magma eruption was bombarding the gstek with bigger chunks of blackened hail, and one of them had punched through a seam around a sensor panel. Dair's eyes widened as she saw the surface of a still-steaming rock.

That was when the hull panel collapsed, and Dair was sucked right out of the ship into space.

*I could be wet now,* Burn thought as he held on to the sides of the container and watched the loader arms reeling them toward the open cargo bay. *Wet, and chasing something tasty. Why in* Duo's *double face did I sign up for this 'shrike-waste duty?*

It was a rhetorical question; the moment Dair had mentioned resigning her commission he had known he would do the same.

It wasn't that Burn disliked military service. Despite the occasional physical discomforts, Burn liked soldiering well enough. He loved playing with the League's ordnance systems—that satisfied urges he still didn't understand—but he had not enlisted for the experience, the excitement, or the career opportunities. He'd taken his oath of loyalty, had his body altered, and learned to kill with weapons simply so he could be at his cousin's side.

Being with Dair was all the excitement any male could want. Watching her back—*well, that, and getting some decent scars*—was all he cared about.

That was how it had been for him since he'd first swum out from beneath his mother's comforting bulk to see the odd-looking little white hovering on the fringe of the pod. She had been only half his size, and her body was all wrong, but she moved like a 'Zangian. *Who is that, Mother?*

*A mistake,* Znora had told him. *The kind someone should have devoured when it was born.*

He searched the narrow row of the helm's view panels, looking for the pale flash of Dair's face. He never liked leaving her unguarded. She may have been the best pilot in the quadrant, but when it came to watching her own back, she was as blind as a pit silter.

*She is not your mate!* his dam would often rant. *Nor will she ever be!*

Burn didn't want Dair as a mate. In fact, he could think of no one he wanted to chase through the breeding caverns less than his little cousin. It would be like mating with a sibling.

"What is that?" Daran asked him over the comline, dragging him out of his thoughts. When Burn glanced at him, the physician lifted a fin. "Over there, by the emergency doors."

Burn turned his head and saw the telltale drift of escaping atmosphere. "It's not good." Judging by the length and amount of the drift, one of the panel seams was separating. He needed to warn Dair, and switched to relay to the helm. "Commander?"

The sound of a warning claxon came over his comline, along with her highly annoyed voice: "Blast, not now. Stand by, Ensign."

He turned to the leader of the miners, who like the other Aksellans had his eight limbs encased in metathermal wraps and carried his oxygen supply in a biospun bubble on his back, and patched his comline through his wristcom so it would translate his language. "What's your name, friend?"

"Mnoc." The big spider, who was black with vivid green patches, made an accompanying gesture with its forelimbs. "Yourz?"

"Burn. Mnoc, how long will your air last?"

"Another hour, perhapz." The big spider's eye clusters rotated toward the ship as he assessed the situation, and his inverted-U-shaped mandible clicked a few times. "You are lozing atmozphere. Do you have rezervez on board?"

"Yes, plenty." Burn wasn't sure of the raider's ability to maintain internal gravity, though. "Our suits are weighted; you should grab on to us as soon as we board."

"We can tether ourzelvez together." The Aksellan extended its pedipalps and spun a short, metallic strand, then handed it to Burn.

He tested the strand, which was flexible but extremely strong. "This almost looks like metal."

"It iz, in part. Each day we ingezt arutanium and combine it with our zilk fluid to create work tetherz."

"That will work."

As Mnoc and the other miners began producing and attaching themselves to the tether strands, Burn scanned the hull, trying to see where the damage was. He knew Dair would have suited up so she wasn't in danger, but if depressurization blew out the engine compartment, they wouldn't be going anywhere.

A shower of alloy fragments exploded outward from the portside midsection of the ship, followed by a large section of the hull panel and a single figure.

*Dair.*

They were on the starboard side, too far for him to reach her, and still he lunged. Only a swift snatch by Daran kept him from tumbling out into space.

"Have you gone sand-belly?" the older 'Zangian demanded.

"Look!" He pointed to Dair's spinning, helpless figure. "I have to get her!"

"She's too far away, Byorn." Daran made him look at him. "I can't let you do it. I'm sorry."

"We have to get her." Burn hit the remote panel on the loader arm clamp and halted the reel. The container stopped rising and began to float. "Come on, help me."

"Zhe'll be pulled pazt uz and down to the zurfaze of the azteroid," Mnoc predicted.

Burn glanced down at the lake of molten rock beneath them, and then back at Dair, whose body was being dragged over the top of the ship. He saw her scrambling, desperately trying to grab anything that would allow her to hold on, but the exterior of the vessel was flat and smooth and provided no handholds.

He should never have left her alone.

"How much more of that tether can you make?" he asked Mnoc.

The Aksellan rattled off something in his native language to the other miners, who bent over to form a circle with their heads. "We have enough fluid between uz to zpin another two hundred meterz."

"That's enough. Attach the end to my midsection."

"Think of what you're doing, podling," Daran said. "If it snaps, we'll lose both of you."

"So you will. Put the ship on autoguidance and it will take you back." He met the older male's gaze. "I'm not letting her die alone."

# CHAPTER
## NINE

"We'll anchor you." The miner encircled Burn with a loop of the tether and secured the end with a small blob of fluid. He wove the other end around two of his legs, and then passed it to the miner next to him, who did the same. "When you reach her, hold on to her tightly. We'll have to reel you both back in very fazt."

Burn climbed up on the edge of the container, tested the tether, and waited. Dair had slipped over to the port side of the ship and would be pulled into open space in another few seconds. He watched her, his muscles bunching with tension, as he waited for the right moment. If he made the leap too soon, he would be pulled down before he reached her. Too late, and the opposite would happen.

"Mnoc?" He crouched, preparing to push off. "Whatever you do, don't drop your end."

"We won't."

Burn waited until Dair's body slid from the hull and there were only four hundred meters separating them, and then he tucked in his fins and shoved hard with his flukes. His body floated out away from the container, and for an instant he had to fight the urge to roll, as he would when he broke surface water.

*You're not falling. Center your head.*

Unlike being in the water, Burn's body encountered no resistance in the vacuum of space, and he had to adjust his reactions and movements to full weightlessness. He felt the tug of the gravity field, stronger than he'd expected, and tried to use it the way he would a steering current.

Dair was tumbling in a slow spin, only fifty meters away from him now. She was turning her head from side to side as she rolled, and he realized she did so because she had spotted him and was attempting to keep him in sight.

*That's it, cousin.* He squinted at the fiery light generated by a fountain of magma below. *Watch me and be ready.*

Grabbing her was too dangerous; his fin ends were already sore from manipulating things through the pressurized gloves of his suit, and his grip might slip.

Burn flashed back to a game they used to play when they were podlings; what Teresa had said was like Terran "chicken." He and Dair would swim toward each other as fast as they could, and just before they rammed into each other they would change direction and use the momentum to propel them up through the surface. Whoever broke the surface first won, and that was always Dair.

This time he couldn't break away, though. This time he had to win, so he could catch her.

Burn made a cradle with his fins as he maneuvered himself to collide with her from underneath. With a little luck the gravity field would help push her into him.

Twenty meters. Fifteen.

Dair was close enough now for him to see her eyes—she looked like he felt—and how she was extending herself within the spin, spreading her limbs out in a star shape in order to make herself as large as possible.

He nodded to her. *Yes, cousin, give me a proper target.*

Burn spread his fins wide as the last few meters between them disappeared, and Dair's body rolled into his chest. She was upside down to him, but that didn't matter. He closed his fins around her waist and turned against the tether, wrapping it around both of them before curling his glove around the strands to secure the loop.

"Pull us in, Mnoc!"

Burn could feel her wrapping her modified fins around his lower body, and tightened his grip on hers. The Wanderer's field clawed at them, making their retrieval a tugging contest, but the miners were many and strong. Another minute passed, and then Daran and Mnoc were hauling them into the container.

The Aksellan righted Dair before they sat her down on the floor of the container beside Burn. He was breathless and shaking, and happier to see her colorless little face than he had ever been in his life. When he would have butted her with his head—the 'Zangian version of an embrace—she held up her hands to keep him away.

Dair's expression turned grave as she made a gesture of formal gratitude. *Thank you for my life, Ensign.*

He rolled his recessed eyes—she was worried about protocol, when she could have been turned into a little pile of white ash?—but he returned the motion. *You're welcome, Commander.*

A moment later he found his fins filled with Dair, who flung herself against him and huddled there, just as breathless and shaky and happy as he was.

Dair didn't react to what had happened until after they had landed at Transport, passed through biodecon, and offloaded their grateful passengers. She held her feelings at bay while she saw that Burn, who had strained several muscles while saving her hide, was transferred to an immersion tank.

She watched him through the clear plas panel. "Are you certain you're all right?"

*I'm sore and hungry.* He finished stripping off his flight suit—an awkward business in water—then swam to press his snout to the plas. *What about you? That was a bloody swim, cousin.*

"Stiff, but I'll survive." She rolled a hand over the back of her neck. "Thanks to you."

*This should be good for a promotion.* He executed a slow but showy somersault. *Sublieutenant mu Znora has a nice ring to it, don't you think?*

"I think you're good at faking injury." She concealed her emotions behind an efficient mask and waved to one of the transport workers standing by the tank. "Go ahead and roll him out of here."

Dair finished the postmission checks on the equipment, briefed Verrig on the damage to the gstek via relay, and then silently secured the access hatch and made her way into one of the lavatory units.

There she knelt and regurgitated until there was nothing left in her belly to come up.

Dair curled up on the floor, holding herself as her body shuddered with belly spasms. She had nearly died. Should have died. Would have died, had her cousin not risked his own life to save hers.

*I could be dead now.*

She had trained to face death, had regularly flirted with it, but nothing in her life had ever scared her as much as that moment when she had been pulled out into the cold, airless blackness. She'd seen the magma below, knew the kind of death it would deliver. She'd nearly yanked her lines so she could suffocate instead.

Perhaps this was why William Mayer and his medical people fought so hard to preserve life—because it could be extinguished so easily.

The persistent sound of a ramp signal drifted over the intercom; someone wanted to board the ship. Dair dragged herself up from the deck and washed the foul taste from her mouth before going out to answer it.

Dair checked the exterior viewer and saw a male in an administrative military uniform waiting outside. She didn't recognize the nubbly-faced humanoid, and enabled the audio. "Yes?"

"Commander mu T'resa, I am Sohrab, aide to Pmoc Quadrant Judge Advocate General Operations Supervisor Njal-Geir." As the thin, reedy-voiced male spoke, the bumps under his greenish derma expanded and contracted. It had the odd effect of making it appear as though his face were riddled with subsurface parasites.

*Or maybe he is,* Dair thought, as she didn't recognize his species, either. "How may I help you?"

He held up a data chip. "I am delivering orders for you. You are to report to Colonial Administration for an emergency hearing."

"A hearing?" Her brow furrowed. "For what purpose?"

A large bump swelled under his right eye, nearly occluding it. "I regret that I am not permitted to discuss that with you." He patted the swelling with delicately fluttering fingertips.

Njal-Geir probably wanted to whine about her not counting miners or something else she hadn't done according to regulations.

*Data pushers.* Her empty stomach constricted. "When do I have to report?"

"They're waiting for you now, Commander."


Dair had never attended a hearing, much less one considered an emergency, so she didn't mind Sohrab accompanying her. He could explain what it meant.

Njal-Geir's aide hardly gave her a chance to ask, however, as he did most of the talking, chattering on about quadrant politics and his curiosity about K-2 and her people.

"—and then the Tingaleans pulled their representatives out of the session without giving warning or reason, and immediately returned to Tinga. The Cordobels regarded their departure as a personal affront, and did the same. From there it was one species after another, until half the assembly had packed up and jaunted homeward." Sohrab shook his head and made a sucking sound that she assumed was some expression of amusement. "This colonial government seems pleasant enough. Do your people take an active part in it? Have you held a council seat yourself? Do you find it difficult to cohabitate with all these nonaquatics?"

"Sometimes, never, and no." 'Zangians didn't yawn, but Dair suddenly understood why Teresa did. Duo, *does he ever shut up?* She spotted the glidehauler that they used to transport the fluid tank from the docks to the coast. The last time she'd seen it, Burn was in the tank, which was now drained. "Why was my gunner brought here?"

"I can't say, Commander."

"I don't understand this need for secrecy." She fastened the last, upper clasps on her flight suit. "Am I in trouble? Can you tell me that much, at least?"

The talkative aide averted his gaze. "I'm sorry, Commander. I really can't say."

They entered the main floor of Administration, where a drone reception unit directed them to a conference room on one of the upper floors.

Sohrab inserted his ID chip into the access panel, which opened at once. When Dair hesitated, his face bumps bulged. "They're waiting for you, Commander."

*They* turned out to be Njal-Geir, Chief Norash, Ana Hansen, and William Mayer, as well as two of the 'Zangian pod elders and a handful of colonial officials Dair didn't recognize. The room furnishings had been organized so that Njal-Geir, Ana, the pod elders, and the officials sat in a row opposite Chief Norash, William Mayer, and three empty places, two of which were set apart. Dair assumed that pair had been provided for her and Burn.

*Like a council meeting,* she thought, *but why?*

The League official looked up from a datapad and nodded at Sohrab before switching his gaze to Dair. His tunic had even more colors and intricate stitches than the one he'd worn during their first meeting, but his expression remained just as dour. "Thank you for reporting so quickly, Commander."

"I wasn't given much choice." Dair came forward. "What's the meaning of this?"

"We will get to that as soon as Ensign mu Znora joins us." He used a small hand to indicate one of the empty seats. "Please make yourself comfortable."

Ana appeared unhappy; Mayer looked as if a smile would make his face crack into several pieces. The pod elders were studying her in a way that would have alarmed her under the water: as a potential threat to the pod. Dair kept her expression blank as she took her place, and a few moments later a dressed, dry-hided Burn joined her.

She bent her head close to his. "Did they tell you anything about this?"

"Not yet." Her gunner nodded toward Njal-Geir. "All I know is he had my tank rerouted here."

Sohrab took the third empty seat and activated a recording drone unit before nodding toward Njal-Geir.

The League official rose. "Let us begin. Ensign Byorn mu Znora, a report has been made regarding actions taken by you that are in violation of Article Eight-eleven of the Allied League of Worlds Military Justice Code: Failure to obey order or regulation;

and Article Nine-fifty-six: Reckless endangerment of civilian personnel." He finally gazed at Burn. "This hearing has been convened to determine the validity of this report and if formal charges should be filed." With that he returned to his seat.

Before Burn could speak, Dair put her hand on his sleeve. "Supervisor Njal-Geir, Ensign mu Znora is under my command, and I can assure you that he has done nothing to violate any articles of the MJC. Ever."

"Commander, I directed Transport Security to monitor your and Ensign mu Znora's transmissions during this latest Bio Rescue mission. It is from that office that the report originates." Njal-Geir held up a disk. "Actions were taken that were inherently dangerous, unnecessary, and displayed a blatant disregard for the lives of the medical personnel and civilians involved."

"Maybe his people monitored the wrong ships," Burn murmured to her.

"What actions are you talking about?" Dair asked.

"Specifically?" The quadrant supervisor bared his teeth at her, but it wasn't pleasant or nonthreatening. It seemed like he wanted to take a bite out of her. "The charges refer to Ensign mu Znora's efforts to retrieve you, Commander, when you were pulled from the helm of your ship into space."

Dair blinked; surely she had heard him wrong. "He saved my life, and you wish to punish him for that? If we'd been in combat, he'd be up for a promotion and a couple of medals."

"By attempting to save you, Commander, the ensign in fact risked the lives of everyone else involved in this mission. You cannot justify that." He drew air in with a sharp sound. "We at quadrant command do not distribute commendations for such reckless discounting of operational regulations."

"Commander mu T'resa isn't required to justify the Bio Rescue project, Supervisor. She does enough serving as one of its pilots." Dr. Mayer rose from his seat, tall and straight in his blue-and-white physician's tunic. "If you want validation, you can talk to *me*."

"Yes. I can see how a *human surgeon* with no military experience who runs a planetary facility would naturally have command of this situation." Njal-Geir's flat face crinkled with displeasure as he sat back and regarded Mayer. "Please, Doctor, do enlighten us with your superior views. Why should the quadrant allow pilots who are vital to the security of this region to risk their lives for this mission?"

Burn winced. "He's going to regret saying that in a minute."

Dair noticed that nearly everyone else present had the same pained reaction. Evidently the fussy little man didn't know Mayer, or he would never have addressed him with such transparent condescension and contempt.

"On my homeworld," Dr. Mayer said, "great men of logic and thought such as John Locke developed a conception of natural liberties, which maintain that each individual has the right to make certain claims against society: to live freely, own property, seek happiness, and consent to be governed." He paused and regarded Chief Norash, who was visibly scowling. "You wish to comment, Chief?"

The Trytinorn shifted his considerable weight, making his specially reinforced seat groan. "Only that I believe you would do better to pick another world as an example, Doctor."

"Indeed. I often forget how my native species' inherent bigotry echoes so well around the galaxy." Dr. Mayer scanned the unhappy faces on either side of Njal-Geir before smiling a little at Ana Hansen. "These ideals are not exclusive to Terra, are they, Administrator?"

"No, they are not." Ana bent forward to address Chief Norash. "The Europa Satellite Accord, the Declaration of Farradonan Independence, and the Kobecian Scroll of Sentient Rights were all founded on the individual's inviolable right to life. I can name others, none of which are even remotely associated with our homeworld or species, if those are not adequate."

The chief's lengthy nasal appendage twitched with embarrassment; clearly he had forgotten that Mayer was not the only Terran in the room. "That is satisfactory, thank you."

"The individual's right to life has nothing to do with this," Njal-Geir insisted.

"It has everything to do with it. When the colony here on K-2 was first established, a charter was also written to address and include such rights for our inhabitants," Dr. Mayer continued. "They are an integral part of our multispecies pluralist society. Life, as we define it, must be afforded protection. Even if it means placing other lives at risk to do so. Those charged with such duties are well aware of the inherent dangers, are they not, Chief Norash?"

The Trytinorn nodded.

One of the pod elders raised a fin. "Physician, you speak eloquently, but acceptable standards of living and freedom are already afforded to the land dwellers who cohabit our world. The situation of these refugees, while pitiable, does not fall within the boundaries of the charter. They are not subject to its provisions."

"Yet many of these refugees go on to become residents of our world, Elder. Are we to withhold humanitarian aid based on whether or not its recipients have been granted residency status?" Mayer's white brows lifted. "I can assure you that such exclusivity will have severe repercussions in many areas, first and foremost the free trade upon which we still depend heavily for the bulk of our off-world supplies."

"Like the Ninrana," Norash said. "They have alienated every merchant within a hundred light-years with their hostility."

Dair personally would have extended that radius another fifty light-years. No one liked the Ninrana, who guarded their planet as if it were made of solid arutanium and covered with gemstones, and who regarded every other species in the system as inferior.

"Let us agree that an individual's right to life includes the right to have direct actions taken to preserve life where it is threatened, and a corresponding duty on others to take such actions," Mayer said. "Chief Norash, who shoulders such burdens every day, will agree with me that freedom—and lives—must be guarded, and defended when attacked by those who would deprive us of both."

The big Trytinorn nodded.

"Implicit in this is the duty not to withhold or frustrate the provision of lifesaving assistance. As a medical rescue mission, Bio Rescue defines our role in relation to these rights—in providing life-preserving assistance, which reflects the reality that those with primary responsibility are not always able or willing to perform this role themselves." Dr. Mayer shook his head as Norash started to protest. "I do not lay the blame on your department, Chief, nor should Colonial Security be held accountable for what war has left behind." His sharp gaze focused on the supervisor's flat face. "I blame your superiors, Njal-Geir."

"Why should you?" The official sounded mortally offended. "We have not sent the refugees through this quadrant."

"That is a matter of opinion, but I am referring to the preservation and enforcement of free passage and safe travel through this quadrant, which *is* your responsibility." Now Mayer folded his arms. "You are aware that I have repeatedly petitioned Quadrant Military Command to address the refugee problem."

The supervisor's receding chin lifted. "No. I was not aware."

"Each time I have been told that the remnant ordnance and traps left behind by the ongoing conflict are beyond your superior's capacity to resolve until after the war is over. Whether this constitutes the quadrant's willful disregard of fundamental legal and ethical obligations, or in truth is a dilemma for which they have not at present the manpower or practical means to resolve, the result has been much avoidable suffering." He approached the conference table, and Dair saw the quadrant official cringe a little. "If you have an alternative solution that will make Bio Rescue redundant, then by all means"—he spread out his clever hands—"replace it."

"I am not here in that capacity."

His grim mouth curled on one side. "Let us pretend for a moment that you are. How would you propose saving the lives of the innocents traveling through this region of space when they are caught in the traps and debris left behind by the League and Hskt-skt? Have you navigational maps showing the danger zones? Charted routes of safe passage? Anything to help these people?"

Njal-Geir opened his mouth, closed it, and then his face turned a disagreeable shade of grayish brown. "This is nonsense. I am not here to address this problem."

"Yet we are, and we have," Mayer told him, his voice low and soft. "Given that there are no viable alternatives, perhaps you should allow us to do this job that no one else wants, until such time that the quadrant can return to this region and clean up its own mess."

Dair knew from her own experience with military command that confronting Njal-Geir with his own inadequacies was not the wisest approach for the doctor to take. Quadrant officials never liked being publicly embarrassed. Yet every word Dr. Mayer had said was true, and more important, the pod elders and Chief Norash were now giving the supervisor very thoughtful looks.

"Very well, I will bring the matter before my superiors." Njal-Geir opted for a change of subject instead of an apology. "What do you propose to do about Ensign mu Znora's actions?"

"We will review rescue protocols and adjust them to ensure that the maximum safety measures are taken," Mayer said, eyeing Burn, "to protect everyone involved in our missions."

"Otherwise you will take no action?" The supervisor still wanted someone's blood, it seemed.

The pod elders conferred in clik, too rapidly and quietly for Dair or Burn to follow; then the senior elder said, "You should be advised, Supervisor, that the 'Zangian council of elders will oppose any disciplinary action taken against Byorn mu Znora."

"As will the colonial ruling council," Ana Hansen added.

Everyone turned to the quadrant official, waiting for his response.

"I will not seek formal charges against the ensign, or make a recommendation to the quadrant at this time." Njal-Geir took out a datapad and made a show of entering some officious data. Without looking up, he added, "However, you will advise your personnel that Bio Rescue is now on strict probation. I will continue monitoring the performance of your crews, and if they endanger any more lives, I will have this project terminated immediately. No matter who objects." He lifted his head and stared not at Mayer, but at Dair. "Is that understood, Commander?"

Dair rose and stood at attention. "Yes, sir."

"Very well. This hearing is adjourned."

# CHAPTER
## TEN

As Shan waited for the colony transport to arrive, he reviewed his unsuccessful encounter with William Mayer the day before. It had taken a week after receiving the transmitted denial of application simply to schedule an appointment with the surgeon, who showed no remorse at having decided against him.

"I have already filled my duty rosters," the elder Terran said.

Shan had little doubt they would stay full, as well, for as long as he tried to be added to them. "You could put me on as a rotational alternate. I am a fully qualified and licensed pilot."

"Let me be frank, Mr. Amariah. Your species has done little but create havoc since arriving here on K-2. You yourself nearly destroyed your ship and three hundred passengers in your care, getting here." The older male's eyes reminded Shan of his father's in the midst of a challenging midwinter hunt. "I have no desire to see you do the same to my medevac teams and patients."

The aquatic transport glided to a stop just beyond the low cliff, and Shan watched its two passengers disembark. As soon as he saw Jadaira he started forward, but hesitated when he saw her assisting her ensign, who was limping.

"If that old Terran feeds like he speaks," Byorn mu Znora—*she calls him Burn*—was saying to her as she walked with him down to one of the low dive-off points, "I hope I never cross his strike zone."

Shan had hoped to meet her alone, of course, but this would have to do. The transponder he had planted in the pendant he had given her had provided some useful information, but not enough.

He needed to draw her in and gain her confidence, so that she would tell him whatever he needed to know. He also needed to start making reconnaissance trips around the system to monitor what traffic was moving in and out of the region. If she couldn't intervene with Mayer for him, he'd have to requisition a ship of his own.

Before they began stripping out of their flight suits, he stepped out from behind the trunk of the scarlet-leafed *arronall* tree. "Commander."

Even injured, the 'Zangian male moved quickly to place himself between Shan and Jadaira. "What do you want, mouth-breather?"

"I must speak to your superior officer." Shan met the young male's fierce dark eyes but kept the amusement out of his voice. "And for your information, I breathe through my nose."

The little pale 'Zangian gave her much larger cousin a gentle push to one side. "Get in the water, Burn. I'll be along shortly."

The younger male made a quick series of tonal clicks that Shan's wristcom didn't translate, but she only shook her head in response.

Shan was gratified to see that Burn was more aggressive than Jadaira. That, at least, was how it should have been. "I am here on official business, if that reassures you, Ensign."

"Nothing about you chokeweed-laden twitchers reassures me, Amariah." Burn checked his wristcom before he said to Dair, "You've been topside thirteen hours, cousin. Don't make it fourteen."

Shan appraised the other male as he stripped out of his garment. According to what he'd learned about the 'Zangian SEALs from the colonial database, he knew mu Znora was actually quite young, and would not physically mature for another revolution.

Burn was one of the largest 'Zangians Shan had seen. When he finished growing, he would likely be one of the largest—if not the largest—male in the underwater colony. It satisfied him on some level to know that Jadaira had a powerful protector.

She did not know it now, but before this was over she might need more than one.

Before he jumped over the edge, the young male turned to Shan. "Touch her and I'll use teeth on you."

*Powerful but not very intuitive.* Shan inclined his head, then shuffled back to avoid the splash as the 'Zangian kicked water back at them. He noted how Jadaira stepped into the spray, closing her eyes and letting it soak her face. "It must be inconvenient, being always obligated to return to the sea."

"Is breathing through your nose a hassle?" she asked.

"Ah, I see your point."

"Excellent." She ruffled her hair—_no, her gillets,_ he corrected himself—and regarded him. "Perhaps you will tell me yours now?"

"I made application to the chief of Medical Services to join your Bio Rescue program. Although I am more than qualified, he has refused to allow me to participate." He watched her expression change. "You are surprised."

"I'm stunned. Why do you want to join? You're a religious leader, not a medical professional, and your people are xenophobes who don't allow you to be touched."

"Six out of ten refugees traveling through this system are, at present, Skartesh." He admired how the green-filtered light from the suns sparkled in the water beading her gillets, creating tiny, perfect rainbows. "And I offered to serve as a pilot, not as a medic."

Her pale eyes inspected him. "I can see why he would turn you down. Your performance with the _Hemat_ was less than sterling." She scratched the front of her chin. "You don't expect me to talk to him on your behalf, I hope."

"My people are angry that my application was rejected." It was a lie, but one she could not prove. "I wished to consult with you on how I might persuade the doctor to change his mind."

"I don't know that anyone can persuade William Mayer to do anything." She sat on one of the chiseled stone benches, rubbed her brow, and peered up at him. "Does your cult consider your rejected application another form of insult? If they do, I wouldn't recommend they try striking the doctor in the face. He'll hit back, and he's strong."

"They will not." He sat on the bench next to hers, where the stone was dry. "You have not rescued any Skartesh yet, have you?" She shook her head. "You will, soon, and when you do, how will you communicate with them? My people do not speak to outsiders."

"We don't . . ." She trailed off and stared at the horizon. "You know, things were so much simpler when the Hsktskt were attacking us. I could just shoot the enemy."

"We are not the enemy." He shifted back as the sea flung a ribbon of spray across the stone. "The Skartesh deserve the right to fair and equal treatment, Commander. More so than other species, when you consider our history."

"You mean being evacuated from your homeworld?" Her brow furrowed. "That's happened to dozens of races since the beginning of the war."

"All of whom were eventually able to return to their native environments. That will not happen for the Skartesh." It was the smell of the water, not the memories of his homeworld, that was making him feel nauseous. "Thanks to the League/Hsktskt conflict, the conditions on Skart are so extreme now that it can no longer sustain our species, or any other life-form."

"How did things get so bad?"

"Skart occupies an important, strategic location," he told her. "The Hsktskt Faction invaded the planet, and used its remote northern polar continent as a temporary command post during their battle with the League to gain control of the region."

Dair visibly shuddered. "What happened to your people?"

"The Skartesh were neutral and took no sides in the conflict. Yet when the League advanced and forced the Hsktskt to retreat, the lizards destroyed their base of operations with orbital thermodisplacer bombardment."

Jadaira winced. "Heat boomers. I've seen the kind of damage they can do."

"These were slightly larger than battle charges, as the Hsktskt also wished to destroy a subsurface weapons cache, which they were unable to retrieve. Until that time, Skart was almost completely icebound. The charges, combined with the detonation of the ordnance, melted the northern cap and created a reaction that decompressed the planet's formerly stable mantle. After the tidal waves subsided, a thousand volcanoes emerged and began to erupt where none had ever existed before."

Her eyes widened. "A thousand?"

"That was just during the initial aftermath. Another two thousand have formed since." He thought of Skart's ash-blackened skies and the endless, filthy rain. "The Skartesh first fled from their mountains to take refuge in the equatorial valleys, but the melt- and floodwater quickly inundated them. In addition to the volcanoes making the highlands uninhabitable, and huge rivers of mud and water eradicating the low ground, a volcanic shroud encircled the globe, escalating temperatures until they nearly doubled. Half the indigenous life on Skart burned or drowned within a few weeks, including five hundred thousand Skartesh. Then the southern polar continent, the very coldest spot on the planet, began to melt, and the process accelerated." He looked out over the wide blue 'Zangian sea. "Skart has since become four-fifths covered with water."

"_Duo._"

Too many thin, starving faces crowded into his mind, and he cleared them from his thoughts. "Society, as it was, might have disintegrated, if not for the unified belief in the Promise. The League arrived to evacuate the survivors, but they did not offer reparations for what had been done to Skart during their war. They gathered up the people, and in essence flung them out into space." Another wave crested at the edge of the low cliff, and he got up from the bench to avoid it.

"Why do you do that?" Jadaira asked. "Move away from water, I mean?"

"I do not like it." He could still recall the stench that had risen from the stagnant brown water at the edge of the lake. The expression on his father's face as he had dragged the bloated, ravaged body of Shan's younger brother to shore.

"How can you not like water? You have to drink it, bathe in it, swim—"

"Swim?" That obliterated the memories of Tarkun, and reminded him of his purpose. "We do not drink water, and we use sonic cleansers only. Immersion in water kills us."

"You mean you can't swim?"

"No, none of us can." He met her shocked gaze and forced himself back into patterns of acceptable thought. "Drowning was an archaic form of execution among the Skartesh. The worst kind.

Historically, prisoners would tear out their own throats rather than face such an end."

"But that's ridiculous! It's just water."

"To you, Commander, it is something you breathe. To a Skartesh, who cannot, it is a terrifying and painful death."

"That explains why your people are so afraid of mine. We must seem like demons to you." Jadaira thought for a moment. "There is no reason you can't learn, though."

"Learn?"

"If you could swim, you might be able to teach some of your people." She gestured toward the sea. "It would help them feel more comfortable living on our world."

"We may not remain here on K-2."

"There are few worlds without water, and the ones I know of are not the sort of places where your people would wish to settle." She glanced toward the colony. "If enough Skartesh conquered their fear of water, and the conditions on Skart someday improve, perhaps you or your descendents can return to your homeworld."

Shan was so shaken by her radical proposal that he was speechless. In all the scenarios he had thought out and planned, returning the Skartesh to their homeworld had never once been suggested. It was unthinkable, and yet in a few years, with dedicated terraforming— quite possible. He masked his excitement by facing the prospect that he would have to carry out the charade. "How difficult is it?"

"For a land dweller?" She itched at the side of her face, which was now flaking slightly. "It requires patience, and persistence. If you wish to dive, you must learn to use specialized equipment, but to swim . . . it would take only a few weeks of lessons, and regular practice."

"Will you teach me?"

Jadaira stopped scratching. "I think you would do better learning from another land dweller."

"You are said to be the most skilled swimmer in the region. I would prefer to learn from the best." This was how he could remain close to her without arousing any suspicions, though it would cost him. *Well, what has not?* "If you do not wish to be viewed associating with a Skartesh, we could keep the lessons private."

"Considering that my pod roams this entire region, that will be utterly impossible." She turned around and focused on a heavily forested section to the west of the colony. "There is a place inland we could use"—she met his gaze—"if you are serious about this."

"I am."

"Then meet me one-half kim east of the main agricultural building tomorrow, midday." She eyed his robe. "And don't wear that."

"What do I wear?"

"To swim?" Her pale eyes gleamed. "Nothing but your hide, Amariah."

Dair left early the next morning for the grotto. Her cousin would have crowed over her plan to teach a Skartesh to swim, and her stepmother wouldn't have approved at all, so she didn't inform anyone of her intentions.

*It is a good idea,* she told herself, even as her 'Zangian side found the prospect of bringing such a hairy, hostile being into the water rather ridiculous. *We can learn more about each other's species this way.* She recalled her promise to Norash. *He might even start confiding in me.*

Dair wasn't sure who had constructed the grotto; likely some enterprising landscaper who had once been assigned to the botanical fields outside the colony prior to the Core plague. It was obvious from the abandoned structures that he or she had intended to re-create something from their homeworld, for there remained the skeleton forms of three capsule-shaped open-sided structures at the north, south, and west sides of the pool.

Yet before more work could be done, something had happened. She was almost sure the builder had died during the plague, for if someone had objected for any official reasons they would have demolished it, the same way they had the towering, animated sculpture of the Rilken's many-phallused god Nuriti that had been erected in the Trading Center's center courtyard some years ago. Although Dair still thought the statue's proximity-triggered ejaculations had been hysterically funny.

In any case, the project had been abandoned and forgotten for years. The centerpiece of the project, a deep-water pool, remained intact, and was still supplied by a pumping system that kept the water sweet and fresh. However, over time the unnatural landscaping had reverted back to its natural state.

Dair had first discovered the little grotto nestled within the wild tangle of overgrowth by accident. She had been hot and tired, walking from Teresa's home to the FreeClinic for a routine exam, and had smelled water. She had followed the scent until she heard the sound of cascading torrents, which the builder had diverted through the feed system from a nearby river. Seeing the narrow waterfall spilling down terraced stone into the private reservoir had been like finding a gift left behind just for her.

Although Dair enjoyed the time she spent topside with her step-mother, and being part of her father's world as well, the grotto was where she came when she wanted peace and solitude. No one and nothing but her, the water, and the absence of worries and duties.

*And now you're bringing an outsider here,* a snide inner voice taunted as she stripped out of her skin shield. *So much for your solitude, Jadaira.*

"Commander."

Onkar's sudden and unannounced appearance made her yelp. She glared at him. "What is it, Lieutenant?"

"Quadrant has sent encrypted data chips, with orders that they be hand-delivered to you." Onkar came to stand beside her, and regarded the pool the way he would a defective strafer he was being ordered to fly. "I hope you are not thinking of swimming in *that.*"

She took the data holder and tucked it in the notch of a branch just above her head. "Why not?"

"It is a puddle."

"It is not." She flung off her skin shield and jumped in, splashing him deliberately. When she surfaced, he was wiping his face. "Why, Lieutenant, you're all wet. Do you want to revise your opinion?"

He flicked some drops from his fin. "It is a deep puddle."

It was a shame that Teresa had never developed a method to transplant a sorely needed sense of humor; Dair would have ordered her second to undergo the operation immediately. "If that's all, you can run along now."

"You wish to be alone. Here." He made both sound highly suspect.

"I like it here." His suspicions, however, were going to drive Dair mad. "It is safer than the outer currents, wouldn't you say?"

"I have never known you to pair yourself with caution." He scanned the surrounding vegetation. "Or privacy."

"I do not pair with anything." She could have been more cautious coming here, though. If Shan took it into his head to arrive early, before she could get rid of Onkar, the situation would turn quickly unpleasant. She swam to the edge of the embankment. "Will you leave me alone, or must I splash you again?"

Onkar crouched down—not an easy thing for a 'Zangian as large and uncomfortable on land as he was—and trailed one of his fins in the water. "I am not your enemy, Jadaira."

"Not unless you are hiding a Hsktskt or a 'shrike under that dark hide of yours." She saw him flinch and draw back. "That was only another joke, Onkar."

"And beneath it?" He met her gaze, and for a moment she had the feeling that she had done him some great, unseen injury. Slowly he rose and backed away from the water. "Regulations require that sensitive communications be held in a secure location until they can be safely reviewed. That is not here. I will keep them with me until you are better situated, Commander."

"Thank you, Lieutenant." She watched him depart and wondered if she would ever understand his prickly nature.

Dair swam alone for another hour, until the suns were directly overhead, and then heard the sound of movement through the tangle of overgrowth. She rose out of the water and met Shan up by the tree line. "You are punctual, Amariah."

"I am grateful for the opportunity to learn, Commander." Shan had changed out of his blue religious robe and wore a standard fitted tunic in muted shades of white and gold. It emphasized his size and form. "I do not think I can do this unclothed, however." He was keeping his eyes fixed on the tree line behind her.

"I have never understood nudity taboos. What are you, deformed under this?" She prodded the front of his tunic.

Shan looked outraged for a moment before he visibly collected himself. "No, but it is as you said of touching your gillets: something that we reserve for a mate."

"I see." No, she didn't. "But how do your kind select a suitable mate if you can't see each other's bodies?"

"We go by scent."

This made even less sense. A good smell was nice, and was said to make mating more pleasant, but a well-built body with plenty of scars counted for more in the water. Scars indicated superior survival skills and robust health. Perhaps the Skartesh did not have to worry about such things as daily defending their territory and their young. "Very well, preserve your notions of modesty, but your garments will likely make you feel weighted down."

Shan made a jerky motion with his head. "I do not think I can do this, even with garments."

*He truly is afraid.* "Easy, pilot." She took hold of his paw and led him to the edge of the water. "Sit here for a moment; you look a little sick."

He took in several slow, deep breaths and looked above her head. "You never told me why you were altered to look like a Terran."

"My dam became infected with Core organisms while she carried me. They damaged my body in utero, and Terran donor tissue was the only kind my body would not reject." She cocked her head. "Do you find me visually offensive?"

"No. Why were you not given 'Zangian transplants?"

"There were none made available for me in time." She sighed. "I was rejected by my natal pod after birth because I was too frail and injured to survive on my own. Such pups are driven off and left to die. That is why when my stepmother asked if she could harvest some organs from other 'Zangians who had died during the plague, the pod elders refused."

"You were a helpless newborn!" He seemed furious all over again. "That is obscene."

"That is our way. Or was, until Teresa saved me." She slipped into the water. "She didn't give up, but took me from the pod and brought me to the FreeClinic. She and Dr. Mayer performed many operations to replace my damaged and missing tissue with transplants and augmentations. After that I lived in a medical immersion tank for a year, until I fully healed and was able to feed and swim independently, and then Teresa returned me to the sea."

"Did your pod accept you then?"

"No, they ignored me for a long time. Almost another year. Look at me." She waited until he focused on her. "You fear the water so much that you avoid seeing it. Why?"

"Unhappy memories of Skart."

Shan had sounded grim when he had told her of his homeworld, but his body language now was different: all coiled and tight and terrified.

"No, that's not it. This is something more personal with you." When he remained silent, she added, "If you do not tell me what it is, I will not be able to help you conquer your fear of it."

The dark fur around his neck bristled, and then slowly smoothed down. "My younger brother, Tarkun, was very inquisitive. Almost from the time he was born he would try to track anything that moved. Just after he was weaned, he wandered away from our camp. A storm came just as he was missed, one so violent we were unable to track him. He never returned, and the rain erased his scent path. My father and I searched for many days before we found him. Somehow he had been swept into a lake." He wrenched his gaze away from her and the shimmering surface around her. "Until Tarkun, I had never seen what water, or the things that dwell in it, can do to a body."

Dair wished she had not pushed him to recall such a painful moment. "Oh, Rushan, I'm sorry."

"It was a long time ago." With an economical movement he pulled off his tunic, revealing a V-shaped torso covered with black fur. Over the left side of his chest were two parallel patches of golden hair. "I would feel more comfortable leaving my trousers on. What must I do first?"

She moved to the shallowest spot in the pool and held out her hands. "Come, join me."

He sat down on the embankment and reluctantly eased his lower limbs in. "It is cold."

She kept her voice soothing and calm. "It is cool but not cold, and when you come in, the water will rise to your waist but no farther. You will feel the bottom with your feet." She didn't pull him in, but waited until he entered the water himself. "There. We will move a little deeper, but only when you are ready."

"I am not as light or small as you are," he said, his voice just as rigid as his body. "I cannot go deeper; I will sink."

"That is the excellent thing about water. No matter what your size or weight, it never has the slightest difficulty lifting and supporting you." She showed him her teeth. "We will not let you sink, Rushan Amariah. I promise."

Onkar had two reasons for holding on to the encrypted data chips delivered by the quadrant courier. The first was to give him an excuse to return to the grotto. The small body of water was less than ideal for what he had planned—large as he was, he never felt comfortable in such constricted areas—but the opportunity to be alone with Jadaira was irresistible.

The second was why he went to the Trading Center and contracted the services of a footgear peddler, who sometimes did illegal program bootlegging on the side. He had to discover what data was so vital that it had to be coded for her eyes alone.

Her behavior earlier had been rather odd enough to make him slightly more suspicious than usual. *She is keeping something from me.* If they were to be together, there could be no secrets between them. He realized he could be overanalyzing the situation; it certainly wouldn't be the first time. *Perhaps it is nothing, and all I must do is be more open and easier with her. Certainly she would approve of that, and it might even prompt her to place more trust in me.*

The front facade of the peddler-programmer's stand seemed to be constructed entirely of the containers in which he packaged his wares. The size and type of the container varied, but all but a few special-order items were displayed through the clear rectangular boxes. Behind them was a privacy screen, which concealed him while he attended to his other, much more lucrative business, and it was there that Onkar paced as he waited.

After several minutes without results, Onkar checked his wristcom. "This is taking too long."

"Keep your flight suit on, Lieutenant." The bootlegger sucked some air in through his teeth as official-looking data began filling his screen. "These chips have TS-five level clearance codes. You sure you want to know what's on them?"

*TS-5?* Now he had to know. "Yes."

"Your court-martial." The bootlegger rapidly tapped his keyboard before he blanked out his display and inserted a data storage chip.

"Why did you shut down the screen?" Onkar demanded.

"If they catch you and you implicate me, I can honestly state that I never saw what was on them. Saves me from spending my best years hacking out minerals in some penal colony mine." He finished copying the data, and exchanged both sets of chips for the agreed-upon credits. "Nice doing business with you, Lieutenant. Come back if you ever get tired of those fluke boots."

Onkar left the Trading Center and went straight back to Dair's puddle in the forest. He was hot and irritable and his hide was flaking, but as he made his way through the trees, he heard her voice. The pure joy in the ringing sound of it sank into him like wasp-netter venom and made him forget everything except being near her again. He began unfastening his flight suit as he drew near, wanting nothing more than to dive in the cool water and hear her speak to him with such pleasure. He was so eager that he nearly stepped out onto the bank before he realized she was no longer alone.

"You're doing fine; don't stiffen your neck." Dair had the Skartesh pilot in the water with her. He was bare-chested, floating faceup, and she had her arms around the center of his body. "Loosen your muscles and let the water support your head."

Onkar drew back into the shadows.

Shan did not seem as happy as Jadaira. "I will sink as soon as you let go of me."

*If he does not,* Onkar thought, *I can arrange it. Easily.*

"No, you won't. Try to relax." Dair stroked the furry surface of the Skartesh's hair-covered, heaving chest with her hand. "Don't fight the water; try to be a part of it."

She had never touched Onkar like that. In fact, she had gone to great lengths to avoid touching him at all.

"How does one become part of liquid?" Shan asked her.

His recessed eyes narrowed to slits. *I could show you.*

"You already are." She moved him in a slow circle around her. "If I were to cut you, you wouldn't bleed sand." She hesitated. "You wouldn't, would you?"

Onkar's teeth ached as he thought of the many satisfying ways in which he could open the Skartesh's veins.

"No." Shan made a low, rumbling sound and brought up one paw to rest over her hand. "You are trying to distract me."

"Yes, and I'm having a very hard time of it."

Rage continued to seethe inside Onkar, burning away every other emotion as he watched them. Soon he felt as if there were nothing left in him but the heat of fury; not since ranging alone in the outer currents had he felt so empty.

Jadaira had always claimed that she would never mate, and here she was, alone with this male who had done nothing but pursue her since he had arrived on-planet. If she had not made her choice, she soon would.

*Let her play with the mouth-breather now,* he decided as he curled his fin around the encrypted chips. *It will keep her occupied while I do what is necessary. And when she brings him into my water, then I will show her what—and how—he bleeds.*

# CHAPTER
## ELEVEN

Dair had hoped to keep her friendship with Shan quiet, and not only because she was trying to find out more about the Skartesh for the chief of security. All her life she had been under someone's scrutiny, and for once she had something that was entirely hers and hers alone.

It was not a 'Zangian trait, to be so secretive. Pod life meant sharing—and knowing—everything that happened to everyone under the water. Dair was not sure why she felt different from her people, but perhaps it was due in part to her stepmother's influence. Teresa so valued things with emphasis on the individual, like privacy, intimacy, and monogamy.

However, unlike Teresa, Dair was a creature of habit, so naturally the woman closest to her was the first to notice that her routines had changed.

"I was hoping to see you at the URD site this week," Teresa said as she finished the last of the monthly medical scans she performed on Dair's augmentations. "What have you been up to?"

"Patrolling, analyzing intel, filing reports, saving lives across the quadrant. You know, the usual." She climbed off the exam table in Teresa's laboratory and began disconnecting the monitor leads attached to her skin. "Why do you need me at the site?"

"I thought you'd be interested to see the final stages of construction. We're almost ready to cut the ribbon and move in." Her stepmother transferred the scanner's readings into the medsysbank. "Burn mentioned you've been slipping off alone after duty."

"Burn spills his gullet too much."

"So you *have* been doing something other than patrolling, analyzing, filing, and saving lives."

Dair sighed and wiped some contact gel from her brow. "You're not going to let me out of here until I tell you, are you?"

Her stepmother smiled. "You got that in one."

"I've been seeing Rushan Amariah off duty." She stepped into her skin shield and began working it up her legs. "Before you start lecturing me on cross-species relationships, we're just platonic friends. There has been no primate business whatsoever."

"Monkey," Teresa automatically corrected her.

"Or that, either."

"Sweetheart, I hate to sound skeptical, but I was just friends with an aquatic male once. Look where that landed me." Teresa came over to help her reconnect the hydro lines that fed a thin layer of water between her skin and the shield and kept it circulating. "I know I'm the last person who should lecture you about falling in love outside your species. But have you really thought about what else will happen if you continue this relationship with that Skartesh? Even if it stays on a friendship-only level?"

"I'll have someone to bring to dinner who doesn't drip or eat live food?" Dair tried to sound hopeful.

"You'll be crossing other, very well-established lines. I should know. I'm one of the reasons that they were drawn." Teresa cupped her cheek for a moment. "I'm going to make a not-too-wild presumption here and guess that you're only trying to be nice to him."

"I am trying to be nice. I am nice."

"You are." Her smile was sad. "Thing is, honey, you're the one who will end up getting hurt."

"You make it sound like I'm birthing his pup." Dair adjusted her collar. "I'm just teaching him how to swim. That's all, Mom."

"You've gotten him into the water?" Teresa looked astonished now. "Without drugging him? Really?"

"Not all the way under yet, but he can float by himself now, minus the medication."

Dair went on to describe how the lessons were progressing. She admitted that teaching a hydrophobic how to swim was not the easiest task she had ever taken on, but whenever she felt like giving up on the Skartesh pilot, she would remember how she felt that first year in the water.

"You remember how many times I tried to approach the coastal pod, only to be driven off or shunned?" She made the fin gesture for loneliness. "He feels like that."

"I thought all that attention your father and I gave you would make up for it. Of course, you're my first and only kid, so I was bound to mess up." She caught Dair's gaze. "Was it so bad?"

The rejection had been like a wound no one could see, but Dair wouldn't tell her stepmother that. "I survived, but Shan and his people are like I was—outcasts." She caught Teresa's hands in hers. "He tells me that the Skartesh are morbidly afraid of the water. Knowing that makes me feel as if these lessons are about more than just learning how not to sink. He's trusting me, Mom. If I turn my back on him now, he might not ever trust an aquatic again."

"Well, you're a grown female, Dair. I'm not going to try to make your decisions for you, no matter how much I'd like to." Teresa gave her a quick hug. "Just be careful. There's still so much about the Skartesh that we *don't* know."

"There's one thing. I haven't gotten him completely naked yet, but"—Dair wrinkled her nose—"I think he has that hair all over him."

Teresa laughed.

Dair's cousin was the next person to grill her, and like Teresa, he waited until they were alone to bring up the subject.

Burn wanted to become a pilot, but he was a little lazy about fulfilling the preliminary requirements before returning to the academy for training.

"Do I have to learn to do the full preflight?" he asked as he took his position on the opposite side of their newly repaired strafer and opened the first hull cowling. "I already know how to check out the weapons array and stardrive. By the way, what are you doing with that mouth-breather?"

"Star vessel *Wavelight*, VID57514719161. Commander mu T'resa, Ensign mu Znora inspecting," Dair said to the hovering recorder drone before she switched it to mute. "If you don't master full preflight, you'll never qualify for pilot training. Which mouth-breather? I'm surrounded by them lately."

"The Skittish one whose dam doesn't like you."

"Oh. Nothing. Pay attention now." She joined him in front of the panel. "When you start the preflight, the first thing you have to watch out for is yourself. You do enough of these, you start getting lazy, and you'll miss things. Especially when you scan the same ship a couple hundred times."

"So the first rule of piloting is, don't get bored with the ship."

"Don't get bored with the checklist and just zip through it. Look at *everything*. Start with the primary control panel here. What do you see?"

"No foreign bodies, no carbon scars and"—he ducked down to look under the ship—"no compartment leaks. What do you mean, nothing? I know you've been doing something; you've gone topside three times this week." He peered inside the panel. "Have you been with him?"

She made an impatient sound. "No, don't just give the conduits and wiring a visual; run your fins along them. Sometimes you can feel chafing and break spots before you can see them. Like this." She took his fin and demonstrated. "Never assume that because it looks okay it is okay."

He glanced at her. "But Verrig said he just replaced all this, and why aren't you answering my questions about the mouth-breather?"

"Verrig can make mistakes, too. Why is it any of your business what I do topside?" She went through the next four compartments with him, but his hurt silence finally made her blow some air through her gillets. "All right, stop giving me those wounded-pup eyes. Yes, I've been seeing the Skartesh."

"I knew it." Burn tested some bolts. "So are you and he . . . ?" He made the fin gesture for sexual intent.

"No, and you're too young and smooth to be flashing that, so quit it. The chief said you could do some maintenance walkarounds with him; that's the best way to learn how he looks for damage and wear. Verrig has the best eyes on the flight line; what he does, you should do." She moved on to the last panel. "And while you're inspecting, always look at the outer spaceframe. When you approach, check the wing tips; make sure the cowlings are correctly seated." She stuck her head inside the compartment to have a look at the drive components. "Everything inside the ship can be fine, but if a chunk of hull gets sucked out you may go with it."

"You would know." He nudged her. "So if you're not chasing each other, what are you doing with that Skittish?"

"Skartesh. I'm teaching him to swim." She emerged and closed the panel. "Let's climb in and start up the thrusters."

Dair made Burn sit in the pilot's seat, while she stood outside to observe. "The first thing you always check is your fuel: gauges, system, backups. Never assume your cells are full; verify with two autonomous sources that they are. Look for any sign of mechanical failure, line collapse, and cell damage. Always pull a sample for a contamination check."

"Verrig keeps the fuelers segregated."

"I don't drive them around filled with water," the flight crew chief said as he joined Dair on the scaffold. "You get a cockpit breach and so much as a trickle of fluid gets into your lines, the thrusters will suck it in and stall, or the water will freeze into a plug and block the line." He used one of his multijointed prosthetic arms to reach in and tap up the fuel screen on the pilot console's display. "Always check your levels twice, here and on the mainsys monitor. Fuel-related accidents are the second-largest cause of pilot/ship losses in the League."

Burn nodded. "What's the first?"

"The Hsktskt." Verrig turned his enormous eyes on Dair. "I'd take her for a test jaunt before you enable her for routine service, Commander. Test and idle speeds on the engines won't give you adequate differential for a proper instrument check."

She nodded. "Burn, signal Transport and get us clearance to launch."

Burn signaled to obtain authorization, while Dair prepared for launch. Just before she pulled on her helmet, she noticed a group of Skartesh on the perimeter of the docks. They all seemed to be staring directly at her. "What are they doing?"

Verrig followed her gaze. "I don't know, but they've been watching you since they got here."

*   *   *

William Mayer considered social events almost as much an annoyance as the formal garb he had to wear to them. He never felt comfortable in crowds or out of scrubs. But as chief of FreeClinic Services, he was expected to make an appearance at the major colonial functions, and the Hlagg ambassador's reception was considered to be the highlight of the cycle.

*At least this time I won't have to pretend interest in the Rilkens' position on the new Jorenian-Aksellan treaty,* he thought as he stepped up to the entry to Ana Hansen's quarters and rang the door chime. "Ana, it's William Mayer," he said to the audio panel, as he was a few minutes early.

"Just a moment," her voice replied.

Absently he wondered why he had never thought to ask the administrator to accompany him before. Ana Hansen was a sensible woman, and far more adept than he was at navigating through the clusters of species at these functions. She was also one of K-2's greatest assets. She had worked tirelessly since the Core plague to salvage the colony, and since her selection to the council had used her influence to stabilize and rebuild their economy. Politicians, merchants, and colonists alike usually went to her first for important consultations.

As he inevitably ended up cornered by some obnoxious, thick-skinned species at receptions he attended alone, he might even make a habit of escorting Ana in the future. Perhaps she could teach him some of her diplomatic conversational self-extraction techniques.

The panel opened. "I'm sorry I kept you waiting." Ana stepped out and smiled up at him. Her face was flawlessly made up, as always, and she had woven her blond hair in an intricate mass atop her head. "You look very well."

"So do you." He inspected the champagne-colored silk gown she wore, which had slashes of nanobeading across the bodice and skirt. The programmed design changed with her movements, making the garment seem alive. He generally refrained from casual touching, but it seemed natural—and polite—to offer her his arm. "Shall we?"

Due to the unusual nature of his species, which were heavily dependent on homeworld life-forms, the Hlagg ambassador had petitioned for the right to build his own embassy on the outskirts of the colony, to provide a type of sanctuary for visiting and resident Hlagg alike. The embassy was rumored to mimic the environment of the Hlagg homeworld while integrating its elements into K-2's natural biosphere, and the reception was being held to celebrate the successful completion of the building project.

"I've never been to the Hlagg homeworld," he said as he parked outside the embassy and helped her from his glidecar. "Have you?"

"Twice." Ana looked up at the embassy, which from the outside appeared to be a large pyramid constructed of vine-covered stone. "William, are you bothered by insect life-forms?"

He thought of his N-jui charge nurse, who resembled a towering preying mantis and sometimes showed a temper to match. He liked T'Nliqinara better than most nurses because of it. "Not unless they're of the stinging variety."

"Excellent." She smiled. "You should enjoy this."

As they approached the front entrance to the structure, William heard a fluttering, humming sound and looked up to see a perfect circle of fist-size insects with large, flashing wings. The circle descended to surround him and Ana, and he automatically put an arm around her waist.

"It's all right." She held out her hand, and one of the creatures flew from the circle to perch on her palm. It was not a living creature, but a drone facsimile made of enameled alloy and plas. "Ana Hansen and Dr. William Mayer to see Ambassador Heek," she said to the small drone, which chirped and flew back to the circle.

William smiled a little as the circle solidified into a Terran-shaped body and, like a polite butler, opened the door panel for them.

"Very clever." Between the outer door and the inside of the embassy was an air lock, which puzzled him. "Will we need breathers?"

"No, the air lock isn't for the environment." Ana guided him inside and sealed the outer door before the inner entry panel opened. "All you have to remember is, don't swat anything."

"I told you that I'm not afraid of insects."

"I'm hoping this doesn't change your mind." Still she put her hand on his arm. "Brace yourself; it can be a little disconcerting at first."

*That's putting it mildly,* he thought as they walked inside, and stopped in the middle of a swarm of hundreds of different insects. The varieties were bewildering: Some were winged like the drones outside, others hopped and glided, still others dangled from the high ceiling on long strands. A squeak from below made him glance down to see a pair of knee-high segmented caterpillar-like creatures swiftly inching away from their feet.

There were so many insects that the air seemed to move with them, creating little currents and eddies to swirl around the assembled guests.

"I take it the Hlagg are fond of their native bugs," he murmured to Ana as he carefully nudged a small mothlike insect from the perch it had taken on the end of his nose.

"Yes, very, and they're an important part of their culture, too. Ah, there's Ambassador Heek." Ana took his hand in hers. "Come and I'll introduce you."

The ambassador was not at all insectile himself, but a humanoid with luxurious copper fur, large ears, and a distinct snout and tail. Instead of garments, however, his body was covered with what William first thought were small, rectangular nanobeaded panels much like the design on his companion's dress. Closer examination revealed that the panels were the shed husks of insect bodies, complete with tiny legs and heads, attached to strands of the ambassador's fur.

William tried to imagine allowing that many insects to attach themselves to his body, but failed.

"Ana!" Heek greeted her with an affectionate embrace before drawing back to study her gown. "You look delightful, as always."

"Thank you, Ambassador." She turned slightly. "May I present Dr. William Mayer, chief of FreeClinic Services?"

"Ambassador." He offered his hand, palm-up.

"Doctor." Heek evidently was familiar with Terran customs, for he joined his paw to William's hand and shook it. "A pleasure to meet you. Come, sit with me and we'll have some refreshment." He gestured toward one of the other Hlagg nearby.

"Dr. Mayer has never been to the Hlagg homeworld," Ana mentioned as they sat down with Heek at a small, triangular-shaped table that was covered with more insects.

The ambassador bared several rows of blunt teeth. "A demonstration is in order, then." He made a low, sharp sound and the insects on the table went still.

William was impressed. "They respond to you?"

"Completely. The Hlagg have always enjoyed a symbiotic rapport with our native insects. Our primitive hunter ancestors would use them to lead hunts, process vegetation, safeguard dwellings, and even ferment tree saps." One of the Hlagg brought a tray of drinks to the table, and Heek offered goblets of a glittering clear liquid. "This is *meksem* sap, fermented in my own family's hives. A wonderful year, too."

Diplomatically William took a sip and found the sap to be as light and luscious as any quality Terran white wine. "The insects, I take it, were the justification for building the embassy."

"Indeed, they were. We knew it could be detrimental to K-2's environment to arbitrarily release our insects, but at the same time we would rather not live without them. Over time we have refined the relationship and the many ways in which we interact." Heek made another, different sound and the insects congregated into several clusters. "They now respond to specific verbal cues, much as any domesticated animal would. Observe."

Heek made a series of short, tonal sounds. The winged insects flew up and formed a whirling column in the center of the table, around a cluster of wormlike creatures that began to glow and filled the column with light. Joint-legged insects began hopping in and out of gaps in the column, and their shiny bodies reflected the light in a symmetrical pattern. At the same time, the hoppers rubbed their forelegs together, creating a pleasant hum.

Ana clapped her hands together. "Gorgeous!"

"Thank you. Most of the lighting on the homeworld is insect-generated, as are our garments, music, and art," Heek explained to William. "K-2 is very beautiful, but when we came here it also seemed very empty and somewhat sterile to us." He nodded toward Ana. "Administrator Hansen was instrumental in obtaining permission for us to build the embassy, you know."

"It was the least I could do, to provide regular access to a more native environment for the Hlagg," she said, "as well as to protect K-2's biosphere."

"You've certainly done that." William looked up and saw that the huge chandeliers were actually alloy racks covered with more of the luminescent worms. "The air locks are to keep them contained?"

Heek nodded. "We are cognizant of the fact that our insects might inflict great harm to the native flora. Also, it would be difficult for anyone but a Hlagg to control them." Someone called to him, and he smiled at them. "I see the Trytinorn representative has arrived. I should clear a space for him; his species have some issues with our small friends. Please excuse me."

When Heek left, the column of moving light dissipated and the insects flew, hopped, and crawled from the table to follow him.

Ana raised her goblet and looked at him over the rim before she took a sip. "What do you think of the Hlagg?"

"They're an interesting people." He checked his own drink for bugs before doing the same. "Although I think I will refrain from mentioning in the ambassador's presence how many mosquitoes I've killed back on Terra." A louder version of the hopper's humming music began to play, and several couples came together in the center of the room.

She followed his gaze. "Would you like to dance?"

"I haven't danced since . . ." He couldn't remember; it had been that long.

"It's either dance or speak with the Rilken representative, who is headed in our direction." Ana rose and held out a hand to him. "I promise I won't shriek if you step on my toes."

He looked at the small, many-limbed alien approaching them. Rilkens were extremely curious, did not wear garments, and, if not frequently discouraged, would slip their slimy tentacles under another species' clothing to feel what was beneath it. He stood and took her hand, which seemed oddly delicate and small in his. "I'll hold you to that."

Ana was an accomplished dancer, so it was easy to follow her movements to the music. As they whirled around the floor, he found himself admiring how graceful she was, and how pleasant it felt to hold her in his arms. Another reason to attend more of these receptions.

The music was disrupted by an incident involving a Cordobel

and the Rilken representative; the latter had apparently attached himself to one of the former's ankles and was trying to crawl up his trouser legs. Rather than going to provide assistance as she usually would, Ana led William from the dance floor and to one of the recessed arches.

"Don't you want to defuse the hostilities?" he asked as they walked into a narrow, deserted corridor.

"I think Heek can handle it," she said. "I want to show you something."

On the other side of the view panels what appeared to be grayish-white sand castles in various sizes filled the room. As they drew near, William heard a proximity sensor blip, and the soft lighting within the enclosure gradually intensified, highlighting the odd miniature structures and the glittering silver specks in the sand used to build them.

"What's this?" He peered through the plas. "A children's playroom? A simulation of a Hlagg shoreline?"

"It's one of their barax colonies. Rather like the ant colonies Terran children used to keep in viewing containers. See the little flashes of green inside the mounds?" She pointed to the octagonally shaped openings in the sand. "Those are barax. They're something a little like a cross between Terran termites and beetles."

"They should be exterminated, like the rest of these pests," a low, flat voice said from behind them.

William turned his head to watch the couple approaching them. He had seen the Skartesh before—on K-2, who hadn't?—yet this was the first time he had heard one of them speak. The two emerging from the corridor were male and female; their robes were a dull yellow instead of the usual white. Both were shedding badly, and patches of their mangy fur sloughed off and fell to the floor with every step they took. From the way their lips were peeled back from their teeth, it was clear that they weren't happy.

He started to reply, but Ana put a hand on his arm.

"Not all insects are harmful, Yersha." Her voice remained as smooth as her expression. "Dr. Mayer, may I present Yersha and Kabod Amariah, the designated Skartesh representatives." To the Skartesh couple, she said, "This is Dr. William Mayer. He's a cardiothoracic surgeon, chief of surgery, and supervises FreeClinic Services for the colony."

"We take care of our own people." Yersha dismissed him with one glance.

"As you are our official liaison, Administrator, we had no choice but to come here," Kabod said. The male Skartesh didn't seem as agitated as his mate, which made his next words something of a surprise. "There is a matter of urgent importance to the Skartesh that requires your immediate attention."

William felt Ana's hand tighten on his arm as she said, "Certainly. How may I be of assistance?"

"That white aquatic female—the pilot—has been making a nuisance of herself over our son." Yersha's voice dropped into a snarl. "You will see that it is stopped at once."

"You may schedule an appointment with my assistant, Carsa, first thing in the morning." Ana sounded impassive, but William could sense her withdrawing, as if her response came more from her training than any desire to help the couple. "She will provide you with the data forms you need to fill out to file your grievance with Colonial Administration."

"That will take too long!" Yersha swiped the air with her paw. "This female distracts our son from his duties and disrupts the faithful with her outrageous behavior. I told her myself to stay away from Rushan, but she did not heed my warning."

"Representative Amariah, I regret your unhappiness over this situation," Ana said, "but there is a standard procedure that must be followed . . ." She trailed off into a sigh as, without another word, the Skartesh couple stalked back into the embassy. "And you're not going to follow it, of course. Damn it."

William knew of only one white aquatic. "She was referring to Commander mu T'resa, wasn't she?"

"I think so." Ana looked perplexed. "I tried to pick up an image from her thoughts, but all those negative emotions she was projecting made it hard to concentrate. Of course, she could just be an overly protective mother."

"Jadaira doesn't strike me as the type to stir up trouble. She's too logical and controlled." He recalled his meeting with Rushan

Amariah, and how insistent the Skartesh had been about being permitted to join Bio Rescue. "If anyone is pushing in the wrong direction, I'd say it's their son."

"Well, there's nothing I can do about it tonight." She shrugged and turned back to the viewer. "So, what do you think of the barax?"

He struggled to focus on the enclosure. "I think you're going to tell me that they're not just pests and they serve some other, useful purpose that will then utterly astound me."

She chuckled. "Actually they are what we Terrans and most species would consider pests, but such insects as barax contribute to the decomposition processes on the Hlagg homeworld. The sand in there is actually fragments of dead wood and other lignocellulose matter, which they eat along with soil, digest, and excrete as building material. Because they're naturally subterranean and tunnel underground, they also aerate and enrich the soil."

"Very useful and pretty pests, then."

"Oh, they're more than just visually appealing. Heek told me earlier that they're ready to start sealing the mounds. Wait a moment until they adjust to the light, and then you'll see." Anticipation made her eyes sparkle as much as the sand, and when she slid her hand down his arm and curled her fingers around his, he didn't pull away.

Gradually the barax crawled out of their mounds and, after a noticeable hesitation, began forming single-file chains by hooking their legs and mandibles together. After twenty or so barax had formed a chain, they moved as one to sculpt the sand up and around the established mounds in artful waves. In their wake they left a silvery substance that sank into the sand.

"The fluid they're excreting hardens the top layer and makes the mounds stable," Ana told him. "When it's dry, they'll do the same on the inside, which makes their little castles permanent."

"A pity they weren't around when we were building the FreeClinic."

When the barax reached the top of the mound, the chain separated and the barax began jumping over the side, sliding down channels like gleeful children sledding down a snowy hill. When they reached the bottom, they turned and raced back up the mound to jump again.

The effect was so charming that he couldn't help smiling. "What are they doing?"

"No one knows, and Heek told me his people have never discovered why they do it. Whatever the reason is, barax watching has a strong positive effect. The Hlagg cultivate barax colonies in their hospitals and use them to help patients recover after physical and mental illness and injuries."

"Happiness termites." He snorted. "Now I've seen it all."

"It's not such a bad thing." She looked up at him, and a dimple appeared in her cheek "You never know, someday you might move a barax colony into your FreeClinic."

"I can't see myself doing that." They were standing much closer now, and the light floral perfume Ana always wore made him breathe in deeply. Remarkable, really, how attractive she was. He had never noticed that about her before. "Did I tell you that you look lovely tonight?"

Her chin dropped, and she stared at his chest. "I don't remember."

Seeing her react like a shy girl was almost as arousing as her scent. He lifted a hand and rested his fingers against her cheek.

"Ana, look at me." When she did, he gave in to the impulse, bent down, and brushed his mouth against hers.

Her lips were as soft as her skin, and tasted of the Hlagg sapwine.

She went very still, and drew back. "Liam, do you know what you're doing?"

"Generally." He didn't like her pulling away from him, and frowned. "Come here."

"I don't think that's a good idea." Ana turned to move toward the corridor leading into the embassy. "I should get back; I think Heek wanted—"

William caught her arm and neatly whirled her around so that her body collided with his. "What about what I want?" He brought his arms up around her to keep her there. "And what you want?"

"If you insist." Her expression blanked as she slid the hands she had pressed against his chest up to link behind his neck.

She was dealing with him, the way she had dealt with the Skartesh.

*Is that what I am to her? Just another situation to be handled?* He was startled by the realization that he didn't know how she felt toward him. She might be an empath, but she kept her own thoughts and feelings well hidden. The same way Rosalind had. Rosalind, the only woman he'd loved; the last woman he'd held like this.

Rosalind, whom he had killed.

"It doesn't matter to you what I feel," his calm, beautiful wife had suddenly shrieked at him one night.

He'd forgotten some plans she'd made and stayed too late at the hospital, as usual. "My patients are more important than the ballet, Rose. We can attend the next one."

"No, we can't. Why did you marry me? Why didn't you just buy yourself a *sexdrone?*"

He had been too arrogant to beg her to stay. That cost him his marriage and, ultimately, Rosalind her life.

*I will not do this to another woman.*

Slowly William set Ana at arm's length. "You're right. This is a bad idea." He ran a hand over the knotted muscles in the back of his neck. "Forgive me." He walked over to the viewer to stare blindly at the barax.

"Liam."

He glanced back at her. She looked cool and utterly poised, as always.

"I wasn't handling you." Her chin elevated a notch. "As it happens, I was handling myself."

His eyes narrowed. "What?"

"There's nothing wrong with your hearing. Before you put your hands on me again, you should think about what you really want from me," she advised him. "Because next time, I'm not going to do this."

Ana walked away.

# CHAPTER
## TWELVE

The ongoing trouble with the Skartesh began to get worse on the day after Dair had seen the group watching her and Burn perform the strafer's preflight.

As she had since the initiation of the mission, Dair flew a daily patrol in Rescue One with the pilots' pod. Although she sometimes went as long as seven shifts without a signal from a ship in distress, she felt the routine was vital. The 'Zangians still needed practice adjusting the strafers' flight patterns and evasive maneuvers alongside the bigger, more powerful gstek raider.

Quadrant had also sent her intel that made her determined to keep the squadron alert. According to the encrypted reports Onkar had brought to her, it appeared as if the Hsktskt were making an effort to take back some of the territory they had lost to the League. All military commanders in the targeted regions were advised to prepare their personnel and resources in the event the lizards made a renewed bid to occupy their territories.

As she put the ship through its paces, Dair also made sure Verrig or one of his senior techs came along to handle any new problems that cropped up.

"I hate flying," the flight crew chief grumbled as they were cleared to disembark after landing. He bent and made a reverent gesture by touching the dock pad with one metallic clamp. "If my gods intended me to zip about in space, they'd have made me an asteroid."

"We like you so much better this way, Chief." Burn gave the back of his prosthetic rig a friendly slap.

"I'm not happy with the flight control adjustments, Verrig," Dair said as she pulled off her helmet. "I should be getting full, smooth deflections off the throttle and it still feels twitchy to me."

The chief stiffened and his small mouth crimped. "I've calibrated it six times."

"Calibrate it again." She shaded her eyes as a pair of Skartesh approached them. "Burn, go file our status report."

Her cousin had already seen them. "Later."

Rushan's parents were accompanied by Njal-Geir and his assistant, and when they were a few feet away it was the official who hailed Dair. "Commander mu T'resa, I must speak with you. A serious matter has been brought to my attention."

She rested her helmet against her hip. "I'm sure you can cope with it on your own. That's why you have all those things on your tunic, right?" She gestured toward the rows of commendation pips he wore.

"You aquatics are so . . . witty. However, this is no time for humor. The Skartesh have concerns that must be addressed at once." He gestured toward a large group of Skartesh waiting outside Main Transport. "I will be happy to mediate, or you can attempt to discuss this matter with them yourself." He leaned closer. "Under the circumstances, I don't believe they'll speak directly to you."

"Yes, well, I'm busy right now. Make an appointment with Flight Control."

Sohrab cleared his throat. "Ah, Supervisor?"

"Not now." Njal-Geir checked his wristcom. "You are off duty now, are you not, Commander? I think this would be an ideal time."

"Supervisor, *please*." The assistant's facial bumps were bubbling with agitation.

Before Dair could respond, angry shouts erupted from the direction of Main Transport. The waiting Skartesh followers were standing in such a way that they blocked the path of a number of cargo haulers. They were also ignoring the drivers' demands that they move out of the way. Other dockworkers stopped what they were doing and headed to surround the impassive, white-robed beings.

Verrig swore under his breath and hurried off toward the group.

"I am off duty, Supervisor, but I'd say you have a more immediate problem on your hands." Dair noticed that the rest of the pilots' pod had assembled in formation behind her and Burn, and were listening intently. "Do you require our assistance?"

"No. Sohrab." The official snapped his little fingers, and strode toward Main Transport, his anxious assistant obediently trotting in his wake.

Yersha and Kabod Amariah seemed to be in no hurry to rescue their followers, Dair saw, so she addressed them. "Did you have something that you want to say to me?"

Burn came to stand at her left side, Onkar at her right. The remaining 'Zangians moved forward en masse to tighten the ranks.

"We are not ignorant of what you are doing," Kabod told her. "You, however, are ignorant of us. So we will educate you, this once."

Burn took a step forward. "Try and see what happens, mouth-breather."

"Ensign." Dair didn't look away from the Skartesh's dark eyes. "At ease."

After a noticeable hesitation, her gunner stepped back.

Dair glanced across the docks. The Skartesh remained indifferent to the threats being shouted at them by the cargo hauler drivers and dockworkers, but there were enough of them to provide a challenge for the pod, if it came to that. Njal-Geir and his assistant were scurrying between the two groups, while Verrig tried herding a number of his subordinates away from the disturbance. Neither was having much success at defusing the situation.

Dair realized that the Skartesh followers were deliberately creating a distraction. *This could get ugly, fast.* "Say what you have to say," she told the Skartesh couple.

"Our son is the Salvager, as was prophesized," Yersha said, her harsh voice softening. " 'There shall be great upheaval visited upon the children of the Promise; violence from above and below the world. It shall cause the children to scatter like seed upon the four winds of creation. This is the time of the Hand of the Salvager, who shall gather them up, and bring them to the Place of Decision, until all who are to be judged shall be seen, and measured, and found wanting or deserving. Only then shall the Salvager choose those worthy of Paradise, and bring life to them through the Great Burning.' "

Dair actually wished she could yawn. "I'm sorry, but I don't know what that means."

Kabod provided the translation, such as it was. "Rushan was chosen to lead our people to Paradise. He has been blessed with the gift of renewal, and will bring the dead back to life. We are gathering here, in the Place of Decision, until all Skartesh have rejoined and are judged. Then we shall return to Skart, and there Rushan will give himself to the Great Burning. His sacrifice will drive back the waters, and transform our world into the paradise that it was."

Shan had never said anything about returning to Skart or . . . "Excuse me? His *sacrifice?*"

Kabod lifted his arms and gestured toward the sky. "Long have we suffered. Long have we journeyed. Long have we waited for the coming day, and the Promise."

"Is anything you mouth-breathers do short?" Dair heard Saree murmur.

"You will not sully our son or blaspheme against the prophecy," Yersha informed Dair. "Keep away from the Salvager or we will see that you do."

They knew about the lessons. They had to, or they wouldn't be staging this scene. Dair wondered if they had said as much to Shan, and then she didn't care. She was tired of being pushed away because she wasn't considered acceptable.

"Don't make threats," Onkar said, his voice strained. "Unless you wish to deal with the consequences."

Dair glanced at him. She had never seen him as furious, or as controlled. For a moment it frightened her to realize she felt the same.

"Thank you, Lieutenant." To the Skartesh couple, she said, "You should take your people and go now."

The reverent expression on Kabod's face ebbed as he regarded her. "We will go now. However, be advised, woman. This is the last warning we offer."

The pilots' pod remained in formation until the Skartesh couple rejoined their followers and, to Njal-Geir's visible surprise, led them away from Main Transport.

"I need to kill something," Burn muttered.

"So do I." Dair turned to the pod. "Let's go home and feed."

Shan was surprised to hear about the encounter when Jadaira next met him at the grotto. Yersha and Kabod had said nothing to him about it, and it was not like them to keep such matters concealed. It did explain why more of his followers were regarding the couple with increased unease. If they continued staging these confrontations, they might lose what little control they had over the cult.

"What is this Promise they were talking about?" she demanded. "What does it have to do with you?"

"It is an ancient and largely meaningless prophecy, that is all," he said as he stripped out of his tunic. He would have to speak to Yersha and Kabod when he returned; they had no business broadcasting the Promise to outsiders. "My parents believe I was born to fulfill it. All the Skartesh do."

"Your father said something about you going back to Skart, and a sacrifice." Her pale eyes met his. "In Teresa's language that means killing something to offer it as tribute to a deity. Is the meaning the same in yours?"

"Yes."

"What are they going to make you kill?"

"Nothing." He walked down to the pool. "Can we begin? The interval I can spend here today is somewhat limited."

"No, I'm not getting in the water with you until you explain this to me." She folded her arms. "*What* do they think you're going to *kill?*"

He looked back at her. If he told her, she would react strongly. On the other hand, if he kept it from her, she might abandon their friendship, and that he could not allow. "Myself. They believe my sacrifice will reverse the conditions on Skart."

"You're serious." Jadaira appeared astonished, and then evidently forgot to inflate her lungs, as she had to gasp for breath before she could speak. "*They're* serious."

He nodded and sat down by the water's edge.

"You can leave them today," she said as she walked down and joined him. "Security can provide guards. If Norash refuses to do something, I'll ask my people to offer you sanctuary. Or you could stay with Teresa."

Her reaction made his mouth curl. "I cannot leave them."

She seized his shoulders. "They want you dead, they expect you to kill yourself, and you can't leave them?" She gave him a single, hard shake. "Are you as demented as they are?"

Had one of his own kind touched him in such a way, he would have been justified in beating her until she couldn't rise. Yet her emotional response, inappropriate as it was, pleased him. "I have no intentions of killing myself, Jadaira."

"You're damn right you're not going to!" She sounded so much like her Terran stepmother that he almost chuckled. She glared at him. "It isn't funny."

"No, it's not." He took a deep breath and slid into the water. "You're starting to flake again, woman. Get in."

Dair's subsequent, flamboyant dive created a huge splash, but Shan didn't try to avoid the spray. Aside from what he was learning about the colony from her, she had actually helped him conquer much of his fear of the water. He had not fully submersed himself yet, but it was only a matter of time now.

*We need to know about the patrols,* his superior had told him. *If they are as vigilant as we have been led to believe, they may interfere with our plans. This Bio Rescue effort is also troubling. Question the female and report back to me.*

"I have not heard of any more Skartesh ships being in need of rescue on their jaunt here," he said as she surfaced. "Have you seen any more on your patrols?"

"No, but quadrant warned us . . . Never mind." She wiped her face and extended a hand to him. "Today we're going to work on breathing and not breathing."

"I like to breathe."

She made the strumming sound that meant she was amused. "Then you'll want to pay close attention."

As the lesson progressed, Shan was able to use casual conversation to coax most of the information he needed about the 'Zangian patrols out of her. She would not comment on the specifics of the warning from her superiors, but that one had been issued was enough to warrant further investigation.

"Next time, we're going to do a little below-surface swimming, and I'm going to show you how to use a breathing rig," Dair warned him as they climbed out of the pool.

"Why the rig?"

"I thought you might like to come and visit my home pod when my stepmother has the opening ceremony for the URD." She nodded in the direction of the coast. "You're a strong natural swimmer, and once you know how to use a rig, you can graduate to bigger water."

The thought of diving into the seemingly endless expanse of K-2's sea made his stomach roll. "I am not sure I am ready for that."

"Trust me, you are. Besides, I'll be right there with you." She nudged him in the same, familiar way she would another 'Zangian. "Come on; it will be fun."

She had no idea how many nightmares he had had about Tarkun since beginning this self-torture. "Very well."

Shan left her and went to the Trading Center, where he had successfully eluded the faithful who had followed him earlier. They were still waiting there for him, although a number of colonists dining in the central courtyard were eyeing them with dislike. When they saw him walking toward his followers, a trio of Yturi plant-beings moved from their table to intercept him.

"You." A leafy limb blocked Shan's path. "You're the one they say is in charge of these dolts, aren't you?"

Shan made a gesture for the faithful to keep their distance. "I am the leader of the Skartesh people."

"I told you they can speak," the second Yturi said to the third. "You owe me fifty creds."

"We don't like them hanging around here," the first said as some of the other diners started gathering around them. "We can't enjoy our meals with them staring at us like that, and they stink of piss." Several voices seconded the opinion. None of them were friendly.

"Then I suggest you take your food and sit somewhere else." He tried to step around the leafy being, but was blocked a second time. "If you have a grievance, file it."

"People say you're mixed up with one of our aquatic females." The Yturi prodded him with a branchlike limb. "We don't like that, either. No one messes with the natives here."

A passing 'Zangian who had stopped to listen made a rude sound that Shan guessed was an agreement.

"You are violating my personal space and my privacy." Shan kept his tone neutral but firm. "Move aside or I will summon security."

"Like to like, dogman," someone else called out. "Stick to your own kind."

*Dogman?* Shan felt his teeth grind. "Move aside."

The faithful, who had obeyed his signal so far, decided to push their way into the crowd and pile their bodies around him. Because most were shedding fur, the Yturi and the other colonists made comments and sounds of distaste and drew back, and they were able to leave the Trading Center, though not without some mildly disturbing threats being shouted after them.

As soon as they were alone, one of the older faithful stopped and turned to face Shan, going down on his knees as he did. Agitation made the silvery fur on the back of his neck stand on end. "I must be educated, Salvager."

Shan, who had been mentally composing his next report to the Elder, made an impatient gesture. "What is it?"

"Why did you not tell those heretics that relations between our people and the aquatics are forbidden, as Yersha has said?" the follower asked.

He reined in a sigh. "I did not tell them that because Yersha is wrong. It is not forbidden."

The old Skartesh looked stunned. "She tells us such things violate the laws of nature. Land is good. Water is cursed." Saying the latter made him shudder, and he released a stream of urine on Shan's boot. "Your mother was very specific."

Yersha and her zealousness were rapidly becoming a liability that Shan could not afford. Also, the Skartesh practice of urinating on each other to ward off evil was one of his least favorite native customs. Yet to maintain his command of the cult, he had to project a certain amount of tolerance, or risk alienating them. "The fact that our kind avoid water does not make it evil. If we are to dwell here, we must show tolerance toward those who do not live as we do. Even those who dwell apart from the land."

This made the kneeling follower look sick. "I do not question the word of the Salvager, but . . ."

"The heretics show no tolerance for our ways," another, younger Skartesh finished for him. She sounded almost defiant as she added, "They taunt us wherever we go, while we must remain silent and accepting."

"Not all of them," a third said. "Some are kind. In particular, those who are furred, like us."

Shan had to suppress this uncharacteristic behavior among the faithful immediately—they could not be allowed to think they could ever question him—but he resented the task. *Is it not enough that I hold your fate in my hands? Would you have me cradle and sing to you while you piss on me as well?*

"You come to the Place of Decision to demonstrate your faith and to be judged." He studied the eyes fixed on him. "Do you believe retaliation against heretics will make you worthy of Paradise? Shall I leave you to find the way on your own?"

His harsh admonition worked exactly as he hoped, driving all of the followers into a circle, in which they began chanting the Promise and urinating on each other. Beyond them, a pair of passing colonists stopped to watch. Shan didn't have to smell their disgust and anger; they wore it on their faces. The same feelings burned and twisted on the other side of his eyes.

*You must be the Salvager.*

Shan looked at the praying Skartesh. They were thin, as they had not yet adapted to the taste of synthesized foods. K-2's humid atmosphere had caused much of their fur to fall out. Memories of disaster and loss haunted their dark eyes, and there was not one of them who had not watched someone he or she loved die on their homeworld. All they truly had left were their beliefs, and they clung to them like the lost, terrified children that they were.

*Their beliefs, and me.* Shan knew that with a handful of words, he could make them pray and dance until they starved to death. He could make them do whatever he wished. *Such is the power of conviction.*

Persuading them to think against their nature was not possible, not now. His superior had warned him not to push the faithful too hard; while he might have the power to save them, he also had the ability to send them over the edge. He would have to go slowly, and carefully, or risk losing them all. He had sworn on everything he believed in that that would not happen.

"Stop."

The prayer circle immediately stilled.

"We need not have relations with aquatics. They remain in their world, and we in ours." Shan put a paw on the shoulder of the old male who had questioned him. "Come now, and walk with me."

The Skartesh stepped up their demonstrations at Main Transport over the next week. They seemed to time them in order to confront Jadaira going to or returning from a patrol, and there were more of them demonstrating every day. The pilots' pod, in turn, responded with more open aggression every time they saw them. Dair was starting to wonder how much worse it was going to get when two security officers showed up at Transport to inform her that her presence was required over at Security.

They didn't let her wriggle out of it as usual. In fact, they escorted her to the security chief's office.

"Thank you so much for stopping in, Commander," Chief Norash said as he stomped back and forth in front of the long wall of monitors. The vids, which served as part of the Colonial Security grid, monitored every major common area in the colony. Groups of dancing, yipping Skartesh filled a quarter of the screens.

They had to be the reason Norash had brought her in. "There a problem, Chief?"

"*You* are my problem. You and the Skittish. If you haven't noticed, they're staging protests." He swept his lengthy nasal appendage toward the monitors. "Religious protests, according to their leaders, and since they're being held in an area designated for public assembly, I can't disperse them."

"Okay." She scratched the side of her neck and decided to play dumb. "And I'm here because . . . ?"

"*You're* the one they're protesting against, Commander." The striped skin around his small eyes twitched. "You and all of the native Kevarzangians. This is because, according to them, you have violated their cultural taboos against relations of any kind between land dwellers and aquatics."

"That's not good." But why was she being blamed for it? Why wasn't someone yelling at Shan? "Anything else?"

"If you'll look at monitor six, you'll see that quadrant official with the Skartesh leaders. He's announced his support for them, and in his spare time even managed to draft an amendment to the colonial charter." Norash's tone made it clear what he thought of that. "If it's approved by the council, anything that violates cultural segregation preferences will be illegal."

She stared at Njal-Geir, who stood with the Amariahs and was addressing a group of colonists "Oh." *Damn.*

"Come with me." Norash led her back to an empty conference room, away from the many curious ears of his staff. "I want some answers."

She met his angry gaze. "So ask the questions."

"There are sixty thousand Skartesh on the planet, which almost equals the League's current species census." He went to the console and brought up the largest group of Skartesh protestors on the display. "Now that they're all here, I have to know what they're planning to do. What have you discovered from Amariah?"

"From what I understand, they've come here to prepare for their final journey to a place they call paradise. I have been unable to determine the exact location, but it's either Skart or a planet close to it," she admitted. "Rushan Amariah is supposed to lead them to this paradise, where they expect him to sacrifice himself, which they believe will then reverse the conditions on Skart."

"A thousand terraformer atmosphere exchangers set on high for a hundred years might reverse the conditions on Skart. Amariah, on the other hand, doesn't have a prayer." He made an impatient sound. "That's all you have for me?"

"At the moment, yes. I'll find out more—"

"Oh, no, you won't." He tapped the display. "I've got twenty thousand protestors assembling in three shifts around the clock. They're pissing on each other and anyone who comes near them, all because of you and Amariah. Your relationship with him ends, now."

Dair knew he was right. Continuing as they had would only aggravate the situation, and placating the outraged Skartesh would prevent more unrest. Yet even as she opened her mouth to agree, another word emerged on its own. "No."

Norash's massive head reared back. "What did you say?"

"No. I'm not going to end my friendship with Shan just because it offends his people." She folded her arms across her abdomen. "He'll have to do it."

Norash slammed one of his massive feet into the floor, creating vibrations that shook the entire room. "The only reason you established this relationship was to gather intelligence for me!"

"Things change. This conversation is over." Dair went to the door panel.

"You want to breed outside your species? Fine." Norash followed. "But I've got potential riots brewing here, Commander, not to mention a health hazard from all the bladder fluid being sprayed around. That's a little more important than your blasted private life."

"Is it?" Suddenly, irrationally furious, she turned on him. "Have I suddenly lost *my* rights under the charter? Am I no longer entitled to the same freedoms as the Skartesh?"

"Frankly, I don't care what you do. The Skartesh can cause a great deal of damage to this colony. They're not only highly unstable, but they now outnumber the rest of the population by two to one. You don't remember the mob riots we had during the Core plague." His gaze became shuttered. "You didn't have to pick up the bodies of the people who were killed."

That was the wrong thing to say to her. "I'm so sorry I missed that. I believe at the time I was too busy being *eaten* by the Core inside my mother's womb."

"If you're trying to anger me," the Trytinorn said between gritted teeth, "you're succeeding. Do I have to remind you that you're a League officer?"

"No. Have you forgotten that there are no regs governing my personal life, Chief? Because no one gets to do that but me." She spotted her stepmother entering the security building. "Why is Teresa here?"

"I didn't send for her, but maybe she can talk some sense into you."

Dair's stepmother saw them and hurried over. She was flushed and a little out of breath. "Dair, I'm so glad I found you. The pod elders are assembling. They've sent a summons for you to appear before them."

# CHAPTER
## THIRTEEN

*I am getting too old for this nonsense,* Dairatha mu J'kane thought as he hovered on the fringes of the swarming coastal pod. Every family underwater had heard the rarely given summoning pulse made by the elders; all of them answered as they would if there had been an attack on the pod. It was fortunate that Teresa had been with him, or he would have had no means to send word of the assembly to his daughter. *Now if only Jadaira isn't up flitting around in space.*

The place of assembly was at reef's end, a region at the southernmost point of their territory. It was held far out from the shore, near the border between the pod's sublittoral habitat and the deeper, bathyal zone of the outer currents. Here the water column turned cold, and the depths swallowed the reds and oranges of the filtered sunlight. It was a symbolic place for the coastal pod, the border between the familiar and the unknown, safety and risk. Few felt comfortable here, and pups were forbidden to stray into the zone by themselves.

It was, as his dam used to say, a place for serious business.

Some of the younger females skirted out of Dairatha's pathway, giving him the usual puzzled glances. As one of the largest and oldest males in the coastal pod, Dairatha should have impregnated a dozen of the best females in the pod over the years, yet he had never chased one of them in the breeding caverns. As a result, Jadaira was his only offspring. He was also older than nearly every male elder, yet he had never been selected to help govern the pod.

Taking a nonaquatic, monogamous mate had rearranged his life in several interesting ways.

Few might believe him, but he did not mind his unusual status. Although she would emphatically deny it, Teresa had sacrificed as much, if not more. And while he did not always understand what drove his unusual wife to do the things she did, he had never once doubted her devotion to him or Jadaira. Not since the night she had run from the surf, screaming for transport as she cradled the ruined body of his newborn daughter in her arms.

*Dairatha.*

He swung around to come snout-to-snout with Nathaka mu Hlana, the elder who had sent out the pulse for the pod to assemble. In their youth they had been rivals; Dairatha had won Kyara from Nathaka during her first time in the caverns. Over time they had become comfortable if somewhat distant friends. *What is it?*

*We cannot delay any longer.* The elder nodded toward the inner circle of the assembly.

*I have sent for Jadaira.* Nath's indifference to the situation angered him. *You waited until she was not in the water to call this assembly; now you can wait for her to arrive.*

*This is not solely about Jadaira. It is about all of us.*

He darted forward, showing aggression for the first time in uncounted years. *You will not drive my child away again, Nathaka.*

*We will do as is best for the pod.* Nathaka didn't wait for a response, but swam back to the inner circle.

Dairatha followed, his tense body language driving other 'Zangians out of his way. No one got near an angry male unless they wanted some new scars, and drawing blood this close to the outer currents might draw other, more dangerous threats.

The elders presented themselves, three males and four females, in a circle. They followed a ritual pattern of complex pulses and maneuvers that displayed both dominance and long experience in the sea. The pod fell silent and hovered, waiting for the first elder to present the matter.

Nathaka moved into the center of the circle. *Some of the land dwellers have sent messages to us. Newcomers are causing strife among them. They wish us to intervene on their behalf, so their territory above remains at peace.*

A female elder joined him. *Since they came to our world, we have welcomed these land dwellers. They in turn have done much for our pod and the other aquatic life here. Rarely do they ask anything of us in return.*

Dairatha could feel unease spreading among the 'Zangians around him. The pact they had made with the first colonists was sacred to them. Aside from bringing several members of the pods into their societies, and training them to do things no 'Zangian had ever done, the land dwellers had been the ones to identify why the aquatics' bodies were gradually changing to tolerate increasingly longer periods topside. Evolution was driving the 'Zangian race from the sea to live permanently on land. Because of this, the pods felt it was vital to maintain healthy relations with those already living on the land. The common view was that anything that threatened the pact threatened the future of the 'Zangian species.

Nathaka went up and breached the surface to take in extra air, then returned and positioned himself vertically in the water, the way he would on land. *The newcomers have made demands of the other land dwellers. They say these newcomers have taboos that make them wish to remain segregated from us. Do we respect their demands, and enforce the segregation, or do we challenge their beliefs?*

Dairatha surged forward. *I present opposition.*

The elders broke the circle and formed a line in front of Dairatha. *We recognize the son of Jakane.*

He tried to recall what Teresa had told him about the Skartesh. *These newcomers fear us because they fear water. These fears will not end with segregation, and neither will their demands.*

Several of the elders made signs of disagreement. Nathaka remained unmoved. *You cannot know the future, son of Jakane.*

*Nor can you, or any of us.* He turned to face the pod, who were milling around still trying to work out how any being could fear them or the water. *When my pup Jadaira was born, many here believed she would not survive. She was cast out of the pod to die. She did not, and today she serves among the land dwellers to protect us all.* He saw the expressions of shame and unhappiness finned all around him. *Jadaira is the reason this matter was brought to us, but she has done nothing but help these newcomers.*

An older female moved forward out of the pod cluster. *I have heard that one of these newcomers wishes to mate with Jadaira. Is this true?*

A small white form darted into the center of the assembly. *No, that is not.*

Dairatha released a stream of bubbles, signaling his pleasure and relief to his child. *I relinquish the opposition to Jadaira mu T'resa.* He swam over to where Teresa was treading water, just outside the pod, and glided his hide against her gentle hands. *Am I glad to see you.*

His mate took her regulator out of her mouth. *Did we get here in time?*

*I believe so.* He nudged her onto his back and, savoring the comforting weight of her, turned back to the assembly.

Dair never got tired of watching the moons set and the twin suns slowly emerge from the horizon. There were a few moments before full sunrise when the skies were the same color as the sea, creating an illusion that there was no topside, and water enveloped the planet.

*Maybe things would be less complicated if K-2 had been a water world,* she thought as she secured the tanks to the breathing rig she had brought for Shan.

Several weeks had passed since the elders had assembled the coastal pod to decide the issue of segregation between the aquatics and the Skartesh. Thanks to her father's opposition, Dair had been able to arrive in time to present her side of the story. What swayed the pod's opinion in her favor was her statement that through her relationship with Shan, she might show the Skartesh that they had nothing to fear from the water or the aquatic population. After an interval of discussion, the elders had elected not to support the move toward segregation, but only by a narrow margin.

Today, with Shan's help, Dair was going to prove once and for all that there was no need for separation between the 'Zangians and the Skartesh. She had helped Shan overcome his fear of the water;

now it was time to help the pod overcome their fear of Shan's kind. By bringing the Skartesh leader down with her and swimming with him among the pod, she would eliminate what naturally separated them, and Shan and her people would see firsthand that there was nothing to be afraid of.

As the horizon brightened from blue to green, she looked up at the male beside her. His expression made her wrinkle her nose. "Stop looking like I'm going to feed you to a 'shrike."

Shan remained still and rigid, the gentle breeze ruffling his fur. He had fixed his gaze on the endless roll of waves rushing toward them. "I do not know if I can do this."

"You can. You've done everything else, haven't you?" She went back to securing the straps of his O₂ rig. "Slip your feet into the flukes. We've practiced with a rig a dozen times now. You're a good swimmer, you've never had a problem with the equipment, and nothing bad happened, remember?"

"We were alone then." His heart pounded under her hands. "The grotto is . . . shallower."

"Water is water." If he went all stiff on her again, the way he had the first day at the pool, she might throttle him. "I'll be right beside you. My pod knows you're Skittish—I mean, they know it's your first time under. They're really wonderful; you'll like them. Plus Teresa and all the researchers will be . . ."

He wasn't listening to a word she said, Dair saw, and the fur over his eyes and his black mane had gone from ruffled to bristling.

"Shan?" She put her hand on his lean cheek and turned his head to make him look at her. The fear he was trying so hard to conceal—that he always tried to hide from her—made her impatience evaporate. "If you don't want to, that's fine. We'll skip it and go when you feel better about this."

"Today is the only day they will be opening the URD." He dragged in a deep breath. "I will go now."

*He says it like a man volunteering for his own execution.* She could keep nagging and make him more nervous, or she could concentrate on getting him into the water.

"All right. Let's go over the fin one more time." She had practiced the nonverbal signals with him so he wouldn't have to take his regulator out of his mouth to speak underwater. That would come later, when he was more comfortable using a rig. "What's the signal if you're out of air?"

Shan lifted his paw and drew it from left to right in front of his throat.

"Something is wrong?"

He extended his arm before him and turned his paw from side to side.

"Come and get me?"

He raised his arm over his head, and then swept it down toward his side.

"I'm okay?"

Shan touched the top of his head.

"Perfect. Remember when you're using the grips that I won't be able to see you, so tug once for 'yes,' and twice for 'no,' and three times for 'help.' Now check your gauges and test your line." She started stripping out of her clothes but stopped as she saw two figures emerging from the surf. "Here's my dad and Burn."

Her cousin reached them first, and ejected the water from his gill vents as he appraised Shan with a skeptical eye. "This should be amusing."

*You-desire-scar?* Dair finned.

Burn snorted some air through his vents and grimaced. "You'll be too busy nursemaiding the mouth-breather."

As Dairatha approached more slowly, his bulk cast a shadow over Shan, who tilted his head back to look up at the huge male. They studied each other in silence, long enough to make Dair start to question her own wisdom in pushing for this visit.

"You're rather small," her father finally said.

Shan nodded. "You are not."

"My daughter has taught me size rarely has anything to do with merit." Dairatha extended one of his fins. "I welcome you, Skartesh."

Seeing her father touch fin to Shan's paw made Dair want to somersault where she stood. Instead, she finished removing her skin shield and strapped on a special harness before she shook out her gillets.

Burn watched the other two males. "You're really not going to mate with him, are you?" he said, for her ears alone.

"I'd sooner mate with you."

"Good." He nudged her. "I'll be close if you need anything."

Sometimes her cousin exasperated her to no end, but there were moments, like this one, when he was more like a sibling. "Thanks."

Burn returned to the surf, dove under a wave, and took off. After exchanging a few more pleasantries with Shan, Dairatha did the same.

Dair itched to run and dive in after them, but she had promises to keep, and a Skartesh to get wet and keep from drowning. In a way she was more nervous than Shan was. "Are you ready?"

"Yes." Shan shifted the rig on his back before he walked with her into the sea. The long artificial flukes on his feet made his gait awkward, but he didn't stop until the water was up to their waists. Only then did he pause to take his last breath of topside air before clearing his regulator and fitting it to his mouth.

They went under the surface together, side by side, and the world turned to cool, liquid blue.

Normally Dair would have kicked off into a fast surge forward, but Shan had to orient himself to an entirely different environment. She limited her movements and focused on him, maintaining eye contact as she had in the pool.

*Can you hear me?* They had had no problems in the grotto, but the acoustics here were much different.

He touched the top of his head.

She glided around him, checking his rig one more time before she came up from beneath him. *Ready? Grab on.*

The harness she wore across her back had been Teresa's idea. She had originally developed it so that 'Zangian workers could help transport equipment and supplies to the URD dome. Since Dair had no back fin, it gave Shan something to latch on to.

Once she felt his paws slide into the harness's grips, she kicked off into a shallow forward dive. As she leveled out and swam slowly toward the seamount ridge, she felt his upper torso brushing against her back as he kicked his legs to help her. A strange but rather enjoyable sensation, rather like carrying a pup, which she had never been able to do.

*Do you want to go a little faster?*

Shan tugged once on the straps.

Dair steadily increased her pace. As she did, her heart rate slowed and her vision sharpened, while her skin and ears began to pick up subtle changes in the current. She could feel Shan's tense muscles relaxing as well.

*Hold on tight,* she said as they moved over one of the bigger coastal reefs. *I want to show you something.*

Teresa had warned her that Shan would respond differently to depth pressure, so Dair kept her dive gradual and easy. *We don't live in structures the way you do, but these are our cities.* She swam over an arc, scattering a small cluster of bright yellow *chinur. Teresa says there are more than twenty thousand different aquatic species on our coast, and that's not even counting the rock eaters and plants.* She pulsed an amused sound. *I'm glad I don't have to count them.*

Dair made a gentle circuit around the oldest part of the reef, where the water had bleached it to a thousand shades of white.

*This is my favorite spot.* She pointed to a squat red *sterbol* facing off with a green-and-black *lenga* bivalve. *You can see their colors so much better against the white.* As a nearly transparent *skimok* used bubbles to propel itself across her path, she caught it with her hand before saying to Shan, *Listen to this.*

The primitive creature held its air, swelling until it released a concentrated jet of bubbles and sound to escape her hold. Teresa had played Terran opera for Dair once, and the sound of an indignant *skimok* was great deal like a soprano hitting a clear high note.

She turned her head to see him studying the reef with narrowed eyes. *Big, isn't it? One of our reefs is about five times the size of the land dwellers' colony. They're so large you can even see them from orbit.*

Dair could have spent all day showing him the reef, but her parents would be wondering where they were, and Shan's tanks were good for only four hours of air. *Better check to make sure he hasn't changed his mind.* She swam to the surface, where Shan released his hold on the grips and began treading water as she had taught him.

She cleared the water from her gill vents and inflated her lungs to speak. "Last chance to go back."

His wet fur looked like a shiny hide now, and he looked much sleeker and, oddly, larger than he did on land. "You will bring me here again?" he asked once he had removed the regulator from his mouth.

"If you want." She glided around him. "Do you like it below?"

"It is . . . I do not have the words." There was true wonder in his deep voice. "Beautiful is not enough. Nor is amazing."

Sometimes she had the feeling that he was not being entirely truthful with her—he liked to hide his emotions—but it was clear that now he meant what he said. Playfully she nudged him from behind. "And you were worried about drowning."

"I think it might be worth it, to die in such a place." He glanced back at the shoreline, and then met her gaze. "I am grateful for this, Jadaira, and all you have done to make it possible."

"You're embarrassing me now." She presented her back to him. "Come on. It's time to meet the family."

Teresa and her team made the final rounds of the main dome room, discreetly checking for last-minute problems.

"Internal atmosphere is stable," T'Kafanitana said as she ran an internal on the envirocontrols. "Heat displacers are running a little above set point, but there are a lot of people here."

That there were. Teresa had invited every scientist and dignitary on colony to the opening ceremony, and not simply because she was proud of the work they had done. There had been a great deal of discussion in the wake of the 'Zangians' refusal to support the Skartesh's bid for segregation, and people were starting to take sides. Since most of the colonists never had the opportunity to view the 'Zangians' natural habitat, she thought it imperative that they see there was no threat from the native aquatics.

She glanced up at the transparent atrium, which allowed natural light into the dome and provided a view of the surface, some one hundred feet above. *Of course, if the roof suddenly decides to collapse, that may sway opinions more in favor of the Skittish.*

Ana Hansen slipped away from a group of representatives to join Teresa. "Everything looks very impressive, Teri." One of her cheeks dimpled. "Now quit thinking about dome breaches."

"If anything is to go wrong," T'Kaf said, "Dr. Selmar believes it will be today. Is this sort of pessimism typical of your species?"

"Only when you happen to be the Terran in charge." Teresa went to adjust the lighting at an emitter panel and then turned and scanned the room. "Okay. Is everyone here?"

"I see your daughter," Ana said, pointing.

Teresa took a moment to wave to Dair before scanning the room. "I think we're still short a few people."

Her assistant checked the guest roster. "There is one more submersible due to arrive."

"Would you go to Communications and check on their status for me, T'Kaf?" Once her assistant had departed, Teresa sighed. "I'm driving everyone sand-belly, aren't I?"

"Today you're allowed to." Ana guided her over to the refreshments table and procured two servers of white wine. She handed one to Teresa and raised hers. "To the future of underwater marine research, and your magnificent new research center."

"To plas ceilings that don't leak." She clinked her server against Ana's and took a healthy swallow. "Don't hit me for saying this, but you look tired. Problems with the council?"

"We're in discussion over the segregation matter, just like everyone else in the colony. The fact that the Skartesh are making this a doctrinal issue isn't helping." Ana cradled her server between her linked hands. "I could cheerfully thump a few of my fellow council members."

"Why are they making it a doctrinal issue?"

"It's actually quite a clever approach. The colonial charter was specifically authored to protect the rights of individual belief systems."

"So long as they don't violate the rights of others," Teresa tacked on.

"Some of the council members believe that by refusing to segregate, the 'Zangians are violating the Skartesh's beliefs." She rubbed her temple. "The debates over legal minutiae are the worst. To tell you the truth, Teri, half the time I don't know if I'm cut out for this position. I've been thinking about resigning."

"Dr. Selmar. Administrator Hansen."

Teresa was surprised to see William Mayer, and didn't bother to hide it. "Slow day over at the FreeClinic, William?"

"Not since I opened it." He looked around. "Do you have a minute? There's something we should discuss." He met Ana's gaze. "You don't mind, do you?"

She lifted her chin. "Not at all."

For a moment Teresa felt as if she had become totally invisible, and then Ana excused herself and moved back toward the other guests. William Mayer's expression was as remote and unreadable as always, but his sharp eyes never left her friend.

*Well, well, what have we here?*

She decided to refrain from commenting and instead took the physician back to the new lab, where she secured the door panel. "I don't know if you had time to read my memo, but I had the crews build some spare holding pens. This way we won't have to keep hauling the bigger aquatics up to the surface for injury and disease treatment."

Dr. Mayer went to the viewer, which showed a wide panorama of the coastal pod's reef system. "You've done an incredible job."

"I'm also likely to bore you to tears talking about it, and you're not here for the tour." She came to stand beside him. "So what's up?"

"We had a minor transport accident yesterday, and my EMTs brought in an unconscious Skartesh. It was the first opportunity I've had to treat one of them." He turned toward her. "She had a mild concussion but was covered with fire-retardant foam, so one of the nurses put her in an immersion tank to clean her up."

"And?"

"She went into shock, and I nearly lost her. Naturally, I did full scans and tox screens." He took out a data holder and handed it to her. "Here are the results. It wasn't due to the concussion."

Teresa turned over the holder. "I'm not going to like reading this, am I?"

"Not if you're in favor of bringing the Skartesh down here. They don't simply have an aversion to water. It can kill them."

She frowned. "How is that possible?"

"The Skartesh's early ancestors probably developed the instinct to avoid the disabling effects of saturated fur in a subzero environment, but over time it apparently has become a full-blown systemic trauma response. Immersion causes radical changes in the central nervous system. The heart, lungs, and brain all shut down nearly instantaneously." He nodded toward the holder. "I've included some documented cases of similar reactions in other hydrophobic species, but nothing to this degree."

"Good thing I didn't invite . . ." She paused and gave him a stricken look. "Rushan. Dair was bringing him today."

William tapped the viewer. "He's right out there, swimming next to your stepdaughter. He appears to be perfectly fine."

She peered out at the Skartesh, who was being circled by a number of curious 'Zangian males. "Why isn't he in shock?"

"That's what I want to know." He paused. "From what Norash has told me, the Skartesh believe that Amariah is the embodiment of their primary deity, and that he *can't* die. His ability to tolerate water may be viewed as justification for that belief. It will also be of great interest to the League."

Like everyone on K-2, Teresa knew about Cherijo Grey Veil, the Terran physician who had saved them all from the Core plague. Since Cherijo's escape, rumors had spread claiming that the Terran doctor had been genetically engineered with, among other things, immortality. After the death of Joseph Grey Veil, the man who had created Cherijo, Terran authorities had ransacked his lab, which contained evidence that she had not been the only clone bioengineered there.

Over the past four years, virtually every species with the technological capabilities had been pursuing the elusive promise of engineered immortality. If Rushan Amariah's DNA had been tampered with, and he was some sort of genetic immortal as Cherijo was rumored to be, that would bring the League back to K-2 faster than a Hsktskt blockade.

"We have to examine him." She checked her wristcom. "I'll speak to Jadaira and see if she can persuade him to agree to it. If he is like Dr. Grey Veil—"

"—then we have to do whatever it takes to protect him." William sighed. "I can't bring him to the FreeClinic. I suspect that my staff and I have been under monitor by the League since Cherijo escaped. They've probably tapped all of our consoles as well."

She smiled. "So we'll break in my new medical bay here."

# CHAPTER FOURTEEN

Once Shan's hold was secure, Dair submerged and headed for the URD site. She was eager for him to meet the pod and to see Teresa's work, and hoped that he felt the same.

*He's not panicking, and he seemed to like the reef. My father and Burn will help see that things go well from here.*

First impressions on both sides were important, however, and Dair didn't want Shan to be perceived as an oversize child clinging to her. When they were a short distance from the home, she stopped and turned under him so that they were face-to-face. *I want you to swim on your own the rest of the way.*

He nodded, then grimaced over the mistake and touched the top of his head.

Dair hadn't misinformed Shan about his abilities; he was a strong swimmer and could keep pace with her if she maintained a moderate speed. As they approached the pod, she clikked her usual greeting to the pilots gathered outside the URD before she swam down with Shan to the dome.

*They'll be opening the outer panels soon.* Dair peered through one of the viewports, and saw her stepmother talking to Ana Hansen. Ana noticed her, and Teresa smiled and waved.

Dair brought Shan back to where the pod had gathered, and mentally crossed her fingers as he looked around them while he treaded water beside her. *Don't be nervous. They just want to have a look at you.*

Saree was the first to approach them. *Jadaira, we were wondering where you were lagging.* She gave Shan a dubious look. *Greetings, Skartesh.*

He made the fin greeting sign Dair had taught him as the other pilots moved in around them.

*He does well, Commander,* Loknoth said. *So you like our water, mouth-breather?*

*There is no need to interrogate him,* Dair said, nudging the male away. She eyed the portal leading up into the dome's center entry pool. *Is my mother coming out, or does she want us to go in?*

*Your dam said for us to wait out here,* Saree told her. *She wants to make remarks before they switch on the power station.*

Dair noticed that most of the pod males were making casual passes over and under her and Shan to get a better look. Because Shan was furred, whatever scars he might have were covered, so they couldn't rank him the way they would another aquatic.

Shan had noticed, too, and seemed concerned.

*It's okay,* she assured him. *Our males are a little competitive, so they're checking you out. They won't hurt you.* She thought for a moment. *Do you have a scar somewhere that shows?*

He pulled back the sleeve of the close-fitting tunic he wore, revealing three parallel breaks in his fur that she had never noticed before.

*Good. Leave your sleeve rolled up; that will impress them.*

The water column brightened as the dome's exterior emitters lit up, and a familiar voice spoke from a specially adapted speaker system.

"Welcome to the opening ceremonies for Kevarzangia Two's very first underwater research dome," Teresa said. "Before we cut the ribbon, I'd like to thank the native Kevarzangians for permitting us to construct this facility here. There aren't many species that are friendly enough to invite two hundred strangers to set up a research lab right smack in the middle of their living rooms."

The pod pulsed their amusement.

"This facility will provide land dwellers with unprecedented access to the 'Zangian environment, and enable us to better understand and explore K-2's oceans and coastal resources," Teresa said. "Not only will it allow our science teams to live among the natives and work on the seafloor for extended periods of time, but the knowledge we acquire from the long-term studies we have planned will help shape the future of all the species that inhabit our world."

Dairatha came to hover beside Dair. *She loves this, doesn't she?* His tone changed from fond to wry. *Of course it means she'll be able to monitor you and me closer as well.*

Dair gave him an affectionate nudge. *I thought that* was *the real reason she built this thing. So she could check up on us.*

He snorted some bubbles. *I wouldn't put it past her.*

"The URD is an ambient pressure facility, which allows us to maintain a seawater interface entrance to the ocean in addition to our six pressurized air locks, to provide easy access for natives and divers." As Teresa spoke, emitters flickered as reference points for the different areas of the domes she mentioned. "The twelve-hundred-ton baseplate covers three acres and supports the five-tiered dome habitat, holding tanks, and laboratories. The facility maintains autonomous communications, database, environment, and life-support systems and provides well over two hundred thousand square feet of living and work space for the staff. Thanks to the latest in conversion and recycling technology, we can support up to three hundred individuals indefinitely. The dome was also designed to be portable, and can be completely disassembled and relocated within five rotations. Although I am hopeful that we won't wear out our welcome."

Dairatha glanced at Shan. *I like your friend better wet.*

*I'm really proud of him.* She finned her satisfaction. *He worked so hard to be able to do this.*

*You're not going to mate with him, are you?*

She gave her father a discreet kick. *I should, just to spite you and Burn.*

"I think that about covers the speech portion of our ceremony," Teresa said. "If my mate would be so kind as to get down here and cut the ribbon, we will officially open the Undersea Research Dome for business."

*At least someone appreciates me,* Dairatha said, and swam down to bite through the little red ribbon Teresa had tacked to the seam of the dome's protective-alloy outer panels.

Mechanical vibrations hummed through the current as the panels began to retract, revealing the large, transparent walls of the interior. The 'Zangians gathered in front of it, as curious to look in as the assembled land dwellers inside were to view them.

*It looks like a big bubble,* Saree said as she came up and flanked Shan. *They made this just so they can watch us?*

*Teresa said observation is just as important as providing the scientists with a natural sense of our environment,* Dair told her. *It's as close to living underwater as any of them will ever get.*

Saree shuddered. *Poor, deprived things.*

The panels were only three-quarters retracted when something made a metallic grinding sound and they stopped moving. From the activity inside and the way her father darted down to the bottom, Dair guessed that something had gotten stuck in the baseplate tracks again. Teresa had had several problems with curious *sterbol* crawling into them during the construction phase.

*Can you watch him for me? I'll go see what's wrong,* she told her wing leader, and then swam in front of Shan. *Stay here with Saree.*

In the outer currents, there were no assemblies. Anything that gathered was mindless food whose sheer numbers perpetuated their species, or whatever wanted to fight each other for the right to take them. And then there were the mogshrikes, most of which spent their entire lives in deep water, never once coming near land. They demonstrated how brutality and bulk defeated thought, and reigned supreme over the kingdom of rogues.

Onkar's years in the outer currents had changed him forever. Even after he had joined the coastal pod, it had been months before he could attend a gathering without feeling his belly knot and his teeth ache.

Now as he watched Jadaira with Rushan Amariah, he welcomed the old hunting instincts.

Onkar had tracked them from the moment they entered the water. It had been child's play to conceal himself in the shadows of the reef arcs, and edge close enough to listen to what she said.

*You can see their colors so much better against the white.*

He could see the Skartesh plainly against the long white length of Jadaira's back, where he clung to her like some overgrown pup. It made the blood pound inside his skull, but Onkar refused to let the fury that had been eating his insides for weeks ride him or make him reckless.

He would not give Jadaira the chance to get between him and the mouth-breather.

Onkar knew the moment he had been waiting for had finally arrived when Jadaira went to investigate a malfunction with the URD dome doors. He didn't speed toward his objective, but left the position he had taken on the outer fringe of the pod and kept his pace to an aimless, casual drift.

There was no hurry. Not until he was close enough to strike.

Jadaira had left Saree behind to watch over the Skartesh, but Onkar had anticipated that. The young female was a capable pilot, but she had yet to mate and as a result remained somewhat naïve about male behavior.

"Sorry about the technical difficulties, folks," Dair's stepmother was saying over the audio. "If you'll turn your attention to the holding tank on the north side of the dome, you can watch the release of our laboratory-hatched wrill."

As she explained the significance of introducing the bioengineered life-forms to the environment, Onkar stopped listening and located Curonal. The young male responded at once to Onkar's fin signal and swam over to meet him when Onkar was halfway to the Skartesh.

*Now?*

*As soon as they release the wrill, draw her away.*

The younger male eyed the pair. *I don't think this is wise, Lieutenant.*

Onkar turned on him.

*All right, all right. I'll do it.* Curonal backed away. *Just don't bloody the water.* He swam off toward Saree and Shan.

A few minutes later the holding tank opened, releasing millions of tiny crustaceans into the water. Their bodies caught and reflected the emitter light, temporarily dazzling everyone looking directly at them, which was the entire pod. By that time Curonal had lured Saree a short distance from the Skartesh.

Onkar shot forward, silent and intent. As he'd hoped, the Skartesh couldn't sense the change in the current around him, and he was able to glance off the smaller male's back without any warning. As he did, Onkar used the broad, sharp hook in his fin to snag the Skartesh's tunic and jerk him along after him.

His teeth ground into each other as he hauled the smaller male away. The urge to turn and attack the mouth-breather was so strong it nearly overwhelmed him. *Don't pierce his skin. Don't bloody the water.*

Onkar could swim faster than anyone in the pod, save Jadaira, and he used that power to drag the Skartesh far from the URD and the pod. He felt Shan struggling and drove his flukes into the mouth-breather's thrashing lower limbs, stunning the smaller male as he rolled into a steep dive straight to the reef bed.

A thousand years of tides had worn the rock eaters' calcium carbonate excretions into a smooth, flattened bed, so Onkar knew slamming the Skartesh into the reef would not puncture his derma. As he released the mouth-breather and pulled up, he watched the impact with intense satisfaction. As long as he did not make him bleed, he could do whatever he liked to him without alarming the others. Shan's body was literally packed with bones waiting to be shattered.

Halfway to the surface, Onkar made a slow turn into the current and used it to hurtle back down toward the Skartesh, who was still lying on his back, stunned and staring up at him. One of his arms was flung out; that became his target.

White flashed in front of his face, and a small, muscular body rammed his out of the current, flipping him head over flukes. *Stop it!*

Jadaira.

He righted himself in time to collide with her a second time as she struck again, but he used his fin hook to catch a strap of the harness on her back and flung her away. *Go back to your dam.*

*He's done nothing to you.* She came at him a third time.

*You think not?* He caught her and spiraled down with her until he had her pinned against the reef bed. She might be faster than he was, but she couldn't break his hold.

*You want a fight?* She bared her teeth. *Fight* me.

There was only one form of battle between a male and female, and another, far older instinct took over. *In the caverns.* That was where he wanted her, where he would have her to himself, where he would hunt her and catch her and take her, and everything would be as it should have been, from the moment he had first seen her. *Come with me to the caverns, now, and I will let him live.*

Jadaira went still as a distress pulse Onkar had not heard since his childhood screamed through the water column. He met her wide, disbelieving eyes and released her at once. The pulse meant the pod was being attacked, and there was only one thing on the planet that did that.

Mogshrike.

Dair swam down to Shan. *Can you get to shore by yourself?* He touched the top of his head. *Our pod is under attack. I have to go and help get the children to safety. I'm sorry.*

He made the okay gesture a second time, and turned toward the shore. Dair swam back to Onkar and without another word took off with him toward the URD.

*Why are they attacking?* From the screaming pulses being sent out Dair knew it was more than one, but still she hoped she was wrong. *They never come in this far, even in the winter cycle.* Then she saw the twin massive fifty-foot forms cutting their way through the darting, frantic pod. *Duo, there are two of them.*

*No. There are three.* Onkar caught her and made her circle to a halt. *By the dome.*

A third 'shrike, the largest, was battering the exposed transparent wall with its head. Its open mouth resembled a cave lined with thousands of teeth, each one as big as Dair's head.

Two were highly unlikely, but there had never been a report of three 'shrikes attacking simultaneously. Given the nature of the vicious, solitary creatures, they commanded huge areas of territory out in the deep water and gave each other a wide berth. Yet here were three in the same space. Not attacking each other, not drawn by some catastrophe that had bloodied the water so as to drive them to madness, but apparently cooperatively hunting together. In water too shallow and warm, according to Teresa, for their primitive circulatory systems to tolerate.

*We have to draw them off.* Frantically she scanned the other 'Zangians, but the biggest males were busy protecting the females and pups and darting around the third behemoth attacking the dome. The 'shrikes would never abandon so many to come after her and Onkar. Teresa might be able to signal topside for help, but it would take too long for the submersibles to reach them.

*There's no blood in the water yet.* Onkar bumped into her and when he had her attention, showed her the gleaming sharp curve of his fin hook. *After I lead them off, get the mouth-breathers to shore.*

Only in the worst circumstances did a male cut into his own hide with his hook and use the bleeding wound to lure 'shrikes away. It was considered the bravest—and stupidest—thing a 'Zangian male could do.

*You can't spill enough blood by yourself and still get away from them.* Dair brought his fin hook down to the soft flesh on the inside of her thigh.

He resisted. *I'm not risking you.*

The scent of his seminal glands heated the water around them. That meant breeding instincts were likely still muddling his thoughts, Dair realized, and that was something that she could use. He would come after her. They could lure them to the breeding caverns at the edge of the sublittoral zone, where she and Onkar could take refuge and wait them out.

*Don't you want to catch me anymore?* She forcibly dragged the end of his hook across her inner thigh, creating a thin, deep gash. *Come on.* As her blood welled out into the current, she moved back a few meters. *Come and get me.*

As soon as she saw him gash his own thigh, Dair darted away, diving down deep until she entered the strongest, widest current within the column flowing toward the URD. The channel would give her an extra boost of speed, but it would also take her very close to where the two 'shrikes were among the pod.

She knew they had picked up the scent of their blood when the sound of the big one ramming the dome ceased, and the two shadows went still. Blood was like an aphrodisiac to the enormous killers; it drove them insane with feeding lust. It was said that they would pursue even the tiniest aquatic for miles while it bled into the water.

Which was exactly what she was counting on.

'Zangians streamed past them as Dair and Onkar approached the two hovering, now almost motionless, outside the dome. The third had turned and was also giving its full attention to the taste of the water. A few hundred yards from the 'shrikes she pulled away from Onkar and swam around them to the right while he did the same on the left.

Being so close to the only predators her kind feared made Dair sick. Mogshrikes weren't just the largest aquatic on the planet; they had been designed by evolution to inspire instant terror. Their bodies were the color of old silt, with short, spiny black denticles covering every centimeter of their hide. Hundreds of mvrey clung to their bloated underbellies and backs, far away from the 'shrikes' cavernous mouths. The eight fins on their bodies were tipped with pointed plating that was even sharper than their serrated teeth, and the two elongated, segmented claspers extruding from their bellies were filled with a paralyzing toxin, which they whipped through large schools of fish to stun several hundred at the same time.

If she or Onkar caught even the tip of one clasper, they would be rendered helpless within seconds.

'Shrike couldn't swim backward, so as she passed them they had to turn to follow the scent of her blood. She streaked past Onkar and glanced back over her shoulder to see the third rejoining its two companions. *They're taking the bait.*

Despite their size, mogshrikes could swim as fast as a 'Zangian, and within seconds the three had eliminated half the distance between them.

Onkar was coming up quickly behind her. *Hurry.*

If they didn't reach the breeding caverns before the 'shrikes caught up to them, they were both dead.

Dair's muscles burned as she poured every ounce of energy into her pace. Swimming this fast blurred the light and colors around her, and she could no longer navigate by sight. She pulsed out a stream of sound and used the echoes that bounced off solid objects as directional signals. Swiftly she located the large rock formations and caverns that formed a wide, labyrinthine network at the end of the coastal pod's territory, and altered her direction toward one end of it.

Dair couldn't look back, but she could feel one of the 'shrikes snapping at her wake. She altered her approach, drawing closer to Onkar so that they left a trail of mingled blood behind them. A final pulse confirmed that she was only a few yards from an entrance to the caves, and as the ominous sound of gnashing teeth drew closer, she plummeted downward, hurtling herself toward that small gap in the rock.

# CHAPTER
## FIFTEEN

The entry cavern shook all around Dair as the huge bodies of the 'shrikes slammed into the outer rock, but she only slowed long enough to see that Onkar was still behind her. The chain of tunnels within the caverns was a maze of twists and turns, some only a few meters wide, but none large enough to admit the mogshrikes.

They were safe, and Dair could stop swimming, and congratulate herself and Onkar. Only she didn't feel like stopping just yet. She had never before navigated through the maze of caverns, and it would be fun to make a final run to celebrate their victory.

Dair glanced back at Onkar, who was still lagging behind her by several yards. He was so arrogant, thinking he could have her. She darted in and out of the maze, using pulses to find new openings and scattering little schools of bulge-eye and fiskates along the way. Feminine delight heated her blood. *I'm too fast for him; he can't catch me; he—*

Onkar surged over her, latching onto the back of her neck with his teeth as he forced her up into one of the small upper caverns. They broke the surface into one of the chambers where the air was kept fresh by a portable exchanger unit. Centuries ago, their ancestors had cultivated chokeweed to grow on the walls, to provide the necessary oxygen. There were still some greenish-brown stalks clinging to the stone.

What the 'Zangians did here required both air and water, but Dair knew he wasn't going to do that to her. They'd come here only to lose the 'shrikes.

She struggled a little against Onkar's hold as she expelled the water from her gill vents, but the exhilaration she felt outweighed her annoyance at being held. The scent rising from the water was having a decided effect on her, too. Males smelled so good when they were aroused. The strong, dark scent of him made her go lax, uncoiling her taut muscles, immersing herself in the feel of the water, of him against her.

They had beaten the 'shrikes. They had survived; they had saved the pod; they had won. She wanted to float in here forever, savoring the triumph.

His mouth left her neck. "I caught you."

"After being bloodied and chased by three 'shrikes." She turned to face him and rested her hands on his sloped shoulders. "You got lucky, Lieutenant."

"Onkar." He bent and nipped at the side of her jaw. "Say my name, Jadaira."

She let her head fall back and her gillets trail in the water so she could see his eyes. "Onkar." He had such loneliness in his eyes. "Why do you look so serious? Didn't you enjoy it?"

"I caught you." He said it with more assurance now.

"Um-hm." They needed to talk about other things, important things, but not here. Not now. It was enough to rest against him and watch his eyes and listen to the sound of his voice echoing low and soft in the chamber. "So what are you going to do, now that you have me?"

"You know what I want." The scent rising from his body intensified, and he wrapped a fin around her hips, urging her to him.

*Males. Always in such a rush.* Dair slipped down and around him, pressing her cheek against his broad back, splaying her hands across his chest. "Not so fast." She could feel and hear his heart this way, trapped between her face and palms. It was strong and rapid, and tension knotted his muscles.

"You delight in tormenting me."

"I do." She used her teeth to gently tug at his hide, following his spine up to where it joined his back fin. He made a sound when she licked the tiny drops of sweat that had formed in the crevice at the base of it, a sound that made her shudder. Parts of her felt suddenly hot and swollen, and she rubbed herself against him, seeking relief.

He groaned. "Don't stop." Slowly he swam forward, taking her to an odd recess carved into the stone just above the water line.

Dair held on to his back fin until they reached the edge; then she climbed out of the water onto it. She wasn't quite sure why she did, only that she wanted to sit there. The recess had been fashioned to support a 'Zangian female form, and while she didn't exactly fit, it was more comfortable than she expected. It also arranged her body in a strange position—at a back angle, with two channels spreading her legs apart—but her head and shoulders were supported, and the stone had been worn to a glossy smoothness.

There was something nagging at the back of Dair's mind; she should be remembering. Whatever it was, she wouldn't worry about it now. Now she only wanted only to tease Onkar some more. "We should get Verrig to design a cockpit seat like this." She wriggled a little. "I like it."

Onkar remained in the water, and stared up at her as if she had suddenly been transformed into some sort of deity. "Do you know how often I have imagined you like this?"

Absently she inspected the gash on her thigh, but it had stopped bleeding. "More than I have." She glanced at the chokeweed growing on the walls. Their seedpods contained a gelatinous substance that would seal their wounds and prevent them from spilling more blood in the water.

"A thousand times." He pressed his face against her belly, and then pulled back with a bewildered expression that swiftly cleared. "I forgot; she changed you around." He nuzzled her between her thighs, nudging and stroking her as he inspected the unique arrangement of her genitals.

"You shouldn't do that." Oh, but it felt so good.

He bit her there, but not hard. Only enough to make more blood rush in that direction. "Slide forward."

Still feeling dreamy and disconnected, Dair shifted. "Like this?"

"Yes. Like that." He dropped back down, but only for a moment. Water surged up around them as he balanced on his fins, hoisting his bigger, heavier body up over the edge and onto hers. He went still. "Jadaira, look at me."

She looked. As big and scarred and tough as Onkar was, she wasn't afraid. He had proved himself. He had chased her, and caught her, and now he would make her pregnant. She wanted to feel their pup growing inside her—

Onkar surged forward, forcing her legs wide as he entered her with the swollen, heavy penis that had emerged from his abdominal slit. Something inside her tore, and she shrieked, arching up under him, but the recess trapped her in place. Only when the outer rim of his slit touched hers did he stop to rest his cheek on the top of her head, his chest heaving as he dragged in air.

Pain induced rationality. This was not some idyllic dream; she was in the breeding caverns. The male buried inside her body had less than an hour ago tried to kill Shan. She didn't even know if Teresa and the others had survived the 'shrike attack. What had she been thinking?

He must have felt her stiffen under him, because he said, "It's too late for regret now. This was meant for us."

"I didn't know." She pushed at him. "I can't."

He lifted up a little and bent his head so that their gazes clashed. "You can. You are." He pulled her away from the rock and held her against his chest. "You will."

Onkar flipped backward, creating a huge splash as he took her back down into the water. She was so angry that she tried to disengage their bodies at once, but he did something inside her body to prevent that. Vaguely she recalled Teresa telling her about 'Zangian phalluses being prehensile, but the water and the smell of him were muddling her head again.

*We have to stop.* She tried to ignore how the pain had ebbed and how good and thick and solid he felt inside her. *Now, Lieutenant.*

*We are not soldiers here, Jadaira.* He flipped her over and over in the water, adding to her disorientation. *We are mates.*

She closed her eyes, fighting the dizziness. She could have protested and fought him, and maybe gotten away. He might not have caught her a second time. But the part of her that was 'Zangian and female wanted only to finish what they had started, to feel him move inside her and to take pleasure from it.

In return, Onkar would give her a strong, healthy pup. One who would not need dozens of painful surgeries to live an abnormal life. A new and terrifying part of her woke in that moment, a primal thing that grabbed her by the soul and demanded that child.

Dair opened her eyes as the spin slowed and they ended in a vertical position, bodies joined, faces only an inch apart. He had no expression, but there was something dark and terrible in his eyes. It was worse than the loneliness. She couldn't put a name to it, but it was something from before, from the time when he had come in from the outer currents.

*I don't know what to do.* Dair reached up and pressed her hand against his dark cheek. *Show me.*

She expected him to be harsh and demanding about it—he was so much bigger and stronger—but he was patient and tender instead. He swam upside down, cradling her against him as he taught her the movements that brought pleasure for both of them. He held her as the intimate friction hurtled her through her first peak, and he murmured wordless reassurance to her as she descended from it. He drew it out, treating her like something precious, and brought her to that place a second time before pursuing his own release.

Watching his eyes as his semen pumped into her made her understand why Teresa put such a high value on monogamy. To think another female would see him like this, would touch him, would feel these sensations, seemed absolutely unbearable.

It also explained why Onkar had wanted to kill Shan.

He swam back up into the chamber and gently disengaged their bodies before moving away. When his gill vents were clear, he said, "I regret that I hurt you. I did not know you would be so narrow inside."

"It wasn't bad, and it went away." She went after him. "Did it hurt you?"

"No. It was . . ." He looked up at the ceiling, then at her. "Do you really wish to know how it was for me?"

She felt suddenly defensive. "Not if you're going to make me feel terrible about it. It was my first mating, you know."

She already knew it wasn't his. Had the other females he had pursued been more appealing? When he caught them, had they pleasured him more? Obviously she had profited from his expertise, but it still made her want to bite him, hard.

Dair looked down at herself. She was nothing like other 'Zangian females. She didn't even have her slit in the right place. Shame and self-disgust swamped her. "I must be the ugliest female you've ever had."

"I keep forgetting how young you are." Onkar glided around her, pulling her back against his chest and supporting her as he had before, when they were joined. "You were beautiful to me."

*Beautiful.* She snorted to cover her pleasure at the compliment. "I'm white, runty, and nothing is in the right place."

"You are fast and strong and you drive me out of my head." He flipped her over to face him. "We will make many fine pups together, you and I."

She wouldn't know if she was pregnant for several weeks. Teresa could test her sooner, but she wasn't sure she wanted her stepmother—or anyone, for that matter—to know about this.

"There may be problems if I carry your child. My body inside is different, too." She looked down to where her belly pressed against his. "I want it, Onkar, but I want it to be normal. If there is something wrong . . ." She wasn't sure how he felt about voluntary terminations.

"Then we will abort it and make another." He nuzzled the side of her throat. "And another, and another . . ."

It was not the answer she wanted to hear. "Do you think Kyara should have aborted me?"

Onkar pulled his head back. "If I say no, you will accuse me of being untruthful. If I say yes, you will say I am cruel and unfeeling."

"Just answer me."

"I think it was a choice that only Kyara and Dairatha could have made. Had they disagreed, then the final decision should have rested with your dam." He nudged her chin up. "It was her body, Jadaira. That she chose to sacrifice herself to give you life was a supremely noble and loving thing, but it does not oblige you to do the same."

Dair's eyes stung. "No one has ever talked to me about it. Not even Teresa."

"There are matters that only a mate can share." He pressed her face to his chest so that her cheek rested over his heart. "Chances are that we will make many strong, healthy children together, so we may never face such a choice."

"I think we have to be practical." She couldn't imagine herself looking after a full brood, like some of the older females in the pod. "With my duties I will barely have time for one." If she had not caught a pup this time, she might confide in her stepmother anyway. Teresa knew a great deal about contraceptive devices; there had to be one that could be modified for her physiology.

"You will have all the time in the world." He stroked her back with his fin. "After you resign your commission, I will take over command of the pilots' pod."

"What?" She lifted her head. "I'm not resigning."

"You cannot remain in the military." His recessed eyes narrowed. "Not if you are pregnant with my pup."

"There are no regulations against it." She broke out of his hold and put some water between them. "Why would you think that I'd surrender my command to you?"

He came after her. "I am your mate now."

The blood in her veins ran cold. Above all else, Onkar was an opportunist, and he would use what they had shared just as callously as he would anything else that would serve his ambition. How could she have forgotten that?

Dair flinched as he slid his fins around her. "I can take as many mates as I wish."

"No." His touch changed, became less tender. "You will be exclusive to me, and you will do as I say."

Had he done this merely to take control over the pilots' pod? Was it possible that he was *that* manipulative, to use her own breeding instincts against her?

"Impregnating me does not entitle you to make my decisions. If I am pregnant." She had to get away from him, to clear the passion from her head and think logically. "The mogshrikes will have left. We should return and see if anyone was harmed. I have to check on

Shan, too." When she tried to slip away, his grip tightened. "Onkar, we're done now. Let go."

"Done?" He dragged her over to the wall and pinned her there. "Do you know what I was? What I can do to you? To *him*?"

On the other hand, perhaps opportunity had nothing to do with this at all.

"I can imagine." She didn't cower, but met his furious gaze squarely. "But that time is over, Lieutenant. You are a member of the coastal pod, and a military officer." She allowed her tone to soften. "You may be the father of my child."

"I will be," he insisted.

"Then you can't go back to what you were, or you will lose everything." She paused, and deliberately trailed her hand across his chest. "Don't you want to see if our pup will be dark like you, or white like me?"

"I don't care what color it is." Her voice and her touch were gentling him, though, and his became tender and considerate again. "Say that you will be mine alone. Say that, if nothing else."

She wanted to. If he had courted her, and established trust, she probably would have. She might have even pledged to be exclusive to him, the way her father had to Teresa. But this was Onkar, who had been her rival for as long as they had been in uniform. "Perhaps, in time."

He released her. "I am going to check if the 'shrikes are gone. Stay here."

"Easy now," Teresa said to Shan as they lifted the litter together.

As they carried the dazed, concussed Cordobel between them to the pressure lock, Shan glanced toward the wall viewer, where a repair team was sealing the last of the cracks caused by the 'shrike attack. Outside, a pair of 'Zangians were doing the same.

The dome had withstood the attack, but not without a price. The power conduits had shut down, leaving only the emergency generators to provide minimal heat, air, and lighting. Impact damage was not limited to the wall viewer; unsecured equipment had been flung everywhere and wisps of smoke still drifted from a bank of shorted consoles. Then there was the mayhem inflicted by the hysterical colonists who had panicked during the attack.

"This is the last one," the Terran woman told the medevac personnel waiting at the hatch. "We'll need three more submersibles to evacuate the uninjured guests."

"They're on the way, Doctor." The medics carried the patient into the lock to depressurize.

Shan went to where he would not be in the way of the repair crew, and looked out at the 'Zangians who had remained near the dome. Most of the females and young had been herded to shore earlier, and it was from them that he had learned how Jadaira and Onkar had lured the 'shrikes away from the dome.

"I tasted their blood in the water," the pilot named Saree had told him. "It was the only thing that could have tempted the 'shrikes to abandon their attack."

The distress in her voice made him want to comfort her, but he didn't know what to say. "Will it work?"

"I don't know." Her eyes had strayed to the horizon. "No one is faster in the water than Dair and Onkar. If anyone can elude them, they can, but . . ." She glanced at him. " 'Shrikes don't swim away from bloody water."

That was when Shan knew he could not return to the Skartesh compound without knowing what had happened to Jadaira. As soon as the medevac teams arrived to launch their submersibles, he had persuaded a nurse to allow him to return to the URD with them. When they arrived at the dome, he found the place in chaos, with Teresa and William Mayer caring for the panic-stricken colonists, many of whom had wreaked havoc and injured each other in a futile attempt to escape the dome.

Teresa joined Shan by the viewer. Blood of many different colors stained her lab coat, and there were strain lines around her mouth and under her eyes. "Have you seen her?"

"Not yet."

"I'm going to suit up and get out there." She hesitated. "I've got an extra rig; do you want to come along?"

He was surprised by the offer, but quick to accept. "Yes."

"Come on then."

Teresa stripped out of her clothing and put on a skintight, charcoal-colored garment. "It's a wet suit made of 'Zangian hide," she told him before he could ask. "I was permitted to harvest it from a pod member who died during the Core plague. It makes my mate's people feel more comfortable around me."

He glanced down at his own, light-colored tunic and trousers. "I should have considered that."

"So you do care what they think of you." She held up the tank harness for him. "Why is that, Skartesh? Your kind seem collectively immune to the feelings and concerns of others."

"Not all of them. I would like to change those who are indifferent."

She *hmph*ed. "Good luck."

After they had checked gauges and lines, Teresa took him to the seawater access pool, where a number of 'Zangians had taken refuge.

"I don't want either of us off our air lines, in case we have to get back here fast," she told him, "so any questions before we go?"

Shan shook his head. He did wonder why the 'Zangians around the pool were directing so many hostile glances toward him, but he would speak to Jadaira about it later. He put the regulator in his mouth and followed Teresa down through the open accessway.

Outside the dome a number of the largest males had formed a widely spaced, hovering line as they kept watch over the darker water of the open sea. Of all the 'Zangians, Jadaira had told him that the oldest males were the most aggressive when provoked, so he understood why Teresa motioned for him to stay a short distance away before she swam to her mate.

*We have seen no sign of them,* Shan heard Dairatha tell his woman. *They would have made for the caves.*

Burn left the line and swam back to Shan. *Why are you still here? Never mind, I know you can't talk. We are watching for Dair and Onkar. They should have returned by now.*

Dair's cousin seemed unusually agitated, but Shan knew how close they were. Carefully he took the regulator from his mouth long enough to say, *She will come back.*

*From your mouth to Duo's ear flaps.*

A large shadow fell over them. *Byorn, get away from this disgust-*

*ing creature.* The female who Dair had told him was Burn's mother gave him a cold look.

Shan frowned as he saw the odd way the big female was swimming—her flukes barely moving, and one fin not at all—but she managed to herd Dair's cousin off toward the front line.

A rapid pulsing sound, like the one Dair made in the grotto when he did something to amuse her, spread out around him, and Dairatha and Teresa hurried out into the darker water. Shan squinted until he could make out two forms approaching. One was large and dark, one small and pale.

Shan's eyes burned, and a silent howl ached in his throat. She was alive. She was safe.

Without thinking, he followed the line of males as they moved forward to encircle Dair and her parents. He needed to see that she was unharmed, and then he would return to the dome and leave her to her people. In his relief he completely forgot what had happened between him and Onkar earlier, or he might have thought twice about approaching them.

He got within only a few yards when the male beside Jadaira shot forward, ramming his head into Shan's chest. The force of the jolt sent him backward and tore the line leading from his tanks to the regulator. The stream of escaping air obscured his vision, allowing Onkar a second, harder hit before there were bodies and voices all around him.

*Onkar, get away . . .*

*His line . . .*

*His fault this happened . . .*

Shan tried to seal the break in the line by wrapping his paw around it, but the tear was too wide, and his regulator had flooded. Instinctively he swam up toward the surface, only to collide with Dair, who grabbed him and hauled him back down.

*You can't; your veins will boil. Hold on to me.*

Water was filling his mouth and nose, but he wound his arms around her waist and held on. As she streaked toward the dome, his heart slowed and he felt his limbs go numb. He barely felt her dragging him up into the access pool, and then he blacked out.

Hard hands pounded on him, and a mouth covered his and

pushed air inside him. He couldn't take it in, couldn't breathe, and then it felt as if his lungs turned inside out and he was choking out a wave of seawater onto the deck.

"That's it," Teresa was saying as she rolled him onto his side. "Get it all out."

Shan coughed and choked until he thought his chest would explode, but finally he ejected the last of the seawater and fell back, gasping in as much air as he could take. Dair hovered over him, her face as white as his ceremonial robes.

"This is the mouth-breather's fault."

He turned his head toward the voice, which belonged to Burn's mother. She was only a few feet away, hovering in the center of a group of 'Zangians who had come up into the access pool. Onkar was circling around them, his gaze fixed on Shan's face.

*If I get back into the water, he will kill me.*

Teresa began removing his rig. "He didn't tear his own line. Onkar did." She grabbed Dair before she could go after her lieutenant. "Settle down, or you'll start a frenzy."

Dair appeared furious. "I don't care!"

"You see? That leech-hided runt of yours should have never brought him here," Burn's mother said, her voice shrill. "He brought the 'shrike here. They would never have come if his stink hadn't been on the current."

"Don't be such an ignorant cow, Znora." Teresa helped Shan sit up. "He had nothing to do with it."

Dr. Mayer knelt in front of him and ran a scanner over his chest. "He'll need a breathing treatment to get the rest of the water out of his lungs."

"You can use exam room two," Teresa said. "We set that up to treat our divers."

"He cannot stay here." Znora heaved her bulk out of the water and limped toward them. Onkar and several of the big males followed her. "Take him back to shore at once, before he attracts more of the monsters."

"That is utter nonsense," Mayer snapped at her. "If his scent had brought the mogshrikes, they would have come as soon as he entered the water."

Onkar stepped forward. "Perhaps they did. If they were far enough away, it would have taken them some time to track the scent." He met Shan's gaze. "You have endangered all of us."

He was a threat to the big male; he could see that much. Something had changed between her and the lieutenant, who was now treating her as if she were a possession instead of a superior. Shan guessed whatever it was had happened while they were luring the 'shrikes away.

Dair put herself between Shan and Onkar. "Back off, Lieutenant." She was still shivering with anger.

"What Znora and Onkar say has weight with us, Jadaira," one of the other 'Zangian males said. "You will take this land dweller topside at once."

Her jaw sagged. "You can't be serious. You can't blame him. Not after what Onkar did."

"I think we're all suffering from delayed reaction to what was a very frightening experience." Teresa turned to her stepdaughter. "Sweetheart, you'd better go. See that your friend gets home safely."

Dair came to Shan and slipped an arm around his waist. "I'm so sorry about this. I never thought—"

"It doesn't matter," he said, his voice rasping out of his sore throat. "Let's just go."

As they walked toward the hatch leading to the submersible, Onkar followed them. "Jadaira."

Dair stopped, and turned. "What?"

"Another can take him back. You will remain here."

Jadaira's species might be polygamous, but her second was acting exactly as a Skartesh male would, defending a mate. The idea that she might have mated with this oversize bully didn't please Shan, either. *She deserves better than him.*

Dair stayed at his side. Her voice went chilly as she asked, "Was this your idea of how it should be, Onkar? Did you do it deliberately, to force me to this?"

The male wasn't paying attention to him anymore; his entire focus was on her. "You know what I want."

"I think I do now." She straightened to her full height. "Pending criminal charges, you're relieved of duty, Lieutenant."

# CHAPTER
## SIXTEEN

Dair said nothing when Shan refused the breathing treatment Dr. Mayer recommended at the URD. He had been through enough this day, and she had the feeling that if she did not get him back on dry land soon that he would never consider putting so much as a toe back in the water.

He was still coughing now and then, however, and once they were alone in the passenger compartment of the submersible heading back to shore, she offered to go with him to the FreeClinic.

"Teresa says water in the lungs can cause infections for land dwellers," she told him. "I don't want to see you become sick because of this."

"I will be well." He studied her. "What about you?"

Her gillets were the only part of her that didn't ache, throb, or burn, and her stepmother would probably want to give her a full physical. She wanted to find Onkar, and kill him. What she needed was to be left alone, so she could sort out her feelings. "I only need to rest." *And decide what charges to file against Onkar.* She gave him an uncertain look. "I'm really sorry about—"

"Don't apologize. It wasn't your fault."

One of the submersible pilots emerged from the helm. "Commander, you might want to come and take a look at this."

She accompanied him to the front of the small craft. Through the viewer she saw the thousands of white-robed Skartesh waiting on the cliffs. They had formed their dancing circles, but this time their movements seemed almost frantic. "*Duo's* light."

"I signaled Security. They've sent a detachment over to monitor them, but they think they're simply waiting for that Skittish you've got with you," the pilot told her. "We can reroute to another drop-off farther up the coast, but I'm sure they've already seen us."

Shan's followers wouldn't come near the water, but if she turned the craft around, they might do something drastic. "Keep going," she said. "Don't disembark with us. As soon as we're on land, take off."

The pilot nodded. "Maybe you should come, too, Commander. Those people don't look very happy."

"They never do." She went back to the compartment and told Shan about the reception committee.

"I did not inform anyone of my plans to visit the pod." He leaned his head back against the hull panel and closed his eyes. "Yersha must have had me tracked."

His dam's behavior made no sense, but little about his kind did. "Are you in any trouble because of this?"

"No, but it would probably be best if you and I avoid each other for a time." He looked at her. "I am not ashamed of our friendship, Jadaira. I think 'Zangians and Skartesh could learn a great deal from each other. But if my people insist on segregation . . .'"

She thought of what Onkar had said to her in the caves, how he had tried to tell her what to do. Shan had the same situation, only instead of one aggravating would-be mate, he had to deal with thousands of bigoted worshipers. "You could leave them." She certainly intended never to have anything else to do with Onkar.

"That would be extremely difficult now."

"I could help you do it." She put a hand on his shoulder. "Shan, you don't have to live like this. I know they think you're sacred and the answer to all their problems, but you deserve to have your own life. You have the right to find your own friends and make your own decisions. As long you stay with them"—she nodded toward the small viewport on the opposite wall—"they won't let you do that. You'll have to pretend to be what they want. Is that how you really want to live?"

He said nothing for so long that Dair was afraid she had deeply offended him. Just as she was preparing to apologize, he said, "You are right, of course."

The submersible came to a halt.

"Then let me help you. I'll tell the pilot to reroute us to another location. He can signal Security to meet us there. You'll probably have to issue a statement so we don't end up with a riot on our hands—"

"No, Jadaira. I need time to prepare them for this." He unstrapped his harness and rose. "My people can be unpredictable when under stress. Any sudden departure by me could lead to things much worse than mass protests."

"But you will leave them."

His dark eyes grew distant. "When they are calmer, yes."

That was all Dair needed to hear. The submersible came to a stop, and she rose. "Great. Let's go."

"You must stay here." Shan coughed and grimaced. "It will be easier for me to disperse them if you are not with me."

He was right, but it didn't keep her from resenting it. "All right."

Dair watched from a viewport as he disembarked and took the lift to the clifftops. There his followers surrounded him, swallowing him within silent walls of white robes.

As the Skartesh retreated, taking Shan with them, she felt a sense of icy foreboding. What had happened today—Onkar's attack on Shan, the attack by the mogshrikes, her mating—would not end here. It would spread, like ripples across the surface of still water, and there was nothing she or anyone else could do to stop it.

The door-panel chime startled Ana awake.

Evacuating the colonists from the URD had exhausted her, and when she had finally made it back to her quarters she had collapsed in her favorite chair. Clearing her mind of the remnant fear and anger she had been bombarded with during the attack had drained her even more, and she'd slipped into a light doze.

One that had lasted only fifteen minutes, she saw when she checked her wristcom. *Can't I have even an hour to myself?*

The chime sounded again. It was probably someone from the council. Onkar's attacking Shan Amariah—the incident was now on record, as Dair had filed a formal report—would not go unmentioned. Ana was an eyewitness; they would be expecting her to give them all the details.

After that, the infighting would start, politely disguised as debate. Council member Ktito would wave his tendrils around and upset council member Govech, who would then demand a recess so that he could soothe his frazzled nerves by eating something, which would make him flatulent, which would then make council member Ver-chitan-ixo ill, and then—

The chime sounded a third time.

"I'm coming." She pushed aside the Navajo blanket she'd draped over her legs and dragged herself to her feet and across the room. Seeing William Mayer on her corridor display made her mutter a word that she never permitted herself to use before she punched the audio. "Yes?"

"Let me in, Ana."

She rested her brow against the wall. *Make the excuse casual, positive, slightly remorseful.* "I'm so sorry, Dr. Mayer, but I'm in the middle of something. You know how it is, serving on the council. I'll stop by the FreeClinic later this week to catch up."

Ana disabled the audio and the chime and hobbled back to her chair. Before she could sit down, however, she heard the door panel slide open.

She swiveled around to face him. He was wearing his white lab coat and carrying a case. "I have a class-ten security lock on that door."

"I have a class-fifteen medical emergency override." He came to her, set down the case, and gave her the once-over. "There's blood on your tunic."

"It's not mine." She picked up her blanket and absently began folding it.

William turned his head, taking in the classic Terran Southwest décor of her living room and the wall of reproduction Anasazi rock art. "I didn't know that you collected Indian artifacts."

"Now you do." She wasn't going to discuss hobbies or her childhood home with him. "There's no medical emergency here, so you had no reason to bypass my lock." Which she would have upgraded to a class sixteen as soon as possible.

He loomed over her. "You were told to report to the FreeClinic for assessment."

That was all? She'd expected him to rant over some bureaucratic inconvenience. "I didn't need to; I'm fine." She went to put the blanket away, but nearly ran into his chest. "Thank you for checking on me, Doctor. I do appreciate it."

He tore the blanket from her hands and threw it aside. "Don't talk to me like I'm some sort of irate politician."

"Politicians don't let people see them become irate, Liam." But she might show him something he wasn't expecting, and soon, if she didn't get rid of him. "I'm sorry that I didn't report for the exam. I try not to use our medical facilities unless I absolutely must."

"You did it to avoid me."

So he wanted her to be candid, did he? "In part, yes." And to avoid making a fool of herself over the man, which would betray the memory of her poor Elars, who had been kind and thoughtful and gentle and *nothing* like Liam Mayer. "We agreed that you and I would do better to keep our relationship as it has been."

"Impersonal. Professional."

"Yes." She couldn't pick up any of his emotions, so what she said must have finally penetrated his thick skull. She put a hand on his arm to guide him to the door. "And now, since I really *do* have a report to prepare for the council, I know you won't mind leaving."

"After I examine you." He plucked her hand from his sleeve. "Remove your garments."

Ana blinked. "I beg your pardon?"

"Strip." He took a scanner out of his case and calibrated it. When she didn't move, he glanced up at her. "I am required to sign off on a security report about the physical condition of the colonists involved in the attack. You're the only one who hasn't been checked."

A laugh burst from her lips before she could stifle it. "Well, I am certainly not undressing, Doctor. You can scan me the way I am."

"But I can't make a visual assessment." He let his gaze drift over her, more slowly this time. "Take off your clothes for me, Ana."

The way he said that didn't even come close to being impersonal or professional.

She hadn't undressed in front of anyone else in years, for good reason. There were a dozen different excuses she could give him; primarily her right under the charter to refuse medical treatment. If she really wanted to be a bitch about it, she could even haul him in front of the council for personal harassment.

Instead, she folded her arms. "No."

"Very well." He pocketed the scanner and reached for the fastener on her tunic. "I'll do it."

Indignation flooded her, and as soon as his fingers touched the bare skin of her shoulder, she opened her mind to his to project her displeasure. Unlike telepaths, generally she could only pick up images and emotions from other beings, but the body contact and the fact that Liam was human made the connection much stronger.

Before she could show him how she really felt, the images and words from his thought stream poured into her head.

Liam wasn't thinking of examining her.

The images that came from his mind were clear, vivid, and shocking. The two of them standing naked in the middle of the barax colony, embracing. A long, erotic kiss. The mound builders sculpting tall sand castles around them. —*stubborn woman hiding something from me not going to walk away this time not like Rosalind*—

She was beautiful in his imagination. Her hair like spun gold, her body enticingly curved, and not a mark on her fair skin.

William Mayer didn't know the first thing about her.

Ana grabbed his hand to keep it from progressing down the row of fasteners. "If you want to keep your pretty illusions intact, I suggest you stop this instant."

"Reading my mind?" He seemed amused rather than offended. "You should have tried last night. I dreamed that I had you on an exam table, in restraints."

"How romantic."

"You had to be there." He focused on her mouth. "Which I could easily arrange."

"You're a doctor. We're colleagues." She wanted to feel outraged, but she couldn't. Not when she had had a similar fantasy that involved the top of her desk. "You shouldn't be thinking of me that way at all."

"I'm a man. We're designed to think that way. But if you don't like my fantasies, stay out of my head." He released another fastener, which made her flinch. "Ana. There's no reason to be ashamed of your body."

God in heaven, if it were only that.

"I'm not." *Show him, show him, and that will make him go.* She lifted her hands and released the last of the fasteners, then shrugged out of her tunic. The soft satin chemise she wore was semitransparent, and did nothing to hide her breasts.

Or her *togmot*.

Liam stared for a few minutes. "You're tattooed."

"I attained *togmot*," she corrected as she unfastened her skirt and let it drop to the floor so he could get the full effect. "Are you familiar with the condition?" When he shook his head, she turned around to show him the intricate red-and-brown patterns that also covered her back and buttocks. "Venyara semen contains an enzyme that alters the skin pigmentation of a female to match that of her mate. Elars was a crossbreed, or I would be completely covered with it, like a true female Venyar."

"Are the marks the same, like Jorenian Clan symbols?"

"No. They're unique to the individual, like fingerprints." Her mouth curled. "Which is why there is very little infidelity among the Venyar."

"Why do you hide it?"

"I'm not ashamed." On the contrary, Ana was proud of the designs that loving her mate had left on her skin. It was like carrying a part of Elars with her forever. "Many species disapprove of crossbreeding, so I dress accordingly. It's a matter of privacy, too. Traditionally Venyara females wear body veils, and don't display *togmot* for anyone but their families and mates." There, all her secrets were revealed. Now he would leave.

Only he didn't go. "I'm not your family." His clever fingers traced the outlines of a pattern that covered her right shoulder like dark red lace. "Were there any side effects?"

Of course he would see it in a clinical fashion. "Yes. Every time I look at myself naked, I miss Elars. Sometimes I burst into tears and cry for hours." She didn't want to discuss her dead love with him, not when she was two inches away from him and nearly naked. "Who is Rosalind?"

"My wife." He dropped his hand.

That startled her. "I didn't know you were married."

"It was a very brief relationship, and not one I devoted a great deal of time to. After I became chief of cardiothoracic surgery at Johns Hopkins, Rosalind accused me of neglecting her and left me. She died shortly after."

"I'm so sorry." She braced herself for a wave of psychic pain that never came. "How did she die?"

"A brain tumor. She never told me about the headaches, and when she left me she never sought treatment for them. Evidently I made her despise physicians that much. The autopsy was the real irony." His mouth flattened. "Rosalind's tumor could have been easily removed with one of the new neural procedures I had pioneered at Hopkins. The same work that I had accomplished while I had been neglecting her."

It broke her heart to hear the calm way he recited the story, as if it were nothing more than an interesting medical case. The fact that he was projecting no emotion at all disturbed her even more. "You shouldn't blame yourself, Liam."

"It was a long time ago." He took out the scanner and passed it over her, then checked the display. "Your heart rate is a little elevated, and your seratonin levels are slightly off, but otherwise you're in perfect health. I recommend that you eat something and get some rest."

He was leaving, just as she had hoped he would, and yet she couldn't bear to see him walk away from her again.

"Don't do this." She took his hands in hers. "Don't give me a glimpse and then shut me out again."

"I have no *togmot* to show you, Ana. Rosalind took it all with her to the grave." He raised one of her hands to his mouth, and brushed his mouth over the backs of her fingers. "You'll find someone again someday. Someone who deserves you."

*He genuinely believes that.* Just as she believed it would be a disaster getting involved with him. They both had tried so hard to keep the past sacred and inviolate, and their hearts safe. Yet the attraction they felt toward each other was only growing stronger, and something had to give.

Ana was used to making compromises, so it might as well be her. *I love you, Elars. I will always love you.*

She had only two garments left on her *togmot*-mottled body. It was a simple thing to shed them, and stand naked in front of him. It was a little more difficult to produce the offer. "I want you to stay. I want you to sleep with me."

His gaze dropped and darkened. "I have to get back to the hospital."

"You will." She pressed herself against him, and smiled as his arms came up around her, and his clever hands stroked her skin. "Later."


Dair ignored the signals from Teresa and spent the night in one of the emergency transfer tanks at Main Transport. Verrig parked it for her in the back of an unused hangar and promised to keep his night-shift crew out of her gills.

"Got a signal from that doc over at the FreeClinic." He watched her peel off her skin shield. "You're supposed to report ASAP for a physical. And before you give me grief about it, you're grounded until you do."

"I'm not surprised. That rounds out what's been a wonderful day." She laughed. "Thanks for the message."

"Go let them suck some blood out of your veins; it makes them happy. By the way, I think I've got that throttle where you want it." He motioned to the gstek with one of his artificial limbs. "If I don't, I'm sure you'll let me know."

"Thanks, Chief." She climbed into the tank. "Night."

It was small and cramped, but it kept her wet and allowed her to fall into an exhausted sleep that lasted until dawn, when the sounds of incoming shuttles woke her. Teresa's last signal was text-only: *CALL ME BEFORE YOU GO ON DUTY OR ELSE.*

Dair dressed and decided to go over to the FreeClinic before she faced her stepmother.

Dr. Mayer came to meet her in the lobby. He looked more remote than she had ever seen him before. "Would you come with me to my office, Commander?"

It seemed like an odd place for a physical, but she followed him into the administrative wing.

"No," he said when they were in his office and she began unfastening her flight suit. "I'll run your physical another time. We have other problems to discuss."

Had Teresa recruited him to grill her about the attack? "Okay."

"I have friends at command level, and one of them sent me a signal this morning." He accessed his console and turned the display screen around so that she could view the message. "Your second-in-command has been reinstated by quadrant."

As jolts went, that was fairly intense. "That's not possible."

"That's not all. Onkar has filed a request to take command of the pilots' pod and Bio Rescue, and after the debacle at the URD, he's probably going to get it." Dr. Mayer cleared the screen and sat down. "If the lieutenant is put in charge, I have no doubt that he will find a way to shut down the project."

Onkar would indeed. He had never approved of the medevac program and considered it a waste of time that could be better devoted to patrolling. He would also consider it appropriate revenge for her rejection of him as a mate.

"He will *not* be put in charge. I am still the ranking officer, and any petition he files is meaningless." Whoever had rescinded her orders was going to regret it, too.

"It means something to him. I've rarely seen anyone as determined as that male is." The Terran's dark eyes narrowed. "Commander, if this is something personal between you and him, resolve it. If it isn't, resolve it. We have worked too hard on this project to have it buried simply because your lieutenant has his snout out of joint."

That stung, but he was right. "I'll see to it immediately."

"There's something else you should be aware of. That quadrant supervisor, Njal-Geir, has also filed a petition on behalf of the Skartesh. They want to form a new, separate colony in the midlands, which will be reserved exclusively for their kind."

The second jolt was no less jarring than the first. "*Duo,* what for?"

"It's their solution to the segregation issue, and they're getting a lot of support for it. I'm not so sure it's a bad idea myself." His expression became bitterly self-derisive. "No, that's not true. I left my homeworld because of this type of xenophobic hysteria. I won't start supporting segregation now." A signal from his console caught his attention for a moment. "You'll have to excuse me; I'm needed in surgery."

Dair left the office and went to the lobby, where she accessed a public console.

Her stepmother answered the signal on the first blip. "Where have you been? Didn't you get any of my signals?" Teresa sounded frantic. "For God's sake, Jadaira, I was worried sick about you!"

"I'm okay. Where's the fire?"

"I should light one under your butt," her stepmother snapped. "For one thing, I need to run a check on your augmentations and give you a complete physical. Also, I'd like to know what the hell is going on with you and Onkar and that Skartesh."

"Dr. Mayer will check me out later. I mated with Onkar. Shan is staying with the cult." She watched her stepmother's face turn red. "I have to report for duty now. We'll talk later."

"You *mated* with *Onkar*?"

"That's what I said." She loved her stepmother, but it was time that she stopped treating her like a wounded pup. "I have to go see what I can do about having him thrown in detention now."

"Dair, wait. I have to run an internal scan on you. He might have ruptured something; you could have—"

She saw Shan enter the lobby. "Not now, Mom." By the time she had terminated the signal, he was beside her. "I didn't expect to see you so soon. I figured they'd make you pray with them for a couple of weeks."

"They might have, but something else happened." He looked around them, and then lowered his voice. "Jadaira, I need your help."

# CHAPTER
## SEVENTEEN

"It's sand-belly to keep doing this," Burn said over the headset. "You know that."

Shan glanced at Jadaira, who had strapped herself in and was running final diagnostic checks on her boards.

"I know," she said, then switched to flight control band. "Transport, Rescue One clear for launch."

He had never been on board a Hsktskt vessel, so it had taken him a few missions to orient himself to the unusual arrangement of the copilot's console. Someone had replaced most of the enigmatic Hsktskt control designations with universal standard, but the staggered triangular module had been clearly designed to accommodate one enormous multilimbed operator.

"I mean it, cousin," the gunner said. "If that old Terran finds out we've been taking your mouth-breather on patrol with us, he's going to detonate. I don't even want to think about what Onkar will do."

"Space Onkar and the old man." Jadaira glanced at Shan. "He's worried about Dr. Mayer."

"He's not the only one." Shan turned his head to look back at the entry panel to the rear section of the ship, where Dr. mu Cheft and the medics were preparing to receive the wounded. So far no one had discovered his presence, thanks to Jadaira and her cousin, but eventually someone would question why the new copilot of Rescue One never removed his helmet or gloves. "Do you really think it's possible to locate the *Kiremaran?*"

"If they're out there, we'll find them." Transport transmitted a go-ahead for their launch slot, and she returned her attention to her boards.

If they didn't find the missing freighter soon, discovery would be the least of Shan's worries. The council's debate over the petition for separatism was reaching a critical stage, and the news that a thousand Skartesh refugees had vanished without a trace just before reaching K-2 hadn't helped.

Shan knew the *Kiremaran* would not respond to signals from anyone but a Skartesh pilot, which was the reason he had used to convince Jadaira to take him along on her patrols. What he couldn't tell her about was the operative on board the ship, or the encrypted signal that had been sent to Shan's superior just before the *Kiremaran* disappeared, with scant details about a pursuing vessel of unknown origins.

Shan had been ordered to immediately determine if the *Kiremaran* had been captured or destroyed, or if the pilot had managed to evade the attackers and conceal the ship somewhere within the system.

Jadaira initiated launch, and the gstek ship rose smoothly into the upper atmosphere. Through the viewer Shan watched the sky turn from green to star-studded black, and the darting flashes of strafer hulls as the pilots' pod arranged themselves into standard escort formation.

"Patrol will take us on a circuit near Ninra, so we'll see what we can pick up from the surface on long-range," Jadaira told him as she leveled out. As the *Kiremaran* had been built on Skart, they had been scanning for one of the alloys unique to the planet. "If they're down there, we'll need to come back with a negotiation team."

*If they're still alive.* "How will the Ninrana treat them if they're discovered?"

"Oh, they'll be discovered." She grimaced. "Ninran has the best planetary security grid in the quadrant. Whoever survived will be imprisoned for seven rotations. If no one comes to negotiate their release, they'll simply disappear."

"Distress signal acquired, Commander," the wing leader reported over the flight band. "Patching through."

Shan adjusted his comm board to pick up the signal, which was

League-automated but sporadic and incomplete, as if the equipment transmitting it had been damaged.

    Space vessel . . . registry ALW76 . . .
    -tress critical . . . multiple injuries . . .
    -tain geographic location data . . .
    -diate evacuation . . . zero oxygen atmosphere . . .

"Shan, stay on monitor and relay a copy of that back to flight control." Dair altered her course to move to the front of the strafer pack and switched to flight band. "Saree, put a halo around the signal and track it to the source. Burn, run the registry; anything with a prefix ALW76 gone missing in this quadrant?"

As Shan transmitted the signal back to K-2, Burn funneled a list of ship registries to their displays. "Six missing vessels with that prefix," he reported. "Four troop, two passenger. The troops are long gone but both of the civvy ships disappeared within the last cycle."

"Three months down in zero oxygen?" She shook her head. "We're not going to find anyone alive."

"Commander, I've tracked the signal back to KOS-11," Saree reported, referring to one of K-2's twenty moons.

"Someone topside should have picked up the signal before this." Burn sounded skeptical.

"It's so faint I had to boost it for intership relay," the wing leader said. "With all the space-surface traffic and signal clutter, Transport could have easily missed it."

Jadaira cut off the audio and turned at him. "Could it be the *Kiremaran*?"

He wanted to say no, because the registry prefix was wrong, but the operative might have altered it to mask the fact that they were a Skart vessel. "It's remotely possible."

"Then we'll have a look." She initiated a relay to the rest of the patrol. I'm making a pass over KOS-11. If scanners pick up signs of life we'll land and assist. Watch my back."

"Acknowledged, Commander. Squadron, alter course and initiate sortie formation."

The strafers broke away from the close-escort configuration they had been flying around the gstek. Shan frowned as he watched them spread out. "What are they doing?"

"Standard sally procedure," Jadaira told him as she adjusted the heading and brought the ship about. "We don't fly escort formation when there's a possibility of attack. There's also our profile." She gestured around the helm. "We're flying a Hsktskt vessel. Anyone who sees us might think we're raiders."

He glanced at the comm panel. "I should start relaying a rescue signal now."

"Good idea. Ask them not to fire at us while you're at it."


Coordinating the repairs on the URD was a priority, but after receiving the signal from Dair, Teresa turned over supervision at the site to her assistant.

"I have to go kill someone now," she told the N-jui as she locked up the lab. "I'll meet you at the dome after he's dead."

"If you are not being humorous, you've just made me a material witness," T'Kaf informed her gravely.

She stopped at the wall where she and Dairatha had mounted all the photoscans of Jadaira at various ages. "I should take you with me," she said, studying one portrait of Dair leaping out of the water and into her open arms. "He's about as big as you are, give or take a hundred kilos. Think you could take him?"

"I could, but I have already eaten breakfast." The chemist grew serious. "Doctor, I think perhaps you should avoid close proximity to the male in question until you are not so . . . distressed."

"Then I wouldn't enjoy the homicide as much." She patted one of T'Kaf's multijointed limbs. "As much as I wish otherwise, I actually *am* joking." She hoped. "I'll see you later."

Teresa drove out to the flight line, and without a single qualm used Dair's own access code to gain entry to the military docks. Circumventing Transport security this way might land her in detention, but her daughter was avoiding her, and she wanted some explanations.

*I mated with Onkar.*

Dair had sounded so distant when she'd told her that, as if she were reporting some odd but not very interesting detail from one of her patrols. Yet mating was one of the most important biological functions for a 'Zangian female, and Teresa had talked to her daughter about it at least a hundred times.

*There's no reason to rush breeding. You're too young. You have your career to think of. You can always have pups later.* She'd even warned her about stressing her SEAL augmentations with pregnancy. *When you're ready, let me know and we'll talk about it.*

The shift scheduled to replace the one currently on patrol were in the main strafer hangar, running flight checks on their ships. The sounds of engines being tested and the smell of heated alloy and fuel blended with the shouts of the flight crew and the lower, more melodic voices of the pilots as they worked together.

Teresa located Onkar by looking for the largest body, and found him inspecting some complicated-looking panel on the far side of his strafer. Although by 'Zangian standards the former rogue male was extremely handsome, to her eyes he was too big and dark and scarred. It also made her feel nauseous to think of him making use of her little girl's body for his own pleasure.

*She's not a little girl. She's a woman. And if he hurt her, I'll kill him anyway.* "Lieutenant."

He straightened and eyed her. "Yes?"

"I'd like a word with you." She nodded toward an empty office to one side. "Now."

"I am busy." He turned back to the panel.

She folded her arms. "I can do it out here, if you'd like everyone to hear about you and Jadaira and what happened yesterday. Which she told me."

The other 'Zangians were making a show of ignoring them, but they had excellent hearing. The other, non-'Zangian flight crew had already stopped working and were staring at the two of them with keen interest.

"Very well." Onkar followed her into the office. "Say what you have to say."

"You really did it. You mated with Jadaira yesterday."

He inclined his head, but brought his fin up to block the punch she threw at his jaw. "Striking me will not change what happened, Dr. Selmar."

"No, but it would have made me feel a whole lot better." She put the length of the room between them. "Do you have any idea what you've done?"

"With luck, I've made her pregnant."

"With luck, you *haven't*." She leaned back against one wall and wrapped her arms tightly around her abdomen to keep from punching him again. "My daughter's body is not simply modified on the outside. After her birth we had to do extensive organ repair and transplantation."

"She told me. I know that there might be difficulties with her pregnancy because of it." He finned indifference. "If the pup is malformed, we will abort and make another."

"Dair might not live long enough to have an abortion." The way he started at that gave her some sour satisfaction. "Puts a whole new spin on the situation, doesn't it?"

Onkar went still and gave her his complete attention. "Explain what you mean."

"All 'Zangian females are born with an extra chamber in their hearts." She tapped the corresponding place on her own sternum. "The chamber is a standby, and only functions during pregnancy, to handle the increased blood supply and oxygen demands that the pup puts on the mother's body. Dair's heart was nearly destroyed by the Core, so we had to replace it."

"With what?"

"A small, modified Terran heart," she said. "We harvested it from one of the human children who died during the plague. It's healthy, but it won't support a pregnancy."

His expression darkened. "You never told her this."

"I thought I had time, her being so young." She threw out her arms. "For God's sake, if she were human, she'd still be in elementary school."

"She is not human."

"I know." She scrubbed a hand over her face. "I intended to implant a contraceptive device as soon as she showed the first sign of coming into estrus, but she never has. Her reproductive system isn't following 'Zangian biology; she's acting more like a human female. It must be the human hormones from the glands we replaced. She's become a selective breeder instead of a seasonal one."

Onkar went to the viewer and looked out at the pilots checking over the ships. "You knew this and yet you did not anticipate her mating?"

"I suspected it. I also thought I had talked her out of it. Until yesterday, she showed no interest in breeding whatsoever." Teresa felt like kicking him. "I also thought that she would come to me before she considered mating with anyone. She always tells me everything."

He checked his wristcom. "Jadaira will be returning from patrol in a few hours. As soon as she lands, take her over to the FreeClinic and run a pregnancy test. If she carries my pup, abort it."

His callousness took her breath away. "I haven't even told her that her life is in danger yet!"

"You had ample opportunity to do so before this. It's too late for explanations now." He left the viewer and paced around her. "After you abort the pup, implant your contraceptive device. I don't want to get her pregnant again."

"Stay away from her and she won't."

"She is my mate." He met her angry gaze. "I know why you came here, Teresa. You want to blame me for this, but the real fault of the matter lies with you."

"Oh, really?" She was going to kick him now, right in the genital slit. "How do you figure that?"

"You knew when you put those human parts in her that they would change her, yet you never told her. Everything you did was out of vanity." Onkar made a gesture toward her body. "You rearranged her so that she would appear physically to be more like a child of your own. Did you take away her ability to have a pup so that she would also be barren, like you?"

He'd accessed her own medical records. Records that he had no clearance to read.

Teresa felt the color drain from her face. "How did you get into my records?"

"Any data can be bought, for a price. I wanted to know what you did to her, and why."

"You know nothing about what I did for her, you bastard, and how *dare* you snoop through my personal data."

"I discovered a great deal about you and what you've done from the database, Dr. Selmar. Terran body parts are not the only organs compatible with 'Zangian physiology. There are a dozen other species you could have used." When she started to speak, he shook his head. "There will be no debate over this. When Jadaira returns, you will perform the abortion. If she does not agree, you will sedate her and then perform it."

"I can't do that," she said through clenched teeth.

"You have made all of her other decisions for her, without consulting her," Onkar said as he walked to the door panel. "If it saves her life, what is one more?"


Dair's neck prickled as they dropped out of the formation to get in scanner range of KOS-11's surface, which was shrouded by a thick orange haze that flowed away from the equatorial center toward the moon's poles, making it appear as if it were about to split in half. "Burn, talk to me."

"Nitrogen-methane-argon atmosphere, with a methane-ethane envelope above the meridional circulation. Surface temp at the equator is minus one hundred eighty-four degrees Celsius, one-seventh gravity. Ice soup." He made a chilly sound before adding, "No sign of orbital mines, energy shunts, or any other war gifts."

She glanced over as her uncle emerged from the back. "Monitor for methane ice storms. What else?"

"I'm reading organic matter and spikes from some kind of subterranean energy font. Stand by." After a few moments Burn said, "There's too much distortion from whatever is radiating down there, but I can confirm that something that either is or was alive is clustered within one kim of the signal source."

Daranthura came over to look at her boards. "Have you found them?"

"Any sign of the ship?" she asked her gunner.

"Negative, Commander."

"Not yet, Uncle." Dair sat back in her harness. "They might

have cannibalized the ship to make the subsurface shelter." She glanced at Shan. "If they did, they've been here awhile, so it can't be your missing freighter."

Shan merely nodded.

"Could they have maintained environment that long?" her uncle asked.

She eyed the position of the twin suns. "If they were smart enough to convert their recyclers to collect the oxygen molecules the nitrogen sheds during sunlight hours and covert them to $O_2$, maybe. This is assuming they had an enviroengineer on board to do it, and they were able to salvage their drive core as a power supply. Most ships carry six months' worth of emergency rations, so they'd still have food and water." She switched to flight band. "Saree, we're descending to three kim. Stay handy." She turned to Daranthura. "Better get your people and equipment secured, Uncle. Entry is going to be a rocky ride."

The gstek didn't like KOS-11's upper atmosphere, and let Dair know it through the helm controls. She compensated, watching her boards as she avoided the denser pockets of methane. Meridional winds buffeted the hull as they descended to within three kilometers of the surface, but the cloud cover didn't thin. "I've got to drop lower; I still can't see anything. Burn, I want continuous scans. You see one jag, we're out of here."

"Comman . . . ignal is . . . up." Saree's voice faded in and out of a wave of transmission static.

"Shan, see if you can boost our signal." She rolled the ship around a midatmosphere hailstorm and finally pierced the shroud of methane smog to get her first clear look at the surface.

Dismissed from surface probe readings as uninhabitable by K-2's colonists, KOS-11 had never been explored by anything but probes, so it was possible that they were the first living beings to see the mountains of fiery red ice rising about the frozen black plains. Evident geothermic activity had created a seething yellow-brown chemical lake that spread over a hundred kilometers, and Dair shuddered to think what might have happened if the lost ship had crashed into that lethal, landlocked sea.

The controls jumped under her grip, and she pulled back on the throttle. "I'm going to thump Verrig for not . . ." Her eyes widened as their course abruptly altered. "Burn? Are you inputting new override coordinates?"

"Negative, Commander. I'm just trying to keep the hull ice-free."

She punched her board, but the new course didn't change. "I've got a console failure," she told Shan. "Switching navigational control to you." Yet when she tried, the console didn't respond. "Burn, did you initiate an override?"

"No. Weapons have just locked down and are offline," Burn reported. "Whatever it is, I can't bypass."

She input the emergency override codes, but the ship's systems ignored them and made its own course adjustments. "Who the hell is flying my ship?"

Shan tried to override from his console; then his head whipped up. "Shut down your comm systems, now."

*Remote access.* All military vessels were equipped with access codes that could be transmitted from a remote location. "Acknowledged." The comm controls were also locked down, so she attempted to cut power to the system. "It's not working."

The ship was dropping lower and lower, barely one kim from the surface now, and was turning. From the smooth maneuvers it was obvious that an experienced pilot had seized navigational control.

She looked through the viewer at the cratered plane they were approaching. Sunslight glittered off the iced-over hull of an enormous alien vessel. "Burn, brief the crew; have them suit up and issue weapons. Disable all exterior access panels; then set up a barricade in the patient compartment."

"What is it?" Shan asked as she released her harness.

"Hsktskt." She went to the arms-storage panel and removed two pulse rifles. "Do you know how to use one of these?" At his nod, she tossed one to him. "Come on; we've got to get into envirosuits before they blast their way in."

"How do you know it is Hsktskt?"

"No one else would know the remote access codes, or have a compatible transponder to send them. Also, there's an abandoned troop freighter out there."

Dair led Shan to the back of the ship, where Burn and two orderlies were dragging heavy storage containers to form a makeshift wall down the center of the compartment. Her uncle was arguing over a pulse pistol with one of the nurses.

"You have to defend yourself," Daran was saying.

"I'm not shooting anything," the female Psyoran insisted. "We're healers, not soldiers."

"Okay." Dair strode over, took the pistol from the nurse, and pointed to a spot between the containers and the outer hull access doors. "Stand in front of the barricade. We can use the extra shielding."

The flower-faced nurse blanched. "But they'll kill me."

"Oh, I'm sorry, I thought you *wanted* to die." She held out the pistol. When she didn't take it, Dair added, "When they bust in here, you can always tell them that you're a healer. I've heard they don't eat medical people right away. We'll try to fire over your head."

The Psyoran snatched the pistol and marched behind the barricade. Dair retrieved two suits for her and Shan and dressed. As she did, she noticed that the other nurse, a placid-looking bovine creature, was directing some angry glances in their direction.

Dair went to her. "K-Cipok, right?" The nurse nodded. "Got a problem with my copilot?"

"He's Skittish." Her broad lips smacked with distaste over the word. "He shouldn't be here."

She slung the rifle over her shoulder. "The ship is under hostile control, we're probably going to be slaughtered like herd animals, and you still find the time to be a religious bigot?"

K-Cipok made a grunting sound. "Maybe he's in with the lizards."

"The Hsktskt toasted his homeworld." Dair cocked her head. "Do you want to know what he *really* is?" She leaned in close. "He's the only other person who can fly this ship. So, just in case I get killed, be nice to him, because you aren't going home unless he takes you."

Burn brought her a spare energy cell for her rifle and watched the bovine nurse hurry behind the barricade. "You don't think I could fly the ship?"

"I reviewed your last sim runs. You could maybe crash it somewhere." She grabbed onto an overhead strap as the gstek touched down. "Everybody behind the barricade. Now!"

# CHAPTER
## EIGHTEEN

Dair sealed her envirosuit and checked her O₂ tanks. Each suit carried three hours of air, and had enough insulation to withstand KOS-11's extreme surface temperature. The water circulating in her and Burn's skin shields would allow them to go another twenty minutes flat-lung before they asphyxiated.

If she took the crew out onto the surface, the envirosuits would keep them alive, but the atmospheric distortions might prevent Saree from tracking them. Dair doubted any of the medical crew were trained to evade capture in a hostile environment, so even if they did leave the ship they'd likely end up being captured or shot.

"I've got readings," Burn said as the gstek's engines powered down. He showed her the proximity scanner he held. "Five life signs, closing rapidly on our position. Faint displacer energy readings."

Burn surveyed the crew, who were bunched up behind the largest, center container in the barricade. "We're not going to make it, are we?"

"Don't swallow before you bite." She nudged him. "Deep with you, Byorn mu Znora."

He bumped shoulders with her. "At your side, Jadaira mu T'resa."

Dair turned her attention to the medics. "Listen up, people. We're going to be boarded by hostiles soon. Spread out and take position like this." She used one of the nurses to demonstrate the correct firing stance. "Keep your eyes on the access hatch but don't fire until I give the order. Hsktskt are poikilothermic, so the outside temperature will likely make them a little sluggish. When you shoot, aim for the upper chest only. Watch your cell meters and replace them before they zero out."

Shan drew her and Burn to one side. "We can hold them off for a time, but if they have superior weaponry and numbers, or use remote access to shut down our envirocontrols, we're finished."

"We can't surrender, if that's what you're trying to suggest," Burn said. "Hsktskt don't take prisoners of war. Dair and I will be immediately executed. You don't want to know what they'd do to you."

"Our priority is to protect the crew." She looked at both of them. "Whatever it takes, we do that."

Both males nodded as something heavy thudded into the outer hull.

"We're out of discussion time, boys. Take your positions." Dair moved to one end of the barricade, while Burn took center point and Shan the opposite end.

It didn't take long for the Hsktskt to pry open the disabled outer doors or bypass the air lock. Dair felt the yank of the pressure change as five gigantic, ice-pelted figures with displacer weapons drawn entered the patient compartment.

The Psyoran nurse let out a tiny, frightened squeak.

The foremost figure used a heavily clawed hand to remove the thermal wrapping from its head. Infolded green epidermal scales gleamed as it surveyed the barricade with huge yellow eyes. A thin black tongue flickered out from a lipless mouth to taste the air. "*Uhsstaaa.*"

Like all officers, Dair had taken a basic Hsktskt language course at the academy. *Uhsstaaa* meant "fodder."

She knew how to respond as well. "*Gjaenseee uhsstaaa.*"

"What does that mean?" she heard Shan ask Burn.

"He called us a meal," he told the Skartesh. "She told him that we're armed and dangerous food."

The other four came up around the first and aimed at the barricade, but didn't fire.

"Hold your fire." Dair watched as the center Hsktskt enabled a flat, triangular-shaped device. "Burn, what is that?"

"I think it's some kind of voice processor."

She frowned. Hsktskt soldiers never used translators; they considered it beneath them to address the enemy.

The big lizard hissed at the device, which produced a metallic voice that repeated a phrase in many different languages, including Terran: "State language setting."

"Terran," Dair called back in the same.

The Hsktskt adjusted the device and placed it on its throat, where it adhered to the scales. "I am LugosVar," he said, the -Var suffix identifying his gender as male. "We are without line. Surrender or die."

His four companions readied to fire.

"Without line?" Burn murmured.

"It means no ties to the faction; they're military deserters. They might have been left here to die." Dair thought fast. "We want to bargain," she said, then swiveled as one of the orderlies popped up and aimed for the speaker. "No, don't shoot—"

The orderly snarled something in his native language and fired at LugosVar. A return blast knocked him across the compartment, into a wall panel where he slid to the deck, leaving a wide trail of dark blood.

"Navas!" K-Cipok dropped her weapon and ran to him.

"Hold . . . your . . . fire," Dair grated. In a louder voice she called out, "What are your terms?"

"We have the ship. We have you," the Hsktskt replied. "There are no terms. Surrender or die."

She glanced back at the nurse, who with her uncle had stretched the orderly out on the deck and were working feverishly to stanch the blood pouring from a fist-sized hole in his chest.

"We have rigged the stardive to implode," Shan called out. "Leave the ship now or we will detonate."

He was lying, of course, but Dair still held her breath.

LugosVar made a sound of reptilian contempt. "You could not use the ship's systems to do so; we have locked out control over them."

Burn glanced at Shan and bared his teeth. "Who said we used the ship's systems?" he shouted at the lizards.

The Hsktskt removed the device from his throat and spoke in his native tongue to the other four, too rapidly for Dair to pick up more than a few words. Still, she got the gist. LugosVar wanted the ship more than he wanted the armed and dangerous food.

They had been left here by their own kind as a form of execution, and had likely endured unthinkable hardships trying to survive; of course they wanted the ship.

"LugosVar." Cautiously she stood, elevating her head above the protection of the barrier. "Bargain with us or we will detonate it. We have nothing to lose. You do."

"We are without line." He regarded her with something like exasperation. "What of your lives?"

"If we surrender, you kill us. If we blow the ship, it kills us. Either way we die." Acting on instinct, she put down her rifle on top of the barricade. "There is one way, however, that we can all get what we want."

One of the smaller lizards hissed something and leveled a pistol at her head. She didn't think it would shoot, and then Burn barreled into her at the same time the Hsktskt fired at her. The impact of his leap and the shot knocked them both to the deck.

"Cousin." Blood sheeted over one side of Burn's face as he rolled off her onto his back. He pressed his rifle into her hands. "At your . . . s . . . ." His eyes rolled back and he lost consciousness.

"Uncle!"

Daranthura was there a heartbeat later, cradling Burn's head and wiping away the blood. "Bring my case over here," he snapped at one of the nurses. To Dair he said, "He has a serious head wound and a cranial fracture. Navas is bleeding internally. Settle this and get us out of here."

She enabled Burn's rifle and walked around the barricade, presenting herself to the Hsktskt even as she targeted LugosVar. "Bargain now or you die."

The smaller one who had shot Burn tried to lunge at her, but LugosVar grabbed the back of its neck and held it. "Terms."

"Take the ship and leave us on the surface with your remote transponder." It had been strong enough to take control of the gstek; she could modify it to broadcast on her own flight band. "I'll signal my patrol squadron to allow you to leave orbit. When you're clear, they can come and rescue us."

LugosVar considered that for a moment. "Your other ships will destroy us before they retrieve you."

"I give you my word as a League officer," she said. "No one will fire upon you."

"We do not depend on the emotional assurances of the warm-blooded." The big Hsktskt nodded toward Shan, who like Dair had also emerged from behind the barricade. "That one will accompany us."

"The council meetings have been running overtime," Ana's assistant, Carsa, told William Mayer. "Administrator Hansen may not choose to return here when the current session ends."

The Tribirrun had nearly completed its gender transition, and the male hormones it had selected to release had made it bulk out, grow some sparse facial hair, and drop its vocal register three octaves. Unfortunately it had not acquired new work garments, so the feminine tunic it had squeezed into spoiled the new masculine effect.

William checked his wristcom; he had no scheduled surgeries and another hour before afternoon postop rounds. "I'll wait."

Carsa stroked his scanty purple beard. "You and Ana are . . . close now, are you not?" There was a distinct challenge behind the question.

"Why?" He could be just as aggressive.

"She has been very patient about my gender-selection process," the Tribirrun said, and folded its muscular arms. The empty bodice of its tunic sagged above them. "I would not be happy to learn that another male subjected her to any sort of emotional abuse."

He stared into the assistant's narrow but still luminous eyes. "Neither would I."

Carsa nodded slowly and went back to work, leaving him to his thoughts.

William almost wished he could get into some sort of verbal sparring match with the Tribirrun over Ana. It would keep him from thinking about the huge mistake he had made. Making love the way they had had been an irresponsible act. He knew he could seriously hurt Ana; he had already inflicted significant emotional damage before he had ever laid a hand on her. Rosalind had been the only woman he had ever loved, and that had ended in disaster.

He wouldn't let that happen again. Not to Ana.

The subject of his thoughts came in some thirty minutes later, carrying a large case of data chips and looking slightly harried. "Liam." She didn't seem surprised to see him. "I'm sorry, have you been waiting long?"

"Yes, he has," Carsa told her before he could reply. The Tribir-run switched off its console and rose. "My transition requires me to obtain some new garments, Administrator. May I be permitted to leave early?"

"Of course." She smiled at her assistant. "I'll see you tomorrow." After Carsa left, she set aside the data holder and went to the prep unit. "Would you like a cup of tea? I have oolong and herb programmed, or jaspkerry if you like Jorenian blends."

"Ana." He came up behind her and gently turned her around. "I didn't come here for tea."

"You came here to tell me that you think this is a huge mistake, and that you want to avoid hurting me, and that you still love Rosalind." She glanced up and made a face. "Sorry. I started hearing your thoughts about a block away from the building. Sex always strengthens the mental wavelengths between an empath and a . . . partner."

Something Cherijo Grey Veil had said about her once echoed in William's memory: *Being around an empath is a pain.* "Ana, let me explain."

She lifted her fingers and pressed them to his mouth. "You don't have to, Liam. I am very grateful that we had that night together. I didn't expect anything else from you, and if you'd rather revert to our former friendship, then I'll be happy to forget all about it."

She knew. She was grateful. She'd be happy to forget.

*The hell she will.* William put an arm across her back and bent to slide one behind her knees. Lifting her off her feet and carrying her into her office took only five seconds, and he was able to hold her and secure the panel lock at the same time.

"What are you doing?"

"It was the top of the desk, wasn't it?" He carried her over behind it, set her down on the edge, and casually swept the contents onto the floor before bending over her and easing her down onto her back. "How did it start again?" He pushed the hem of her skirt up over her thighs and pulled her hips forward so that the crotch of her undergarment rested against his erection. "Like this?"

"Liam!" Her whole face went pink.

"The huge mistake was waiting this long to see you as a woman. I've wasted too many years alone." He slipped his hands under her skirt so he could feel the silky patterns of her *togmot* against his palms. Making love to her had been like being caressed by a thousand satin ribbons. "It was irresponsible, having unprotected sex the way we did."

"Unprotected? But I—"

"I checked your medical records. Your contraceptive implant expired six months ago."

"Oh, God." Her eyes went wide. "I forgot to renew."

"I think we're a little old to start a new family, but we can always discuss it later." He nodded as he slid off her undergarment and cupped her damp mons. "Quite frankly, I can't love you the way that I loved Rosalind. I ignored her and neglected her and dismissed her concerns as unimportant." Gently he used his fingers on her. "I want to give you my attention and my affection and my companionship, whenever you want them." His mouth curled. "In between surgeries, anyway."

She reached down and covered his hand with hers, and her thoughts echoes clearly in his head. *Every day for the rest of our lives.* Out loud she said, "Does this mean next time we try out restraints and the exam table?"

Before he could answer her, or take their present position to a more satisfying level of intimacy, an emergency signal alert came in over her comm panel.

"Your patients *and* my politicians," she said as she reached over to answer it. "Ana Hansen."

"Administrator Hansen, security reports four-oh-seven in progress at Transport. Militia are responding."

"I'll be right there." She terminated the relay and sat up. "I have to go deal with this; I'm on call for prelim detention rulings, and they'll probably have a lot."

He tugged down her skirt and helped her to her feet. "Why are they using numeric codes?"

"To prevent widespread panic. We haven't had any of these since the plague." She took a stunner from her desk drawer and tucked it into her tunic pocket. "Four-oh-seven is the code for a civilian riot."

Although Dair had been forced to give up Shan as a hostage, LugosVar had kept his end of the bargain and escorted them back to the cannibalized troop freighter he and his men had been living in. Once there, he had allowed her to raise the strafers using the Hsktskt's powerful transponder. Dair had ordered the pilots' pod to allow the gstek to leave KOS-11 unmolested, and they had obeyed her. Once the Hsktskt had left orbit, it had taken a little more time to coordinate the evacuation of Rescue One's crew from the surface, as each strafer could only take one passenger. Eventually they had picked up everyone and returned to K-2, where Dair planned to drop off the crew and go after the gstek.

Her luck ran out as soon as she disembarked from Saree's strafer and saw Njal-Geir waiting for her, along with several thousand Skartesh.

"Appropriate a ship for me," she said to Saree as they walked down the ramp to the docking pad. "The fastest, most heavily armed ship on-planet. I don't care what it takes."

"Acknowledged." Her wing leader changed direction and headed toward Transport Admin.

The quadrant supervisor took his time walking over to her. "Commander mu T'resa. You seem to be short one vessel." He made a show of looking around. "Where is Rescue One?"

"I'll send you a report later." When she tried to move past him, two armed security guards got in her face. "You are interfering with an active military operation. Step aside."

"Flight control reported that you encountered a group of Hskt-skt marooned on KOS-11." Njal-Geir's smirk disappeared. "Are they presently in possession of Rescue One?"

He already knew, the fat little slug. "There were extenuating circumstances involved—"

"Please." He held up one of his pudgy hands. "Did you voluntarily turn your ship over to the enemy, Commander? Yes or no."

She was wasting her time even attempting to explain the situation to him. "Yes."

He shook his head like a disappointed parent. "And is Rushan Amariah still on Rescue One?"

"Yes."

"Commander, I'm placing you under arrest for multiple violations of the Allied League of Worlds Military Justice Code." Njal-Geir turned to guards beside him. "Take her to security for immediate interrogation."

She looked for Saree. "You can arrest me when I get back. Right now I have to go and get him."

"The only place you're going, Commander," the supervisor told her while Security seized her arms, "is a detention cell."

She struggled. "If I don't go after them, they'll kill him."

Njal-Geir appeared unmoved. "You should have thought of that when you surrendered your ship."

One of the Skartesh stepped away from the restless circles of white robes. It was Kabod Amariah, Dair saw as the guards secured her wrists behind her back, and he was headed directly for them.

Maybe the cult's avid devotion to Shan could be useful for once. "The Salvager was kidnapped by the Hsktskt," she called out in her loudest voice to the followers. "If I am released I will take a ship and bring him back to you."

Kabod's lips peeled back from his teeth.

"Shut up." Njal-Geir gave her a shove in the back. "Take her out of here, now."

Dair jerked away from the guards' hold. "If I don't go after him you will never see Rushan Amariah again. Your people will never find paradise."

The followers stopped dancing and stared at each other. Some began howling and tearing at their fur, while others surged toward Dair.

By then Kabod had reached them. "Idiot female!" He tried to strike her in the face, but Dair dodged out of range. "I will have the faithful tear you apart for this!"

Yersha emerged from the sea of white robes. "Kill the aquatic!"

"No!" a young female Skartesh shrieked. "She says she can save the Ennobled One! Release her!"

Other voices rose and more of the followers spilled onto the docking pad. The Skartesh began clawing and biting at each other. Nearby transport workers seeing this dropped what they were doing and rushed over to keep the Skartesh at bay, while the pilots' pod stepped between Dair and the mob.

"Pull your lines!" Dair heard Saree shout, and watched as the 'Zangians yanked the water supply lines from their skin shields and began hitting the Skartesh with the spray. The lupine species reacted as if they were being pelted with acid, staggering back to avoid getting wet.

The howling and shrieking rose in waves as Shan's faithful followers tried both to get to Dair and to protect her. Njal-Geir had pulled the two guards away from her and was hiding behind them while shouting entreaties for the Skartesh to calm down and let him handle the situation.

Someone came up behind Dair and released the bonds around her wrists. "I didn't think you guys were allowed to throw wild parties on the flight line," her stepmother said as she tugged Dair away behind a nearby abandoned cargo transport. "I heard what happened. Are you injured?"

"No." She scanned the available ships in the area, but the only ones fast enough to pursue the Hsktskt were the strafers. Luckily her fighter, the *Wavelight,* was docked only a few yards away. "I have to launch, right now, and get Shan back."

Teresa followed her gaze. "How are you going to do that in a fighter vessel?"

She closed her eyes and tried to block out the noise from the rioting Skartesh. "We modified the gstek for in-space docking so we could transfer injured from ship to ship. I can latch onto the hull, board the ship through the strafer's refueling hatch, and grab him."

"They'll either blow up your ship or kill you the minute you try to board them."

"Not if I can come around them blindside." She looked around the side of the hauler to see security forces moving in on the rioters.

"I'll take a couple of pulse grenades with me when I board. If they don't give me Shan, I'll set them off and destroy the ship."

"And yourself, and Shan?"

"They fell for one bluff. They'll fall for another." She reached over and hugged her stepmother. "I love you, Mom. If I don't return, tell Dad not to gorge too much, okay? He's getting as big as one of your houses."

Teresa clutched at her. "Don't do this, baby. Let someone else go."

She pulled her stepmother's arms away. "Tell Onkar . . . tell him I'm sorry." With that she got up and ran to her strafer.

# CHAPTER
## NINETEEN

Shan knew that he was going to be executed as soon as the Hskt-skt cleared Pmoc Quadrant space. The lizards had no use for him once they left League-occupied territory, and alive he would remain a liability that they didn't need.

It was not the end he had envisioned, but it was an honorable death. His superiors would find another way to save the Skartesh from outsiders and themselves. Even Jadaira would forget him, once she forgave herself for sacrificing him to save the others.

While he rationalized and accepted what was about to happen to him, a familiar, long-ignored voice snarled inside his skull. *Once you would have fought to your last breath, and now you go to your death like an old, toothless female.*

"You are quiet, warm-blood."

Shan looked up through the alloy lattice over his cramped cell to see LugosVar peering down at him. The Hsktskt leader had been the one who had tossed him in here after several of his men had knocked Shan around the compartment a few times.

A black tongue flickered out of the Hsktskt's toothy jaws to taste the air. "That female who bargained you away to me; was she yours?"

Jadaira had been as close as he had ever gotten to having a mate. He shrugged. "She might have been."

"She is strong and wise, as well as decisive. Her line will produce many fine warriors." LugosVar looked around the patient compartment. "What use were you warm-bloods making of this vessel?"

He saw no reason not to tell him. "Medical rescue of refugees and nonmilitary personnel injured in space."

The Hsktskt's tongue flickered out a few times. "You lie."

"Check the database. All the mission information is recorded." He rested his head back against one wall. "Will you be the one who kills me?"

LugosVar thought it over. "I can be."

"I am a warrior," he said, finally freeing the words he had buried inside him for so long. "I would ask you for a warrior's death."

Something like admiration gleamed in the Hsktskt's enormous eyes. "Then I shall grant you one." Someone hissed something close by, and LugosVar went away.

Shan closed his eyes and thought of the moments he had spent underwater with Jadaira, exploring the reef. There had been much ugliness in his life since Tarkun had drowned, and despair and anger over that ugliness had been the making of him. Yet from the moment he left the air and descended into that silent blue world of hers, he had felt cleansed of it. He could let go of the horror of Tarkun's death and remember the happy, energetic child his brother had been. He could forget those long months gathering survivors on Skart and herding them into ships to take them away from the only world they had ever known. In that brief time by her side, he had become himself again. His only regret was that he would now never have the chance to tell her how much she had given to him.

A claxon went off, signaling a hull breach. He braced himself, expecting to feel the air being sucked out and wondering wildly if this was to be his death, when something blasted the lattice hatch off his cell and a clawed hand yanked him out of the compartment.

As LugosVar held him dangling over the deck, Shan saw Jadaira standing at the far end of the compartment. She held enabled pulse grenades in both hands.

"Never trust a warm-blood to be truthful," the big lizard snarled.

"I kept my word, Hsktskt. You were allowed to take the ship, and leave KOS-11, and take Rushan with you. No one took a single shot at you." She glanced at Shan for a moment, evidently checking him for injuries. "Now I want him back."

"If I do not turn him over to you, you will release the grenades."

When she inclined her head, the clawed hand holding Shan by the neck tossed him across the compartment. "Take him. Once you are back on board your ship, we will attack."

"You would do better to get out of here." She calmly handed Shan one of the grenades before using her freed hand to help him up. "Time to leave. Through the hatch behind me."

At the doorway, he paused to look back at the Hsktskt leader. "Her line deserves to continue."

LugosVar's eyes narrowed. "Get off my ship."

Dair faced the Hsktskt as she backed into the hatch after Shan. Once inside, she sealed the door and bolted up the access ladder. "Hurry!"

He took the gunner's position behind the helm and looked through the viewing bubble that provided a 360-degree view of surrounding space. Somehow Jadaira had landed *on top* of the gstek. "Woman, you are insane."

"And you're welcome. Man the weapons; we might need them." She sealed the accessway, released the dock clamps, and rolled the strafer around in a maneuver so fast and radical that Shan nearly slammed into the control console. "You should also put your harness on, right now."

As they came about, a rapidly approaching formation of ships glittered off their starboard. He initiated long-range scanners and read twenty League strafers heading directly toward them. "Jadaira, your pod is here."

"No, no, no!" As they shot away from the gstek, she switched over to flight band. "Patrol, this is the *Wavelight*, Commander mu T'resa. I order you to break off your attack and take evasive action. Repeat, break off your attack."

"Negative, Jadaira," a harsh voice said over Shan's headset. "You are no longer in command of this squadron." Onkar began issuing orders to the other pilots to close in on the gstek and open fire from all sides.

She broke in on the channel. "Lieutenant, I have Shan on board. He's safe. Let them go."

Shan heard a curious sound over his headset before the channel went dead and Jadaira began to swear softly. "What is it?"

"He's jammed our transmitter." She maneuvered the *Wavelight* so that they were headed toward the patrol. "Are the Hsktskt enabling weapons or their stardrive?"

He checked his panel. "Not yet, but they're coming about."

"They're so distracted by me that they're not seeing the pod ships." Stars blurred into jagged streams of light as she rolled the strafer and dropped down, effectively flipping the ship around. "Fire on the gstek but don't hit anything important."

"What?"

"You heard me. Do it."

Shan targeted a nonessential portion of the storage level beneath the ship and fired. Pulse energy flared briefly at the point of impact, and then the proximity energy readings on his board began to climb. "They're enabling the stardrive."

"Finally." She changed course and flew away from the gstek, but kept the strafer between the gstek and the patrol.

Shan understood what she was doing. By positioning them between the Hsktskt and the 'Zangians, Jadaira was shielding the gstek, which would give LugosVar time to escape. "Why are you protecting them?"

"I don't renege on a bargain."

The patrol reduced speed, but one of the strafers broke formation and shot forward, firing at the gstek as soon as it had streaked past the *Wavelight*.

"Lieutenant!" Jadaira banked sharply to pursue him, and switched to an emergency signal downlink used only to transmit one-way distress calls. "Onkar, listen to me. They're deserters, not soldiers. Jink out of here before they lock onto you."

The rogue strafer never wavered, and a moment later the Hsktskt returned fire, landing multiple hits along the fighter's port side. Onkar's ship went into an uncontrolled spin while the rest of the patrol flew past the *Wavelight* and closed in on the gstek, firing from all sides.

An enormous ball of light briefly blocked out the stars on the port side, and Shan felt the hull shudder.

"The gstek has been destroyed," she said, her voice flat. "I'm going to get Onkar. Initiate shepherding procedures."

\*    \*    \*

Landing at Transport with Onkar's strafer in tow took two passes, as flight control spotted fuel leaking from the damaged strafer and redirected Dair at the last possible moment to the most remote pad. She set down in the center of a cluster of emergency response vehicles but didn't wait for biodecon or control clearance to exit the fighter.

Someone called out to Dair as she hoisted herself up onto Onkar's strafer and punched the canopy release. "Why did you do it? They let us go." The sight of her second effectively strangled the rest of her tirade.

The attack had damaged the cockpit's seals, and the interior liquid was gone. 'Zangian blood was spattered all over the navigational console. One of the displays had exploded and the shards had reduced Onkar's flight suit to shreds. Beneath it, his skin shield was ruptured in a hundred places and leaked reddish-brown-stained water.

His face was a raw, horrific ruin.

"*Duo*, no." Seeing him like this made Dair swallow bile. Onkar was the strongest and most aggressive male in the pod; he had lived rogue and endured things she could not imagine. Could he survive this? What would she do if he did not? "Why did you do it?" she asked again, her voice breaking.

"They were attacking you." Onkar blinked away some blood oozing into his remaining eye. "I defend my mate."

Just as she had tried to protect him. "Don't move. I'll get help." Dair jumped down to the pad and looked at the approaching response team. "He's badly injured and needs immediate evac to the hospital."

Six armed security guards with weapons enabled surrounded her. "Commander, you will come with us now," one of them said as he took out a pair of restraints.

She glanced over at the *Wavelight*, but Shan was gone. "I want the rest of the pilots checked for injuries as soon as they land."

Verrig came around the nose of the strafer. "I'll take care of them, Commander."

The guards restrained her before marching her to a glidetruck used for transporting prisoners, where they secured her in the back and posted two guards on either side of her. From Main Transport they took her to Security headquarters, where she was processed and escorted to a detention cell.

Dair remained silent throughout the entire process, and was not surprised when a somewhat bruised and disheveled Njal-Geir appeared outside her cell.

"I'm here to inform you of the charges being brought against you, Ensign." He removed a datapad from his tunic.

*Ensign?* It didn't register at first, until she realized that he must have used his authority to have her demoted. "File your charges," she said. "I don't care what they are."

"You should. The riot you caused spread throughout the colony. Aside from the property damage and injuries, the violence has created a significant bioenvironmental hazard." He gave her a nasty smile when she looked up. "The Hlagg embassy was attacked, and in the confusion many of their insects escaped. They have been unable to retrieve all of them."

The flooring creaked as the gigantic figure of Security Chief Norash approached the cell. "Supervisor, this is a maximum-security area. Unless you are volunteering to serve as counsel for the prisoner, you have no business being here."

"I will be prosecuting her," the little humanoid informed the Trytinorn.

"No, you won't. Quadrant command has refused my recommendation to try Commander mu T'resa before the colonial council. They have placed her on administrative suspension and have surrendered jurisdiction over her case to the ruling 'Zangian elders." As two 'Zangian males from the coastal pod joined them, Norash released the locks on the cell. "She will now be placed in the custody of her own people and tried by them."

Nathaka mu Hlana and the other six elders had already assembled the pod at reef's end and appeared to be in middeliberation when Dair arrived with her 'Zangian escort. Upon seeing her, however, the seven broke the ritual circle and led the pod around her as though they were retreating. No one finned a greeting; no one looked her way.

Being shunned as a pup had been bewildering, but Dair hadn't been a part of the pod at the time. Now that she had spent years among them, it felt a hundred times worse.

*Come.* Ethana, one of the guards, nudged her around.

*Where are we going?*

*To the looking dome,* he said, using the common 'Zangian term for the URD. *Your dam and some of the other mouth-breathers are there.*

Teresa would be there to defend her, as always, but if there were other land dwellers present, they had come only to condemn her. She flipped around to face the dark water of the outer currents, and wondered for an instant how it would be to turn her back on everything and swim away to lead a rogue's existence. Onkar had done it.

*We will make many fine pups together,* he murmured from the shadows of her memory.

Dair pressed a hand to the curve of her abdomen, and then slowly turned away from the outer currents and swam with her guards to the URD.

The aquatics assembled in and around the seawater interface entrance, with the older, larger 'Zangians staying in the water for comfort while the young joined the SEAL pilots on the surrounding deck. Teresa and her father were present, as well as her uncle and Dr. Mayer, but Ethana prevented her from greeting them.

"You are to remain silent unless you are directly addressed by the elders," he told her, and ushered her over to an unoccupied corner.

After making a pulse calling for attention, the elders, who had also remained in the water, gathered in a semicircle, signaling that they had reached a conclusion.

Dair had heard of things like this happening—she was fairly sure it was the way Onkar had been driven from his natal pod—and felt the numbness spread inside her. *I won't be given a chance to defend myself. Neither will anyone else.*

"The land dwellers are displeased with us, as we are displeased with them," Chetori mu L'noru, one of the female elders, said. "It is agreed that Jadaira mu T'resa and this Bio Rescue effort are the cause of both. Jadaira incited the Skartesh newcomers to riot, and is responsible for the theft and subsequent destruction of a valuable space vessel. Alien insect life-forms were released that were not recovered and may pose a threat to the land dwellers' health and food supplies. These are not the ways of the land dwellers. Our pilots have risked their lives and have sustained serious injuries while attempting to save near-dead beings, while one of the newcomers brought here attracted three predators to attack our pod. These are not our ways."

"If we had maintained proper distance and respect between our kind and the land dwellers," one of the older males called out, "none of this would have happened."

"This abominable alterforming that has been done to our kind is the true source of the trouble," Znora said. "We can never be land dwellers, and it should not have been permitted." She jerked her head toward Dair. "Cast her out, I say, and cease these unnatural modifications on our young."

"You are wrong, Znora. The 'Zangian species is in evolutionary transition," Dair's uncle said. "Our pups have larger, stronger lungs. The size and shape of our bodies are changing with every generation. We are becoming land dwellers, and we will have to leave the sea someday. All know this."

"In a thousand revolutions, yes," Znora sneered. "Every member of this pod will be long dead by then. We must decide for our time and our people who live *now*."

Saree stepped forward. "We pilots volunteered to become SEALs so that we could help defend our world against the Hsktskt forces during the war." She gave Burn's mother a hard look. "Are we now to be considered abominations for doing so?"

"Other ways to serve could have been found!" Znora insisted.

"You *still* have not forgiven Burn for not seeking your permission before he underwent alterforming?" The female pilot made a sound of utter contempt. "His umbilical cord snapped long ago, Znora. *Duo,* stop trying to sew it back together."

Strums of amusement swept briefly through the pod.

Saree addressed the other aquatics. "Even if we wished to return to our former selves—which we do not—the process cannot be reversed. We are SEALs forever. If you cast out Commander mu T'resa for being an alterform, you will have to do the same to the rest of us."

Dair straightened as Saree came to stand as close to her as the guards would allow. The rest of the pilots' pod followed.

"Very well, what of this ridiculous effort to save the near-dead?" Znora demanded. "As you said, Chetori, it is against our nature. We should not be involved in it."

"You cannot expect other beings to adhere to what you decide is natural or not," Dr. Mayer said. "We land dwellers value life above group convenience. For you to pass judgment on Bio Rescue is as ridiculous as it is for me to decide that all 'Zangians should become lifelong monogamists."

Dair noticed a disturbance in the pool, and saw Shan emerge from the water alone. He climbed out and Teresa went over to help him remove his breathing rig.

"What is he doing here?" Znora demanded. "Was there not enough damage the last time he polluted our waters with his stench?"

"I am to blame for the loss of the ship and the tensions between our people," Shan said, ignoring the big female. "I asked Commander mu T'resa to take me with her on patrol. My presence put the crew in danger, and my rescue caused the gstek ship to be destroyed and the injuries to your pilot. If you wish to censure someone, it should be me."

Chetori eyed Saree. "There was another injured?"

"It was Onkar. He was taken to the trauma facility as soon as we landed."

The elder female turned to Dr. Mayer. "Do you know how serious these injuries are?"

"The lieutenant lost one of his eyes and suffered extensive tissue damage to the upper extremities, torso, and face. As soon as his condition stabilizes, I will be performing his surgery." He gestured toward Dair. "Commander mu T'resa saved his life. She towed his ship back to Transport and alerted flight control to ready emergency evac for him."

"She also told him several times not to engage the Hsktskt vessel," Saree added. "He would not have been injured had he followed orders."

"She was relieved of command, was she not?" Chetori asked.

"Yes, but—"

"Onkar then had no obligation to follow her orders. He was protecting a mate, and her efforts to recover him are yet another example of going against what is natural." Chetori motioned for Dair to be brought forward, and the guards guided her out of the corner. "Jadaira mu T'resa, do you dispute any of the charges made against you by the land dwellers?"

"No."

Chetori gave her an odd look. "We will allow you to speak in your defense if there are circumstances to be considered that have not yet been raised."

Dair could argue reasons, but the truth was that she *had* caused a riot and she *had* stolen a ship. The pod was already shunning her; all the elders had to do was make it official. "I have nothing to say."

The seven retreated under the water to confer, but it didn't take them long.

Nathaka mu Hlana delivered their decision. "The seriousness of Jadaira mu T'resa's offenses merits permanent exile from the pod. However, the involvement of the land dwellers, the intentions behind her actions, and the fact that this female is part land dweller herself are considerations that must be weighed in the balance. It has been decided that Jadaira mu T'resa will leave the pod and live on land in exile for one season. At the end of that time, the elders will decide if she should rejoin the pod or remain with the land dwellers."

Dair closed her eyes.

"The pod agrees to segregate ourselves from the Skartesh, and any future alterforming or physical experimentation of any kind on our kind is prohibited." Nathaka turned to Dr. Mayer. "Further participation by 'Zangians in the Bio Rescue effort will be determined by Onkar when he has returned to duty."

The guards moved away from her, and Dair saw the pilots avert their eyes as she walked toward the pool. Behind her Teresa was protesting, but nothing she said would change the elders' decision. Until they decided otherwise, no 'Zangian would come near Dair, speak to her, or even look at her.

Once again she had become invisible to her own kind, but this time it might be forever.

Dair slipped into the water and let the numbness take over as she darted away from the URD. After one last, long look at the dark water of the outer currents, she turned and swam toward the shore.

# CHAPTER
## TWENTY

"I never thought I would hate any species more than my own," Teresa said as she sat staring at the food that had grown cold on her plate. "But 'Zangians are passing them fast."

Ana finished her own meal and signaled the attendant. "You haven't met an Ichthori yet. They make xenophobia seem as offensive as a facial tic."

The two women sat in one of the new full-service multispecies restaurants that had opened on the perimeter of the Trading Center. Ana had insisted Teresa meet her for lunch, although she had yet to tell her why.

Teresa knew her friend hadn't found a legal precedent that would overrule the elders and allow Dair to rejoin the coastal pod. Over the last week she and Dairatha had already exhausted all possible avenues of reconciliation with the 'Zangians.

Ana had quickly picked up on her frustrations, judging by the sympathetic look she gave her as she asked, "How is Jadaira?"

"Devastated. She went off to that forest retreat of hers and hasn't come back. That they could do something like this to anyone is wretched enough, but to Dair? After what she's been through?" Teresa shook her head. "It's horrible."

"It's politics, Teri. Even underwater, they have them." Ana nodded to a hovering attendant, who removed their plates from the table before giving her an inquiring look. "Just coffee, please."

"Nothing for me, thanks." Teresa gave him a vague smile before propping her cheek against one hand. "How do you stand it? Deal-ing with all these pompous asses day in and day out?"

"Someone reasonable has to," Ana said. "Otherwise, the pompous asses take over and then you'd have little Terras springing up all over the galaxy."

"Amen. So why am I here wailing over bureaucrats and my poor kid?"

"Two reasons." Her friend lowered her voice. "I need your opin-ion on something personal, and something classified."

Teresa perked up. "Personal? Since when?"

"Since Liam Mayer and I became lovers." Ana templed her fin-gers and tapped her lips.

"You and Dr. Dignified, lovers? Get out of town." Teresa chuck-led, and then stared at her. "God, you're serious. When did this hap-pen?"

"Right after the 'shrike attack at the URD. We're debating whether we'd like to share quarters or not." Blond brows arched. "Is it so hard to believe?"

"You? No. Him, yes." She rolled her eyes. "Okay, so I have to know—what sort of a lover is he?"

"If only the desk in my office could speak." It was Ana's turn to laugh. "Your jaw is going to bounce off the ground any minute."

"Actually I might be dragging it across it for a while." She pressed a hand against her heart. "On your *desk*?"

"And his. We're trying to be considerate of each other's work schedules." Amusement gleamed in her eyes. "Here I thought you and Dairatha had already gone through the underwater version of the *Kama Sutra*."

"We probably have." She regarded her friend. "Seriously, I think if you and William want to live together, you should do it. You'll both have to make some adjustments and compromises, but life is short, Ana. Second chances are few and far between."

She nodded. "Thanks. I'll let you know how it goes. On the classified front, Chief Norash met in private session with the coun-cil yesterday. He received an alert from quadrant regarding Jadaira's flight records, which showed that she had accessed reports of miss-ing ships. Someone at command noticed something odd about the list and decided to follow up." Ana accepted a server of her favorite dark brew from the waiter and took a test sip before she added, "Thirty-two ships in the last cycle have vanished."

She frowned. "That sounds like an awful lot of ships."

"For a noncombat zone, it is. It's also interesting that they were all following the same basic route through our system." Ana set down her server. "They sent no distress signals and left no energy trails or debris fields. They simply disappeared without a trace."

Teresa saw a cluster of Skartesh exiting the Trading Center, followed by a group of adolescent male Omorr, each of whom bounced along on a single leg. "What's the quadrant planning to do about it?"

"Since the missing ships' last known positions were all within a few light-years of K-2, they've asked Chief Norash to investigate. They're worried it's a move by the Ninrana." Ana followed her gaze and rose from the table. "I'd better go have a word with those boys."

"I've got the tab." Teresa paid the waiter and left the restaurant with her friend.

Outside, the Omorr youths had encircled the Skartesh group and blocked their only exits from the immediate area. The oldest of the adolescent males was bouncing back and forth in front of the largest of the lupine beings.

"Segregation by definition means to uphold practices or policies that separate beings of different races, classes, or ethnic groups in education, residential, commercial, and/or public amenities," the boy was telling the Skartesh's apparent leader. "For a species so strongly in favor of such discrimination, you do not restrict yourselves or your movements in the least and yet you expect us to do so when in proximity to you. Why is that, Skartesh?"

"Damn, that's one smart kid," Teresa murmured.

"They're all like that," Ana told her. "You should see some of their mathematical graffiti." As they drew closer, she politely cleared her throat to draw the attention of the Omorr boys. "Gentlemen, do we have a situation here?"

"That depends on your perspective and interpretation of the charter, Administrator Hansen." The oldest boy's gildrells, which formed a white, beardlike mass around his mouth, undulated lazily.

"Our parents have told us to avoid this species, yet they continually choose to invade areas designated for common use by colonials. They spray their body fluids around indiscriminately, which constitutes a biological hazard. They seek to amend our charter with a clause that will allow them privileges and territories superior to those afforded to every other resident species, yet protest against such is considered by governing officials such as you to be illegal."

Ana looked directly into the boy's angry eyes. "I will wager my entire compensation for the cycle that your DNA matches the Omorr cells found at the scene of some fairly nasty algorithms calculating the generational incidence of brain-damaged offspring produced by the self-fertilization techniques among lupine species."

"Cells shed all the time. One can't ambulate through life in a plas bubble." The Omorr youth made a casual gesture with one of his three arms, and his companions moved away from the Skartesh. "However, if such devices are available, you would do well to place the Skartesh inside them."

"You asked why we wish distance from you," one of the young Skartesh said in a rasping voice. "This is why." One of the older females tried to silence him, but he faced the Omorr. "We do not wish you to be incarcerated. We only wish to be left alone."

"So you are capable of speech. Could you also control your bladders?" the Omorr demanded. "I for one am weary of hopping over your puddles of piss."

The young Skartesh male bared his teeth. "It is our custom."

"On my homeworld, it is custom to challenge to the death someone who offends as you do," the Omorr said. "If I can refrain from my customs, you can refrain from yours."

"I am not afraid of you, One-leg," the Skartesh male sneered.

"That's enough," Ana said. She turned to the group of Omorr. "I know you boys don't think this is fair, but one of the challenges of living in a multispecies society is to develop tolerance and patience. I've always thought your species was too evolved for this type of petty behavior. Just because the Skartesh are unwilling to change does not justify this kind of harassment."

"We are not unwilling," the Skartesh male said. "We are prevented by our elders." When the older followers made sharp sounds of protest, he eyed the Omorr. "I will be beaten for speaking to you. Will your parents do that to you?"

"No." The Omorr looked uncertain. "They *beat* you?"

Before the young male could say another word, the older Skartesh dragged him off with them.

Ana sighed. "The next time you boys try to pick a fight, remember this."

The oldest boy muttered a low affirmative and led his friends off in a direction opposite of that taken by the Skartesh.

"Nicely done." Teresa watched the elegant bounce-strides of the Omorr youths as they retreated. "Want to have a go at Dair for me?"

"I'd like to talk to her tomorrow, if you don't mind. I think this situation with the missing ships justifies reactivating the Bio Rescue program. I know Norash could use Dair's help finding them."

"Did he ask for her?" Teresa knew the security chief had been particularly upset over Dair's involvement in the Skartesh riot at Transport.

"Not yet." Ana checked her wristcom. "But he will, in about an hour. After I finish meeting with him."

What had been Dair's sanctuary had become her prison. She could no longer take any pleasure in the seclusion and quiet of the grotto, or the confines of the pool that now seemed unbearably small. Denied the sea and the sky, she felt as if the world had contracted around her, forming a suffocating cell.

The elders had chosen their punishment well.

Now that Dair was a disgraced exile, she had nothing to do. Teresa had come to see her several times, her manner surprisingly tentative, and had repeatedly asked her to come and stay at her dwelling. Her stepmother had promised to enlarge the immersion tank as much as possible and even to stock it with some live food.

"I know you're upset, honey," Teresa said, "but you can't stay out here forever."

She had little interest in what the future held, and said as much when she refused Teresa's offers. Instead of arguing with her as she

usually would, her stepmother had expressed her love and then retreated, promising to return.

None of the pilots' pod came to see her, not even Burn, who had
been released from the FreeClinic, according to Teresa. She felt sure
it was more due to the elders than anything she had done. Zangian
adherence to a decision to shun one of their own was absolute. Dair
felt no animosity toward her squadron. Had she been told by the
elders to shun one of them, she probably would have done so.

It was bitterly amusing that she had finally been granted her secret wish. All these months while she had been so consumed by carrying out her duties, making Bio Rescue a viable operation, and
managing the balance between the pod and the land dwellers, she
had often wished for time away from it all. To be more like Teresa,
with her quiet solitude and her need for privacy. Now she would
have all the time to be alone that she could want. Maybe even the
rest of her life.

"Jadaira."

She clearly heard Shan call to her as she floated on the surface of
the pool, but staring up at the lacy green-and-red canopy of the trees
seemed more interesting than conversing. She heard the rustle of his
tunic as he removed it, and felt the ripples of surface displacement
as he slipped into the pool.

"Jadaira, please answer me."

She lifted her head a little. He looked gaunt, tired, and had lost
a small amount of weight. There was a part of her that took pleasure
in seeing that. "Why?"

"I am your friend."

"You *were* my friend." She let her head drop back to its pillow
of water.

"This happened because I took advantage of our friendship." He
swam over and treaded water at her side. "I wish to make amends."

Another who wanted to "fix" things. "You cannot. Go away."

"If you had a choice, would you have your body restored to its
natural state, as it should have been when you were born?"

Dair changed her position from horizontal to vertical. "I have
had enough surgery to last a lifetime."

"It is not surgery. It is touch healing." He was utterly serious. "You know the Omorr practice it, don't you?"

"Did you not hear anything the Elders said? I am *shunned*, Rushan." She flung a hand in the direction of the cliffs. "The pod are no longer permitted to see me, and if I violate this ruling by returning to the sea, my people will make my exile permanent. Some three-armed shaman putting his membranes on me isn't going to change that!"

"What about your child?"

"I have no pup."

He shook his head. "I saw the change in you after the 'shrike attack. You carry a child inside you."

There was no way he could have possibly known that. Even Teresa admitted that it would be another month before they could determine whether Dair was pregnant or not. "If I am, then I will have it here, alone."

"There is something wrong with your heart as well." He put a paw to her chest. "Even now I can feel it laboring. You must be healed, and soon."

Why was she listening to his ridiculous predictions? She shoved his arm away. "Leave me alone."

"You have to let me help you."

She had needed him a lot sooner than this. Now it was too late. "You want to help? Go away."

Dair looked over and saw Burn and several of the other pilots standing on the bank before she averted her gaze. "I am not permitted contact with you."

"We will not tell anyone. The Skittish will not, either," Burn said as he began to strip. "Will you, mouth-breather?"

"Go and talk to your stepmother," Shan said to her. "Tell her what I said. It's important, Jadaira." He swam to the bank and climbed out.

Burn deliberately splashed him in the face as he dove in. With only a few flips of his tail, he made a complete circuit of the small pool and joined Dair in the center. "How can you tolerate this? It is a puddle."

"Onkar said the same thing." Still, it was *her* puddle.

"Ah, yes, Onkar. He returned to duty yesterday and assumed command," Burn told her. "His first order was to shut down all Bio Rescue operations indefinitely."

"I don't care." She looked over at the other pilots, who were watching them. "Why did you come here?"

"You are still our commander, and we need you." Burn went on to detail the briefing they had been given by Security Chief Norash, who had reports of more than thirty ships vanishing within K-2 space. "We will be actively searching for them."

"Not as Bio Rescue."

"No, we go as a military patrol. We intend to file a request for your full reinstatement with command." He gave her a nudge. "No one knows the region better than you."

So they wanted her back, but only because she knew the system better than the rest of them. "Don't file any request on my behalf. I am not rejoining the League."

"Thousands are missing and possibly stranded somewhere. Command expects us to find them." He made an exasperated sound. "We agreed when we started this that we would help these people. Now, because of some misunderstandings, you would ignore so many in need?"

First Shan, now Burn. "None of them have ever helped me. They have taken away my rank, my work, my family, my friends, and my home. Now I have only my life and this puddle." She met his confused gaze. "Would you have me sacrifice what little I have left to provide aid for people who will never be grateful for it?"

"We never did it for the gratitude, cousin," he reminded her. "You said it was the right thing to do. That is enough for us."

Two alien butterflies flitted over the grotto. Dair looked up at the insects and felt her heart harden. "Then you should have no difficulty in following your orders. Just keep me out of it." She turned her back on him.

Burn left the pool and, after a brief discussion, led the pilots' pod away from the grotto. Dair swam to the opposite bank and hoisted herself out. Her heart did seem to be beating a little faster than usual, but she was angry with the pod, and disgusted with herself.

*I will tell Teresa about it the next time I see her. It will make her happy; she can run more of her tests.*

She stretched out on the grass and returned to her study of the canopy, but she no longer found any amusement in trying to arrange the patches of light that shone through the leaves into stellar constellations. She flung an arm over her eyes. Driving away Shan and Burn had given her some temporary satisfaction, but now she felt more alone than ever.

Dair fell into an exhausted, uncomfortable sleep, waking only when the green sunlight had dimmed to a dark purple. As she listened to the unfamiliar sound of insects chirping around the grotto, she scratched at her shoulder. Her skin had grown unbearably dry. Although she should have jumped back into the water, she only turned onto her belly and buried her face in the cool, sweet-smelling moss.

A strange appendage curled over her shoulder. "You need to get wet."

*Onkar.*

Dair flipped over, prepared to taunt him for not shunning her as he should, but the words died in her throat.

Before attending the academy, Onkar had submitted to the same amount of alterforming as the rest of the pilots. Now much more work had been done, replacing his missing eye, gillets, and facial tissue. The new eye was completely black; new, matching gillets sprouted like Terran hair from his formerly bald scalp; and paler new skin had been grafted to his upper face. His fins had been modified as well, and made to look and function like hers, but were also covered in the same, lighter skin as his face. Barely healed scars covered his fins, neck, and jaw.

"What have you done to yourself?"

He tugged her to her feet. "You are flaking. Get in the water." He started to give her a nudge in that direction, but by then she had her hands on his face, and he stilled. "I am recovered."

"You are . . ." There were no words for it.

"Ugly?" He lifted a modified hand to his transplanted gillets. "They're Ylydii; they feel strange. I thought you would like me better this way."

Better now that he looked more like her.

Dair backed away from him, turned, and dove into the water. She stayed down for several minutes, hoping he would not follow, trying to decide what to do. She wanted to bite him. She wanted to fling herself at him and pull him down into the water with her. She wanted to kill him. She wanted to—

Dair rose slowly and looked through the surface. Onkar sat waiting on the bank, the same way Shan had when he was too afraid to enter the water by himself. She emerged and cleared the water from her gill vents to speak. "I have been cast out of the pod."

"I know."

When he said nothing more, she swam a little closer. "I have been discharged from the military as well. No one wants anything to do with me. I am utterly disgraced."

He simply looked at her.

"You knew this would happen; don't you want to gloat about it? Hear me say that you were right about Bio Rescue, and the land dwellers, and becoming involved with the Skartesh?" Her lungs burned, and her heart felt like it was careening out of control in her chest. She paused to steady her breathing, then released the rage and sank back into bitterness. "Well, congratulations. You have what was mine. My command, my pilots, even my family pod. I have nothing."

"Do you care about the breach between our people and the land dwellers?" he asked.

"You mean the one I am now powerless to heal?" She gave him an ironic look. "I was the cause of it, and I might have stopped it. What do you think?"

Onkar slid into the water, still fully clothed, and swam to her. "I will have you reinstated as a League officer and turn over command of the squadron to you. I will do what I can to reverse the elders' decision and see you reunited with the pod. I will even reactivate the Bio Rescue effort, so that we may use the other modified gstek vessels to search for these missing ships. There is but one thing you must do in return."

*Reverse the elders' decision?* "There is no way you can do that. . . ." She trailed off as he came up behind her and slid his new hands across her belly. "What do I have to do?"

Onkar turned her to face him. "You agree to become my mate for life."

Dair blinked. "And if I don't?"

"I remain in command of the pilots' pod, you sit in this puddle for the next season, and Bio Rescue is no more."

Hope gnawed at the edges of her depression, but she refused to let it feed just yet. "I don't understand. You have everything now. Exactly the way you've always wanted."

Onkar's new face displayed some of the old arrogance. "How little you know me." He bent his head and bit her shoulder.

A humanoid might have screamed, but biting her was a show of male dominance, a mark of possession. In the sea Dair could have wriggled away and taken off for the breeding caverns, where he could chase her properly and prove he had the right to mark her as his. But they were nowhere near open water, and Onkar had already caught her once. If they had made a child, by 'Zangian custom she was considered his, and was expected to be exclusive to him until she weaned their pup.

No male ever had the right to demand she be his life mate.

Onkar knew her parents and their unusual arrangement, but he had never shown approval or disapproval toward them. He rarely showed any emotions toward anyone except her. Something warm slid down her arm and she turned her head to see blood oozing from his teeth marks.

"I'm bleeding," she said, confused even more. Males did not bloody the water unless they were fighting another male for possession. They never drew blood from a female.

"There is no end to this wanting you and fighting you and chasing you." He sounded disgusted with himself. "You have to decide it, Jadaira. I cannot."

"Why?" She pressed a hand over her shoulder. "Why me? Why for life?"

He didn't respond, but took her hand from the wound and suckled the blood from her fingers, then did the same to her shoulder. A component in 'Zangian saliva helped their blood coagulate faster, and within seconds tiny clots formed.

"Why won't you answer me?"

Onkar released her and returned to the bank. After he climbed out, he looked down at her. "I have given you the terms. Give me an answer."

A week of exile had nearly driven her insane. What would life as his mate do to her? "I agree."

# CHAPTER
## TWENTY-ONE

Burn resented Onkar for being the one who had convinced Dair to return to duty, but he was too grateful to have her back to complain about it. Dair had already been subjected to enough haranguing, as both Norash and Dr. Mayer had had plenty to say to her before they allowed her to return to duty. Dair's dam had given her a full physical and then had taken Burn aside and ordered him to watch over his cousin.

"If she starts having trouble breathing, feels dizzy, or her hide turns blue around the eyes and mouth, you must have the copilot relieve her and have the doctor on board examine her at once," Teresa had told him.

"Is she sick?"

"No, but she could become ill without warning." She had seemed almost angry. "If I could suspend her from flight duty I would, but all of her test results are negative."

Burn had asked what the tests were about, but Teresa had refused to elaborate further.

Now, as they were preparing for their latest mission, he found himself constantly checking Dair's face to see if she was turning different colors.

"I still don't understand why they call it a 'sting operation,' " he said as they walked around the newly modified gstek. "We are not using wasp-netters or tube snakes," he added.

"It comes from a policing procedure that originated on Terra," Dair said as she secured one of the camouflaged hatches. "It refers to using an elaborate ruse to gain the confidence of an offender to facilitate apprehension."

He glanced at her mouth, but it had still not turned blue. "How will we gain their confidence by stinging them?"

"The sting is a metaphor for what we will do *after* we obtain their trust." She handed him a scanner. "Make sure all the emitters are projecting the correct energy signatures, and quit staring at me like that; it's annoying."

By disguising the crew and ship to appear to be nothing more than ordinary immigrants, Norash had told the pilots' pod, he hoped to lure whoever was responsible out into the open. Dair had already plotted a course that would send them along the same routes taken by the missing vessels.

Burn had expected Onkar to lead the mission, but his recent injuries still had him grounded, so he was coordinating the operation from Security headquarters. He noticed that Dair had nothing to say about her second-in-command, either, but knew that she would eventually tell him what Onkar had said that had changed her mind.

All this secrecy was starting to get on his nerves, though.

By the time Burn had finished checking the gstek, the medevac crew had boarded. Like him and Dair, they were dressed in their ordinary civilian garments, and he thought the variations between the native designs gave the mission something of a festive air. Dr. Dloh, the Aksellan physician who was leading the team, had even donned a miner's work belt and head protector.

"I zpent my winter breakz from MedTech working my family'z azteroid fieldz," the arachnid being told him. "Feed me zome arutanium and I can even zpin you zome dezent tetherz."

Burn had heard that Rushan Amariah had volunteered to serve as copilot, but that Norash had turned him down and appointed Saree to fly along with them. He felt a tiny amount of resentment that he had not been considered adequate to serve as gunner and copilot, but if Dair did become ill while they were under attack, it would be impossible for him to fly the ship and operate the weapons console at the same time.

Once in space they flew a long, roundabout course to circle outside the system and merge into the trade route that the missing ships had followed.

"Keep the comm channels open and don't use long-range scanners," Dair reminded him. "I want us to appear nice and harmless." She then became involved in a lengthy discussion with Saree about the differences between flying the strafers and the gstek.

Monitoring the civilian frequencies was much more interesting than listening to the females and their pilot chatter, Burn discovered as he eavesdropped on a pair of cargo haulers squabbling over where to put in for shore leave. One wanted to keep going to make up some time lost at a previous stop, while the other was having a problem with a particularly offensive group of passengers.

"Confine them to quarters with a prep unit and seal the door panel until we get to N-jui," the first relayed.

"I would, except they've slimed most of the common areas and corridors already," the second replied. "My maintenance crew just went on strike."

"I told you not to let Ghindarik on board, didn't I? I told you they always track their ooze everywhere."

Burn was tempted to break in on the transmission and offer some advice—he'd known a couple of Ghindarik during his academy days and they shed mucus only when they were overheated—but a new transmission came in over the emergency band.

ALW SID relay 426900726/esdistr/ott9754301: ALW passenger transport *Jilmehar* requests immediate assistance from any/all vessels within response range. Present location Pmoc Quadrant sector 564372. Stardrive disabled; all propulsion systems failing. Entering geostationary orbit at coordinates 93.27.60.003. Repeat. ALW passenger transport *Jilmehar* requests immediate assistance . . .

Burn checked the list Norash had downloaded into the gstek's database, and found a match. "Commander, I'm receiving a distress call from one of the missing ships." He copied the relay to her console. "It's the most recent known to have disappeared."

"Acknowledged." There was a pause. "Track transmission source and compare to transmission of last known position, Ensign."

He didn't know why she wanted him to do the comparison until the source came up on his star chart. "Verified. Source and LKP are a match. The vessel is in orbit over Ninra."

Dair could not establish orbit over Ninra without official permission, but she could get close enough to track the missing vessel. As soon as it appeared on her screens, she tried raising them, but no one responded to her signal. With a sinking feeling she had Burn initiate a structure scan.

"Scanners show no life signs on board, Commander. All of the shuttles and emergency evacuation pods are gone."

She flew by the planet and turned the gstek around slowly to make another pass. "Give me a time lapse on that distress call, please."

"Stand by." Burn ran the signal through the database, analyzing the message for transponder encoding. "Distress call signal originated from this location six days ago."

"That long?" Saree looked alarmed. "We can't leave them down there another day."

Dair knew that if she relayed the information to Norash, he would recall them. She thought for a moment. "We could go after them pup-tailed." The maneuver was risky, but she preferred it over retreat.

"We could." The younger female pilot eyed the red planet that seemed to swell on the viewer. "We could also get caught in the grid zone and blasted out of the sky."

"Put me through to the crew." Dair waited until her gunner had opened their secured channel so that the medevac team could hear her. "This is Commander mu T'resa. We've received a distress call from one of the missing ships. Their stardrive failed, and it appears that the crew and passengers were forced to put down on Ninra six days ago." She contemplated her console for a moment. "Standard procedure would be to contact K-2 security, who would send a diplomatic team to Ninra, where they would have to obtain official permission to establish orbit, land, and retrieve these people. It usually takes a couple of days."

Dr. Dloh's voice came over her headset. "Iz there zome problem with that, Commander?"

"After seven days, the Ninrana consider anyone who has landed on their planet without permission as their property. We don't know if they kill them, sell them to slavers, or imprison them somewhere, but they're never seen again. The few diplomatic teams that have been allowed to land found no trace of them." She paused. "These people have been down there six days. A retrieval team won't get to them in time."

There was some discussion among the crew before Dloh asked, "Our orderz are to locate the mizzing zhipz, iz that not correct, Commander?"

"Yes, those were our orders."

"Can you locate where they are on the zurfaze?"

Burn broke in. "I can use the differential scanner to weed out their life signs from the Ninrana. If they're still breathing, I can get us to within one hundred yards of their position."

"Then if you can find zome way to land without attracting the notize of theze people," Dloh said, "I zuggezt we go and rezcue them."

Dair already knew how to get in through the security grid. "Please secure yourselves and any loose equipment, Doctor. This is going to be a fast, ugly descent." She brought the ship about so that they paralleled the empty vessel. "Burn, I need you to take out the *Jilmehar*'s orbital stabilizers. Make it look like a meteor hit."

"Acknowledged."

After Burn fired, the abandoned ship's orbit began to immediately decay. Dair brought the gstek up behind the vessel and extended the cargo loader arms to clamp onto the *Jilmehar*'s fuselage.

"I'm shutting down the main engines and engaging maneuvering thrusters," she told Saree. "Burn, keep your short-range scanner activated and tell me as soon as we've passed through the grid sensors."

"You *are* going to restart the engines once we're through," he joked.

If she didn't, they would end up a blackened smear across the face of Ninra. "Yes."

"I'll watch for new launches." Saree turned her attention back to her console.

Dair used the maneuvering thrusters to push the empty vessel into reentry position. As she did, she spotted the satellite ring that used powerful emitters to generate the security grid's sensor field around the entire planet.

"Entering outer grid in ten seconds," Burn warned her. "Nine, eight, seven . . ."

Dair shut off all power to the ship's thrusters and propulsion systems, making the gstek appear as inert as possible. Because they were physically attached to the *Jilmehar,* the grid would read the two ships as one vessel falling out of orbit.

"Inside security grid zone," Burn muttered. "*Duo,* it extends two kim."

She knew the Ninrana were paranoid, but keeping half their atmosphere cloaked in sensor fields seemed excessive, even for them. "Saree, are you picking up any low-atmosphere patrol vessels?"

"Negative. Just a lot of empty space." The younger pilot sounded puzzled. "No surface-to-air or air-to-surface activity at all."

"I've heard they curtail their travel to ground-only." As reentry burn flared bright orange and red along the outer hull of the *Jilmehar,* the empty ship also shielded the gstek from most of the heat. She watched their altimeter, which was dropping fast. "Burn, how much longer?"

"We should exit the zone at three kim, in about fifteen seconds."

As soon as he relayed that they were clear, Dair restarted the engines and released the *Jilmehar,* which began to break up as it hit the lower atmosphere. She changed their trajectory to come in at an easier angle to prevent the same from happening to them. "Find me those people, Burn. When he does, Saree, locate a landing site for us."

Shan told himself that stowing away on board the gstek was the only way to accompany the Bio Rescue mission without causing more trouble for Jadaira, but as the ship began a rapid descent he decided that hiding was not as important as discovering if they were about to crash somewhere.

It was not time for him to be on Ninra, or to reveal himself, but the mission might leave him with no choice. Unless he could get them off the planet before the others arrived.

The medevac team reacted to his entry into their compartment with varying degrees of surprise and dismay.

The Aksellan physician Dloh released his harness and came over to block his path. Huge fang-shaped mandibles stretched wide, ready to bite. "I know you were prohibited from joining thiz mizzion. Explain yourzelf."

"A thousand of my people on board a Skartesh ship are also missing. Since I was not permitted to join the mission, I boarded illegally prior to takeoff and concealed myself to prevent discovery." He glanced through a viewport but saw only space turning to a fierce, clear shade of blue. "Where are we?"

"Ninra. We're going down to rezcue zome ztranded jaunterz." Dloh's eye clusters rotated. "Commander mu T'reza iz not going to be happy to zee you."

Shan saw that no one else was, either. "I would not wish to distract her during this crucial part of this mission." He couldn't stay on the ship, not under the circumstances. He turned to one of the insect nurses and gestured toward the hooded cloak she carried. "May I borrow that?"

"Amariah." Dloh raised one of his eight appendages and prodded Shan's chest. "My poizon zacz are full. You would do well to remember that."

He did not mistake the Aksellan's statement as an attempt at humor. "I will."

Dloh made a waving gesture at the nurse, who handed her cloak to Shan, then climbed back into his harness. Shan covered himself and took a position at the back of the compartment, where he would be least likely to be noticed. The hull shuddered as the gstek entered the lower atmosphere and leveled out.

Through the viewport beside him, Shan caught his first glimpse of the planet's surface. Ninra was a desert world, utterly devoid of surface water. The surface temperature was so hot near the equatorial regions that all life had been long ago driven or burned away.

He knew from the intelligence reports his superiors had sent him that the Ninrana had been in trouble for some time, but seeing it for himself brought home the real dire straits. Over the centuries, the thinning atmosphere, changing surface winds, and rapid decline in negligible vegetation caused Ninra to absorb more and more of the twin suns' radiation.

The reality that surrounded them was a massive, hostile wasteland.

"They don't want outziderz to zee thiz, I think," Dloh murmured.

Shan studied the elaborate drilling rigs that the Ninrana had built in their endless pursuit of water. "How deep do they have to go now?"

"Az low az the water table dropz, I imagine." The arachnid physician peered out. "You can't help but pity the poor wretchez. Zlowly dying of thirzt is not a pleazant end."

Shan had been assigned to scout Ninra if possible, and he recognized the region they were approaching as the Red Basin Range, a heavily populated region. Seeing the series of interconnected basins, divided bizarrely shaped mountain ranges produced during ancient shifts in the strata, brought home the desperate situation on this world.

"Thoze basinz were onze lakez," Dloh said. "You can ztill zee the old irrigation zyztemz their anzeztorz uzed for their cropz, there." He pointed to the decaying machinery left behind to frame the empty tracts of now-barren red soil.

Dair used the cliffs as cover, flying behind them to conceal the ship from the Ninrana settlement they were rapidly approaching. After they landed and the engines shut down, she emerged from the helm with her copilot and gunner, and briefed them on the route they would take to retrieve the passengers and crew of the *Jilmehar,* who were being held a short distance away in an area set apart from the settlement.

Superheated air flooded the compartment as Burn opened the outer hull doors, and once outside Shan's fur became soaked with sweat within minutes. The bone-dry atmosphere, low oxygen levels, and scorched appearance of the predominantly red soil gave him an immediate, almost unbearable thirst, but one of the nurses wordlessly pressed a container of water into his paws.

The temperature had the direst effect on the three 'Zangians, whose exposed facial skin had dried and was beginning to crack. He almost said something, and then heard Dair call a halt. Everyone was startled when Dair took a drink from her water container and then spit in Burn's face. After he rubbed it into his skin, Burn did the same to her and Saree.

While the rest of the team stood and drank in the shade of a forty-foot column of displaced earth, he recalled that the word *Ninra* roughly translated to *thirst,* and the inhabitants had appropriately called themselves "those of thirst."

Shan studied the distant settlement, which was primitive but quite ingenious. Primordial deposits of erosion detritus skirted the lowest elevations, forming rectangular outcroppings, the southern faces of which the Ninra had carved out to form large recesses. The overhanging portion at the top of the recesses protected the odd dwellings they had built within them from the direct rays of the sun.

The dwellings, which were nestled in the back of the recess, were likely the coolest spots on the surface. The earthen berms used the thermal stability of the earth to lower ambient temperature, while exterior, shaded areas allowed the Ninra to work outside in shade while the steady wind blew through to cool them. The high-mass structure of the dwellings seemed to be used primarily for storage and shelter, as the inhabitants were currently using the low-mass outer areas for gathering and what appeared to be food preparation.

Between the irregular clusters of dug-in dwellings were sprawling roads leading to and from each outcropping and around what appeared to be a series of elevated, tiered stone lattices built in the very center of the basin. The lattices were horizontal instead of vertical, however, and completely bare of vegetation. More remnants of a past burned away beneath the blazing twin suns, Shan guessed, and stayed at the back of the medevac team as Dair led them toward one of the outcroppings fringing the settlement.

"We'll evacuate any zeverely wounded firzt," Dloh was telling his nurses, his buzzing voice just above a whisper now. "Make zure the onez who are fit and ambulatory help carry out the injured. Watch for zignz of heat exhauztion; it happenz quickly in thiz zort of environment."

The shaded outer areas of the dwelling they approached were deserted, but Dair and Burn produced pulse pistols and enabled them as they drew close. Shan tucked his paw inside his cloak and kept it on the stock of his own weapon.

There was no door panel at the front of the dwelling, only a narrow opening draped with a light-colored panel of woven material.

Dair tugged the edge of the drape to one side, looked in, then motioned for them to follow her as she entered the structure. Shan stayed to the back of the medevac team, listening intently as they filed inside. The fur on the back of his neck rose as he heard alloy sliding against stone, and froze.

Someone was waiting inside.

There were a few short bursts of pulse fire, and a nurse screamed. As strange, harsh voices called out orders, Shan moved quickly back into the shadows cast by the dug-in.

He held his breath and remained still as Dair exited the dwelling with her arms up and her hands laced behind her head. She was followed by a tall, dark-skinned humanoid who held a rifle trained to the back of her head. Another humanoid in a light-colored cloak walked up to Dair and her captor, and tugged back the hood covering his head.

"Commander mu T'resa, how lovely to see you again." Sohrab, Njal-Geir's assistant, smiled. "Welcome to Ninra."

# CHAPTER
# TWENTY-TWO

Dair said nothing as she and the Bio Rescue team were marched at gunpoint away from the dwelling and toward the center of the basin.

Sohrab, on the other hand, hadn't stopped talking since he'd appeared. "You don't speak the native lingo, do you? Unfortunately your wristcom can't translate it, because the Ninrana have never allowed their language to be recorded. A shame, too, because they have a fascinating culture. For instance, the male walking behind you—his name is Urloy-ka, by the way—is the chief of the Red Basin Range's largest warrior clan. He's the one in charge around here, so he'll be performing the ritual sacrifices."

Saree heard him and walked a little faster to come up beside him. "What sacrifices? What are you talking about?"

"Didn't I mention? You're all to be killed. They do that with captives and other oddities; evidently they see it as their way of purifying the universe and appeasing some of their deities, who happen to be extremely bloodthirsty. And don't be fooled by all the stoic expressions; they're actually very excited to have captured you and your 'Zangian cohorts."

Saree caught Dair's eye and then moved her gaze to Sohrab's throat and bared her teeth. Dair shook her head.

Njal-Geir's assistant said something in his native tongue to Urloy-ka, who responded with a terse statement.

"I asked him why they think you're such a prize, in case you're wondering," Sohrab said. "He says your alterform bodies are so offensive to his god of creation that your executions will bring back the rains that went away thirty years ago." He giggled. "I haven't the heart to tell him that they're never coming back, no matter how many offworlders they slaughter. Why spoil their fun?"

The skin on Dair's brow cracked and oozed blood that the blazing temperature instantly dried. "Why are you here?"

"Wouldn't you like to know?" He gave her a sly look. "Perhaps you'll live long enough to find out."

A huge crowd of Ninrana had gathered in the center of the flat basin, and stood in clusters around a number of horizontal multicolored stone racks. As they reached one, Dair saw that the stone was actually bundles of long, polished bones. There were too many variations in shape and color for the bones to be from one type of animal, and she had seen nothing but Ninrana on the surface.

The people who had disappeared on Ninra hadn't disappeared at all.

Dr. Dloh came to stand beside her. "They're not animal remainz," he said, as if reading her mind. "They're humanoid."

"To which yours will be added, as soon as your corpses are butchered and picked clean." Sohrab sighed. "That's the only problem with visiting this world—the meal intervals. You just never know who you're going to be eating."

"I know who I'm going to eat." Dark fluid dripped from two hollow-tipped fangs that had emerged from Dr. Dloh's front appendages, the drops from which sizzled as they hit the sand and began melting it.

"You have no bones, so you're of no ritual value to the Ninrana." Sohrab removed a block-shaped device and enabled it. "But they won't mind if I squash you, if you'd rather not watch the festivities."

Urloy-ka jerked Dair over to a small series of steps that led to the top of the first tier of the bone rack. The Ninrana escorting the other two 'Zangians followed. The crowd surrounding the base of the racks shouted their apparent approval.

"I'm so sorry we weren't able to chat longer," Sohrab called out over the noise. "One last bit of advice for you and your friends, Commander: Don't struggle, and they'll be satisfied with decapitating you."

Burn suddenly lunged and threw himself into the Ninrana chief, knocking him off the steps onto the sand. "Run!"

Dair grabbed Saree and ran with her up onto the tier rack, jumping from one bundle of bones to the next, trying to gain some distance.

"Oh, dear." Njal-Geir's assistant shook his head. "Now they'll definitely take their time chopping you up."

Dair saw other Ninrana armed with long swords leap up onto the racks to form a deadly circle around her. "Use your teeth," she told the younger female. "Bite through the big vein on the left side of their necks."

Someone called out what sounded like a warning, and the circle of Ninrana around Dair and Saree went still. Dair turned toward the call and saw Shan striding toward the bone rack, pulling off a cloak as he crossed the distance. He made a sweeping gesture and shouted something in Ninrana.

"What is he doing here?" Saree whispered. "How does he know their language?"

Dair could only stare as everyone else did while Shan climbed up on the first tier and pulled off his tunic. The sight of his bare, furry torso with the two golden marks on it seemed to amaze the Ninrana even more.

*Not his chest,* she thought, looking at the twin symbols tattooed on the brow of every Ninrana male. *The markings on it.*

Sohrab hurried up onto the rack. "You are not supposed to come here yet," he hissed at Shan as he picked his way over to him. "It is not time to do this. You'll ruin everything we have planned and then what—"

As soon as he was close enough, Shan calmly picked up the babbling humanoid and tossed him over the side of the tier, then issued what sounded like an order to the nearest Ninrana, who handed him a strange, curved dagger. He held it up over his head and shouted out to the gathered natives, who fell silent.

*His sacrifice will drive back the waters. . . .*

*What do they think you're going to kill?*

*Myself.*

"No." Dair watched his arm sweep down and started jumping

bundles to get to him. The Ninrana were so mesmerized that none of them tried to stop or chase her. "No, Shan, don't!"

The Skartesh thrust the hooked blade in his own chest, and then twisted it before he dropped to his knees.

She screamed his name.

"Stay back, Jadaira." He gasped before he pulled out the blade and let it fall from his limp, bloodied paw. "Stay . . . ba—" He slumped over and was still.

"*Duo,* please, no." She staggered and nearly fell through the bone rack before she regained her footing and made the final leap to reach him.

His blood ran over the convoluted bundles of bones and dripped onto the upturned, rapt faces of the Ninrana standing directly under the rack.

Dair sank down beside his huddled form, over which Urloy-ka now stood. When she reached to touch Shan's fur, the Ninrana caught her wrist and uttered a terse phrase.

She yanked her arm away. "How could you do this to living beings? How did you make him do this?"

Shan's body shifted beside her, and then he groaned.

Urloy-ka hauled her up and away before he turned his head and shouted to his people, but his voice died away as Shan slowly lifted his head.

"Forgive me." With slow, painful movements he rose to his feet. Dair's gaze went to the horrific wound on his chest, which was now closed and appeared to be shrinking. He pressed his paws to it, then spread his arms and turned to face the Ninrana chief, showing his chest to him. No wound showed now.

It had to be some sort of trick. He'd faked stabbing himself.

Urloy-ka released Dair and backed away, shaking his head. Around and beneath the racks, the Ninrana began shrieking. Some fell to their knees, babbling and tearing at their clothes; others ran away screaming.

"What have you done?" Dair heard Dloh say.

"I have shown them that there is life after death." Shan looked down at the fleeing natives, apparently unmoved by their hysterics. "I have just destroyed everything that they believe in."

"You should have waited for us, my son." Yersha Amariah climbed up onto the bone racks.

Dair saw ships landing all over the basin—hundreds of them—and her eyes widened as eager, white-robed Skartesh began pouring out of them to do battle with the frightened Ninrana. "What are they doing here?"

Shan gave her a strangely distant look. "We are taking control of this planet."

"The occupation is going well," Kabod Amariah said as he looked out from the open window of the chief's dwelling. "We have grounded the bulk of the Ninrana fleet, and we should be able to launch our own within the week."

Shan finished washing the dried blood from his fur and took the clean tunic Yersha was holding for him. "We will need Ninrana crews if we are to utilize all of their vessels." He pulled the fresh garment over his head and began fastening it.

"They will be willing to serve by the time we are ready," Sohrab said from the chair he was lounging in. "Once we have defeated the Ylydii, we can use our combined forces to take control of K-2." He sipped from his flask of spicewine before he gave Shan a hard look. "You should have waited to commit suicide until the faithful arrived. They needed to see it as much as the Ninrana."

Yersha sniffed. "They heard enough about it. They will do as they are told."

"They are becoming agitated. They challenge Yersha's and my authority." Kabod turned from the window. "Perhaps you should perform the self-sacrifice a second time, Rushan."

He stopped fastening the tunic and looked down at the unmarked place on his chest where he had buried the ceremonial dagger only a few hours ago. "No, that will not be necessary."

Armed Skartesh guards waited outside to escort Shan, his parents, and Sohrab out to the front of the chief's dwelling, where the prayer leaders of the faithful had assembled and were dancing in prayer circles. As the suns were setting, the temperature had dropped to a more tolerable level. Although the Skartesh were unaccustomed to the intense heat, Ninra's arid climate was far more comfortable than the thick, humid conditions they had endured for so long on K-2.

The sight of Shan emerging from the chief's dwelling caused the dancers to halt and turn their attention toward him.

Sohrab lifted his arms toward the metallic blue sky. "Today begins our journey—"

"Today you will begin nothing!" Njal-Geir shouted as he pushed through the followers to make his way to the front. "You people will return these stolen vessels to K-2 at once."

"I knew I forgot to do something before I left that planet," Sohrab murmured to Shan. "Forgive me; I was in a hurry."

"Sohrab?" The quadrant official's tiny eyes went wide as he recognized his assistant. "What are you doing here? Did they take you hostage?"

"As it happens, no, Supervisor. You see, I am one of the faithful, and I helped them steal those ships." Sohrab walked up to him and clapped a hand on the smaller male's shoulder. "Come inside and we will explain everything."

Shan, Yersha, and Kabod accompanied the two quadrant officials into the dwelling, where Njal-Geir began demanding explanations.

"I have tried to support your efforts, but this is outrageous. I can't endorse a separatist movement that allows its membership to indulge in such felonious activities. Gods above, man, you've invaded a free world."

"We only did what the Ninrana were planning to do to the rest of the system," Sohrab assured him.

"That is irrelevant." He gave his assistant a disgusted look. "I'm afraid I will have to take some severe disciplinary action against you."

His assistant's mouth curled. "Yes, I suppose you do."

"Representative Amariah, I respect your religious beliefs, but you must do exactly as I say now," Njal-Geir continued. "If we are to salvage this situation and protect the rights of the Skartesh—"

"Supervisor, we are not interested in religion," Kabod told him. "We are taking control of this sector of space."

The official paled. "But your followers . . . they believe you are leading them to a better world. They won't continue to participate in this coup of yours when I tell them the truth."

Yersha laughed. "The faithful are as stupid as you are. They will do as they are told, and we will continue to use them until we have gathered enough trained replacement forces from the other worlds we occupy."

Njal-Geir turned to Shan. "This was your doing, wasn't it? You are behind all of it."

"Don't take it so hard, Supervisor." Sohrab patted the official on the shoulder. "You can have all the power and importance you have ever wanted now. Just go on doing exactly what you were doing, until we're ready to take K-2. When we do, I'll even set you up as a provisional governor."

"I will not." Njal-Geir flung off his former assistant's hand. "You and your accomplices are going to put a stop to this illegal aggression at once, or I will see to it that you spend the rest of your days mining fuel ore for oversize spiders!"

Sohrab sighed. "I was afraid that buried somewhere under this thick-skinned moronic exterior there was a small but tragically honest soul. Very well." He swept an arm toward the opening. "Shall we?"

They followed Njal-Geir as he stalked outside.

"Will you tell them that this is over?" the supervisor asked his assistant. "Or shall I?"

"Sohrab." Shan stepped forward when he saw the glitter of a blade, but Yersha put her paw on his arm and shook her head.

"I'll do it," Sohrab said, turning Njal-Geir around to face him. "You've talked enough."

"Wha—" The supervisor's voice became a gurgle of agony as he looked down between them, and grasped the hilt of the knife Sohrab had driven into his chest. "Gah . . . guh . . ."

"Amazing. You still won't shut up." His former assistant tugged out the blade and turned the supervisor away from him before he reached around and made a quick slash.

Shan saw Njal-Geir's body jerk and a wave of blood spatter the sand, and closed his eyes briefly.

"No one threatens the Salvager and lives," Sohrab intoned solemnly for the benefit of the faithful as he let the supervisor's body crumple. "Now, who will be the first to bring tribute for our savior?"

A trio of Skartesh males dragged a heavy cargo container to the front of the crowd, and one of them opened the top panel to display the mound of pistols inside. "We offer two thousand pulse weapons for the journey to paradise."

A lone female presented a wooden chest filled with glowing amber gems. "I bring five hundred *golarn* crystals." She gave Yersha and Kabod an uncertain look before she smiled timidly at Shan.

As more offerings were brought forward, Shan saw Urloy-ka and several other Ninrana dignitaries appear at the edge of the crowd. They looked pale and sick, but were also carrying heavy bundles and caches.

"I see those who did not believe in the Promise." He gestured toward them. "Come forward."

"If it is permitted," the Ninrana chief said in halting Skart, "we would make new offerings to the One Who Brought Truth."

"It is permitted if you join the faithful and follow the Salvager," Sohrab said in Ninrana, his voice a smooth purr. "Are you and your people prepared to do so, Chief?"

"Most are. Some have . . . fled." Urloy-ka bowed as Shan approached him. "We who remain behind will do as you command."

"Rise." Shan placed a paw on the Ninrana's shoulder. "You will join us and bring the truth to all those who do not believe."

Urloy-ka looked at the armed Skartesh, and then back at Shan. "As you say, Salvager."

The tribute continued, and Shan acknowledged the many weapons, gems, and supplies the Skartesh had been stealing and stockpiling for months from the colony on K-2. Guards brought torches when the suns had dropped below the horizon and darkness covered the settlement.

Shan looked out at the exhausted faithful and turned to Sohrab. "Where is the 'Zangian pilot?"

"We put her in with the other prisoners. Why?"

"Bring her to me. It is time that I repay her for all that she has done to prevent the fulfillment of the Promise."

Sohrab issued orders, and within a few minutes Jadaira was dragged out of one of the dwellings and hauled up to Shan.

He studied her face, the skin of which had dried and cracked until she appeared like an ancient crone. "You do not look so well, Commander. Beg me for some water, and I might let you have some before you die."

Dair's mouth worked for a moment, and then she spit a small amount of saliva in his face.

"Take her inside." When Sohrab made a sound of protest, Shan eyed him. "I wish to enjoy myself. You can feed her remains to the Ninrana tomorrow." He turned to the faithful. "Guard our encampment well. Tomorrow we will be one day closer to paradise."

A third guard was required to force Dair inside the chief's dwelling and into the chamber the Ninrana had used for interrogations. Yersha accompanied Shan and directed the guards to gag the 'Zangian female and chain her securely to the wall.

"Let me have the honor of killing her for you, my son," the older woman said as she took a pistol from one of the guards and then dismissed them. "I have long waited to see this one dead."

"No, Mother." He took off his tunic and tossed it on the chair. "I want pleasure before blood."

"You care to sully yourself with her?" Yersha leaned against one wall. "This I would watch."

Shan approached Dair slowly, watching her eyes as he reached out and tore open the front of her flight suit. Water from her skin shield sprayed out as the lines tore.

"Ugh." Yersha scuttled out of the way. "How can you stand to touch her? Sloppy, disgusting thing."

Shan shoved one paw into Dair's torn uniform. "She amuses me." He used his body weight to press her writhing body against the wall, and fingered her gillets. "I think I will remove the gag. I want to listen to her scream as I take her."

"I do not." Yersha shuddered. "Do not put yourself in her mouth unless you break her jaw first; her teeth look sharp." She glanced through the window at the reveling faithful. "I am going to find Kabod before he drinks himself unconscious. Shall I send in a guard?"

"No." He tugged sharply on a handful of gillets, making Dair produce a muffled groan. "I don't need an audience."

Shan waited until Yersha had departed, then lifted himself away from Dair and went to the door and window to drop the draping cloths. He grabbed the largest container of water he could find in the supply chests brought from the ships and carried it to her.

"I'm sorry, Commander." He opened the container and poured it over her head. "I had to make it look real for her."

Dair closed her eyes and lifted her face into the stream. Before the container was half-empty, Shan carefully peeled away the adhesive gag and held the container to her swollen mouth.

Dair drank down the rest and then sagged back against the wall, gasping for breath and staring at him. "Why?"

"I'm not Skartesh." He looked at the door before leaning close. "And I'm not Rushan Amariah."

Dair watched him work loose the manacles the guards had used to chain her to the wall. "Who are you? *What* are you?"

"I'm Maj. Shon Valtas from Quadrant Intelligence." He released one of her wrists and went to work on the other. "I was assigned to an undercover investigation of the Skartesh cult by Col. Oriah Triak. My SID is seven-two-eight."

An SID was a SEAL identification number. "You're an alterform?"

He nodded. "My people, the oKiaf, come from the same region of space as the Skartesh. We're also the only species genetically close enough to accept the required DNA modifications. I was alterformed so that I could pose as Rushan Amariah, infiltrate the cult, and find out what they had planned. We didn't know they would take it this far, or be this successful."

His entire manner had changed, from his facial expressions to his speech patterns. It made Dair's head spin. "Where is the real Rushan?"

"He went back to Skart alone after the population was evacuated by the League and killed himself, trying to fulfill this idiot Promise they believe in." He removed the last chain and eased her arm down.

"We were able to conceal his death from his followers and use DNA from his remains for my alterformation. I'll brief you on the rest when we return to K-2. Do you need more water?"

"Not now, but I need to take some to Saree and Burn; they're in worse shape than I am." She glanced toward the draped doorway. "We have to get off this planet tonight, and we have to send help for the Ninrana."

"We'd better free the others first." He paused and pulled together the torn front of her flight suit. "Forgive me for what I did, Commander."

Her heart was still pounding from the terrifying assault. "Wait until I'm assigned to impersonate a messiah, and *you* have to be the frightened captive."

He grinned at her. "Grab as much water as you and I can carry from the supply chest. I know how to get to the holding cell without being seen."

While she collected the water containers and stowed them in two carryalls, Shan—*no, Major Valtas,* she corrected herself—left and returned with two Skartesh robes and Ninrana cloaks to wear over them. They dressed and concealed the carryalls beneath the cloaks, then went through a back corridor and out into the night.

Although there were armed guards posted at the perimeter of the encampment, the Skartesh inside the settlement were drunk, and none paid any attention to them as they crossed over to the dwelling where the Bio Rescue team was being held. The major removed his cloak as soon as they were inside, and the Skartesh guard reacted instantly to the sight of him by dropping to his knees.

"Brother, I have brought a relief guard to take your place," Shon told him, slipping easily back into Rushan Amariah's more formal persona. "Leave your weapon and go and join the faithful. This is a night for all to rejoice."

The guard stuttered his thanks before handing his rifle to Dair and departing.

"You are really good at this," she said.

He checked the other two corridors. "I had to watch archive vids of the real Rushan for months."

They went to the sublevel holding cell, where the medevac team was draining water from the 'Zangians' skin shields to dampen cloth and apply it to their exposed, damaged skin. As soon as Dair pulled back her hood, Dr. Dloh sprang toward the barred door. "We need water dezperately." He drew back at the sight of Shon and bared his fangs. "Why iz he ztill breathing?"

"He's an intelligence officer and he's on our side. Here's water." She handed her carryall through the bars, then raised the rifle. "Everyone, stand back." Once the team was out of the way, she shot out the locking mechanism and tugged open the door. "We have to go to the gstek and get out of here. Can you walk?"

Burn was already staggering to his feet. "I can run."

Shon went over to help the nurse sluicing Saree with water, but the young 'Zangian female was semidelirious. He swung her up into his arms. "I'll carry her. Let's move."

Once they emerged from the sublevel, Dair went to the door to check outside. "There are still a lot of Skittish out there."

"Dair will take point; I'll bring up the rear," Shon told them. "Follow her, keep absolutely silent, and stay out of the light." He checked once more outside before he nodded to Dair.

She stayed in the shadows on the outcroppings and dwellings, leading the team along the most direct route back to the gstek. As they crossed the last several yards over open sand to the ship, Dair felt the pounding in her head diminish. They were going to make it.

The boarding ramp had been closed, but there were manual controls to release it tucked behind one of the engine cowlings. Just as she lowered the ramp, a large shadow moved in front of her.

Urloy-ka and a dozen Ninrana stepped from behind the ship. The chief looked at Shon and asked a question.

Dair showed them her rifle. "Step away from the ship."

Every one of the Ninrana instantly produced swords and pistols.

"They're confused. Let's take advantage of it," Shon said in a casual, conversational tone. "Ensign, take Saree from me. Jadaira, don't lower your rifle but walk backward toward me." After he handed the unconscious 'Zangian female to Burn, he addressed the Ninrana leader in a harsher tone.

"Everyone move as close as you can to the ramp," Dair said, never taking her eyes off Urloy-ka. "Be ready to jump for it."

"Hand me your rifle slowly," Shon said. When she had, Shon enabled it and pointed it at Urloy-ka's head. "Now get on board." He started walking toward the Ninrana, away from the ramp. "Hurry up."

Dair started to follow him. "I can't leave you like this."

"That's a direct order, Commander." As the natives surged forward, he leveled a shot at the ground between them and glanced back at her. "Dair, you have to get them out of here. Tell Norash everything that has happened. *Go!*"

# CHAPTER
## TWENTY-THREE

"We've got company," Burn said. "Forty ships on a direct inter-cept course, and more coming up behind them."

Dair altered course and speed. "Point of origin?"

"Ninra. Looks like they've sent their entire fleet after us."

She had already tried to send a distress call to K-2, but someone had disabled the transponder while the gstek had been on the planet. "Time to intercept?"

"Four minutes, fifty-one seconds." Burn took in a sharp breath. "I was wrong, Commander. The ships aren't Ninrana. They're the ones the Skittish appropriated."

At top speed, it would still take another ten minutes to reach their homeworld. The Skartesh ships would cut them off halfway there.

"Program a recording drone with all the information we have on the Ninrana/Skartesh plans to attack Ylyd and K-2 and launch it," she ordered. "If we don't make it, maybe the drone will."

"We can still use ship to ship downlink and receive signals," he advised her. "You should talk to them."

"Excellent idea." She enabled the emergency downlink. "Skartesh fleet, this is Bio Rescue Two, Commander mu T'resa speaking. Pmoc Quadrant Command has been apprised of your in-vasion of Ninra and your plans to attack other planets in this sector. You can avoid serious consequences and further loss of life by re-turning to Kevarzangia Two now and surrendering the stolen vessels to authorities."

"I think we'll be too preoccupied with blowing up your ship, Commander," the voice of Njal-Geir's assistant drawled. "You're a terrible liar, you know. I disabled your transponder myself. You didn't know what was happening when you landed on Ninra, and you haven't had the time or means to warn anyone since you left."

There was a small burst of energy off the starboard side of the gstek.

"They just destroyed our recording drone," Burn advised her. "Time to intercept two minutes, fifteen seconds. Powering displacer array."

"Hold your fire until I give you the order," Dair snapped before she resorted to the downlink one last time. "You may take temporary control of this region, Sohrab, but Command will eventually send troops and ships, and they have a hundred times as many as you. Why waste thousands of lives in a war you can't win?"

"Our allies will be sending troops as well," the former official told her. "Maybe you remember the last time they visited this region. Tall, green, scaly, and they kill everything that moves. They're going to come as soon as—"

She cut off his relay and sent one of her own back to the medevac team. "The Skartesh have sent all their ships after us, and they're about to intercept us. They have enough firepower to destroy us before we can reach K-2, and that's what they intend to do." She looked through the viewer as the small sphere of her home planet appeared in the distance. "I'm sorry I wasn't able to bring you home this time."

"We are honored to have zerved with you, Commander," Dr. Dloh replied.

Dair reduced power and turned the gstek about to face the advancing ships. "Burn, I'm going to fly into them. I want you to take out as many ships as you can. Reroute all power from the systems as needed."

"Acknowledged, Commander."

There was so much she wanted to say to him. "You have always been the brother of my heart, Byorn. I hope you know that."

He made a rough sound. "At your side, Jadaira. Always."

Dair studied the arrangement of the Skartesh fleet. Flying a course straight through the middle would allow Burn to hit multiple targets and perhaps deflect some of the pulse fire directed at them onto surrounding ships.

"Rezcue Two," a buzzing voice unexpectedly came over the receiver. "Thiz is Akzellan freighter OH423, Field Zupervizor Mnoc tranzmitting. I waz leading a caravan of ore haulerz back to ztation on Ylyd when I picked up your downlink relay. May we be of azziztanze?"

"That's one of the miners we picked up from the *Wanderer*," Burn told her, and then he gasped. "*Duo*, he has a lot of friends."

Dair saw seven huge ore freighters appear on her port side, and eight move in on her left. Because they often carried heavy amounts of valuable ore, the gigantic haulers were heavily armed and shielded. Their propulsion systems enabled them to move quickly as well, to avoid ore-hungry raiders.

They were more than a match for the Skartesh fleet.

She enabled the downlink. "Field Supervisor Mnoc, if you would relay our situation back to K-2 security and flight control, and help us hold them off until help arrives, we would be extremely grateful."

"Acknowledged," he replied pleasantly. "Pleaze maintain your current pozition, Commander." He maneuvered his freighter in front of the gstek, effectively shielding it.

The other ore haulers opened fire on the Skartesh fleet, targeting each ship's weapon arrays and destroying them. Because the ore haulers were just as fast, the Skartesh were unable to execute effective evasive maneuvers. A few were able to fire on the freighters first, but the Aksellan ships' dense, buffered hulls absorbed the hits with little or no apparent damage.

Within minutes the entire Skartesh fleet had been effectively disarmed and rendered harmless.

"I have a signal coming in from K-2 flight control, Commander," Burn said. "It's being relayed to the Skartesh vessels."

Dair tapped into the transmission, which was apparently a recorded dialogue.

*Representative Amariah, I respect your religious beliefs, but you must do exactly as I say now.* Dair recognized the speaker as Njal-

Geir, the quadrant supervisor. *If we are to salvage this situation and protect the rights of the Skartesh—*

*Supervisor, we are not interested in religion,* a male Skartesh said. *We are taking control of this sector of space.*

*But your followers . . . they believe you are leading them to a better world. They won't continue to participate in this coup of yours when I tell them the truth.*

A female Skartesh laughed. *The faithful are as stupid as you are. They will do as they are told, and we will continue to use them until we have gathered enough trained replacement forces from the other worlds we occupy.*

"That signal is fraudulent!" Yersha Amariah shrieked over the open channel. "It has been doctored by our enemies!"

"This signal was sent to us by Njal-Geir shortly before he was killed," Dair heard Security Chief Norash say. "He was carrying a transmitter on his person when he went to Ninra, in order to collect evidence against Commander mu T'resa and the members of the Bio Rescue team. What he discovered, in fact, is that Yersha and Kabod Amariah have been manipulating their own people through their religious beliefs to stage a coup of this region. We have also found evidence that this coup attempt has been financed by agents of the Hsktskt faction, who were responsible for the surface bombardment of Skart."

There was a long silence over the channel, and then a vid was transmitted from one of the Skartesh vessels. It showed Yersha, Kabod, and Sohrab being dragged to an air lock by a group of young followers. Other, older Skartesh were trying to stop them, but they were outnumbered.

Dair enabled the downlink. "Unidentified Skart vessel, this is Rescue Two. You must turn these criminals over to the proper authorities. Please acknowledge."

The three coup leaders were thrust into the lock and the doors secured. Some of the younger Skartesh began attacking the older.

She tried again. "Skart vessel, this is Rescue Two. Do not, repeat, do *not* execute your prisoners. We will rendezvous with you and remove them from your ship."

Yersha's mouth formed a silent scream just before she and the two men were sucked out of the air lock into space.

A young Skart voice responded with, "We have turned the traitors over to God."

A new voice came over Dair's headset. "Commander, this is Chief Norash. We have to convince these people to return to K-2. We have a full diplomatic team en route from the quadrant, as well as a cultural disaster response team coming in from Omorr. We will do whatever it takes to find a peaceful solution, but they must surrender the ships."

Supervisor Mnoc broke in. "The Zkartezh have not rezponded to any of our zignalz. They are regrouping and changing their courze."

Dair blinked as a second vid from the Skart vessel appeared. The followers who had cast the Amariahs and Sohrab out into space had surrounded another figure. It was a battered-looking Rushan, but from his expression and slow movements he appeared to be either dazed or drugged.

A young female Skartesh looked into the screen as Shan was led away. "Commander, we were ignorant of what was done by our elders and those who betrayed us. Please convey our regrets to your people, the colonists, and all those who were affected by these deceptions."

"What happened isn't your fault. Let us help you now."

She shook her head. "We are young, but we understand what is happening to us. Our leaders have been judged and found wanting. Through the mercy of the great powers that watch over us, the Salvager has been returned to life. Now only he can save us in the Great Burning. Farewell, Commander." She terminated the signal.

Dread seized Dair as she checked the Skartesh fleet's new heading. "Burn, I want every ounce of power you have routed to the engines. Now."


Norash and a security team were waiting at Transport when Dair landed.

"Welcome home, Commander." The Trytinorn inspected her. "You look well and truly fried." In a lower voice he added, "Good work."

She ignored him and went to the flight crew chief. "Verrig, have every strafer we have ready to launch in five minutes."

The chief looked over her shoulder at Norash, who had followed her, then nodded and went into the pilots' hangar.

Norash regarded her with something like pity. "Commander, you need to have medical treatment for those burns."

"Later." As Burn disembarked with the crew from Rescue Two, she waved him over. "I need you to get Rescue Three ready to launch."

"Rescue Three hasn't been fully modified yet," Burn told her. "All the raider components haven't been removed."

"It doesn't matter; I can still fly it." She'd fly an Oenrallian junk ship, if she had to, to get Shan and stop the Skartesh.

"I can't authorize a second rescue mission," Norash said from behind her.

She whirled around. "Do you know what the rebel Skartesh are going to do?" When he nodded, she added, "Do you know that Maj. Shon Valtas from Quadrant Intelligence is on one of those ships? He's the SEAL QI sent to impersonate Rushan Amariah and stop the cult."

"I know about Valtas." His voice softened. "I know you were his friend, but it makes no difference."

"Of course it does. The Skartesh still think that he's their messiah," she told him. "They believe that if they sacrifice him and themselves that it will restore their homeworld and he will somehow bring them back to life."

"Major Valtas knew how dangerous this assignment was when he volunteered," Norash told her. "Saving one life doesn't justify endangering an entire squadron to do so."

The pilots' pod exited the hangar and gathered around Dair, Burn, and Norash.

"You misunderstood me." Dair clamped down on her temper. "I'm not talking solely about rescuing Major Valtas. I'm talking about preventing an entire species from committing suicide."

"By the charter, we're not permitted to stop them," Norash reminded her. "Self-termination is not illegal."

"It is if some of them are unwilling. The young Skartesh have seized control and they will be murdering their elders." She looked at the pod. "We have about an hour of flight time before it's too late. If we catch up and dock with the ships, we can board them and take over helm control from the pilots." The expressions on her pilots' faces infuriated her. "Why are you just standing there? Move it, people."

"Commander." Onkar drew her away from the others. "We've already discussed the matter. No one is going after the Skartesh."

"You would see them die like this?"

"No, but I will not sacrifice our pod to save them." He touched his modified fin to her burned cheek. "They wouldn't come back with us anyway, Jadaira. Let them go."

It was like being shunned all over again, except this time it was being done with regret and misplaced kindness. She could see it in their eyes.

She glanced at her gunner. "Burn?"

"I am with you," he said, but not with the same conviction that he had when they had faced death themselves.

Dair turned to Norash. "Do you really think it will be better this way for them?"

"I believe that they will find the peace they have been denied since leaving their homeworld," the Trytinorn said. "The young ones have suffered enough, Commander. That they are taking their abusers with them seems like justice to me."

Dair nodded slowly. The young Skartesh rebels were sick, and as such they had to be abandoned. It was, after all, the natural order.

"I'll take you over to the hospital," Onkar said, and put one of his new arms around her. "Teresa signaled and said she would meet us there."

"I forgot; I brought you back a memento of Ninra." She patted his chest. "Let me get it."

He glanced over at the gstek, where Verrig and the flight crew had already started working to repair the damage. "Verrig has disabled the stardrive, so you won't be able to launch the ship."

"I'm not going to try to steal the gstek," she said, and walked away from him. As she reached Burn, she halted and gave him a Terran-style embrace. "In ten seconds," she whispered against his ear flap as she hugged him, "I want you to reel around and then faint."

He stiffened for a moment before he rubbed his cheek against hers. "You're sand-belly, you know. Be careful."

Dair released him and strode to where Verrig and the crew were working. Casually she waved to the crew chief as she went around them to the entry ramp. As soon as she heard the thud of a heavy body hitting the docking pad, she ducked under the ship.

The strafer she wanted was Saree's ship, the *SandPearl*. Dair knew her wing leader didn't like flying double, and had modified her ship to allow her control over weapons and navigation.

She heard the first shout just before she closed the canopy over her head and started the engines. "Control, this is the *SandPearl*. Request immediate emergency launch slot."

"Commander, you are not authorized to launch. Power down your engines."

"Control, give me a slot or I will launch without one." She glanced through the viewer at the gstek, where Norash and Onkar stood gesturing and shouting at her. "I promise I'll bring this one back, and all the other ones that were stolen."

The controller reluctantly relayed the slot trajectory, and cleared her for launch.

"Thank you, Control." Dair eased the fighter out of the dock position and enabled lifting thrusters. As soon as she had enough height, she angled the nose up and engaged the main engines. As the fighter shot up into the sky, she checked her console and calculated the flight time.

She had forty-two minutes to reach the young Skartesh rebels and convince them to turn back.


Shon Valtas dreamed of oKia.

His family lived in the northern reaches, far from the crowded cities in the tropic regions. Ice and snow regularly covered their lands for three of the four annual seasons, and made it impossible to grow anything but minimal crops. The Valtas survived by hunting, trading, and raiding, and were regarded by many as the fiercest and most terrifying of oKiaf's many warrior tribes.

His ancestors, who were more religious and close-ranked than even the Skartesh, had emigrated to the colder clime to escape the advance of technology and what they viewed as the wanton destruction of their traditions and culture in favor of profit and convenience. To this day his parents and the rest of the Valtas tribe still clung to the old ways and refused to build a permanent dwelling or permit any but the most basic of machinery within their borders.

When Shon had left, he had never wanted to return. He never had, except when he closed his eyes.

In his dream he was walking with Tarkun, who had somehow grown to adulthood and carried a spear bow decorated with hundreds of kill notches.

The sight of his dead sibling as a man didn't alarm him. *I thought you drowned, brother.*

*I did.* Tarkun stopped by a mound of black fur and crouched to inspect the carcass. The summer-fattened *praa* had a magnificent quartet of tusks, over which his younger brother ran an admiring hand. *I only live in your dreams, Shon. Like oKia. Lend me a blade.*

Shon handed him his best gutting knife. *I should have watched you closer. If I had—*

*You would have tracked me to the lake, and followed me into the water.* Tarkun drew the edge of the knife expertly down the center of the *praa's* underbelly, cutting through the hide and fat while avoiding the musk glands and bladder. *Had you, we would both be dead.*

Shon looked through the trees at the horizon, where a strange amber-red light had appeared. *I'm not dead?*

Tarkun eyed him and uttered a sharp laugh. *Only to your people.*

It had been his parents who had driven Shon away. Not because of their prejudices and backward thinking, as some thought, but because they never saw him. Tarkun's death had robbed his mother of joy and had reduced his father to an embittered, silent man. His brother had died, but Shon had become a ghost the two of them refused to see. Had his parents not wallowed in their sorrow, he might never have left to search for what he believed they were denying him.

*You are in the eyes and hearts and minds of thousands of children now, brother.* Tarkun lifted a bloodied hand and offered him a chunk of the *praa*'s raw liver. *Will you run from them, too?*

"Salvager."

He opened his eyes to see a young Skartesh female bending over him. The last thing he remembered was the gstek taking off from the surface and someone hitting him from behind. Now he felt thick-headed and muddled. "Where . . . ?"

"We have left Ninra," she told him. "We the younger have taken control of the vessels. The truth was revealed to us."

That made him sit up and look around him. He was in a medical bay on a ship. "What truth?"

"That you were surrounded and used by betrayers." She pressed her brow to the back of his paw. "Forgive us, Salvager. We did not know. We have set things to rights now."

"What things?"

She lifted her face, and her expression turned to one of utter rapture. "All of our transgressions will be cleansed in the Great Burning, and we will be worthy to follow you to Paradise."

"I would know precisely how the faithful intend to cleanse themselves," he said, choosing his words carefully.

"It came to us as the truth did. Our eyes became unveiled and we saw the way to Paradise." She gestured toward the viewer panel to one side of the bed. There were more ships around them, and just beyond, K-2's binary stars loomed, larger than he had ever seen them. "We will cast ourselves into the heart of creation, where we will know the Great Burning together and be reborn."

The Skartesh were flying their ships directly into the twin suns.

# CHAPTER
## TWENTY-FOUR

Once Dair had cleared the stratosphere and left orbit, she began plotting her course. The most direct route to get to the Skartesh ships would require her to fly through some of the worst war traps, including a stretch of derelicts that she had never navigated through before now.

Any one of them could shred her ship to pieces, and she didn't have Burn to blast anything that tried.

It was dangerous, it was foolhardy, and she didn't even know how she would turn the Skartesh back when she reached them. *If* she reached them. The best she could hope for was to shoot out the propulsion systems—thanks to the Aksellans, the Skartesh couldn't fire back—and render the ships powerless until reinforcements from K-2 could arrive.

Only reinforcements weren't likely to come, and if she destroyed their engines too close to the suns, solar gravitation would simply suck them in.

"I'll figure out that part when I get there." She transferred power to the weapons array as she approached the first obstacle. "It's not that bad. I've had worse days."

Something much larger blipped on the edge of her screen, and she switched to long-range scanner to see what was on the other side of the free-ranging minefield.

A formation of three scout ships, five raiders, and a command cruiser skirted the opposite edge of the field. All nine ships were in recon positions and had weapons arrays powered and ready.

All nine ships were Hsktskt.

"*Duo,* I really didn't need the damn lizards right now." She fed the coordinates into her panel and extrapolated their destination.

If they didn't change course, the Hsktskt ships would reach K-2 at roughly the same time she got to the Skartesh.

"Okay. This is, officially, the worst day of my life."

Dair hunted along the frequency bands until she found the one they were using for intership transmissions. The navcomm was able to translate Hsktskt, and, along with the decryption key Verrig had extracted from the captured gsteks, she was able to listen in on the exchanges between the ships' pilots.

From their transmissions, Dair discovered that the Hsktskt knew their captured gstek raiders were being used for medevac. This apparently had outraged one of the faction's regimental commanders, who had sent the attack unit with orders to retrieve or destroy their ships.

The two unit pilots discussed the various ways they could retrieve the ships, most of which included wiping out the colony on K-2.

Dair could risk only one short transmission, so she encoded all the data she had on the Hsktskt force and sent it in a quick, encrypted microburst back to the homeworld. With luck, no one would ignore her signal and the pilots' pod would get off the ground before the Hsktskt reached the planet.

She could improve their chances, too, if she could slow the Hsktskt down. *It's a shame their displacer mines aren't programmed to blow up Hsktskt ships; I could lure a couple of them in and let the field do the work.* She adjusted her course to keep from straying too close herself, and then thought of the day she and Onkar had bloodied themselves to draw off the 'shrikes.

*Burn is right.* Dair's shoulders shook with silent laughter as she edged closer to the mines. *I am sand-belly.*

She had to fly slow, nearly lurching along the way a large troop freighter or cruiser might, in order to trigger the mines' proximity sensors. She also changed her emissions to make the strafer read much larger than it was. As soon a pair of mines detached themselves from the field to come after her, she increased her speed. Not enough to elude them, but to string them along after her. The active trailing mines triggered others, and in short order she had an entire string of them tagging after her.

She came around the field and flew under the edge of it, coming out underneath the Hsktskt ships and pulling up sharply. At the last possible minute she rolled out and away from the unit. Her long tail of mines, which were not capable of such maneuvers, did what they were programmed to. They clustered on the nearest objects—the Hsktskt ships—and exploded.

Dair had barely cleared the field when two raiders came up behind her and opened fire. She took two hits before she made it to a neighboring asteroid belt, where the pilots' pod had regularly trained. Although the raiders had superior weaponry, they couldn't match her speed or experience flying within the belt, and eventually broke off their pursuit and rejoined their unit.

"One little fighter isn't as much fun as a whole colony," Dair muttered as she took stock of the damages to the strafer. She had lost one engine entirely and most of her scanners were fried. The Hsktskt had her seriously outgunned and she was running out of time; if she went after them a second time she could kiss her tail and the Skartesh good-bye.

All she could do was hope that she had given Onkar enough time to get into space. Reluctantly she changed course and exited the belt, resuming her pursuit of the Skartesh fleet.

As Jadaira's last, terse transmission ended, Onkar sent out the emergency signal to the pilots' hangar to scramble all available fighters.

"Civilian launches are canceled until further notice," he told the head controller. "Initiate recall procedures for all military personnel on colony." He sent a direct relay to Verrig. "Chief, we have incoming hostiles. I'm taking out the first detachment. Launch the next two in five-minute intervals."

"Affirmative, Lieutenant."

He turned to Norash. "You'd better move your ground forces into defense positions and evacuate all nonessential personnel. If they reach the planet, it will get bloody."

"You haven't been medically cleared to fly," the Trytinorn pointed out. "Not that I believe that will stop you, but are you the best pilot to lead this attack?"

"Our best pilot is up there now." He spotted Burn crossing the docking pad. "You'll have to settle for her second."

Since discovering the Hsktskt on KOS-11 and decrypting the data sent to Dair from command, Onkar had worked quietly with Norash over several weeks to establish emergency response procedures in the event of a direct attack by the Hsktskt on K-2. Although Command would not have considered such extreme measures appropriate, Onkar had had the feeling that of all the targeted regions, theirs would be the one the lizards tried to retake.

What he hadn't planned for was Jadaira being the one who would tangle with them first. That she was facing them alone made his blood freeze.

He caught up with Burn on the flight line. "Ensign, have you been assigned a pilot?" The younger male shook his head. "I'm taking point, if you're interested."

Burn's eyes darkened with primal pleasure. "You're on, Lieutenant."

By using every pilot present, Verrig was able to send out twenty strafers with Onkar. Aware that they were flying into combat, the pilots' pod quickly assumed their attack-formation positions and kept the frequencies open and silent, waiting for orders. Once they had reached orbit, Onkar was able to transmit a downlink emergency-signal warning to the other worlds within the system of the Hsktskt threat.

There had been no time for a briefing, so Onkar relayed the data about the Hsktskt attack unit. "Squadron, center eight ships will engage, with right and left flanks providing cover and replacement. Engaging ships, watch your weave patterns and avoid cross-fire zones. We have nine ships on a direct course for the planet. That means we're going to make nine clouds of space debris. Acknowledge your orders by the numbers."

Each of the nineteen other pilots signaled in turn, and Onkar turned his attention to his console and plotted an intercept course based on the elapsed time since Jadaira's transmission and the last-known position of the Hsktskt ships. "Ensign, power the weapons array."

Dair pushed her engines beyond their limits, and caught up with the Skartesh fleet when they were a little more than 150 million kim away from the binary stars.

Aside from the unpredictable gravitational fields, planet-size flares, ion and magnetic storms, and the fierce solar winds generated by the twin suns, by far the most dangerous aspect of flying in such close proximity was the possibility of encountering a randomly ejected solar mass or one of the coronal loops. Both commonly occurred within 50 million kim from the twins, both were often hotter than the surface of the stars themselves, and both could change frozen space into lethally superheated zones.

The young Skartesh rebels believed they could fly into the suns, but in reality they would burn up long before they got near the actual surface.

Dair had been signaling the fleet since she had come within range, but none of the ships responded. That was why she had decided to make use of the last of the space traps she had encountered, an energy shunt concealed in the middle of a small sea of derelict ships that had drifted away from its original purpose, which had been to barricade one of the busier trade routes during the war.

Luring the shunt's power-leeching probes had been a lot like triggering the displacer mines, except that Dair had to use different bait. Allocating as much fuel as she could spare, she vented a concentrated, continuous trail of it for the probes to follow. Since the Skartesh would not respond or turn back, she decoyed the probes to the first vessel, where she got as close to the fuel cells as she could before she abruptly cut off her own vent trail.

Deprived of her fuel, the leech probe immediately searched for the nearest source of energy, and attached itself to the fuel cells. Because its collection rate compensated for the amount of energy available, it would drain the cells.

It was slow, tedious work, luring the probes out one by one and then leading them to each vessel, and Dair was already exhausted.

An odd numbness on her left side and a sporadic flutter of pain in her chest only added to her discomfort. She kept moving from ship to ship while she sent the same message to them, over and over.

"Skartesh fleet, this is the *SandPearl*. Your ships are in immediate danger. Alter your course and turn about before you enter the coronal zone. Please acknowledge."

No one responded, and by the time she had run out of leech drones she and the still-functioning vessels were nearing the outer band of the twins' gravitational field. With a clenched jaw she flew through the fleet, shooting out fuel cells on the remaining dozen ships still capable of flight.

On the last pass she misjudged the range and one of the protective hull panels exploded out, crashing into her port side. Emergency sealing panels slammed down as she rolled out of the spin just in time to avoid colliding with one of the inert ships. Her viewer and panels went black as all power to helm controls abruptly terminated.

"*Duo*, not now, not here." In the dark she punched her safeties, trying to bypass the ruined circuits, but the ship's backup systems were also down. The only way for her to regain helm control was to perform a manual bypass.

The nagging pain in her chest grew steadier as she fumbled with the console. It had been years since she'd physically worked on a strafer panel, but she was a pilot, not some addle-brained mechanic. Working by touch made her even more impatient, until the pain in her chest moved into her lungs and she began to feel hot.

At last she closed the bypass and reinitiated her console. Light illuminated the cockpit as the control panels fluttered back into operation, allowing her to level out, but then a warning light flared on her propulsion panel. Lack of control and proximity to the twins had caused her remaining engines to overheat, and now they had shut down. The ship was still moving, however, so maybe she was getting bad readings. She enabled her viewer, and then whipped her head to one side as the blinding light of the twins filled the screen.

She groped along the panel until she felt the correct keys and shut down the viewer. Her heart hammered inside her chest as she checked her scanners. The ones still functioning showed that she had drifted much farther from the fleet than she'd thought.

The Skartesh ships were still inert and maintaining a safe distance, but now the *SandPearl* was caught in the outer gravitational band, and being slowly dragged forward into the coronal zone.

"Skartesh fleet." As she sent out the signal, Dair used her maneuvering thrusters to bring the strafer about so that comm hardware faced away from the twins. "As you are probably aware by now, I have disabled your engines to prevent you from flying into the suns. Unfortunately, my own engines have become disabled. It appears that I will be making the sacrificial trip for you."

A very young male Skartesh voice answered. "We are sorry, Commander."

Dair thought of the dark water of the outer currents, and how alone she had felt when she had thought of swimming into them. She had the same feeling now. "If you really want to change things, boy, try living. I really liked it; I think if you give it a fair chance, you will, too." She took a steadying breath. "Would you relay a message to my people for Lieutenant Onkar and Sh—Rushan Amariah for me?"

"I'm here, Jadaira." It was Shon.

"Hey." Flakes of skin from her brow drifted down in front of her eyes as her skin reacted to the rapidly increasing interior cockpit temperature. "Guess whose turn it is to stay behind?"

"You shouldn't have done this, Dair." He sounded miserable.

No, she should have stayed with her pod and listened to Onkar. She could have been a good mate to him, and he would have given her strong, beautiful children. For a moment she wished she could change every decision she had made since leading the *Hemat* out of the minefield.

But there were some things more important than a safe, happy life. She had given thousands of others a chance for the same, and that was a more than fair trade for her own.

"Yeah, well, I guess you were a bad influence on me." She waited until a short burst of static cleared from the channel. "Listen, I'm getting close and I won't be able to transmit much longer." The heat made her eye ducts flood, and tears streamed down over her cracked cheeks, and she made herself remember the time in the breeding cavern, when Onkar had made her feel so good and so cherished.

"Tell my second-in-command . . . tell Onkar that it was quick and that I wasn't afraid."

"I will, Dair. Don't be frightened."

She took in a quick, sobbing breath. "Acknowledged."

"Dair, we see—" Interference erased the rest of his signal.

She didn't try to raise him again, but shut down the transponder. Her whole body was burning now, and she wanted to scream, but she had no breath. She kept her eyes closed, praying it would end now, but the burning became eternity.

Time passed, and she waited, but the end never came.

Dair had to try a few times before she could open her eyes. The Skartesh ships looked small now, but it seemed as if there were a lot more of them. Maybe the corona distorted the images the way water did sometimes with things above the surface. Glowing bands of pretty light enveloped the strafer, sending it into a slow, languid spin. As she switched off the viewer to protect her eyes, she wondered if she had gotten caught in the end of a loop. No one had ever survived such a thing, so she couldn't be sure.

The heat was more like Ninra now, terrible but tolerable, even though each breath she took in seemed to fill her lungs with plas shards. The ship was spinning faster and faster, and she braced herself, expecting it to break apart around her.

Her engine panel flickered.

Dair squinted at it. It was difficult to see, but somehow, the engines were reading back online. *Surely they've melted by now.* She reached out, seeing her gray, desiccated right hand as if it belonged to a stranger, and slowly tapped the keys. The strafer shuddered and strained as if were wrestling with some greater power; then Dair was thrown into the console as the engines engaged and the fighter shot forward.

Where was her harness?

Her left hand wouldn't work at all, so she lifted her right to push herself back from the console. The viewer showed her moving at minimal speed through deserted space. When the planet Ylyd swelled to the starboard, she tried to blink, but her eyelids wouldn't close now.

*If that is Ylyd, then the suns are behind me.* Dair used the last of her strength to set a course for K-2, and engaged the autoflight system before she sagged back in her seat. Aside from the burned condition of her body, the pain in her chest felt crushing now, and her vision was wavering.

Dair knew she was dying; that wasn't what bothered her. It was the fact that she had escaped the corona for no apparent logical reason. A number of blips appeared on her scanners, and she switched the viewer to wide-angle front view.

She was flanked on both sides by the pilots' pod and other ships she didn't recognize. There seemed to be hundreds of them; 'Zangian, Aksellan, Ylydii, even some Ninrana, but she couldn't trust her eyes, either. How had they pulled her out of there? She wanted to know before she died, but she could no longer speak or use the console. It took everything she had simply to keep breathing.

The course Dair had set would take her where she wanted to go. Maybe she would live long enough to see it, and that would be enough.

"Why doesn't she respond?"

Onkar never took his eyes off the crippled strafer. "She's engaged the autoflight; she's probably unconscious. We'll follow her down and get her out." He hesitated. "I owe you a great deal, Ensign."

"I'll collect someday, Lieutenant."

Obliterating the Hsktskt unit had cost them two ships, but as soon as the last raider had been destroyed the pilots agreed to follow Onkar and find Jadaira and the Skartesh. They had quickly found the forty ships she had disabled, and even more surprising, they also found as many ships from neighboring worlds that had docked with the Skartesh, and were evacuating them. Even some of the Ninrana fleet had been dispatched to help.

There was nothing they could do for the *SandPearl,* however, one of the Ylydii pilots told him, and indicated the position of the strafer, which had crossed over into the coronal zone.

Onkar had almost gone in after her despite the hopelessness, until Burn proposed a radical solution that was merely a large-scale version of one of Jadaira's more unconventional maneuvers.

With the assistance of the other ships, the gunner coordinated a simultaneous firing of all the ships' pulse weapons at the same time that a coronal loop extended out toward the *SandPearl*. The pulse energy reflected off the cooler base gases of the loop then whiplashed up and knocked the strafer out of the loop with such force that it threw her completely clear of the outer gravitational band. Once away from the deadly heat, the strafer's engines cooled down enough to restart, and Dair had flown away from the suns.

Now all Onkar had to do was get her home and to the hospital. She would likely be burned, and her augmentations stressed, but Teresa would know how to deal with that. He would suspend her from duty until she was completely well, and by then they would know if they were to be parents.

"Her trajectory is wrong," Burn said, sounding worried. "Lieutenant, she's not going to land at Transport."

Onkar punched up her coordinates. "She's flying to the sea." There was only one reason she would do that. "Signal Trauma and advise them we have an emergency water landing."

"They can get a team out there on a submersible," the gunner told him. "She's probably not as bad as she thinks; you know how females are."

Onkar ordered the rest of the pod to land at Transport while he followed Dair down. They ignored his orders and stayed with him, pulling up as he entered the lower atmosphere to set down on the shore.

Dair's ship slowed, but not enough. It crashed into the water and began to sink.

"I'm dumping the ship," Onkar said as he brought the nose down to do the same. "Prepare to open and exit through your emergency hatch."

He barely felt the jolt of the impact or heard the noise of the engines as they flooded with seawater. He was out of his harness and through the emergency hatch before Burn had time to open his. Dair's ship had sunk a few hundred yards away from a place Onkar had only heard of but had never seen.

The most sacred place to the coastal pod beneath the water had no name; it was not visited or discussed. It was an immense, solitary cavern made of the most ancient white reef rock, and was set apart in a place no one but 'Zangians who were old or sick went.

Dair had come here to die.

# CHAPTER
## TWENTY-FIVE

Onkar was prepared for the worst when he released the cockpit canopy, but the sight of her made him release a pulse of sheer agony. Her harness and flight suit had been burned to cinders, and her skin shield had melted onto her. Most of her facial hide was burned away, and her eyes had shrunk far back into her head.

Her voice was gone, but her mouth formed his name. *Onkar.*

Carefully he reached in and lifted her out. *I caught you again, Jadaira.*

He swam with her cradled against him into the narrow stone entrance. Inside, the water was soft and cool, and light from the surface filtered through a million tiny holes in the porous white rock. Carrion-eating *crestars* clung to the walls, waiting patiently for the time to do their work and add to the pile of 'Zangian bones that covered the floor of the cavern.

It was a beautiful place.

Onkar surfaced and swam with her to one of the curved rock ledges. Unlike the ones in the breeding caverns, these were fashioned so that 'Zangians could stretch out and let the weight of their bodies on their internal organs help hasten the end.

He cleared the water from his gill vents. "I was hoping to take you to a different cave when you returned," he told her as he lifted her to the smallest of the dying ledges. Suddenly he knew he would never leave this cave unless she came with him. "If I get Teresa here, she could—"

With great effort, Dair lifted her hand and touched his mouth, then shook her head once.

Pulses came through the water, swelling up around him. He dropped down, and through the holes in the white walls he could see the hovering forms of the pilots' pod, and other 'Zangians of the coastal pod. He saw Jadaira's dam, and Teresa's mate, who was holding her against him. He saw submersibles filled with land dwellers.

He returned to the surface. "Jadaira?" Something broke the surface behind him, and he turned to see Shon Valtas, the Skartesh he had tried to drown twice, along with Dair's uncle and the rest of the Bio Rescue team.

*He is not a Skartesh, but an officer and a soldier, like us.* As Onkar watched Shon and the others remove their regulators, his animosity toward his rival disappeared. Whatever this male was, Jadaira had cared deeply for him, and he would not challenge his presence.

Daran and the nurses climbed up onto the ledge, but Onkar already knew there was nothing they could do.

"She has come here to die," he told Shon, and submerged for a moment to give them all time to say their farewells, and to prepare himself for losing her.

No great healing power here, however. *So much for his dam's legend.*

As he looked out through the walls, Onkar saw that the 'Zangians were moving in ritual watch circles. The pilots' pod remained separate, in the upright position similar to that of attention during a military inspection. They were honoring her and praying for her, and in that moment he would have given anything to be the one on the ledge, while she waited for his last breath.

He heard the sound of something falling into the water from above, and then something else flashed all around him.

The latter was not sound or light or movement, but it was something of all three. Whatever it was, it held Onkar motionless for several heartbeats. It spread out and did the same to those gathered around the cave.

Then it was gone, so completely that it was as if he had imagined it.

*We go to die in a nameless place, Onkar. It is small and white and beautiful. And there, if we are worthy, a great power heals us and returns us well and whole to the sea.*

He darted up to the surface, and saw that everyone was in the water. The nurses were hanging onto the ledge, their eyes wide. Dairatha was swimming fast, agitated circles around the cavern. Shon Valtas treaded water in the very center and looked dazed.

The ledge was empty.

All hope died inside him. "She's dead." He could not bring himself to look down at the bottom.

"No," a melodic voice said. "I'm not."

Onkar turned to see Jadaira treading water behind him—a different Jadaira from the one he had placed on the ledge. Her face was completely healed, and at the same time, altered.

She was no longer white. Her flesh was pale and radiant and flawless and . . . a silvery color.

He was afraid to touch her, afraid that he had gone mad and was hallucinating her. "Are you real?"

She nodded solemnly.

"Not a dream." He dared to lift his hand and touch her face.

She pressed her hand over his. "It's me."

Onkar took her down into the water with him, whirling around and around with her before streaking up with her to the surface. He hardly remembered to inflate his lungs. "You're alive. How?"

A sound drew Jadaira's attention to the shore. There a wall of young Skartesh in white robes stood chanting. Behind them, more were gathering. They were not up on the cliffs or far back on the sands, but instead they stood at the very edge of the water, mere inches from the thing they feared.

This time they were not chanting Rushan Amariah's name. They were chanting Jadaira's.

"I think they helped," she told him.

"How do you list a divine and mysterious burst of power under the treatment section on a medical chart?" Teresa asked William Mayer.

"I believe it's spelled G-O-D," he told her as he helped Dair down from the exam table.

"There is no precedent for this, you know." The Terran woman sighed. "I know some of the old 'Zangian legends speak of a healing power, but that's just arcane superstition."

"Not anymore." Mayer gazed at Dair. "You passed the last of your scans, Commander. You are completely healthy. And only God knows why."

Dair understood the uneasy looks he and everyone else had been giving her since the day in the cave of the dying. Whenever she saw her reflection, or looked down at herself, the same expression was on her own face.

The experience had altered her physically on several levels. Her skin had changed color, now no longer white but a shade that appeared to be a blend of white and the dark gray of normal 'Zangian females. Her eyes were no longer pink, but the same ghostly gray shade.

Internally, all of the Terran augmentations her stepmother had transplanted had been mutated and now could no longer be differentiated from the native parts of her body. Even her genetic structure, once half 'Zangian and half Terran, had been transformed into an entirely new sequence that had never before been recorded. Dair was able to stay out of the water for much longer periods of time, and suffered no ill effects when she did.

"I still think it's some form of radiation she was exposed to in the coronal zone," Teresa said as she finished the chart entry. "Look at how much her DNA has changed. No living being has ever survived that kind of exposure, so this could be a perfectly natural phenomenon."

"One that will have you stuck in your lab until you've identified it," William predicted.

"Just think of the potential treatments," her stepmother told him. "It would change the future of rehabilitative and transplantation medicine, and take alterforming to a whole new level. *If* we can figure out where it came from."

"Well, whatever you do," Dair told Teresa as she dressed, "don't start flying aquatic patients into the sun to see if they turn different colors and stop flaking."

Dair was not the only one who had been changed. Witnessing what was now commonly referred to as "the great healing" had eased the tensions between the Skartesh and the 'Zangians. The Skartesh were great believers in miracles, and the 'Zangians believed their presence on the shore must have contributed to the startling event.

The cult had entered into new talks with the council, this time to arrange community service to make restitution for the ships they had stolen and damaged. Ana had been instrumental in getting counseling for the traumatized young Skartesh and their elders, hoping it would aid in mending the breach inside the cult itself. The other land-dwelling colonists were not as forgiving as the aquatics had been, but there were fewer public confrontations and reports of harassment.

The Hlagg, whose embassy the Skartesh had vandalized during the riots, had gone a step further. As the lupine species were excellent hunters, the Hlagg were working with the Skartesh to track and recover the escaped insects. Ambassador Heek had also set up a barax colony inside the Skartesh compound, and trauma counselors were using it as part of their efforts to deprogram the cult.

The Ninrana were not doing as well. While they had survived the brief Skartesh invasion, Shon's staged suicide had seriously damaged the very foundations of their culture, namely the ritual sacrifice and consumption of outsiders. Quadrant was still deciding what sanctions to bring against the desert world on behalf of all their victims.

Scientists who visited the desert world to retrieve the remains of the Ninrana's victims had also dropped a bombshell: Within twenty years, there would no longer be enough water on the planet to sustain life. Some of the Ninrana's more stable tribal leaders had agreed to enter into talks with the Ylydii and Kevarzangians to address the renewed Hsktskt threat, but the twenty-year death sentence on top of the collapse of their religion had created tribal splinter groups, who were now threatening to tear Ninra apart with a civil war.

Dair had just finished dressing when Shon Valtas appeared in the doorway. "Good morning, Major."

"Commander." He nodded to Teresa and William. "I heard that you were being discharged and thought I'd stop by."

"Come on, William." Dair's stepmother took the doctor's arm. "You've never shown me your office. I'd like to see if your view is better than mine."

When they were alone, Shon studied her. "How are you feeling?"

"Healthy, but pretty confused. One minute I'm dying; the next I'm perfectly fine, but different. Everyone has a theory but no one knows why." She frowned. "I know I'm the same person I was, but at the same time, I'm not. Does any of that make sense?"

"Not really."

She laughed. "Okay, just checking. So why are you hanging around this place? I would have thought QI would have turned you loose by now."

"It's not going to be that easy, I'm afraid. I've volunteered to stay and help the counselors deprogram the Skartesh." He came over to her and took one of her hands between his paws. "Dair, when I was impersonating Rushan, I was never able to step out of character, not even for a minute. We're trained to immerse ourselves in an undercover role."

She nodded. "You had me and everyone else fooled."

"It's why I couldn't treat you any way except the way he would. It made me a little crazy at times, not being able to laugh or share war stories or tell you how much I simply enjoyed being with you."

"Well, now you have." She nudged him. "I still want to hear about all the cloak-and-dagger stuff you QI guys do, too."

"Actually, I was thinking of quitting intelligence and applying for a permanent transfer to K-2 as a patrol pilot." His grasp tightened a degree. "The truth is, I'd like to stay and be with you. I care deeply for you, and I'd like you to become my life mate."

Dair's physical alterations had changed one other thing: the muscles in her face. Since the day of the crash, she had been able to smile the way a Terran would. She only wished now that she could. "Shon, you have been a wonderful friend, and I trust you with my life. But friendship is all I've ever felt toward you. That is one thing about me that won't change."

He sighed. "I thought that was what you might say, but I had to be sure." He bent over and pressed his furry cheek against her brow. "Be happy, Jadaira."

Dair watched him leave with a faint pang of regret. It was a shame that she didn't have deeper feelings for him; they would have done well together. As for being happy, despite her own feelings, she wasn't entirely sure that was guaranteed, either.

The door panel opened and Onkar came in. He looked rather agitated. "I saw Shon leave. Are you ill? Are they keeping you for more tests?"

"No, I'm perfectly healthy, and I've just been discharged. See this?" She smiled for him. "This is the weird thing that my face does now when I'm happy. You're going to see it a lot, because I'm pregnant, so get used to it."

"I was standing outside and I overheard you speaking to him." He looked at the floor. "Jadaira, I made you promise to be my life mate under duress. I release you from that."

"You do?" She folded her arms. "Why are you being so generous? Don't you like the new me? Don't you want our child?"

"I know I am the reason that you refused him, and, if you are free, you and the major can be together." The words were polite, but he looked like he wanted to regurgitate something. "The child . . . we will share."

"You *are* the reason that I refused him, but Shon and I are just friends."

He glanced at her, unsure. "I don't understand."

"Think about it. It'll come to you." She strolled past him and out of the exam room.

Onkar didn't catch up to her until she had left the hospital and was almost to the coastal transport pickup. "Are you saying that you prefer me over him?"

She had all but clubbed him over the head with it. *Males.* "Yes. I prefer you, period. I just want you."

"You want me." He seemed stunned.

"Well, you, and this pup, and joint command of the pilots' pod, and help keeping Bio Rescue in operation." She linked her arms around his waist. "I can negotiate on everything but the you part. You, I have to have."

"You want me." It was as if he couldn't get past those three words.

Dair started to tease him again, but she remembered the day she had been shunned by the pod, and how she had contemplated leaving and swimming into the outer currents. Onkar had spent most of his life out there, and in many ways he was still there.

It was time for that to change.

"Come on." The transport pulled up beside them, and she tugged him to the access doors. "I want to show you something."

They were quiet on the ride out to the coast, and just as silent as they stripped at the top of the cliffs. Once she was naked Dair noticed Onkar looking at her the same way he had in the breeding caverns. Which was good, because that was the second place she wanted to take him.

They dove together over the edge and plunged into the sea. Dair stayed at his side as they swam over the reefs and out to the ridge. She finned greetings to the other 'Zangians, but she didn't stop to socialize.

When they crossed into the sublittoral zone, Onkar glided around her. *Where are you going?*

*You'll see,* she said, and kept swimming until they had passed the URD and reached the place of assembly. It was deserted, and beyond it, so were the outer currents.

There had been more reports of mogshrikes in the area since the attack on the dome. Even more disturbing, the 'shrikes were grouping and hunting in packs of three and four. The scientists at the URD were working closely with the 'Zangians to discover what had changed their behavior, and several deep-sea expeditions to observe 'shrikes in their natural territory were being planned.

Dair stopped just short of crossing into the darker water, and faced him. *When I was being dragged into the suns, I thought about this place. I was so afraid, Onkar. I never knew how it felt to face dying alone. That's how you felt every day you were out there, wasn't it?*

*When I lived as a rogue, I tried not to feel.* Onkar looked out into the emptiness. *But yes, I was afraid.*

*You're still afraid.* She moved until she was between him and the outer currents, and she looked directly into his dark eyes. *That's why I wanted to come here. I want you to look at me. I want you to hear me. Who am I?*

*You are everything to me.*

*Yes. I am. I am your life and your mate and your home. As you are mine. It is the same for me. No matter what happens, that will not change. We made a child. We are one.* She swam away from the dark water, and entwined her body with his. *Do you understand now?*

*Yes.* Dair could feel him trembling, and then he wrapped his arms around her and pressed her head to his heart. *We will never be alone again.*